# ONCE MORE

## The Sayen Falls Series
### Novel 1

To Rhoda,
Keep writing with
the Spirit!
—Rebecca J Berry

# Rebecca J. Berry

"Once more unto the breach,
dear friends, once more."
William Shakespeare
Henry the Fifth

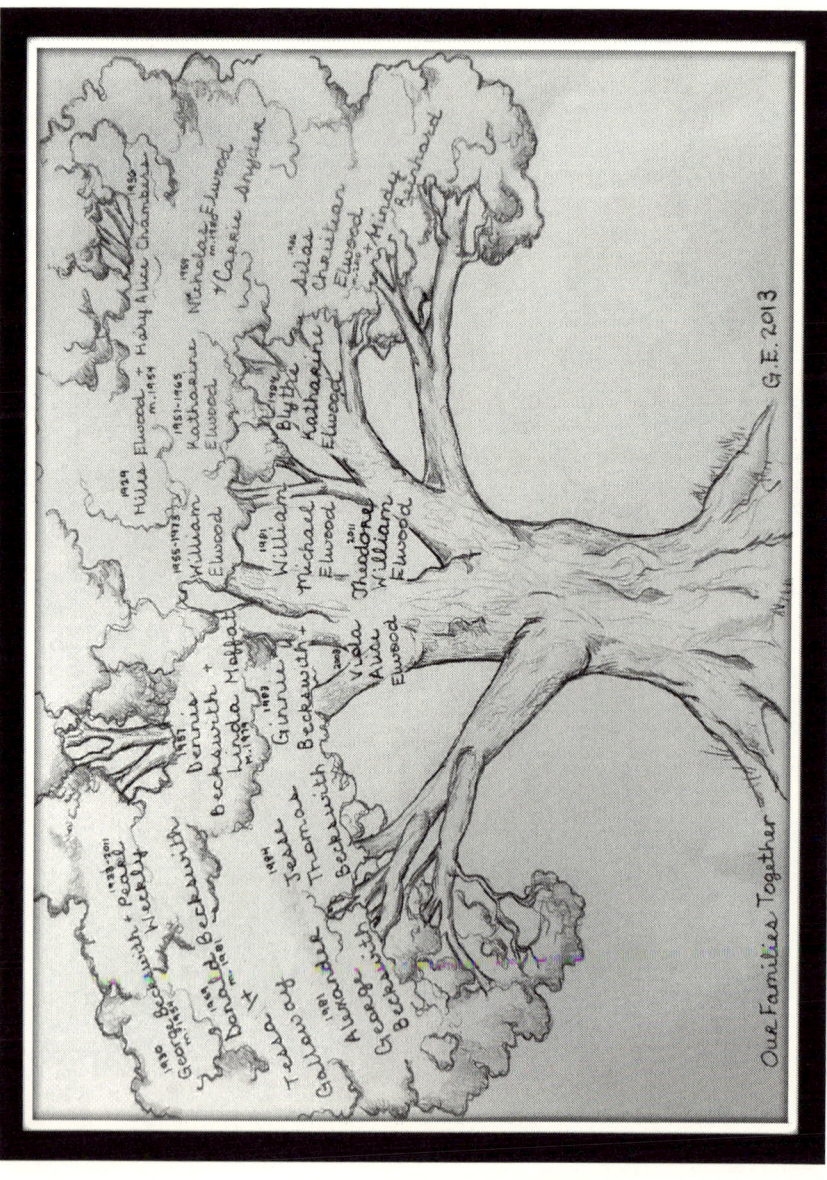

Printed in the United States of America

First Printing, 2018

ISBN 978-1-7326926-0-2

Rebecca J. Berry, publisher
Plotting Possibility
plottingpossibility@gmail.com

# DEDICATION

My very first complete published novel is dedicated to my parents.
You taught me to love words and stories.
You encouraged me to be a wordsmith and craft stories of my own.
You even named me after a literary heroine.
I'm pretty sure words and stories are just in my blood.

I hope I make all of you proud.
Thanks for everything

# ACKNOWLEDGMENTS

First, I must thank Holly Taylor Roberts. You served as the midwife to Sayen Falls. It's been a labor of four years bringing this book to completion. Without your constant encouragement and honest feedback, Blythe would've wandered into a field of daisies to recite poetry to the ladybugs. My characters thank you for pushing me to dig deeper and write harder. And I thank you for understanding my vision and dream for this story.

Special thanks to Charlotte Cottier. I cannot thank you enough for your thorough feedback and advice. Your notes were invaluable to me in shaping the story into its best self. With your insights, I felt like a sculptor removing excess to reveal the statue inside the stone, as the saying goes.

I also want to thank my mother, Amy Schulz, and my dear friend, Marybeth Drodofsky. You two are my champions, my cheerleaders. You helped me find mistakes—both in grammar and in the bad plot ideas. You urged me to stay true to myself in editing. It means the world to me to have your encouragement. You believe in me when I stop believing in myself.

The graphics on and inside this book were contributed by several old friends. The gorgeous Elwood–Beckwith family tree was sketched by the talented Holly Metesh. I will forever be in love with that tree. The images of the river on the front cover were given to me by Andy Kuzas and Holly Taylor Roberts. Andy made a special stop at the Cuyahoga River to get the shots I wanted. Additional photographs of the river and the Cuyahoga Valley were provided by Joey Locicero. It means so much to me that you helped me out!

This book wouldn't be here without my husband and our kids. I started writing again when our son was two years old. I needed something just for me, as many moms do. And writing is my thing. Thank you, Curtis, for all the evenings away in the last four years. You gave me precious time to escape into Sayen Falls. And, kids, I wouldn't be who I am without you.

Last, it's a bit cliché, I fear, but I want to thank my readers. I know that reading is an investment of sorts. In this busy world, there are many other things to do. And in this crowded market, there are lots of other books to read. Thank you for giving *Sayen Falls: Once More* space on your bookshelf (physical or digital). I hope you'll want to return to Sayen Falls many times to have a cup of tea with the Elwoods!

# Prologue

March was holding spring hostage in Sayen Falls. Usually, school children would cheer for snow and the romantic at heart would smile at its beauty, but this year each and every person in town was over it. It wasn't fun or beautiful anymore. It was annoying. In fact, it seemed to fall already gray and slushy and used up.

For Blythe Elwood, March was generally a gross month anyway. Historically, this was when life became abnormally complicated. There was no reason for it other than the wheel of fortune spinning around to mess things up again. It was like someone had put a gypsy curse on March where Blythe was concerned. And she'd really like to stick a pin in the voodoo doll of whoever had done it. If she actually believed in such things.

Thus far, the month had been a flat calm, aside from the snow. Blythe didn't really care how much it snowed, so long as no one dropped any bombs on her. No parents breaking up the family, no fiancés breaking her heart, no medical emergencies, no major decisions, no drama of any kind. In the absence of upheaval, life felt downright boring this year. For a creative like Blythe, the monotony was detestable, and it was wearing thin now, but at least she could catch her breath.

It was on this particularly nondescript snowy, blowy day that Blythe found herself carefully creeping along memory lane. Until recently she had taken leaps and somersaults and major dance breaks down memory lane that always left her winded. The reckless wandering opened her up to be wounded again by past hurts, to be reminded of past regrets, and to be left wistful for what might have or should have been. So, it was with great care that she started down that road. What she discovered—much to her surprise—was that she had more power over the memories than they had over her. By standing at a distance, she could keep from toppling back into the darkness that licked her feet in those old moments.

This past Christmas she had made a resolution of sorts to live differently. Three months later life looked no different on the outside. She still lived above The Yellow Bowl and spent nearly every waking hour in the coffee shop to make ends meet. Her left-hand ring finger was still bare. Her relationship with her parents still strained. Yet, something about the act of living was different. She was pretty sure it had to do with her memories finally staying where they belonged—in the past. The resolve to be done with darkness did much to free her tired spirit.

She loosed her dark hair from a messy ponytail and shook her head slowly. Combing her fingers through her hair, she began gathering it up again. There was no thought as to what she was doing. Her mind was comparing memories of dancing with Jesse Beckwith in *Kiss Me, Kate* and the day Ian told her that writing was a stupid waste of time.

1

The shop phone rang. The memory bubble burst as she answered it, "The Yellow Bowl, coffee, books, and tea. This is Blythe, what can I help you with today?"

"I hoped you still answered the phone that way."

"Alexander George Beckwith," she smiled wide. "What in the world are you calling me for? Although I'm relieved it's you and not your brother."

"What did Jesse do now? I didn't know he's even in America, much less Ohio."

"He's not. He's in London. He saw a show yesterday in the West End and called to tell me I should finish my play. He went on and on about it."

"My brother? I'm shocked," Alex quipped with heavy sarcasm. The Beckwith brothers were three years apart in age, but all manner of brotherly love had escaped them. "So, you're not immediately dropping everything to do what he thinks you should do?"

"No, I have a shop to run and people to care for."

"I'm sure Jesse is taking that well. Oh well, he always finds a way to nurse his wounds."

"Yes, he does. And the nurse is usually drop-dead gorgeous."

"Don't be jealous, Blythe. You're leagues above him. He's an idiot."

"You know there's never been anything real between Jesse and me. Just a lot of talk and inflated expectation from our grandfathers," Blythe said a little too brightly. Her tone rang just a smidge false. She changed the subject, "So, why are you calling me?"

"I have a favor to ask of you. Actually, I can pay you for your trouble, so I suppose it's more like a job."

This was a most unusual statement. Alex was a corporate lawyer currently living on the east coast and making loads of money. Blythe had no idea what kind of favor or job she could do for him, so she asked. He explained,

"I have a friend looking for a good place to start over, so to speak. He's opening a pizza place so I set him up there on the riverfront in Sayen Falls."

"Why Sayen Falls? Of all the places in the world, why here?"

"I'm surprised you of all people are asking that question. Sayen Falls is as good a place as any. And the people can't be beaten. Believe me. I haven't lived there in—what?—thirteen or so years, and I've not been impressed with my sampling of humanity outside of the Falls."

"You could come home more often then you know, you big dummy," Blythe laughed. The word 'dummy' was not one Alex heard regularly and he had to share in her laugh.

"Duly noted. Anyway, the contract has been signed so it doesn't really matter what the reasons are, Sayen Falls is the place. And more accurately, it's the shop connected to yours."

2

"I get to have a neighbor? It's been over a year since that shop was rented."

"You do get to have a neighbor. He's not just opening the shop, he'll be living upstairs too. And that's where the favor comes in. There's not a lot of time for prep and landing, so to speak, so I was wondering if you'd mind setting up the apartment? He's packing things now and we'll ship those boxes out soon. I'm ordering some furniture to be delivered. You don't need to unpack for him or decorate or anything like that. Just make sure a bed is where a bed goes and a couch is where a couch goes, stuff like that."

"I can do that, I think. I'll have Finn help me move the furniture around."

"Finn McCartney is still around, huh? I thought he graduated from seminary already."

"No, he graduates next spring. Thankfully I have his help here at the shop another year."

"Tell Finn he'll be compensated for his time. I am paying you for your help, Blythe."

"You don't have to do that. It's the right thing to do. I can find some cups and plates, and household stuff in the attics. Between my grandparents and your grandfather, there's enough for two or three apartments."

"I planned on ordering everything. Money is really no object."

"Can I ask? Why are *you* making these arrangements?"

"Gracen isn't really focused on the details right now. I told him I'd take care of everything to make his life easier."

"Gracen. Does he have a last name? Anything I need to know?"

For the rest of her life when she looked back on this moment Blythe would answer the question herself that there was a lot she needed to know. But in the present tense, Alex answered.

"His name is Gracen Hall. We were roommates for a while at Princeton and have stayed friends. Oh, and you'll like this, he's moving from Summerstead Isle."

"New Jersey?"

"That's the one. But there's not much to know. I think he'll keep to himself, so you won't really even notice he's there."

"Like a hermit crab."

"That seems appropriate for a guy coming from Summerstead."

Summerstead Isle had been a favorite vacation spot of the Elwood clan for generations. Up until Blythe's parents divorced anyway. Every year her brothers wanted to buy hermit crabs, but Blythe used to think they were creepy. Still, hermit crabs aside, Summerstead was her favorite place in all the world. They had been happy there.

"I'll take care of things, Alex. Just let me know when to start expecting stuff. It will give me something to do," she shrugged. "It's been slow down here on the riverfront."

"Of course, it's the off-season. But spring should be coming soon. The Gala is next month, right? I think Gracen will arrive about that time."

"My invitation for The Gala just came today. It's exactly a month away."

"Well, I'll do my best to keep you busy over the next few weeks then. I really appreciate your help. I knew I could count on you."

"I should hope so. The Elwoods and Beckwiths have been there for each other for three generations now."

"Like I said, you can't beat the people in the hometown crowd," Alex said warmly. He was momentarily distracted by someone else speaking to him, and then he said to Blythe, "Hey, I gotta run. I have a meeting with a client. It was good talking to you though. I'll keep in touch."

"You know where to find me."

She hung up the old rotary phone that was The Yellow Bowl's landline and she sighed. This was where anyone could find her. Every now and then someone might have to drive a few blocks to find her at her grandparents' house. Her life would be an easy play to block; very few changes in scenery.

However, the scenery doesn't necessarily have to change for things to get shaken up. A new character can change everything. Or perhaps a change of circumstances. Or even just a break in the weather.

Blythe looked out the front window of her shop and smiled when she saw the sun was shining. It was the first burst of sunshine in a month of gray days. Things were changing already.

# Chapter 1

It doesn't take much to fill a 1967 Shelby Mustang. They were designed for speed and style, not storage capacity. Consequently, when Aunt Grace attempted to hand Gracen his guitar, he had to refuse.

"I doubt I'll be playing much in Ohio. Stick it in the guest house with the rest of my stuff."

"Uncle Harry would never have wanted this," Aunt Grace said sadly. It still seemed so impossible that Harry was gone and buried. She was certain he was in peace on the other side of paradise, but he was the only member of the family with peace.

"I know, but maybe it's for the best. I've tried to make life work here on The Isle for thirty-two years and it hasn't stuck. Time to try something new," Gracen said. His optimism was a thin veneer over his anger. "Uncle Harry was always telling me to make changes."

"I still don't understand how this happened. You were supposed to inherit the company."

He swallowed a fit of ugly words at this reminder, and instead put his arm around her. The top of her gray head barely reached his shoulder.

"Listen, Uncle Harry did everything he could for me. Without him, I wouldn't be able to have this fresh start. He taught me everything he knew about the business, about pizza, and he did manage to leave me the recipe. It's okay. I'll be okay."

She took his hand so she could see his forearm. The ink on his tattoo was healed so it didn't hurt when she placed a knobby finger on the words she had heard so often from the husband she lost.

"I know you did this to spite your grandfather—"

"I did this to remember Uncle Harry," Gracen insisted. Roy had said the tattoo was a waste of money just like the Shelby. And Gracen had responded that the waste was the point. He could make it without Roy's hush money. Or at least, without all of it. Still, that wasn't the only point. Gracen legitimately wanted to honor the memory of Uncle Harry.

"He'd be relieved to know that something got into that head of yours," Aunt Grace said, reaching high to tousle his hair. Looking into his stormy eyes, she saw not the grown man, but the little boy. She tried to steady her breath, but the tears would not allow it. Her voice quivered, "I can't help but be afraid I won't see you again. I know when you cross that bridge that you don't intend to come back. Losing you like this ... I just lost Harry."

Very little had the power to break Gracen's heart anymore; it had been crusted and calloused so many times that it was hard for a real emotion to find its way in. But this moment cut deep. The loss was mutual. Walking away from Aunt Grace just six weeks after burying Uncle Harry was an intense blow. And Roy knew it.

At this point, however, Gracen no longer had the option to stay. An agreement had been made, and there was a storefront with an attached apartment waiting for him in Ohio. There was no choice but to go forward.

"We'll see each other again," he promised. "I don't know when. It's going to take a lot of time to get a business established and viable before I can even think about coming back."

"Gracen, just remember to make time for people. Harry tried to teach you about people, even more than the business and the pizza. But there's no recipe for people."

"Alex Beckwith assures me that the people in Sayen Falls are very friendly. You know Alex, from Princeton?" he smiled, laying the charm on thick. It was one of his best tricks.

"I know all about Alex Beckwith," Aunt Grace scoffed. "Another workaholic like you. Your charm doesn't distract me a bit."

She hugged him tight, so afraid to let him go. Yet the time had come. He had a new life to get to, so Aunt Grace had to trust that all the love she and Harry had poured in, and all the prayers they'd lifted up would amount to something now. "You should go. It's already afternoon. It'll be the middle of the night when you get there."

"I planned it that way. Rush hour around Philly will be rough, but after that, it'll be fine," he said, then he added, "I'll be fine."

Her arthritic fingers fumbled with the clasp as she removed her silver cross necklace from around her neck. She had worn it every day since she was sixteen. Now she pressed it into Gracen's hand.

"I know you're not religious, not like Harry and me were … are," she faltered. She'd yet to determine how to speak in the proper tense with her other half gone. "But I want you to hang this from the mirror in that car you bought. That way when you see it you'll think of me and you'll know that I'm thinking about you."

"Praying for me," he corrected as his fingers closed around the necklace.

"Don't forget it," she told him. "Well, I won't ask you to call when you get there. I know you hate that. But let me know that you're alright in the next couple days."

"You know I'm not supposed to have a lot of contact with the family," he reminded her. "After the thing with JJ."

"You let me worry about that, okay? I can handle your grandfather; I've been doing it since we were kids."

Gracen nodded. He knew as well as Roy that Aunt Grace wouldn't let him dictate who she could and could not speak to. Evidently, she was the only one. His mom was lying in bed with another nervous breakdown, and his three siblings were fairly indifferent to his departure. They'd never been close. This was his only tearful goodbye as he packed up the remnants of his life in Summerstead and headed west to Ohio. Only Aunt Grace.

He slid into the driver's seat and hung the necklace on his rearview mirror; it sparkled in the midday sun like sunlight shining on the ocean waves behind him. This was the one place he would miss, Aunt Grace and Uncle Harry's homey beach house. Then again, without Uncle Harry half the life had gone out of it anyway. He had passed in February, and by April, everything was changed. A lump caught in Gracen's throat. He cleared it with a cough and adjusted his glasses. Most of the time he wore contacts, but he wanted to give his eyes their best shot at not getting worn out from the long drive ahead. Contacts don't tolerate tears well.

Gracen gave a short wave before he punched in the clutch, slid the gearshift into reverse, and departed Summerstead Isle, New Jersey, the best family beach in America. He'd never understood the moniker himself. Sure, there was a nice beach, and the boardwalk was interesting with shops and mini-golf and eateries. But tourists chattered about it being their home away from home, everything was better at the beach—it was all lost on Gracen.

As he crossed the bridge onto the mainland it sunk in that this was really happening. It wasn't just big talk. The weeks since Uncle Harry's passing had been filled with talk. This was action. He was finally taking hold of his own life. Glancing at his tattoo, he read it aloud,

"'Once more unto the breach, dear friends, once more.'"

A single line lifted from Uncle Harry's favorite play, Shakespeare's *Henry the Fifth*. The last time Gracen visited him at the hospital, he'd given him this speech. His voice had been frail, but still, it was a battle cry, a call to arms. And now that Harry was gone it was exactly what Gracen needed.

Gracen's very existence was a breach in the family. No matter how much he poured into the hole, it served only to tear them further and further apart. The fallout after Uncle Harry's death was the final blow. Now he was punching a new hole in the universe. He would not stop until he had the life he wanted. If not for himself, then to honor Uncle Harry. He was headed west and leaving his problems behind him. Full speed ahead.

* * *

Just as planned, it was not quite midnight when Gracen arrived in Sayen Falls. Bleary-eyed from continual driving, he nearly drove past his new digs. Alex had told him the building was yellow brick and split with another business with an upstairs apartment. It was the light coming from that apartment that got his attention. A warm glow poured through sliding glass doors, spilled first onto the balcony then cast a dim light into the parking lot. He turned the dial back on his radio as he suddenly realized how loudly his music was emanating from his car. Getting the vintage car with the upgraded sound system had been worth it.

With one eye on the yellow building, Gracen threw the gearshift into reverse and effortlessly backed into a parking space. He had many to choose from; only one other vehicle was in the lot, a red Jeep Wagoneer. The year was hard to place—Jeeps aren't really collector cars like his Shelby—but he figured it was a '60s model. He wondered if an old man or a young hipster lived in the apartment next to his. In either case, hopefully, they wouldn't interfere with him too much.

Right now the idea of going into his newly acquired storefront or his apartment made his skin crawl. Being crammed in the Shelby for over eight hours—thank you, rush hour—had pent up too much of his nervous energy. He startled himself accidentally slamming his door, then he leaned against the car to stretch his legs. A simple jog through his new surroundings should do the trick. Evaluating both directions, he decided to run west since he had come from the east. As he turned his head, he caught a glimpse of a shadowy but decidedly feminine figure at the sliding glass door above. The car door must've startled her, too.

Then, he remembered. Alex said an old childhood friend of his lived next door. She had a weird name that Gracen couldn't recall. A girl, he mused, not an old man or a hipster. He figured a girl was more likely to meddle with his business, so that was preemptively irritating. On the other hand, girls could be useful for clearing the head.

But not when they live and work next door. Nope, this one was off-limits. Gracen drew a firm boundary line in his head. That settled, he slipped off his glasses to rub his eyes as he walked to the end of his building. There he found a stone staircase recessed into a grassy embankment. The staircase led into the cobblestone plaza that he would soon learn was locally known as "the riverfront". This was where he was making his new life.

As Gracen jogged through the plaza it seemed like a sad version of the boardwalk in Summerstead. It was about three city blocks long, and his place was pretty near the middle. Unlike the boardwalk, where an ocean view was always to the east, businesses lined both sides of the cobbled road. Retro marquees and wooden signs protruded from the brick-and-plaster storefronts, awkwardly modified from factories of the past. Roughly a third of the shops were empty. There were ruts in the pavement where cobbles had loosened. The overall aesthetic of the place felt like the eighties had pasted its postmodern flair onto an otherwise very nineteenth-century setting. It was disjointed, it was underutilized, and it felt like an incredibly stupid place to start a new life.

By the time he circled back to his building, his reserves of energy were spent, and all he wanted was sleep. Since he was on the plaza side he staggered up the front staircase. At the top, he found two doors, one to the left and one to the right. If it hadn't been for the wreath on the left door, he would not have known which one was his. Just as Alex had said it would be, the door was unlocked for him. For a second Gracen wondered if

What's-Her-Name had unlocked it and if she had a key, but he was too tired to really get to the bottom of that mystery. He crept into his new place and collapsed onto the first soft surface he could find, a supple brown leather sofa. Eventually, he would appreciate its quality, but not tonight. Within seconds he slipped into unconsciousness, fully dressed, shoes still on his feet, glasses pressed into his face.

Sometime late the next day dehydration stirred Gracen from his fog. It took a full minute to remember where he was since the view was entirely new. The apartment had faded brick walls, exposed ductwork, and retro filament lighting. As he stretched into full awareness Gracen decided that his money—or rather his grandfather's money—had been spent okay. Not wanting to bother with any details Gracen had transferred an obscene amount of money to Alex to cover the cost of renting the storefront and apartment, and furnishing the place, all of it sight unseen. Alex had done well enough on the apartment. The storefront remained to be seen, and Gracen had his doubts based on his run last night.

As he rolled off the couch his phone slipped from his back pocket. One missed call. Alex.

"Hey, I hope you got into Sayen Falls and your apartment okay. If you have any questions, reach out to Kyle Farriss. His office is in city hall. I'll be hard to get ahold of for at least a few days. I'm in the airport now waiting for my flight to Vancouver. I'm meeting with some clients and will be in Canada for about a week or so. I'm sure you'll be fine though. It's just Sayen Falls. Enjoy The Gala tonight. Alright, I'll talk to you later."

Kyle Farriss. His name was the other signature on the lease Gracen had signed for the property. He was the community developer in charge of the riverfront plaza. Alex had spoken well of him so Gracen assumed that it was more of a personality thing than a professional thing. Because the man clearly had no idea what he was doing with the riverfront.

Running his fingers through his hair, he could feel that it was curlier than he preferred and greasier than was socially acceptable. He needed to shower but first, he needed to hydrate. In the kitchen he found exposed cupboards stocked with cups, plates, and other accoutrements but nothing in the way of groceries. There was a letter on the counter with an envelope.

*Welcome to Sayen Falls!*
*No one feels like cooking after they move. And if you're opening a pizza place, you should know what the competition tastes like.*
*—Blythe Elwood*

Gracen tore open the envelope to find a gift certificate for Roman's Pizza. At the bottom of the letter, she'd jotted simple directions to find the pizza place. Blythe. That was her name. She must've been the one who had left the door unlocked. For that matter, she was probably the one who had filled the cupboards. Gracen shouldn't have been surprised that Alex had found someone so thorough. He was a real stickler for detail. It's what made him such a proficient corporate lawyer.

Well, at least dinner was covered. Water. He needed water. He found a heavy tumbler in the cupboard by the sink. Above his kitchen sink was a window that offered a fair view of the river beyond the parking lot. The Shelby gleamed in the sunlight, sparkling in her always-coveted glory. And then there was that vintage Wagoneer. Surely it didn't belong to the girl, Blythe. Maybe she had a boyfriend? As he set his glass in the sink and turned away to find his bathroom, an unexpected sight demanded a double take. A young woman dressed in a pink cocktail dress and white kitten heels climbed into the driver's side of the Jeep. Then she shifted into reverse and sped out of the private lot. Not only did it belong to the girl, but she could drive it in an evening gown. Gracen was starting to wonder what kind of odd pocket of old-school Americana he had moved into.

The dress. The Gala. That was all happening today. And soon it seemed. Or else Blythe just really liked to be dressed up.

When Alex had told him about The Gala, or rather, warned him, Gracen had shrugged it off. He figured he'd probably miss it anyway, but as luck would have it, he'd arrived the very same day. And judging by the way Blythe was dressed, this was no Podunk affair. Luckily, the boxes of clothes and other personal effects that he'd sent ahead had arrived. He remembered the box in the back seat of the Shelby—a box of important documents and things Uncle Harry had set aside for him—and made a mental note to bring it up before he left for dinner.

He looked at the stack of boxes with a disgusted sigh. It wasn't like him to leave something disorganized and unlabeled, but he had been angry when he packed so "stuff" seemed to be a good enough descriptor. He was irritated with himself for this waste of time. Then, he quickly shifted blame to his brother. After all, JJ was the reason he'd been angry in the first place and provoked into this inefficiency.

He started digging through boxes and first found movies and books. After three of those, he finally found a box of shoes and belts. He was getting closer. At last, he found clothes, but not the right kind. Shorts, t-shirts, jeans, nothing even remotely appropriate for a gala, even a gala at Sayen Falls. Not surprisingly Gracen had left his tux behind on Summerstead. It hadn't been high on his priority list. With growing frustration, he tore open another box.

"Finally," he muttered, "something here will work."

Rummaging through the box he pulled out a blue pin-striped shirt, the same midnight blue as his Shelby. Below the shirt, he found a pair of charcoal-gray pants. He turned back to the box of shoes for a pair of high-end blue boat shoes, then spied a thin black necktie with a square bottom. He wasn't sure it was formal enough but that was as good as it was getting for Sayen Falls' newest arrival. These suburban types could be cliquish and judgy, so he hoped there would be someone who would take it easy on him. Maybe Blythe; she certainly looked nice and the pizza was a friendly gesture. But Gracen knew that usually, the nicer a girl looked the bigger headache she was in the long run. Not that it mattered; he'd drawn a line.

Showering did wonders to bring Gracen back to something that felt more like life. He dressed quickly in jeans and a t-shirt, left his evening clothes out for later. Then he headed out to his car with directions and gift certificate in hand. Blythe wasn't back yet. Looked like that little meet 'n' greet would be happening later, which was probably for the best. He'd be relying on the cocktails to layer on the charm and survive mingling. There was no way he could do all that on an empty stomach.

## Chapter 2

Blythe completely forgot about the electric bill until she flipped the switch to her bathroom light and two of the bulbs flickered out in a rather dramatic fashion. The bill was due by five o'clock, so she had to leave right that minute to get the payment in the box before they emptied it for the day. She'd have to do her makeup and hair in the Jeep at stoplights. That was distracted idling, not distracted driving, right? She grabbed her makeup and a fistful of bobby pins before tearing out the door and down the stairs. There was a momentary pause in her rush when Blythe skirted past the vintage Shelby. It wasn't what she'd been expecting based on the modern furniture Alex had selected for her new neighbor. But that was something she'd have to ponder later.

Of course, traffic was congested. It was a Friday evening at rush hour. At last, she made it to city hall, mumbling the whole way about online payments and paperless billing being a thing now. After throwing her bill in the utility box she grumbled against the traffic clogging her way to the riverfront. She arrived just as The Gala was starting. The Shelby was gone and an old Honda was in the lot instead. Finn was here. She breathed a sigh of relief as she entered through the back door of The Yellow Bowl and called out for him.

"I'm up front," he shouted. His Irish accent was thicker when he raised his voice. Blythe walked through the shop, passing crammed bookcases; the smell of coffee and tea filled the air. This was home. More than any house, The Yellow Bowl was Blythe's home. It was the one place that felt right.

Finn McCartney, as usual, was keeping busy and making himself useful refilling sugar dispensers at the front counter. When he finished he looked at Blythe, his eyes lit up and he grinned, "Good night, woman."

"You only get away with calling me that because of your accent."

"I stand by my statement, woman, you're stunning."

"Thank you. You clean up pretty good too, for a poor seminary student," she grinned. He smoothed out his pink and gray tie with a shy smile. "Although you didn't have to match me," she said, holding his tie up to her dress. "It's a little prom night don't you think?"

"I didn't have a lot to work with. Apparently having an entire wardrobe of suits is no longer a requirement for taking a pulpit, so I'm in luck," he said. Finn washed his hands in the small sink then came around the counter, "So has the new guy arrived?"

"About midnight last night."

Finn raised his eyebrow. He opened the front door of the shop to escort Blythe outside. She rolled her eyes, "I had my balcony door open since it was such a warm night. March was frigid, but April is more than making up for it."

"How very *Romeo and Juliet*, balcony and all."

"Shut it."

"I promise, that's my only one."

"Good. Because you know I've been getting giggles and knowing glances from my grandmother and Ginnie for a month now. It feels so Jane Austen."

"Oh, have you been reading Jane Austen again?"

"You know I don't have time to read. I just sell the pretty books, I don't get to read them," she grinned. She looked up at the strings of fat round lightbulbs strung from side-to-side across the plaza. They were glowing warmly against the twilight sky. The riverfront wasn't much to look at, in all honesty, but it did get prettied up for The Gala each year.

Finn locked the door to The Yellow Bowl as he spoke, "I do know. But I also know that you've turned a page this year. You're not dwelling on Ian as much."

There was a poky jab at her heart at the mention of his name. "It's been about eighteen months since I saw his face or heard his voice. And I finally don't miss him. I think I finally see him the way the rest of you do. If he showed up tomorrow asking me to take him back again I'd say no. I'm done. *Finis.*"

"Well, you definitely mean it if you say it in Latin. So, we'll just put a period on the statement with a toast," Finn said as he motioned to a waiter and selected two tall champagne flutes.

"I'm an Elwood, I'm not supposed to drink," she said. Her grandparents had strict ideas about alcohol and the grandkids at least claimed to toe the party line.

"We all know that Miles and Mary Alice make exceptions for special occasions."

"Like their granddaughter taking her life back?" she asked, accepting the champagne.

"Well, I was referring to The Gala, but if you want to be that dramatic, I'll toast anything," Finn replied. His eyes teased her over the rim of his champagne flute. Blythe smirked at him as she took a sip of champagne. Lowering the flute, she glanced around the plaza.

"Liam texted me. He and Ginnie are coming after all."

"They managed to find a sitter on Gala night?"

"A student, Lily Morgan. I sorta know her dad. He used to come in the shop, but that was ages ago now. Anyway, I'm just glad it worked out and they could come."

"Remind me again why Ginnie's parents didn't just watch Teddy and Viola?" Finn asked.

"Dennis and Linda are out of town for their anniversary," Blythe replied.

13

Through the thickening crowd, she caught a glimpse of her petite grandmother wrapped on her grandfather's arm. Miles navigated Mary Alice toward Blythe and Finn where they stood just outside The Yellow Bowl.

"Why didn't you park out back?" Blythe asked Miles as she pecked his weathered cheek.

"The stairs are getting to be too much for your grandmother to climb," he told her quietly. It was easier to park in the ground level of the parking garage and take their time crossing the plaza than to struggle with the stairs just for a private parking space.

Blythe nodded at him, then turned to hug her grandmother. Mary Alice pressed a small ring box into her hand.

"I found this today when I cleaned out the junk drawer," she explained. Finn took the champagne flute from Blythe, receiving a sideways glance from Mary Alice. Blythe fiddled with the lid and found inside a gold Claddagh ring with an emerald set in the crown. According to Irish tradition, the Claddagh searches for true love. It is a symbol of loyalty, friendship, and honor, which perfectly described her grandparents' marriage. They were everything Blythe ever hoped to be. She slipped it easily onto her left-hand ring finger.

"Just fits," she said, salty tears tingling her eyes. She batted fiercely so her mascara would not even consider running.

"I don't know where that ring came from. I've never seen it before," Mary Alice said, "but I thought you'd like it. I know you're devoted to your work here at the shop, so maybe the ring can do some searching for you. No one should do life alone."

"Thank you, Grammy," Blythe murmured. She hugged her grandmother gently, so she wouldn't crunch her with the swell of emotion she felt.

"Hey, where are those pearls I gave you?" Miles asked as he realized Blythe's neck was bare. "You always wear them to The Gala."

"I must've forgotten. I had to dash down to city hall to throw the electric bill in the mail slot," she sighed, thankful to now have a reason to slip up to her apartment for a moment.

"You work too hard," Mary Alice clucked, shaking her gray head.

"I'll run upstairs and get them on."

"You want me to wait?" Finn offered. He was officially invited to The Gala as an employee of The Yellow Bowl, but he was really just there for Blythe. She shook her head.

"I'll catch up. You've waited on me enough today."

She took the steep staircase up to her apartment landing two at a time, rather ungracefully in her vintage dress. In the kitchen, she ran a glass of cool water in her sink as she steadied her breathing. These weren't exactly sad tears she was arguing with, but they weren't exactly happy tears either. They were the kind of tears that come from emotions held deep inside, like hope and the desire to be loved and the feeling of being loved.

While she examined the ring sparkling on her finger Blythe told herself it wasn't that she was unloved, it was that she wasn't loved yet. There was a difference. And now the Claddagh could do the searching for her. She scoffed at herself; it was just a fairy tale.

She smoothed her dark hair in the mirror, her French twist still intact save for a few romantic wisps framing her oval face. Then she remembered why she was up here in the first place and retrieved her beloved string of pearls.

PapPap had given them to her on her Sweet Sixteen. Her grandparents had hosted a big birthday party for her at The Yellow Bowl. They'd invited all of their friends and her friends for a cross-generational blowout. The Glenn Miller Orchestra and The Dave Matthews Band took turns on the stereo, but it worked. The whole thing worked. Blythe felt loved, which was a fleeting emotion in those days. And those pearls were a lasting reminder of how important she was to her grandparents.

Her ensemble was now complete with PapPap's pearls. Blythe smiled. She was loved. Maybe not by the brooding romantic hero that she once dreamed of, but she was loved very much and that was something. She descended the stairs much more calmly and in a style much more befitting the pink tea-length dress, made full by the hot pink crinoline just peeking out from the hem. At the bottom, she rounded the corner out of the stairwell and smacked into a tall man unknown to her.

He was four or five inches taller than Blythe, which impressed her as she was rather tall herself. The sleeves of his blue pin-striped shirt were rolled up to his elbows, revealing a tattoo that she couldn't quite read without staring. His top button was undone but he wore a loosened black necktie, slate-gray pants, and blue boat shoes.

"I'm so sorry," he said, taking her elbow into his firm hand. Her left hand extended to steady herself, and he grasped it, his fingers brushing the Claddagh. Their eyes met; Blythe had never seen eyes like that before. They weren't one color but several—blue, green, hazel, gray, gold—like a picture she'd seen of a galaxy, perfectly framed by black-rimmed glasses.

"It's alright. I wasn't watching where I was going," Blythe breathed, suddenly aware that she had been holding her breath.

He released her elbow and extended his hand, "I'm Gracen Hall."

"So you're Gracen Hall," she said, slipping her hand into his. "It's good to meet you. It was a little weird setting up your apartment without even knowing you."

One look at that striking dress and Gracen realized this was the young lady he had seen getting into the Jeep. He grinned, "It was a little weird moving into a place I'd never seen, but I appreciate your help."

"It's not every day that Alex Beckwith asks me for a favor, and I

15

couldn't say no. Becky would never forgive me," she laughed. She paused a moment when Gracen's brow furrowed. "I'm sorry. You're going to get a lot of names thrown at you tonight. Becky is a nickname for George Beckwith, Alex's grandfather. He owns that donut shop across from me."

"There's one name I haven't had thrown at me yet."

"Oh good grief," Blythe muttered at herself. There was no reason for her to be so rattled by this man, even if he was giving off some very confident vibes. "I'm Blythe Elwood."

"As in 'Hail to thee blithe spirit'?" Gracen asked, quoting a bit of Percy Shelley. He gestured as he said it and Blythe was able to read his tattoo. She smiled to herself.

"Shelley?" she asked. "Not quite. More like Gilbert Blythe, *Anne of Green Gables*. My dad categorically ruled out Gilbert for my brothers, but my mom talked him into Blythe because it means happy."

Gracen blinked at her. She'd identified the reference without so much as a pause and then countered it. Dropping a line of poetry or fine literature was one of his favorite tricks. It never failed to make a pretty girl smile. But when Blythe had smiled, it was different. Momentarily, he considered the possibility that Alex had primed this girl just to mess with him. Then realized Alex had better things to do.

"Well, it's quite a name, either way," Gracen said at last.

"I know, it's unique. I was the only Blythe in a school full of Ashleys and Amandas."

"I feel your pain. I was surrounded by Mikes and Ryans."

"I like Gracen though," she said. Her nerves settled. No reason to be emotional over a ring or rendered speechless by her handsome new neighbor. There, she was making progress. She turned her head coyly, "It suits you."

"You think?"

"For knowing you five minutes, sure," she quipped. "Besides, what's in a name? 'A rose by any other name' and all that."

"Shakespeare?"

"Less impressive than the Shelley reference, admittedly, but I figured you'd appreciate it," she pointed at his arm. Gracen peered at her incredulously. She grinned, "What?"

"I just ... wasn't expecting anyone to know it."

"I love *Henry the Fifth*."

"You've read it?"

"I wrote my senior thesis on Shakespeare and the movies. I focused on *Henry the Fifth*, *Romeo and Juliet*, and *Much Ado About Nothing*. Of course, that was years ago now."

This was met with a stare. He'd only ever discussed literature and the fine arts with Uncle Harry. No one Gracen knew wanted to talk about old

16

words penned in centuries past, particularly, none of the women he knew. At least, to his knowledge, maybe he'd never given them the chance. So Blythe with her impromptu Shakespearean small talk startled him and it took a minute to recover.

In that minute, she laughed at him, "You seem surprised, shocked even."

"To be honest, this is not exactly the small talk I expected tonight. I've been to many galas, balls, and whatever, but I don't recall ever discussing poetry at any of them."

"Well, you started it. But I'm glad I could surprise you and offer you a new experience."

"I appreciate it. It's not often I get to put my English minor to good use. The business major, the MBA, *those* I use every day."

"Good ol' Princeton, right? That's how you know Alex."

"Right, we were roommates."

"But in between business classes, you took in Shakespeare?"

"Something like that."

"And did you study poetry?"

"Some, but my preference was nineteenth-century literature."

"Like Dickens and Twain, or like Emerson and Thoreau?"

"Some Dickens, a bit of Emerson, but mostly Austen and the Brontes."

A bubble of laughter escaped Blythe's lips, "Chick lit?"

"I think that's a bit insulting to them, but *Pride and Prejudice* is the key to understanding women," he said with a devilish smile. Blythe pursed her lips, trying to figure out just what he meant by that.

Just as she formulated the perfect retort to the notion that literature could unravel the mystery that is woman, they were interrupted by Mae Houser.

"Oh the dress fits you just perfectly," she gasped. "I am so glad. I knew you would look just gorgeous in it the moment it came into the shop."

"You always know what I'll love, Mae," Blythe replied. "Have you met Gracen Hall? He's opening a pizzeria in the shop next to The Yellow Bowl."

"Good to meet you, Gracen. I've been wondering about that place. It's a good location next to The Yellow Bowl. The Elwoods are good people," Mae said.

"So I'm finding out," he winked. Blythe tried her darnedest to squelch the blush rising in her cheeks.

"Mae owns the vintage dress shop in the next block, near The Chatterbox," she explained. He nodded; he had noticed the explosion of taffeta and lace in the display window on his jog.

"Hey, don't stick around here all night. The band they hired is pretty good. You should go down that way, cut a rug. Don't let your brother have

17

all the fun! He's giving Ginnie quite a night out," Mae laughed before joining Sam Buterbaugh. Sam owned Buterbaugh's Antiques across from Houser's Dress Shop. He was a widower and she was a widow and Blythe thought they'd make a good match. She was pretty sure Sam did too but didn't know how to woo a woman after being out of the game for forty-some-odd years. Maybe he needed a primer in Jane Austen, Blythe thought with a smile.

"Cut a rug?" Gracen snickered.

"I'm surprised she didn't say it was groovy. She's sweet but not very … modern."

He looked around, "That could be a tagline for the whole plaza."

Blythe laughed and Gracen liked it. He liked everything about her. Stunning looks aside, this girl was sharp as a tack. Uncle Harry always said it would take more than a pretty face to finally turn Gracen's head. Nope. That line had been drawn and it was firm. There would be no toying with the girl next door, no matter how interesting she was.

"Come on," Blythe said as she took a step east toward the amphitheater, "I'll give you the unofficial tour of the riverfront and I'll talk slow so you can keep up. I wouldn't want to overtax that very educated brain of yours."

Gracen rolled his eyes but held out his arm for Blythe. She hesitated for a moment before slipping her arm around his. He stifled a self-satisfied sigh. There was a line between flirting and trifling, even if they were all the same letters just mixed up. This was flirting; this was safe.

# Chapter 3

"I might need you to write this down," Gracen said as he and Blythe ended their tour at the amphitheater at the end of the plaza.

"I'll draw you a map," she grinned. Her arm left his side as she returned a wave to a couple on the dance floor. "Oh good, everyone is here so you can meet them all at once."

"That won't add to my confusion at all," he said with thick sarcasm.

"I have a hard time believing a seasoned businessman really struggles with names and places as much as you're alleging," she replied. He shrugged away a grin.

Blythe led the way towards her grandparents who were sitting in the amphitheater with Finn and Becky. They were joined presently by her older brother, Liam, and his wife Ginnie—the couple who had waved at them from the dance floor.

"What do you think of the band?" Blythe asked her brother. He raised an eyebrow.

"You know I'm not much of a Beatles fan."

"Hey, didn't you go out with Ringo?" Ginnie asked, somewhat discreetly pointing towards the stage. Blythe took a good look at the tribute band then smothered a laugh.

"I did for a hot minute. He was a good kisser."

"More than I needed to know," Liam grunted. He turned his attention towards Gracen who was looking very amused. "I assume you're the new guy in town."

"That is me. Gracen Hall."

They shook hands and Gracen was keenly aware he was under scrutiny. As he glanced at the other members of this small party, he could see they were all evaluating him.

"This is my brother Liam and his wife Ginnie. They have two kids, my little god-monsters," Blythe said with obvious pride. "Ginnie happens to also be Alex's cousin."

"Right, he told me that, I think. There were a lot of names and details," Gracen said as he took Ginnie's hand.

Blythe continued, "These are my grandparents, Miles and Mary Alice Elwood. They actually own The Yellow Bowl, I just manage it for them. And this is Finn McCartney. He works for us between classes at the seminary school in Oak Grove and interning at First Church here in town."

"You can just call him Father Finn," Becky said, deliberately irritating Finn.

"And this is George Beckwith, but everyone calls him Becky like I said before. That's a real nickname, unlike Father Finn," Blythe said as Finn scowled.

"Alex's grandfather," Gracen said as he shook hands with the old man. "It's good to finally meet you."

"Likewise," Becky said. He shared an obvious look with Miles. Inwardly Gracen sighed. He liked talking with Blythe, but clearly flirting with her in front of the hometown crowd was going to be a rookie mistake.

On stage, the band started up again with "Eight Days a Week". Blythe put her hands on her hips as she said to Liam,

"Let me guess, this one bothers you because it's not numerically correct?" Then she explained to Gracen, "Liam teaches math at the high school."

"It's numerically fine, it's just not calendarly correct."

"Calendarly?"

"You were the English major, not me."

"There's a reason one of you handles the books and the other one of you balances the books," Miles joked, rather pleased with his pun.

Mary Alice patted his arm, "Very clever, dear."

"Anyway, you have to admit this is better than last year," Blythe insisted.

"Oh that was painful," Liam readily agreed. The mayor's nephew thought he was the next singer-songwriter superstar, but he had bombed terribly. Blythe had called their younger brother Silas that night and made him listen to the music through her phone. Silas was the musician in the Elwood family. All agreed that it was cringe-worthy.

"Why didn't you date that guy longer?" Ginnie asked as she studied pretend Ringo Starr drumming his heart out. "He's cute."

"He was cute in high school too. I guess we were a thing for maybe like a month."

Gracen almost laughed out loud. The idea of a month being short-lived was absurd. He was too focused on his work and himself to put any time into a relationship.

"I don't remember you dating much in high school," Liam said.

"This was after you left for OSU," Blythe told her brother. Still, Liam was right. She really hadn't dated much in high school. In those days Blythe was outspoken and sassy. Girls despised her confidence, and guys didn't really know what to do with it. Besides, Blythe was in an undefined, unofficial, nearly non-existent relationship with Jesse Beckwith. And that mess was enough to keep most potential boyfriends far, far away. Jesse was nothing like his older brother Alex. He was impulsive, demonstrative, even dramatic if he thought it'd get him what he wanted.

Blythe shook her head, casting off those thoughts. Then she laughed, "I guess he wasn't very interesting ... other than the kissing."

This had the desired effect on Liam who made a face and took his wife's hand to lead her back to the dance floor. Blythe stuck her tongue out at him as they left. When the band transitioned into "When I'm Sixty-Four" her eyes lit up, and she looked at Finn hopefully.

"Of course, it's why I'm here," he smiled.

Finn took Blythe onto the dance floor with confidence. She laughed as he slipped a hand around her waist. They were comfortable dancing together, and Gracen noticed how effortlessly Blythe moved. It wasn't exactly ballroom dancing, but there was grace there.

"It was very kind of Blythe to set up the apartment for me," Gracen remarked to her grandparents. "I'm sure she's very busy and I appreciate the extra work."

"Finn helped with the furniture and heavy lifting. He's probably the most helpful young man I've ever met," Miles said.

"They were glad to do it. We look after our own," Mary Alice said. "We fools on the river have to stick together."

A waiter offered a tray of drinks, nondescript cocktails, which Gracen took with gratitude. This was nothing like the formal events he'd attended thus far in his life. Maybe the mayor and the members of the city council would be more self-important; perhaps a pack of college professors could be snobby just to make him feel at home. But as he looked around he just saw a crowd of people being nice to each other. It was very unsettling.

"That's what this gala is about," Miles explained. "The winter is hard on the businesses. People don't like to walk from the parking decks to the shops, or going shop to shop."

"They just want to be able to run in and out and get what they need," Becky grumbled. "Something someone should've taken into consideration when they designed this place."

Gracen couldn't have agreed with him more, but he kept that to himself.

"Seven or eight years ago Kyle Farriss and Mayor Holland came up with this Spring Gala idea," Mary Alice said. "The business owners, their staff, family, and whatnot are able to attend free. Everyone else here pays."

"Like a fundraiser?" Gracen asked. His eyes skirted around the plaza; this place could really use some charity.

"No, the ticket money pays for the band, the drinks, the finger food," Mary Alice told him. "It's just a celebration that the riverfront made it through another winter."

This was insane in Gracen's not-so-humble opinion. It would make much more sense to use this event to generate actual money for the businesses; money to repair and replace, or maybe just to bulldoze it and start from scratch. He sipped his overly fruity cocktail. No chance they'd go for the demolition idea. They seemed to like being stuck in a time warp.

He looked back to Mary Alice, but saw her nudging Miles and discreetly pointing towards the dance floor. Following her gaze, Gracen saw that Finn had been sidelined with a phone call. Judging by his expression, a call he wasn't happy to get. Blythe was talking with Ginnie; Liam looked bored.

"Ireland must be calling," Miles said. "Never a good thing."

"Particularly tonight. Finn gets out about as much as Blythe does," Mary Alice said.

"And he had one job to do," Miles added. Gracen felt his insides grimace. The way they finished each other's sentences, taking turns with the sideways glances in his direction, it was practiced and perfected. It was just like Aunt Grace and Uncle Harry. A ripple of grief shot through Gracen's heart as he realized again that Aunt Grace wouldn't be sharing this banter with Uncle Harry anymore. He finished his cocktail.

"Dance with Blythe," Gracen sighed. Miles and Mary Alice looked at him as though they had no idea what he was talking about. "Finn's one job was to dance with Blythe."

"It's just a joke, dear," Mary Alice smiled.

"I thought that was something that kids say," Miles said to Becky. "One job to do."

Becky shook his head with a frown, "I'm still figuring out why everyone's obsessed with that book of faces thing. It's not even a book."

Gracen couldn't help the snort of laughter. He wasn't sure if Becky was trying to be funny or not. In either case, he caught the hint about Blythe and figured he'd put all of them out of their misery.

He hadn't planned on doing any dancing that night. It wasn't really his scene, and he didn't want to toy with Blythe too much. Then again, this was more of a social club than nightclub situation. So what was the harm?

So, severely underestimating the power of conversation, Gracen stepped onto the dance floor. As the look-alike John Lennon began singing "If I Fell" he took Blythe's hand into his. Starting at the touch she turned to see who had hold of her.

"I didn't really think you'd be the 'dancing at a gala' type," she said.

"With the right partner, maybe I am," he replied. "You move like a dancer."

Blythe blinked twice. No one had ever told her she moved like a dancer. Like a she-buffalo trying to dance, yes, but not a real dancer. She'd spent hours and hours rehearsing dance routines, with calloused feet and very sore knees.

"Let me guess, community theater, lead in the school musical?" he continued.

"I killed myself to learn the routines. I don't have a naturally graceful bone in my body."

"Could've fooled me," he said. As he put his hand around her waist, she naturally shifted towards him. Her fingers were slender and felt delicate in his hand. He added softly, "I told you, you move like a dancer."

"Just following your lead."

For a moment, she could have sworn that he smelled ever so faintly of salt water. With Summerstead Isle at her fingertips, her resolve to live now instead of in yesterday and in what might have been was immediately diminished.

Smiling, she asked, "So tell me, why Ohio?"

"Why not Ohio?"

"Okay then, why not New Jersey?"

He wanted to keep his reasons close to the vest, so he replied simply, "It's not everything it's cracked up to be."

"It probably is different when you live there, but I always loved it. My family used to vacation there every year. We'd rent a condo on Kelsey Avenue, stay a whole week. One year I read seven-hundred pages of *Gone with the Wind* sitting on the beach. I mean, who goes all the way to New Jersey to read *Gone with the Wind?*"

"Not a bad way to spend a week."

He'd spent countless hours sitting in a lonely spot on the beach with his head in a book, listening to waves crashing and seagulls calling, and getting lost in a story better than his own. "It seems this isn't the first time we've been in the same place at the same time."

"Just the first time we're aware of it."

"I don't know, maybe I noticed you before."

"Well, if you remember a gangly teenage girl with a sand-covered copy of *Gone with the Wind,* that was me."

"Nope, I'm afraid I don't remember that."

"I'm relieved. It was not a good hair year for me."

Gracen had found his avenue for getting the conversation away from himself. "And do you read when you're away from the beach?"

"I used to, but there isn't much time now. The shop is my life," she said, lifting her hand to gesture in the direction of The Yellow Bowl. As her hand rested again on his broad shoulder, he reflexively shifted his hand on the small of her back. Blythe hoped that shiver she felt didn't come through to the outside of her body. She shrugged to hide it, "I don't think I've finished a book in years."

The truth was Blythe wasn't just busy. She had come to avoid the things she loved so much; the books that brought her such joy, such inspiration, such depth of emotion. Her life at The Yellow Bowl was an inexhaustible mess of paperwork for filing, piles of teacups for washing, stacks of books for sorting, and customers for sweet-talking. There simply wasn't time for the things she loved, for the things that helped her feel. Or perhaps she had stopped making time. Instead, she allowed all the empty spaces to be filled in with obligations so she didn't have to feel anything. Ian had been the last straw, and now it was just better not to feel too deeply or expect too much.

Yet that sun-bleached memory of reading under the shade of a wide beach umbrella, her toes buried in sand, made Blythe want to curl up with a book and get lost again. Maybe find herself again.

"You should make time," Gracen said as if reading her thoughts. She looked up at him, her green eyes bright, and she blinked slowly. Every other Elwood had brilliant blue eyes, as dazzling as sapphires, except Blythe. Her eyes were an ever-changing shade of green.

"I should," she said breathlessly, feeling all the air go out of her lungs.

Abruptly, almost abrasively, the band switched to "Twist and Shout". With near relief, Gracen chuckled when Blythe actually jumped and her eyes betrayed her surprise.

"What a strange transition," he said. "You should have a word with your ex about how to pick a set list."

"I'll get right on that," she retorted. Gracen lifted her hand high in the air to spin her. This was more surprising than the music. "So you, like, actually dance?"

"Not often, but when I have to. My aunt and uncle used to dance in their living room. I learned a few things."

"They sound like fun people."

"They were the best people."

"Were?"

"Uncle Harry passed in February."

"I'm so sorry," Blythe told him sincerely. This was becoming a rather incongruous conversation for the music.

His nerves told him he was talking too much and needed to stop. As the band nailed the shouting part of "Twist and Shout" Gracen took a beat to clear his thoughts and blink away his grief. Then, he spun her again. "He'd be happy I'm with people."

The truth was Uncle Harry would be over the moon that Gracen was dancing with a beautiful woman on this fine spring evening instead of holed up with work. It was a shame the evening would come to an end soon. About a block away, church bells began to chime. It was a strange sound to hear above the band and the murmur of The Gala.

"It's ten o'clock," Blythe said, looking up as if she could see the music notes. "The bells at First Church play hymns at ten in the morning, twelve noon, six in the evening, and ten at night. I think every kid in Sayen Falls goes asleep to those hymns."

"Those are not even intervals."

"Not at all, but it's pretty. I've missed hearing it. It's harder to hear the bells in the winter with all the windows and doors shut up."

"Hey," Ginnie interrupted, "we gotta head home. Hopefully, the kids are asleep, but who knows. Lily Morgan seemed too nice for my terrorists."

"It was good to meet you," Liam said, shaking Gracen's hand again. The women shared a look, Ginnie said quite a lot with her eyes. She was high on expectations for her sister-in-law that Blythe did not harbor for herself.

24

In the amphitheater, Miles helped Mary Alice up from her chair. He made eye contact with Blythe then gave her a little wave. They would be taking their leave too. It had been a nice evening out with the young people, but it was time to go home and get settled. Becky had already returned to his quiet house.

Blythe pushed a few wispy hairs out of her eyes, "I should probably find Finn. If he's still on the phone, that's not a good sign."

Gracen held his arm out to Blythe, "Can I walk you home?"

Blythe slipped her arm around Gracen's, "I was counting on it."

## Chapter 4

"Gracen seems like a nice boy," Mary Alice said. Her old bones creaked as she eased herself onto the couch. While she had taken her teeth out and washed her face Miles made up her makeshift bed, laying a sheet over the couch cushions, arranging her pillows just the way she liked, and getting her favorite quilt ready. She'd told him a dozen times that he didn't have to fuss over her, but he just kept doing it. He was a stubborn one.

He turned on the eleven o'clock news as he joined his wife on the couch. He sighed and collected his thoughts, "He does seem nice enough."

"You're worried about Blythe."

This was a redundant statement. Miles lived in a constant state of worry for his three grandchildren. The amount ebbed and flowed, but it was always there.

"I just don't want history to repeat itself. So you and Ginnie are going to have to go easy on Blythe. Don't shove her at that boy."

"I've never shoved anyone in my life," she countered. "I might nudge a little when my grandchildren need some prodding though."

"I wish you'd nudge Silas a bit more," he confessed. Of the three grandchildren, his youngest had him the most worried. Silas's marriage was in trouble, but, true to form, he wasn't opening up about it. Silas was typically the secretive one. Miles respected that was the boy's nature, but he would rather be privy to the information and tailor his prayers properly. As it was, he would just have to pray vaguely. Praying, Mary Alice insisted, was the only response to worry.

Miles and Mary Alice prayed every night for their family and had for over fifty years. Sometimes they wondered if it did any good at all, but then in just the right moment, the prayers would be poured out again and answers would come.

"It was nice that Ginnie and William were able to come tonight," Miles said. He only ever referred to their eldest grandson by his full name.

"It was good for Ginnie especially. I think it's hard for her to be at home with the kids all day long. She was always so outgoing."

"We'll see what we can do," Miles promised. After fifty-nine years together he knew that there were times to simply trust his wife's instincts. If she was concerned for Ginnie, there probably was a reason to be. Just like he felt about Silas.

The TV news cycled to the sports and Miles muted it. Mary Alice slipped her careworn hands in his. Together they bowed their heads to pray.

* * *

When Liam and Ginnie arrived home their children, much to their surprise, were tucked snugly in bed where they'd been sleeping for the last hour.

"How did you do it?" Ginnie was astonished; her children had a special knack of transforming from angels into wolverines at the witching hour. "They never go down quietly for sitters."

Lily lifted her shoulders shyly, "I guess I just wore them out. We were outside most of the evening. I had Teddy do jumping jacks, well his version of jumping jacks, before we came in. And then we did a craft and read stories."

"I've never had a babysitter bring crafts before," Ginnie smiled. "I bet Viola loved it."

"She was very excited. Teddy did a good job too. He really likes stickers."

"He does. He can get a little carried away," Ginnie said, remembering the great sticker debacle just a month prior. Teddy had gotten a package of stickers in the mail in a card from Liam's mom and stepdad. When Ginnie left him alone to switch the laundry from the washer to the dryer Teddy had gone nuts, putting stickers on every available surface he could reach—the fridge, the cupboards, the TV screen. Careful peeling and essential oils had removed most of the damage.

"They're sweet kids. I hope I can come back sometime," Lily said softly.

"I'm glad this worked out, Lily," Ginnie assured her.

"How was The Gala?" Lily asked. "My parents go every year."

"It was nice. The music was a little lame but you'll have that," Liam said, loosening his tie. Ginnie shook her head with a teasing smile.

"My husband isn't a Beatles fan, and they hired a tribute band."

"Oh, my father doesn't like The Beatles either," Lily said. She liked the easy affection between Liam and Ginnie, the winks, and nods, and poking at one another.

"Isn't your dad English?" Liam asked. "Shouldn't he like The Beatles?"

"Well, it's not a requirement," she replied. She picked up her backpack and the keys to her sporty Lexus.

"Thank you for your help," Liam said as he opened their front door, "and thank your parents for letting you be out this late."

"You don't have to worry about getting home early for me," Lily told them. "My parents don't worry, so if I get to sit for you again, please just take your time and enjoy yourselves."

Her words struck a chord in Ginnie's heart. Her own parents' wildly over-protective behavior used to drive her crazy. Now as an adult she was grateful for their provision and protection. It made her sad that this sweet young girl didn't feel that at all.

After Lily departed, Ginnie tiptoed into her kids' bedrooms to make sure they were still breathing and carefully kiss their heads. Being a mom was hard sometimes, like being smothered in loud, sticky, blessings. But those blessings were always angelic in their sleep.

* * *

The Morgan home was all show and no heart. It was not a place Lily missed, certainly no home sweet home despite all the material things she could imagine. She parked her car next to her dad's in the spacious three-car garage. His Jag was still making those clicking sounds as it cooled, so Lily knew they hadn't been home long.

She cracked open the door from the garage into the laundry room and listened. Her parents were upstairs. They weren't yelling, but their voices were … animated. Silently she dropped her backpack in the laundry room, careful to not cause an obstruction—as her parents had pointed out to her before.

Using her cell phone to light the way, Lily navigated through the dining room toward the staircase. Her room was the first one at the top of the stairs. She'd often been thankful that she didn't have to creep past her parents' room when they were fighting, or the guest room where her father often slept.

After she succeeded in her mission to her room, she threw open the door to the walk-in closet that her mom had insisted be added to her daughter's room. Lily stared at her options: high-quality pajamas, a hand-made nightgown from her English grandmother, or one of her oversized t-shirts. Tonight she wanted simple. She pulled out a built-in drawer and chose a pair of shabby pajama pants and her dad's threadbare Eton t-shirt. For a second she wondered what her dad was like as a teenager, and then she figured he'd probably been stuffy and boring then too.

She flopped onto her four-poster antique oak bed and scrolled through her phone absentmindedly. Nothing interesting anywhere on social media. Big surprise. Lily's thoughts cycled back to the Elwoods, the quintessential American family, two loving parents, two adorable children, they even had a dog and a white picket fence. Mr. Elwood obviously loved his family, adored his wife. And it was no wonder, as Ginnie was the model of the loving wife, and mother. She saw the love between them and wished that her own parents adored each other the way that they did. As much as she wished on every last star, she knew that wasn't possible.

Her thoughts were interrupted by a loud slam of a door. Lily knew that door. She had heard it so many times before. Her father was a very buttoned-up man, in true keeping with his English nature, but he had his limits. When Julian Morgan finally reached his boiling point he exploded like a geyser. Lily rolled over. She knew what was coming next. Unable to resist a fight Mom always followed, and then the real fighting started. If Julian was thoroughly English then Karen was completely American. She didn't understand a man who couldn't just talk things out and say how he felt. She was done dealing with his issues.

Lily took a breath. There has to be more than this, right? She clicked on her TV for a distraction. Maybe she could binge watch something with happy people in it. She was tired of the arguing—she wanted resolution, she wanted more.

Just as she selected a show, her phone lit up with a text message. It was from Brady Carmichael, the twenty-year-old boyfriend her parents barely acknowledged. She'd met Brady a few weeks earlier when she'd taken her car in for an oil change. He had flirted with her, and she had soaked up his attention like a wilted sunflower. As far as she could tell, Brady was the only person who took an interest in her; he was the only one who cared.

* * *

"Gramps?" Jesse said slowly. His grandfather's phone call woke him up even though it was late morning in Hong Kong. Despite the fact that he basically lived in hotel rooms, Jesse did not sleep well in strange beds.

"Boy, you should've come home for The Gala," Becky told his grandson. He was sitting on the edge of his bed, about to turn in for the night. It had been two years since Pearl had passed and it was still so hard to go to sleep alone.

"I know, but I couldn't pass this job up. I'll be home soon though."

"You better come home soon."

"Is this because of the new guy?"

"So you know about him?"

"I talked to Alex about a month ago, when he was setting it all up," Jesse sighed. That call with his brother had been so strange. That's why this one felt normal. Everything between the Beckwiths was strange. "Look, Gramps, if this is because of Blythe—"

"I just don't want you to come home someday and regret it all."

"Gramps, trust me. And stop worrying. You spend too much time with Miles. And Ginnie. The three of you are going to worry yourselves into anemia. I'll be home soon. That's a promise."

"I'll hold you to it, boy."

* * *

"Do you have a pen?" Blythe asked Gracen as she snatched a cocktail napkin from an empty bistro table in the plaza. Gracen fished in his pocket and produced a ballpoint pen. She grinned as she took it, "I'm surprised it isn't gold-plated and engraved."

"Do I give that much of a little rich boy vibe?"

"No, but you are that much fun to tease."

As they approached The Yellow Bowl they found Finn leaning in the doorway, listening intently and not saying much. He looked very frustrated.

Cupping the phone to his shoulder he apologized to Blythe, "I'm sorry for leaving you stranded, it's Bridget."

"Enough said," Blythe replied. Finn didn't talk much about his family, but Blythe had managed to learn the names of his four siblings and which ones specialized in drama. Bridget was his youngest sister and the worst offender. "Do you want to talk when you're done?"

"I'll probably be a while yet. She's really upset."

Blythe hugged him, "You can use my office if you want, just lock up when you're done. Thanks for coming tonight."

"Anything for you," he winked. He juggled the phone then held out his hand to Gracen, "It was good to meet you."

"Likewise," Gracen nodded.

Finn returned the phone to his ear, "Yes, Bridget, I'm listening, go on."

He smiled again at Blythe and Gracen, then slipped into the darkened shop. A light went on in the back where her office was. Blythe and Gracen were left alone.

A park bench was in the middle of the plaza under a bright lamp, the kind of lamp C. S. Lewis wrote about in Narnia. With a flourish of her skirts, Blythe sat on the bench and, using it for a table, began sketching.

"Is this my map?" Gracen asked, peering. "Am I meant to be able to read it?"

"I am not known for my artistic talents. If you wanted a realistic map, you should have asked Ginnie."

"That would've been good to know before she left with her husband."

"Yup. You're stuck with me now."

She began labeling the images on her map. Then she frowned, turned the napkin over, and began drawing again.

"Didn't like that one?"

"That was the riverfront. You also need to know Sayen Falls."

"My phone has GPS, you know."

Blythe stared at him flatly, "This is better than GPS."

"Better than a map given to me by a satellite that knows everything?"

"Yes. It doesn't know everything. I do. About Sayen Falls anyway."

She presented him with the makeshift map. He straightened his glasses and began to read. The labels made him laugh.

"Student Ghetto—don't go there. Main Street—AKA bars with foam parties and tattoo shops for sorority girls."

"I told you, your little GPS doesn't know what I know. That's the other end of town, where the university is. It's like a totally different world over there. Not without its merits."

"I can see that. Sayen Falls University—the seat of academia and binge drinking. What is Crystal Creek—Snob Paradise?"

"It's very upper middle class. There's a country club and it's all very la-dee-dah."

"Oh, so that's where I'd find my people?"

"I hope not. Those people make me sad."

"They make you sad?"

"Yes. There's more to life than lots of money and big houses and seeing who can work the most hours."

She felt a slight twinge of hypocrisy with that last statement. In bare-bones honesty, she had to admit that she was becoming a workaholic herself. Her life was the shop and little else.

Gracen, on the other hand, knew he was a workaholic. This was why he felt a little like Cinderella at the ball tonight. It had been fun, surprisingly, to talk and flirt with Blythe and to meet her people, but it had to be one of a kind. There would be no time for people in the days and weeks ahead. If he was going to be successful, he'd have to work nonstop.

"Thank you for this map," he said as he put it in his pocket. "I should turn in. I lost an entire day between sleeping in and this gala."

He gestured for Blythe to go up their staircase ahead of him. At the top of the stairs, she rested her hand on her doorknob and stood with one foot on pointe behind the other.

"If you need any help, just let me know. I'm almost always here."

Precisely. And that's why Blythe was going to stay on her side and Gracen was going to stay on his.

"You've been a lot of help already, thank you," Gracen told her as he opened the door to his apartment. She said good night and he said the same, then they disappeared through separate doors.

As he walked through his apartment, he could see her touch on all his things; the arrangement of the furniture, the neatly organized cups and dishes, the folded towels in the linen closet. He hadn't noticed it before. Now Gracen was keenly aware that Blythe had been in his place, ordering his things, and leaving her mark. Whether or not he liked it, she had infiltrated his life. A breach had been made before he even arrived.

Well, starting tomorrow the perimeter would be secured. Gracen had to get down to business, literally. And he didn't foresee dropping into The Yellow Bowl for friendly chats over tea happening anytime soon. Even if she was a wealth of information, surprisingly well-read, and witty. She was a distraction. All people were distractions. And Gracen had no time to spare for distractions.

31

## Chapter 5

By force of habit, Gracen woke at six-thirty the following morning. Lying in bed he swiped through his phone—no missed calls or texts, no new emails, not surprising. He made a mental note to give Aunt Grace a call today, tomorrow at the latest.

With a sigh and a long stretch, he rolled out of bed. He put on his glasses, pulled on gym shorts and a white t-shirt, and slipped into his running shoes. It was time for his run. He had discovered that if he ran first thing in the morning it gave him time to order his thoughts, and plan his day. Gracen had several tips and techniques for getting his head cleared; running was probably the healthiest one.

The riverfront was isolated in the morning, the shops dark, the plaza empty. Gracen decided to run on the boardwalk that followed the river. In Summerstead he avoided the beach and the boards, too many tourists, too many seagulls, too many memories. Here the river was fine. It was new and meandering and demanded nothing of him.

As fresh cool air burned into Gracen's lungs, rhythm started pushing his scrambled thoughts into place. The first order of business would be a shower and something quick to eat. That could be tricky, he still needed groceries. Rather than The Yellow Bowl, he decided to head into Beckwith's Donuts shop. He filed that under 'expanding connections', not 'avoiding neighbor girl'.

Alright, next up on the docket was finally looking at his storefront. Truth be told, Gracen had been dreading this. Maybe it was only recently vacated and wouldn't be in complete shambles. He made two different mental lists depending on the state of the restaurant. With any luck, he'd be able to use the quick and easy list.

Twenty minutes later Gracen circled back to his apartment. The Yellow Bowl was open now and he could see Blythe inside wearing a red gingham apron and smiling at her customers despite tired eyes. It would be easier to just pop in next door for a cup of coffee and a bagel or something. Gracen rarely did easy.

After showering and finding some clothes he could work in, he dashed across the plaza into Beckwith's. There were a half-dozen retirees sitting on stools at the counter. A couple of perky college girls were serving up fresh, hot donuts. Gracen expected regular yeast donuts made more or less assembly style behind the scenes. Instead, Beckwith's boasted fresh cake donuts fried in oil. The donuts were covered in either chocolate, strawberry, or vanilla icing, or sprinkled with powdered sugar, or cinnamon and sugar. They did offer yeast donuts, also made on site, but most people passed after a taste of a hot cake donut. Gracen made his selections and also ordered a coffee to go.

"Aren't you guys and The Yellow Bowl direct competition?" he asked the girl as she entered his order.

"Mr. Beckwith and Mr. Elwood thought of that when they opened," she explained. "We serve their tea and coffee, and they serve our donuts. Not the made-to-order ones though."

Clever. And similar to the business arrangements that had existed between Uncle Harry and Roy. Two separate businesses, helping each other out to maximize the bottom line for both. Until Uncle Harry got sick and Roy finally got what he wanted. Complete control.

Disorder was starting to disrupt the carefully structured thoughts in Gracen's mind. Enough of that mess, he commanded himself, focus on what needs to be done. He thanked the girl, then ducked out of the shop and back towards his own place. As he fiddled with the key, he caught a snippet of Dean Martin's boozy vibrato coming through the front door of The Yellow Bowl. It made him smile, Uncle Harry loved the Rat Pack, but the moment his front door opened and he saw his shop for the first time, that smile vanished.

Imposing cobwebs hung from the corners and dated light fixtures, shabby tables accompanied by worn and tired chairs littered the dining area. A grimy display case mocked him and his goals. He swallowed hard, willing himself to walk through to the kitchen and office. The kitchen was in sore need of cleaning. No, it needed to be torn out and replaced entirely. The office was the best part of the place; it was empty.

Rapid thoughts pushed and shoved for attention. Gracen rubbed his brow with the hand holding hot coffee. It sloshed through the tiny slit in the lid and stung his hand. The small jolt of pain won his attention. He licked the coffee from his hand and then headed out through the back door. There was no way he could think in that environment.

Outside the sun had warmed the air temp just enough to be comfortable. He found a couple of empty buckets between his back door and the door of The Yellow Bowl. That would do for a chair. He slumped onto a bucket, leaned against the yellow brick wall, and took a bite of his vanilla iced donut. As he chewed, Gracen pulled his phone from his pocket, opened his note-taking app, and created a fresh list.

- Demolition—make a separate list to detail
- Clean—hire company?
- Install new fixtures—all kitchen appliances, lighting
- Buy furniture—dining area, office
- Paint
- Décor
- Name the place— Harry's? G.H. Pizza?
- Hire staff

He snickered to himself. The notion of working with a crew of bored suburban teenagers or rowdy college students in need of drinking money was laughable to him. It was a far cry from the middle management white collar job he was used to. No wonder Roy laughed when he'd given him the money. Gracen's life was a joke.

Still, this was all he had. This run-down shop and a recipe. Gracen hoped that elbow grease, smart planning, and good food would be enough to make this work. Returning to Summerstead with his tail between his legs was not an option.

So, he finished his coffee and donuts and started to work. He made more lists in greater detail as he scrutinized his shop from top to bottom, and side to side. Making good use of his smartphone assistant feature, he looked up businesses that could demo, clean, or install for him. As he expected, it would be the most cost-effective to do it himself. It would take all of his time and energy to get the shop in working order, but that was alright with him. He hadn't planned on anything else.

* * *

By the end of the week, Gracen had all of the demolition work done and arrangements were made for the scrap to be picked up. The demo took longer than he planned since he had to be careful not to damage the counters and cupboards that were staying. He spent the weekend scrubbing the storefront clean of all its grime and neglect. It was monotonous and disgusting, but oddly satisfying to see it come clean. Mercifully the floors didn't need to be replaced, and the walls could be salvaged with paint. There were no signs of water damage or other decay. It turned out that his shop had good bones under all that dirt.

On Monday morning he found his work at a standstill. His freezer and refrigerator units were back ordered until Wednesday. Another phone call told him that his pizza ovens, two used ones from outside Pittsburgh, were also delayed. This meant that everything would arrive on Wednesday—the day he had scheduled the stove top and industrial dishwasher to arrive. And it meant he had nothing to do for two or three days. Nothing to do but think.

With a grunt, Gracen threw his phone onto his couch and darted down the stairs for a jog. Time to clear his head, make a new plan. He headed west toward The Chatterbox, a fancy restaurant at the end of the boardwalk. As his mind emptied of concerns for the shop, he thought about the one and only conversation he'd had with Aunt Grace since his move. She had reminded him to be a real person, not a workbot, as she called him. He felt that he was letting her down by being so engulfed by his work. And yet, no one was going to do the work for him and it had to be done.

His legs started to tighten up—much like his brain—so he stopped to stretch his calves against the side of an empty brick building. Closing his eyes and breathing deep, he tried to order his mind again. He was startled by the feel of fur and a wet tongue on his fingertips. A black-and-white border collie was licking his hand and prancing with much excitement over his find. This dog clearly had no idea that Gracen wasn't a real person.

"Bandit! Stop that!" a familiar voice shouted, followed by a laugh. "Oh, it's just you."

"Just me?" Gracen replied. He knelt to scratch the dog's ears as he picked up the leash the dog trailed behind him.

"Yeah, Running Man, just you," Blythe said, her smile teasing him.

"That's a dance move, right?" he stood and handed her the leash. "I assume he isn't yours?"

"No, dogs are a little impractical here. Bandit is Ginnie and Liam's dog. I volunteer to take him after he goes to the vet. The poor guy hates going and he's edgy afterward. My nephew—Teddy the Terror—isn't exactly the best therapy for calming Bandit down."

"Teddy the Terror?" Gracen asked with amusement.

"He's two years old, and a ball of colossal energy. Bandit is normally great with him, but sometimes he needs a break. And I miss having a dog; we had a dog growing up," she explained. Bandit was tugging on his leash, so Blythe started walking. She led them towards the boardwalk. "Bandit likes to bark at the ducks on the river. Did you have a dog as a kid?"

"No, my grandfather didn't see the point in having pets." He looked at Bandit and his tail wagged happily. Roy thought dogs were impractical at the beach and a general nuisance. Anyone who takes but doesn't contribute is a nuisance. There's no quantifiable value for love in Roy's economy.

"So why aren't you at the shop?" Gracen asked.

"It's Monday. We're all closed on Mondays."

"Mondays, closed. Good to know."

"And you? How are you doing? Making any progress?"

"Sort of. I'm stuck on aesthetics. I keep thinking of my uncle's place."

"He owned a pizza place on Summerstead? Which one?"

Gracen's lips quirked into a shy half-smile, he ran his hand along his jaw. Blythe narrowed her eyes, "Don't even tell me, Louie & Lucy's? That's the best place on the Isle."

"Yes, it is. Family owned and run since 1956."

"So why are you here and not, I don't know, *running* it?" she said with emphasis.

"I see what you did there," he smirked, then he explained, "Because it got absorbed into Wallace Corp when my Uncle Harry died."

"Wait a second, Wallace? As in Wallace Wonderland, Adventureland, Bike Rentals, Pirate Golf and Go-Karts?"

"You forgot Wally's Lemonade that started it all. Yes, that Wallace."

"So does that make you a Wallace? Are they like real people?"

"My grandfather is Roy Wallace. We are real people. Sort of."

"I see," she frowned. "And no room in the family business? Explains why you're here."

"Sort of. It's at least the simplest explanation."

"Sort of. Really, Gracen? Is that all I'm getting out of you?"

"We're one of those stereotypical dysfunctional wealthy families," he said dryly.

They had reached the spot where the boards above the river gave way to pavement along the riverbank. Gracen stopped short when a curious assembly of cement pylons of varying heights appeared, leading up towards curved rows of seats like a strange Roman amphitheater. Blythe looked at his face and laughed, "Don't ask, no one knows why they constructed this."

"It's like some kind of eighties drug-induced yuppie Stonehenge."

"It was aliens, had to be," Blythe said as she sat on one of the pylons. She looped Bandit's leash around her ankle. He sat at attention, just waiting for a duck to show up.

"Yes, aliens. Yuppie ones," Gracen nodded.

"So you're stuck on a vision for your shop," she said, bringing the conversation back around. "What will you call it? Maybe there's some inspiration there."

Her interest entertained him. With amusement, he looked down at her from where he was standing, "I don't know. Got any big ideas? You're my resident expert on the riverfront."

"You'll probably think I'm crazy, but I think you should call it Summerstead Isle Pizza, you could call it SIP for short. A lot of the Sayen Falls townies vacation on Summerstead. If you can give them a slice of the beach, they'll give you their money in a heartbeat."

"A slice of the beach," he considered. It was an intriguing angle. "It seems far-fetched. Ohio is basically landlocked."

"We have Lake Erie ... an hour away from here," she pointed out. "Besides, a name doesn't have to make sense. It gets people in the door. I mean, who calls a tea room The Yellow Bowl?"

"Is there a yellow bowl?"

"Yes, but that's not really where the name came from." She looked up at him, he was impossibly tall anyway plus he was standing above her. "You know, I wouldn't get a crick in my neck if you'd sit down."

Shaking his head, he sat down. "So there's really a yellow bowl?"

"There is," she smiled coyly, "and if you ever set foot in the shop I'll show you."

"Why does that sound like 'come into my parlor said the spider to the fly'?"

"I promise to only show you the bowl and not to eat you."

"Then I'll consider it," he nodded. "So you really think a beach place would work?"

"We have a boardwalk and a river, not exactly Summerstead, I know, but people will like it if you can sell it."

He looked at the river as it rushed over rocks and swirled around the pillars holding the boardwalk in place. It was a far cry from Summerstead Isle. But maybe he could carve out one spot here in the river that could remind people of the place they loved. The trickiest part was that Gracen had no idea what they loved about it.

Blythe added, "For what it's worth, my grandparents have an attic with an entire corner of things from Summerstead. I'm sure there's something that could work for your place."

"Why would they let me use it? They don't know me at all."

"Well, we look out for each other down here; we're our own community within Sayen Falls. It sounds lame, but it's true."

"Your grandmother said that at The Gala, about looking out for each other."

"My grandparents sort of set the tone for the riverfront shops when all of this was overhauled and new shops opened up in the eighties. I grew up with the idea that we help each other. Although, I can tell this is a foreign concept to you."

"It's not foreign. It's just," Gracen fumbled through his thoughts, and what he realized made him profoundly sad, "the only person in my life who helped others and accepted help from others was Uncle Harry. And he was taken for a chump in the end."

"That's heartbreaking," she replied gently. "Look, I know it's strange to ask for help from near strangers, but you can't be a maverick and do this all yourself. It's impossible. You're going to be dead before the festival season even starts."

"Festival season?" Gracen asked. This was new information.

"Good grief, did Alex tell you anything? There are festivals throughout the summer down here—Irish Fest, Italian Fest, Music Fest, Rib Fest, blah blah fest, you get the idea. I assumed your grand opening would be Summer Fest, the first weekend in June."

"That moves my timeline up by a couple weeks," he sighed. This made the setbacks even more frustrating.

Blythe stood and Bandit jumped up, his paws thumping her in the abdomen. She scratched his head then pushed him down. "If you want help, or want to bounce ideas around, you know where I am. If not, it's not gonna break my heart. I try to resist it, but Elwoods are a bit pushy by nature. We just like to help."

Now it was Gracen looking up at Blythe, "Is that why you agreed to set

37

up my place?"

"I told you when we met—I couldn't say no to Alex. Becky would never forgive me," Blythe grinned. "But yeah, it's just who I am."

There was a third reason. The moment Alex had revealed that Gracen was from Summerstead, Blythe had begun to hope deep down inside that a little bit of the peace she'd always found in Summerstead would be available next door. However, Gracen had turned up with peace in very short supply, and so Blythe was grasping at straws yet again.

# Chapter 6

That evening, after delivering Bandit safely home, Blythe decided to drop in on her grandparents. Talking about Summerstead had made her nostalgic. Per usual she found Miles and Mary Alice in the kitchen. Miles was taking a cookie sheet from the oven. After Mary Alice's stroke which had limited her mobility, he pitched in a lot more in the domestic duties. Under his wife's direction, he had become a pretty proficient cook and baker.

"Chocolate chip. It's almost like you knew I was coming," Blythe said as she picked up a cookie from the plastic tray where Miles was laying them out to cool.

"How was your day with Bandit?" Mary Alice asked.

"Good, you know I'm his biggest supporter when Liam starts grumbling about him," she grinned. "And while I was walking him today I ran into Gracen. We talked about his shop. He's struggling with a name and a real vision for the place."

"I figured he arrived with all that sorted," Mary Alice said.

"I think he's had a lot of details to deal with. I'm not sure aesthetics are his thing. Anyway, I suggested Summerstead Isle Pizza, which I know is a little crazy, but I think it could work."

"It's no crazier than The Yellow Bowl," Miles said off-handedly.

"What did he think of your idea?" Mary Alice asked.

"He thought it was crazy," Blythe laughed, "but just in case it grows on him, I thought I might look through the attic?"

"Help yourself," Mary Alice said. "Someone should use our old junk."

"It's hardly junk, Grammy, just because you don't use it anymore," Blythe replied. "Besides, I doubt he'll go for it. I just thought it'd be fun to look at again."

"You are our most sentimental grandchild," Mary Alice said fondly.

"When these cookies are done, I'll come up and join you," Miles said as Blythe headed towards the stairs.

"It's alright, I won't be very long. I'll be back in time for *Murder, She Wrote*," she grinned. It came on at eight o'clock on one of the throwback stations they pulled in with their antenna.

Blythe felt them exchange a look behind her back as she climbed the stairs. She was used to the knowing looks Mary Alice and Miles gave each other. They'd been doing it her whole life, and the number had only increased in recent years.

The attic was unfinished space on the second story just off the blue room that had been her uncle's. It had a regular door that could easily be mistaken for a closet until opened. Once inside the attic, three dim lightbulbs on pull chains illuminated the cluttered catch-all. Neither Miles nor Mary Alice believed in purging.

There was a small aisle of patchwork carpet slowly being encroached upon on either side by towering stacks of a lifetime of memories. To the left of the door was an elegantly appointed pump organ littered with framed photos and old knick-knacks. Beside it was a tall oak bookcase with glass doors housing dusty volumes of school books, encyclopedias, and a handful of sensational novels. Blythe had always wondered how they'd gotten such large, heavy pieces of furniture up the stairs and into this jammed space.

But this visit to the attic wasn't about strange furniture storage. Just beyond the bookcase was a stack of paintings leaning against the wall. This was what she was after. When she found the one she wanted tears filled her eyes. She had expected them and that's why she wanted to be alone. Blythe couldn't help but become emotional when sifting through the storehouse of her favorite memories. Summerstead Isle and happiness were synonymous to her. And she wanted a piece of it here in Sayen Falls now more than ever. Now that it was attainable.

But only through Gracen. And he was irritating. The night they met Gracen had been so charming, friendly, even flirtatious, and then a week of literally running past her. Blythe had decided that she wasn't going to chase after him. She'd wait for him to come to her, or for their paths to cross naturally. For pity's sakes, they were neighbors. Still, it was vexing all the same. She liked talking to him, he made her laugh, she got to use her brain and not feel bad about it. Ian had hated that Blythe was clever. And furthermore, Gracen had the recipe for Louie & Lucy's, the best pizza she ever tasted.

She'd have to wear him down, one way or another, though it wasn't going to be obvious and desperate. Gracen couldn't think this was about him. It wasn't. Nor was it about her single status. Whatever. This was about Summerstead and getting her good memories back to the present tense. After all, this year was going to be different.

\* \* \*

A downpour on Friday morning washed out Gracen's morning run. It also made the jaunt across the plaza to Beckwith's unappealing. Still, his mind demanded caffeine in no uncertain terms. He felt that he had no other choice; the time had come to check out The Yellow Bowl.

A silver bell tinkled as he opened the front door. He was overcome with the smell of freshly brewed coffee and tea, complemented by the aroma of old books and sugar. The Yellow Bowl was brightly colored with its bookcases, tables, and chairs all in shades of yellow. It felt cheerful and inviting like going to a good friend's house, or maybe like coming home. Precious few places had ever felt like that to Gracen.

"Be still my heart," Blythe laughed as she came into view. She held a stack of vintage picture books in her hand, the red gingham apron tied around her waist, her hair pulled into a ponytail.

"I figured it was time to grace you with my presence."

"You just want to see if the yellow bowl really exists."

She set the stack of books on the end of the counter as she stepped into place and gestured Gracen to sit. As he slid his lanky legs over the stool he noted a ceramic yellow bowl on a shelf behind her. He pointed to it.

"Yes, this is the yellow bowl. It was my great-grandmother's. A lot of pies and cookies were mixed in that bowl. So what'll you have?"

"What do you recommend?"

"I make lousy coffee," she admitted, "so I drink the tea."

"Hit me," he said, tapping the counter. Blythe pulled a tartan plaid cup and saucer set from the shelf behind her and poured from a cream-colored teapot with beautifully painted forget-me-nots. She slid him a yellow Depression glass sugar bowl and a silver souvenir spoon from Summerstead to stir.

"How is it the granddaughter of a coffee shop owner makes lousy coffee?" he asked, adjusting his glasses.

"The Yellow Bowl was meant to be a tea room. My grandfather had an aunt—Aunt Nan—who ran a tea room in the 1930s called The Yellow Bowl. Some of these teacups were actually hers. We keep the usual serving cups below, see," Blythe said as she slid open the bottom portion of the back counter to reveal countless sets of plain cream-colored cups and saucers as well as tall glass mugs.

"So why am I drinking tea from a plaid teacup?"

"Because, despite your rudeness, I like you," she said with a feisty smile.

"My rudeness?" he repeated. As he scooped two spoons of sugar, he noticed the sugar had sprinkles in it. Cute. Blythe leaned on the counter and he could smell her perfume, something warm like vanilla but woodsy like sandalwood. He liked it.

"Yes, you've been living here for almost two weeks. We've spoken twice, this is the first time you've been in my shop. I consider that a bit aloof, if not rude."

"I'm focused," he protested. He hadn't expected her to call him out.

"I know your type. I grew up with Alex. And he's worsened with age."

Gracen took a sip of the tea. He'd never been much of a tea drinker, but this was delicious. "What is this?"

"It's Earl Grey crème made from loose-leaf tea. Finn orders all of our tea—we have loose leaf and tea bags. For a tea room, we were actually pretty pathetic before he came."

"He seems like a good guy."

"He's my right-hand man. I couldn't run the shop without him, especially in the summer."

"I hope that's because summer is the busy season. Please tell me there is a busy season because I haven't seen much activity."

"It's not really like what you're used to on Summerstead," Blythe replied, grateful for the chance to mention it, "but the festival weekends are very busy."

"So not every weekend has a festival?"

"No, just a couple a month. Honestly, the store owners down here couldn't handle it otherwise. Most of them are retired, and this is a hobby. Only a couple of us actually need to make this work for a living. Of course, the restaurants are a little different from the shops."

"Just like the shore," he said. Since she had suggested Summerstead Isle Pizza he hadn't been able to get it out of his head. Only the name. He still couldn't see how it could work here, in Ohio, on a river without a beach.

"Have you settled on a name?"

"No, unfortunately, I've had an earworm crowding out all other thoughts."

"That's because it's a good idea. And the right idea."

"I just don't see it, Blythe. I name it Summerstead Isle Pizza, and then what? Make some papier-mâché seagulls and throw sand everywhere?"

"Only if you're crazy. What I would do, if you're asking, is whitewash that old paneling. It'll be like that place downtown on the Isle—"

"The Varsity Diner."

"Yes! And then dotted Swiss curtains like the place named for the shipwreck, The—"

"The Lucinda?"

"Yeah, that's it!"

"But no one will know that," he said, refusing to share Blythe's vision.

"Yes, they will. A lot of people here have been to Summerstead, I told you that. Besides it doesn't matter, it's a feeling. It will feel right."

"Okay, so after you've made it a white wonderland, where does the beach part come in?"

Blythe bit her bottom lip as she considered her next move. Might as well bite the bullet and look completely crazy, she thought.

"Come with me," she said. Leaving his cup on the counter, he followed out of sheer curiosity as she walked the length of the shop and through the back door to the parking lot. The rain had let up some but was still drizzling steadily. She opened the hatch of the Wagoneer and it served as a shelter from the rain. Gracen had to stoop considerably to join her.

She explained, "I stopped by my grandparents the other night and picked up a few pieces. I figured if you didn't want them, I'd hang them in my apartment or something. They should be in the light of day."

Carefully, Blythe slid a large painting to the edge of her Jeep, and two more paintings appeared beneath it. Gracen stepped forward to consider the artwork and was startled by the feeling it gave him. He'd seen hundreds, maybe a thousand, paintings of his hometown; the sandy beaches, the bright boardwalk, the waves crashing on the shore. None ever moved him. He surveyed them all rather cynically, but not this one. Maybe it was longing, maybe it was grief, but something put a lump in his throat.

The artist had set the scene just before dusk, so some families were meandering up from the beach, and others were coming out to the boardwalk in their evening attire. In days gone by, folks dressed up to walk the boards, men in coats and ties, women in dresses, children scrubbed and polished. The details of this painting felt so earnest and hopeful. It was a vintage piece now in this day and age. Some of the places depicted on the boardwalk scene had gone out of business or rather had been bought out by Wallace Corp.

"Isn't it perfect?" she said softly. "They bought it on their twenty-fifth anniversary. It hung above the couch for ages but my dad bought them a new piece a couple of years ago so they stored it in the attic."

"I could never take this," Gracen swallowed. He could almost smell the caramel corn and cotton candy filling the air with sugar as the sea rolled billows of salty perfume to shore. The longer he studied the swirl of blues and grays he could hear the cry of seagulls and the boisterous music from the amusement park.

"Consider it a loan," she offered. She asked him to help her move the large painting so she could show him the others. "Grammy painted these ones herself. She went through an art phase around the same time Liam was born."

These ones weren't quite so masterfully done but there was that same earnest quality to them. He could see that Mary Alice had painted these with fondness. One painting featured the sand dunes, which had since been washed away in a hurricane. And the other painting was of the fishing pier standing on spindly legs at high tide.

"Blythe, I really can't take these. These are meaningful to your family."

"Yeah, so meaningful we had them in the attic for the mice to enjoy. We're considerate that way," she quipped. "Anyway if you want them, I figured that would set the tone pretty well."

"I would say it's a good start," he mused.

"I had some other ideas. We have lots of old photos from Summerstead. My family's been going there for generations. My grandparents honeymooned there. And my great-grandparents went there in the twenties. I thought of selecting some of the vintage photos, making them posters, maybe doing some color replace work on them to make it feel modern."

"You've put a lot of thought into this," he noted. His voice was colored with surprise.

"That's just how my brain works. You're hyper-focused, I'm hyper-creative. It's still okay if you don't like it. I know it seems pretty out there."

"Actually, the more you show me, the more I like it. But this isn't the Summerstead Isle I know."

"You weren't a tourist," she shrugged, sensing there was much more to it than that.

"No, I wasn't a tourist. And I wasn't really a townie. I was just ... me," he said vaguely. The idea was crazy. A beach-themed pizza place almost five hundred miles away from the ocean. On top of that, Gracen being the proprietor of such a place—it was absurd.

However, it wasn't his vision. It was hers. And they weren't his memories they were using. They were hers. And her vision was clear and her memories were good. There was enough here to work with.

Mistaking his indecision for rejection, Blythe began to slide the paintings back. Gracen put his hand on her arm to stop her,

"If it's alright with you, I think I'll take those."

Her eyes widened, "Seriously?"

"Yeah, I need a name and a look. I haven't come up with anything else, so why not?"

"I think it'll be great," she beamed, "and I can help you pull it all together if you want. You only have a month before the opening."

"Well, whether or not I like help, it seems that we're collaborating on this. It's your vision and your memories after all, not mine," Gracen said, quoting his private thoughts to her. And that was precisely what Blythe wanted to hear. Her vision, her memories, Summerstead Isle finally where she could reach it again.

# Chapter 7

"Wow, it's looking good in here," Finn said with surprise. He carried a large cylinder package with him. "It looks really good, very beachy."

"We're not quite done," Blythe said without giving him so much as a glance. Gracen was up on a ladder holding a wooden sign with 'SIP' written in rope lights. The sign was as long as his own wingspan so his spot on the ladder was tenuous. Blythe was determining whether or not it was centered and straight. "A little up on the left, just a little. Okay, there."

"And now we say the magic words and it stays up here?" Gracen asked as he grimaced trying to keep it still.

"Just a sec," Finn said. He set the package down on the counter and slid the other step ladder to one end of the sign. Blythe handed him a drill. Gracen could feel the weight lessen as the screws went into the wall. Finn moved the ladder to the other end, and when he was done, he handed the drill to Gracen so the center could be secured.

"Thanks," Gracen said when the work was finished. "Perfect timing."

"I'm very impressed. It's come a long way in a short time," Finn said.

Light reflected off the whitewashed walls making the shop feel open and airy. Valances made of white dotted Swiss framed the windows without blocking the natural light. The stunning watercolor was mounted just above a long white shelf decorated with thrift store vases she'd painted to look like sea glass. A small nook just to the right of the main door housed Mary Alice's paintings with a fishing net strung between them holding two pieces of faded driftwood. Blythe had found several long strings with big round bulbs that reminded her of marquee signs on the boardwalk. She hung them across the restaurant, back and forth like long laundry lines. The effect was simple, crisp and clean, and very beachy.

"There are some finishing touches yet. I'm waiting to get some poster prints," Blythe said. She'd used an editing program to doctor some of the snapshots of the shore and placed the order at the beginning of the week. She spied the cylinder package Finn had with him, "Maybe those are the prints."

"I doubt it, label says it's from Summerstead Isle," Finn replied, offering the package to Gracen. "It came while you two were at the hardware store, so I signed for it. I hope that's okay."

"No problem," Gracen said. He glanced at the package but made no motion to take it from Finn. Instead, he took out his phone to tap in a few notes. Blythe raised an eyebrow.

"Aren't you going to open it?"

"I know what's in it."

She narrowed her eyes, but only the top of his head received the glowering look. She'd spent all week watching him tap notes into his phone.

"I have no idea how you keep it all straight on your phone."

"It's an app."

"Thanks, got that much. I guess I'm more of an old-fashioned paper and pencil type."

"That makes sense," he replied without looking up. She sighed. He commented, "You can open the package if it's bothering you."

"Your nonchalance is bothering me."

He flashed her a wide grin. Blythe tried to look annoyed but she couldn't make it stick. That stupid smile. And he knew it. She seized the package and slipped a utility knife from her back pocket.

"Wait, before I open it, why don't you tell us what's in here?"

"To see if I'm right? It's a couple of classic movie posters."

This piqued her interest so without further delay, Blythe carefully slid the contents out of the package. A brief note on rose-scented paper fluttered to the floor. She picked it up to hand to Gracen. He scanned the note, made no faces at all, then turned his attention back to her. Blythe was quickly learning that Gracen visibly reacted to very little.

She handed the top of the rolled documents to Finn then began to carefully unfurl them.

"*To Catch a Thief*," Blythe read slowly as the poster unrolled.

"And *North by Northwest*," Finn supplied as he snuck a peek at the poster underneath.

"So you're a Hitchcock fan?" she said eying the posters with some skepticism. She had never understood the fascination with Alfred Hitchcock.

Gracen folded his arms as he eyed her with an equal amount of skepticism, "You're not?"

"I've only seen *The Birds* and *Vertigo*. I wasn't impressed."

"We'll just pretend you didn't say that."

Gingerly he took the edge of the posters from her and rolled them back up to slide them back into the tube. This was the first interest of his that she didn't share. At one point in the past week, Gracen had started wondering if Blythe was just faking all their shared interests, but her utter lack of enthusiasm for these posters confirmed that she was not. A strange compulsion surfaced to share what he loved with her and see if he could make her love it too. He overlooked the feeling as mental exhaustion.

Blythe examined the posters more closely, "Are these originals? They don't look or feel like my cheap reprint of *Breakfast at Tiffany's*."

"Audrey Hepburn. That figures," Gracen stated simply. "And yes, they're originals."

"What do you mean 'that figures'?" Blythe demanded.

He grinned again and disregarded her question, "Aunt Grace said in her note that since I'm settled in, she'll be mailing me some of my things."

"So I should expect more mystery packages?" Finn asked.

"Yes, and you're welcome to sign for any and all of them. And, Blythe, you have my official permission to open them."

"You really aren't into surprises," Blythe noted.

"There won't be surprises. I know Aunt Grace too well," he replied. And he knew exactly what he had left behind.

"Speaking of packages," Finn said to Blythe, "so still no plans for your birthday?"

"That was a lame transition," she said weakly. She hadn't mentioned her birthday a single time all this week, which was unlike her. With all of the sideways glances and needly elbows going around, Blythe feared that Gracen would read into any mention of her birthday.

"It's your birthday and you didn't even tell me?" Gracen asked with genuine surprise. Now Blythe felt like an idiot.

She gave him one of her sassy smiles to cover, "Friday, tomorrow, actually. And don't get offended. I just forget that you're new and don't know anything."

"I enjoy it when you remind me that I don't know anything."

"It keeps you humble, Princeton," she teased. "Anyway, no. No big plans. My grandparents will probably stop by the shop. My parents may or may not call."

"Yeah what's the story there?" Gracen asked. Any references to the Elwood parents were few and far between, and always very, very brief.

"It's complicated," Blythe replied flatly.

"That's an understatement," Finn remarked.

"I'm trying to not live in the past remember?"

This was not the same. This was emotional stuffing so Blythe didn't have to deal with how much it still hurt her. Particularly on her birthday, and major holidays.

"Ginnie will bring the kids. We'll eat donuts and they'll sing to me. It will be hilarious. And Silas will probably call and brood."

"Silas, the younger brother," Gracen noted. There was usually a fondness when Blythe talked about him.

"Yup. And that pretty much accounts for everyone," she shrugged.

"Except me."

The familiar tenor voice of her oldest friend filled her ears and she spun on her heel to see him. He'd grown a thin beard which was a shade darker than his light brown hair. The tattoos on his arms were looking more like sleeves. Blythe was the only one who liked his 'artwork'.

"Jesse Thomas Beckwith!" she cried, throwing her arms around him. "You drive me crazy when you do this and you bloody well know it."

"Bloody well? Pretending to be English again, are we? It's all the tea and books," Jesse teased in an exaggerated English accent.

"Enough with the tea and books already."

"That's what I keep telling you."

"What are you doing here? I thought you were in India."

"I finished that two days ago. And what do you mean? It's our birthday. The last one of our twenties. You think I wouldn't be here with you?"

Blythe turned to Finn, "Did you know about this?"

"He called me last night to clue me in."

"I needed his help to catch you off guard," Jesse cackled.

"It was easier today," Finn said, "she's been busy with Gracen."

Gracen had been taking in the scene with equal parts wry amusement and selfish annoyance. So this was the Jesse Beckwith that he'd heard so much about over the years and especially lately. The first time he'd heard about Jesse was from Alex, years ago when they were roommates. Alex had talked often about Sayen Falls. He had high remarks for the Elwoods and for his grandparents, of course, but Gracen never heard him say a kind thing about his own nuclear family. There seemed to be nothing but open disdain for Jesse. Then, since coming to Sayen Falls himself, Gracen heard Jesse talked about many times. Always wistfully, as if all the Elwoods and all the Beckwiths wished they could just pin him down and make him behave.

Now, as Gracen watched Blythe fawn all over him and the easy way they flirted and laughed, he understood why. It was painstakingly clear that these two had been meant for each other. They evidently even shared their birthday. Yet, they were not together. It seemed very strange.

"So you're Gracen Hall," Jesse said as he extended his hand. "All of Sayen Falls has been talking about you."

As Gracen accepted the handshake, Blythe simultaneously gave Jesse a thud, "Just because Ginnie gives you regular reports doesn't mean all of Sayen Falls is talking."

"The Sayen Falls I know and love has been talking," Jesse replied.

"You're annoying."

"As you so often tell me."

"Gracen, this pest is Jesse Beckwith, Alex's brother."

"Becky's grandson and Ginnie's cousin," Gracen nodded. "You're well-connected."

"Only here in Sayen Falls. Out there in the world, I have to beg for my bread and butter."

"Oh, shut up," Blythe laughed. "Your expenses are paid almost everywhere you go."

Jesse shrugged, "True, and this is why I'm taking you to dinner tonight."

"Our birthday is tomorrow."

"I'm aware our birthday is tomorrow, but our reservations are tonight."

"You're leaving tomorrow, aren't you?"

"Not quite that quick. I just wanted to surprise you and I didn't want you to spend all of tomorrow moping."

"I don't mope."

"Sure you do. You mope, you weep, you watch old movies and drink tea. And I just couldn't stand the thought of that."

The very last thing Blythe wanted to do was reward Jesse with a smile. He was being incorrigible and irritating. Of course, that was his superpower.

"What time is dinner?" she asked trying to smother that smile and sound disinterested.

"Six o'clock."

"Fine. But you're helping me stock books tomorrow."

"Exactly how I always wanted to spend my twenty-ninth birthday. With tea and—"

"Don't even say it."

"Books," he winked. "I'll be at the shop just before six. I'm heading to Gramps for now."

The door swung shut behind Jesse, and the shop felt strangely awkward. All of this had left Blythe flustered. She didn't know why. It just felt so odd having Gracen and Jesse together in the same room. That was stupid. This was Jesse's hometown and this was Gracen's new home. Of course, their paths would cross sometimes and Blythe would be right there in the intersection. Why should that be awkward?

"He's nothing like Alex, is he?" Gracen said.

"Nothing. And it's been that way forever," Blythe answered.

"Does he do this often?"

"Just turn up from the middle of nowhere? Yes. I think it amuses him to see us all be constantly surprised."

"And he also knows you're all constantly let down," Finn muttered.

For every three promises to come home, only one was ever fulfilled. By and large, Blythe had stopped asking. She just let Jesse turn up whenever he turned up and the rest was a wash. However, Becky and Ginnie still asked and invited and tried to talk him into coming home. It was simply Ginnie's sweet nature to want Jesse to always know he was welcomed and wanted. It was harder to watch Becky be disappointed by his only grandsons—the big shot lawyer and the big shot photographer who almost never come home.

"I'd defend him but it's true," Blythe conceded. "Don't ever tell him I said this, but he's too much like his father."

"He'd never forgive you for that," Finn noted.

"There's one similarity," Gracen remarked, "Alex would hate that too."

"Have you ever met Donny Beckwith?"

"I met Donny *and* Tessa when Alex and I graduated with our bachelors."

"They *both* came?" Blythe asked incredulously. "How did that go?"

"About as awful as you're imagining. It was the only time I ever met Donny, I've been around Tessa a few other times."

"I know Tessa has a lot of issues. Okay, well, one main issue. She really should not drink alcohol. But I have a soft spot for her," Blythe explained. "When she was sober, she was really thoughtful and sweet. She taught me how to wear makeup and how to flirt with boys."

Retelling the memory brought a girlish smile to her face. It'd been a long time since she'd thought about Tessa's little lessons.

"I can see that, having met Tessa," Gracen replied.

"Donny and Tessa aren't all bad, neither one of them. Donny is very charming, I think my first crush was on him. I was maybe five," Blythe said, laughing at herself. "That was before I understood it all. Hmm, maybe that's why my taste in men is so questionable."

It was Finn's turn to chuckle, "You may actually be onto something. If Donny Beckwith was your first heartthrob."

"That's really awful, isn't?"

"It is. And it explains so much."

They shared a rather cynical laugh, but Gracen could not join in. He wasn't privy to the background stories that had shaped Blythe. He had so far only seen her as the good hometown girl, the sweetheart of Sayen Falls. It was a strange notion that there was a streak in her that liked the bad boys and had been hurt by one or two.

Maybe that's why she's not running from you, his inner voice hissed.

There was no time for that kind of pointless self-talk. Immediately he silenced that inner voice and focused all of his attention back to the task at hand: his shop. The actual shop was just about complete, but he'd yet to hire staff or train them. Time was ticking until the first festival. Blythe could go have dinner and share laughs with her old friends, but Gracen needed to stay focused. His livelihood was at stake.

"So, Finn, I wondered if we could chat later about who you think I should hire. You mentioned yesterday you had some leads."

"Come over whenever you want. I'll be holding down the fort tonight, but it should be quiet. Thursdays are usually when I catch up stocking."

"I'll help you out then, and we'll talk."

"That's kind of you to help," Blythe said to him. "You really don't have to though. You're so busy getting this place ready."

"I owe you. You've been a workhorse for me this week."

"We take care of our own here on the river."

"So I've heard."

# Chapter 8

The most remarkable feature of The Chatterbox was the enclosed glass deck which stretched over the Sayen Falls. The waterfalls themselves were rather small, but it was still awesome sitting on top of them with nothing but a glass floor beneath your feet. The view from the deck was impressive as floodlights illuminated the waterfalls in rotating shades of red, blue, and green. Inside the main dining room, a tuxedoed pianist tinkered at the baby grand piano providing nondescript background music for the murmuring customers and bustling waiters. The chandeliers were dimmed for the dinner service; candles flickered on the tables for mood lighting.

As Blythe entered on Jesse's arm she remembered their first dinner together at The Chatterbox, just the two of them. It had been homecoming their sophomore year. Jesse had saved his paychecks from the donut shop for a month to pay for it. Now, he made enough in an hour to pay for their meal easily.

"I requested our regular table."

"We have a regular table?"

"I decided that we should."

"I think for that to work you have to be here regularly."

"Well, I walked into that one, didn't I?"

Blythe grinned as Jesse pulled her chair out for her before taking his own seat. They were sitting on the glass deck in the far corner where it felt cozy and private.

"I remember when they built this deck," Jesse said. "Gramps thought they were nuts."

"I think he still thinks that."

"I'm sure he does. No one in Sayen Falls changes much."

"I'm sorry to disappoint you."

"That's not a disappointment. It's a comfort."

A waiter appeared to fill their water glasses and ask what they wanted to drink. Jesse ordered champagne for them both and the waiter left.

"You still hate wine, right?" he asked. She nodded as she lifted her water glass to take a sip. He caught sight of the Claddagh ring, "That's new."

She set the glass down and he took her hand, "Where did you get it?"

"Grammy said she found it in the little table in the living room."

"That marble-topped one?"

"Yeah. She said she doesn't know where it came from. I think it was hers, though, and she just doesn't remember."

"Why would it have been in that table?"

"Who knows? Her memory is fading and things end up in weird places. It worries me."

"You're not usually a worrier."

"I don't usually have to be; PapPap and Ginnie worry about everyone enough. But I'm the chief worrier in resident for my grandparents. You know that."

"It's why you never leave."

"Where would I go?"

"There's a whole big world out there, babe."

"There's a whole big world right here, Jess."

"Perspective, eh?"

The waiter returned with the champagne and took their dinner orders. Jesse ordered a steak with lobster tails and Blythe ordered lamb chops. Alone again, Jesse lifted his champagne flute to clink with Blythe.

"So is the Claddagh working?"

"You mean, has it found my one true love? I don't think so, do you? I mean, I doubt I'd really be having dinner with you if it was working."

"Well, that's harsh. I hope you always have time for dinner with me."

"It's not about time."

"Oh, you mean, another guy wouldn't put up with me?" he smirked. "Depends on the guy, I suppose. I think Finn would be okay with me."

"Finn? Are we still entertaining that idea?"

"I didn't know you ever had. Officially, anyway. I did assume that deep down you thought about the good father that way at least a time or two."

"He hates that nickname. And you don't worry about what I think about deep down."

"Oh, but I do, Blythe. I do worry about it."

"Here we go."

"What?" he asked innocently.

"I knew you came home for a reason and our birthday has nothing to do with it."

"That's not true. You know our birthday is special. After all, I waited around for you."

"It's practically folklore at this point," she giggled. "You were two weeks late, and I was one week early."

"Born just hours apart."

"Shared a crib for nap times."

"And the occasional bedtime, when my mother was too sloshed to drive."

"Or when my father was at the racetrack."

"When you put it like that it sounds like we grew up in a den of vices."

"Don't think that we didn't, Jesse, we did. Your father's womanizing, your mother's drinking, my father's gambling."

"No wonder your mother was so self-righteous," Jesse snorted.

"Pride was her vice."

"And yours?"

"Tea and books, as you so often remind me."

"Better than mine," he mumbled. And Blythe knew. She knew that Jesse was repeating so many of his father's behaviors, the very same ones that he hated so much.

Their discussion was interrupted briefly again by the waiter delivering their food. It was piping hot and perfect. There was silence between them for a few minutes as they enjoyed each mouth-watering bite. Jesse insisted Blythe try the lobster, and although she was sure she wouldn't like it, she let him pop a bite into her mouth.

"Good, isn't it?"

"Better than I expected. I'm just not a seafood eater, you know that."

"I'm determined to make you adventurous one way or another."

"Good luck with that."

"So, is Gracen offering any seafood at this Summerstead Isle Pizza place he's opening?"

"That's what you're leading with? Seafood? Just ask what you want to ask," she told him bluntly.

"I'm trying to act casual. Play along."

"Alright. I'll play. No, I don't think so. No seafood."

"Don't get moody, I'm just … concerned."

"Concerned."

"Blythe, what does anyone really know about this guy? He lives right across the hall from you. It's not even a hall, actually, it's a cement landing."

"He's never even been in my place."

"Well, that's a relief."

"Are you serious?" she asked, eyes narrowing. Jesse knew that look. It meant she was going to get hot-headed and very stubborn quickly.

"I can't help it. I worry about you. I'm the chief resident worrier about *you*," he said, echoing her own words.

"No, you aren't, because you aren't *here*."

"Well, maybe that's the problem. I just hear things from Ginnie and from Gramps."

"Right, because your grandfather doesn't have an agenda."

"I know he does. I know he still wants us to be together. You know it's because he adores you so much, right? No one is good enough for you, in his eyes."

"Except you."

"Believe me, the irony of that isn't lost on me. I know you deserve better than me," Jesse admitted, "and that's why I'm concerned about this Gracen Hall guy. I'm not sure he is better than me."

"I don't even know what that means. He's just a guy living next door and trying to open a pizza place. It seems pretty low threat to me."

"And look at what happened the last time you trusted the new guy in town," he said hotly. That cut Blythe to the quick, her eyes darkened.

"The last new guy in town was Finn. Not Ian. You knew Ian. We all hung out in college. You never said a word. And yet when it all fell apart you claimed you always knew he was a bad guy."

"I did. In my gut, I knew he was a creep. And that's why I won't let it happen again."

"You just met Gracen, how could your gut know anything?"

Jesse swallowed hard, "I looked him up."

"What do you mean," Blythe enunciated slowly, "you looked him up?"

"I used the interwebs to see what I could find about your new friend."

"Jesse, that's insane."

"Why are you angry? Are you afraid I found something bad?"

"You invaded his privacy!"

"It's the internet. If I could find it without paying for it then it's not private. It's already out there, waiting to be found."

"You don't have to do this. Being overly suspicious won't make up for the fact that you're never here. Nor will it undo the fact that you checked out when I chose Ian."

"I never understood why you chose him. You could've had Linus Huxley." He grunted, "You could've had me."

"Well, Linus rolled over and played dead. At least Ian made an effort."

"Yes, Ian made a really great effort," Jesse spewed. "That worked out beautifully."

"And where were you? You were busy adventuring while I was drowning with Ian."

"I'm sorry, I didn't mean to bring all of that up. I just can't watch you hurt like that again. It killed me. It killed me that I couldn't get back home when you needed me."

"I survived. Some of it I survived on my own, and some with Finn, and some with you, and some with my family. That's what survival is. It's a group effort in parts but it has to begin and end with me. And that's why I don't want you digging around on Gracen."

"I've learned how to dig for a story and look for the truth. I do more than take pretty pictures sometimes, you know. And when it comes to you I'm going to do my job."

"You don't get it. This isn't about Gracen. It's about me. I need to learn how to trust again. And I have to do it on my own terms. Fact checking Gracen doesn't help me."

"But how do you know he's worthy of your trust?"

"It's not about him," she repeated. "I'm a better person when I trust people and I'm not closed off. I'm learning to trust myself again."

"Look, I'm not saying don't trust the guy, I'm saying ..." Jesse hesitated; that was exactly what he wanted to say. "Just find out some things."

"I will. In my time, in his time. I'm not worried about it," she insisted.

He let it lie while he finished his steak. Then, he took a sip of champagne and said disinterestedly, "Did you know he's only worked for Wallace Corp? Never anywhere else."

"Jesse, who cares?!"

"Okay, okay, I'm done, you win. You do it your way. You're the reason I come back here at all. I just want you to be okay."

"Oh, please, save it for another day."

"You're that mad at me?"

"I'm irritated, but I'm almost over it."

"You can never stay mad at me for long."

"You're not home long enough for any feelings I have for you to be more than passing."

"Well, that's hurtful," he said, only half teasing. He fished in his suit coat pocket, "And I brought you a present and everything."

"I thought dinner was my present."

"It's like you hardly know me. I always bring you something."

He slid a small brown paper package tied with string across the table to her. The reference was not lost.

"I like the wrapping."

"It seemed to fit."

Her lithe fingers unwrapped the package and in her hand, she found a delicate silver chain with a pendant. Inside the pendant was a clipping of edelweiss.

"I got it in Austria last month," he explained. "When I finished my job, I took the *Sound of Music* tour. Blythe, there's so much I wished I could share with you. I feel that everywhere I go."

"That's funny. I feel that way too."

"I hate that we're always at this impasse."

"Me too," she sighed.

She handed the necklace to Jesse, and he stood to come around to her side of the table. Carefully, he pushed the hair off her neck, then put the necklace around her throat. His fingers brushed her skin as he fastened the clasp. Before he returned to his seat, he leaned to kiss her cheek. She turned her face toward him, and their lips met for a moment. But just a moment. They both knew it was just that moment.

"When do you leave?" she asked as he took his chair again.

"Saturday morning."

"I'll take you."

"You don't have to. I rented a car this time."

"I'm taking you," she repeated. She slid her hand into her clutch handbag. "And since we're giving gifts, this is for you. Hold out your hand and close your eyes."

"This brings back terrible memories of fishing with our brothers."

"I'm not going to put a dead snake in your hand. Good grief, I still have nightmares."

"Me too," Jesse grinned as he closed his eyes and opened his hand. Blythe dropped a flash drive in the shape of a tube of lipstick in his hand. His eyes popped open, "I'm not sure this is my shade."

"It's a flash drive. It's my play."

"Your play? Have you worked on it?"

"Not really. But seeing as you keep nagging me about it, I wanted to give it to you. It wasn't easy. The original is on a floppy disk."

"You started writing it that long ago," Jesse busted up laughing. "How in the world did you get it off a floppy disk?"

"The library has a converter thingy."

"Is this the only copy? I won't take it if it is. I want you to work on it."

"It's not the only copy. I have it saved in a cloud and another thumb drive with some other stuff from the past."

"You could have just shared the file with me."

"I could have, but I wanted you to have this."

"What else is on here?"

"Just some pieces of us."

"That's cryptic and vague."

"That's my gift to you."

"We have a very weird relationship," Jesse said as he leaned across the table to kiss her cheek. This time their lips did not meet.

"Yes we do, my old friend."

"Saturday morning will be hard."

"It always is."

# Chapter 9

Machines hummed as Jesse worked to prepare one large chai tea latte and one large vanilla cappuccino. As he pulled a lever down warm frothy liquid filled the glass mug he was holding. He repeated the action for the other. He could tell by looking that they were perfect. The customers who had ordered them paid for their drinks and took the table closest to the window for a chat. Jesse turned to Finn with a proud smile.

"I still got it."

"Congratulations."

Finn and Jesse were manning the shop while Blythe ran to the bank to do a cash drop. They were mostly talking and working a little on the bookshelves, but Jesse had jumped at the chance to wait on customers. Back in their college days, Jesse helped Blythe quite a bit between classes. He'd lived across the street above the donut shop. Life seemed busy then, but those were simple days in comparison.

On the plaza, a young man, about twenty years old, crossed to the parking deck. Momentarily Gracen entered The Yellow Bowl.

"That kid was number seven today. And a dud. No way he'd work out," he sighed. Looking around he noticed Blythe's absence and Jesse's presence, "Where's Blythe?"

"At the bank. She needed a break from this loon," Finn smirked, to which Jesse only shrugged as he loaded a few dirty mugs in the dishwasher. It seemed strange to Gracen that Jesse was behind the counter. There was something territorial about it. Or maybe Gracen was just used to a more cut-throat atmosphere.

"You've had seven interviews today? Weren't you just thinking about hiring yesterday?" Jesse asked as he wiped the counter with a rag.

Gracen explained, "Evidently having Blythe Elwood and Finn McCartney on the job means things can happen at warp speed."

"We just know the right people," Finn said. "So did you interview anyone you liked? I assume this is the college crowd, the high schoolers are still finishing their day."

"I think there were four or five good ones. I'll have to see how many of the high schoolers I like. There's six of them coming in for interviews today. I'm hoping for a staff of eight or ten that I can rotate. Especially the minors and labor laws and all that."

"You don't sound excited," Finn noted.

"I'm just concerned at how young my staff will be. Don't get me wrong. I've seen some hard-working seventeen to twenty-two-year-olds. But it can also be a lot of drama. And feelings."

Finn laughed, "Something tells me you don't do feelings very well. Or drama."

"It's not my favorite. And I never know what to tell people about their problems. If you can't rub dirt in it or walk it off, I have no idea what to do," Gracen said dryly.

"You need a den mother and I know just the person," Jesse piped up. "My cousin Ginnie."

"Ginnie Elwood?" Gracen asked. Immediately he felt stupid for asking.

"Yeah, she usually works in the summer to supplement their income while Liam is off," Jesse explained. "She's really good at feelings and drama. Mrs. Elwood was everyone's favorite teacher when she was at the school. They all came to her to talk about their hopes and dreams and fears and boyfriends and girlfriends and frienemies."

"I think he gets it," Finn interjected. "You have to stop him. Jesse monologues."

"Ginnie Elwood. I think I could work with Ginnie," Gracen nodded. He'd only met her the one time at The Gala, but she had certainly seemed nice enough. And Blythe hadn't mentioned any terrible things about her sister-in-law. If anyone would know something bad about her, it would be a sister-in-law. After a pause, he said, "I'll give her a call this evening."

Grabbing a napkin, Jesse jotted down Ginnie's phone number from memory. There were three numbers Jesse knew by heart, other than his own: Ginnie's, Blythe's, and Becky's. He almost had Miles and Mary Alice's number down pat but kept flipping the last two digits.

"Here's her number. They usually have dinner around six and try to get the kids in bed around nine," Jesse told him. "But Teddy the Terror complicates things."

"Thanks," Gracen said slowly. He wondered why Jesse was being so very helpful. Maybe he just wanted to help his cousin out. Or maybe there was some other reason.

"When's your next interview?" Finn asked, glancing at the clock above the counter. It was metal bent into the shape of a teapot which Blythe had spray painted a bright sunshine yellow, and it read a quarter 'til three.

"In fifteen minutes. I better head back and get ready. The monotony of interviews is making me forget important questions," Gracen said. He slipped Ginnie's number into his back pocket and gave a nod to Jesse. More customers were heading in the front door so he exited through the back. Just before he opened his own back door, he saw the red jeep coming through the parking lot.

"Hi there," she smiled as she slammed the door.

"Hey, I just left your place."

"Are the boys hard at work or hardly working?"

"Both. You have some customers."

"Well, glory be."

"How was last night?" he asked casually. That stupid feeling returned.

"Oh, Jesse is always Jesse. He drives me crazy but we've been friends forever," Blythe shrugged. She made it sound so meaningless, but the very fact that she was trying to make it sound that way meant that it was not. Gracen might not know what to do with drama or feelings, but he could spot it.

"He suggested that I hire Ginnie to be a den mother for my staff."

"Did he now?" Blythe asked with a smirk.

"Any reason that's a bad idea?"

"No, not at all. Ginnie's amazing. I'd hire her myself for the summer, but she really needs to make more in tips. I think she's the perfect fit, given the other names Finn gave you."

"I'm about to start interviewing the high schoolers. Ella is my first one."

"Ella Buterbaugh will seem like a silly girl, because, well, she is. But she's also a hard worker. Lily Morgan will keep her grounded, from what I hear. I don't actually know Lily very well, but my brother has high remarks for her. That says a lot. Liam is hard to impress."

Gracen had sensed that at The Gala, but he didn't comment on it now.

"Thanks for the insights," he said, placing his hand on the doorknob.

"Let me know if you need any other help."

"Will do," he grinned. "And happy birthday."

"Thanks," she smiled. "It's been an uneventful day, but not a bad one."

* * *

All airports buzz with the same low hum of digitized announcements crackling through overhead speakers, luggage wheels skidding across shiny floors, people rushing and people snoring between flights. The air is always laced with coffee and French fries. And while some airports boast a wider variety of shops and restaurants than others, they're pretty much all the same at their essence: a place to exist between engagements. Jesse knew this well. His home was the pantheon of airports around the world. Thus he stood, carry-on slung over his shoulder, in the airport, home at last.

"I'm glad you came to visit," Blythe said.

"So am I. I feel bad for Gramps though. He always hopes that I'm home for good."

"He misses you. We all do. But I keep telling him that someday you'll fall in love with some exotic girl and only come home for Christmas."

"I'm not out there looking for Mrs. Jesse Beckwith."

"I wish you'd find her anyway. Maybe then everyone would let it go."

"Like we did?" Jesse said quietly. He dropped his carry-on and took both of Blythe's hands into his. Her hands were cold. Her hands were always cold.

"We were ten when you asked me to marry you," Blythe said with a laugh that belied her. Jesse had climbed the tree in her backyard to carve their initials high in the trunk where no one would see their secret pact. "That was a lifetime ago now."

"Only nineteen years."

"Don't remind me that we're almost thirty. Especially here in the airport where the world is waiting for you, and I'm going to go home to my tired little shop."

"Sometimes I don't want the world."

"Yes, you do. You're happy out there, meeting new people, going to interesting places. You were never happy here in Sayen Falls."

"I need to know you'll be okay."

"Without you? You've been doing this around-the-world gig for six years. I've been fine," she grinned, "and now you have a spy so you should be able to relax."

"A spy?" he replied with mock disbelief. "Do you mean Ginnie? She would never spy."

"No, she wouldn't. She has too much integrity. But she will tell you everything all the same because she wants you and Alex both to feel like you're not missing anything."

"Well, that's not my fault, is it? Besides, it should only bother you if you have something to hide."

"As of now, I don't."

"That better not change, Blythe Elwood. Maintain some distance, for my sake," Jesse said as he pulled Blythe into his arms.

"You better get going. Security will take a while," she sighed. This was the worst moment of every short-lived visit. "Let me know when you land. I'll worry."

"You sound like Ginnie."

"I said I'd worry, not imagine sixty-three ways you might've died until I hear from you," she retorted. Her eyes flitted to his ink-covered arms.

He winked, "The next one is for you."

"You've been saying that since you got your first one."

"Maybe they're all for you."

"You always have a line," she whispered. For a moment the hum of the airport hushed to near silence and the world around them whirred to a near stop. Jesse gazed into Blythe's green eyes, slipped his hand into her dark hair, and drew her lips to his. She kissed him in return, gripping his arms and leaning into him.

"Let me know when you land," she repeated quietly, slipping her hands from his.

Slowly Jesse picked up his carry-on and took one long last look at Blythe. Whatever he felt for her would remain unsaid. There was simply no point when he had a flight to catch.

# Chapter 10

On the morning of Summer Fest, Gracen woke up before his alarm with his brain in absolute shambles. He dressed quickly and headed out for a long run to try to put things in order. But as he jogged through the plaza his thoughts only grew more anxious.

This was such an unlikely spot for a triumph. Maybe he should have stuck it out in Summerstead Isle. He could've worked for Roy if he'd just swallowed his pride and ignored what he knew. Sometimes he thought that's what Uncle Harry would have done. Then he had to wonder if that is exactly what Uncle Harry *had* done and how Roy had managed to take so much in the end. In any case, none of that mattered now because Gracen was here in Sayen Falls, Ohio. The die was cast. The Rubicon was crossed. And all other dramatic sayings about fate.

This run was doing him no good. When that had happened in Summerstead, he usually found a girl to help clear his mind.

He stopped dead in his tracks at that thought. His feet had brought him back home even though his mind had been elsewhere. He was now yards away from his building. There he plainly saw Blythe leaning against the yellow brick. She sipped from a takeout cup as she looked dreamily up into the sky. At her feet sat another takeout cup. Her head turned and she saw him. She began walking his way and Gracen met her.

"You ready for this?" she asked as she handed him the cup.

"I guess I have to be."

"I think you'll be surprised. You're going to knock it out of the park."

The bells and whistles in his brain went on high alert as she stood there smiling at him. She laid her hand on his arm, covering his tattoo. "He'd be proud of you."

Oh, how he wanted to believe her. He wanted to be sure that he'd done the right thing in leaving. He wanted to know that everything he was doing here in Sayen Falls would be right. But he just didn't know. And somewhere in the back of his brain came the nagging idea that it wasn't all about business.

They talked for another minute or so before Gracen made his excuses to go upstairs and get ready for the day ahead. Staring at himself in the mirror, he only saw inadequacy.

"Here goes nothing," he sighed.

\* \* \*

The littlest Elwoods had the audacity to wake up at six-thirty on the first Saturday of the summer. Liam really felt that it should be a punishable offense but reason prevailed, so he found himself eating sugary cereal and watching lousy cartoons with his kids. Teddy had tossed and turned all night and cried at regular intervals. None of this bothered Liam, he was a deep sleeper, but Ginnie had been up most of the night soothing their two-year-old. When the kids padded into their room bright and early Ginnie had given her husband one menacing look and he knew it was his turn. Besides, it was her first real day of work.

As the theme song of Teddy's favorite cartoon started the little dynamo began to clap his hands and jump in a stilted dance. As he shouted the last word of every line, his version of singing, Liam burst out laughing. These were the anecdotal moments he missed during the school year. Maybe it wasn't so bad to be up with the kids on a sunny Saturday morning. It was sort of nice to have them all to himself, the way Ginnie had them all day every day. Liam was glad that Ginnie was working again this summer. She needed to get out of the house. And he needed to make some memories with these little early-rising monsters.

* * *

"You know, I never considered what it would be like to be on the other side of a festival," Ella Buterbaugh said as she punched another order into the system. It was only half past eleven and already the place was full.

"I had no idea this many people even came to the festivals," Lily Morgan added.

"This is insane. But in a good way," Sawyer Charles agreed. He carried a plastic tub of sauce from the fridge to the front counter where Gracen was throwing dough. These three were the core of Gracen's high school crew.

"You guys really got the word out about SIP," Gracen said as he caught the dough. A crowd of customers smiled as they watched him work. With great flourish, Sawyer pushed up his sleeves and began kneading another lump of dough. He'd gotten pretty good at throwing the dough in a short amount of time. The two of them were a pair of showmen and a throng of festival goers crowded into SIP to catch a glimpse.

"I just hope we can keep up," Lily said as another group of four sat down in her section.

"Just keep smiling and they'll never know that we don't know what we're doing," Gracen nodded as he poured a ladle of sauce onto a pizza. He remembered how Uncle Harry used to tell him in the theater there was a saying about thirty feet. It only had to look good from thirty feet away because the audience wouldn't be close enough to see the details.

The first couple of hours went by in a blur of activity. The orders kept coming in and the pizza kept going out. If every weekend was like this, Gracen stood a chance.

He smiled at Lily as she came to the counter with another order. He'd had his doubts about Lily because she was so shy, but she was doing well so far. She was good with customers, very sweet and very accommodating. He noticed that no one minded waiting a few more minutes on their pizza if Lily was serving them.

"Can you spare a couple of minutes to help Sawyer cut up some more lemons for the lemonade?" Gracen asked Lily. Her eyes flitted to her tables.

He remembered that Blythe had told him people needed to care about him for the business to work. That still seemed strange to him. In Summerstead, tourists didn't care about the people behind the product, or how many generations the recipe had been in the family, or how hard they had to work to bounce back from Hurricane Sandy. They just wanted their pizza fresh and hot. However, Sayen Falls was not Summerstead Isle so he figured he should make an effort.

"I'll take care of your tables," he said. As Lily disappeared into the back, he approached a table of teenagers, drinking lemonade and munching on doughy breadsticks while they waited for their pizza. Before long, a man from another table interrupted.

"Hey, you the owner?"

"I sure am, what can I do for you?" Gracen asked, plastering on his most charming smile for the two middle-aged couples sitting at the table.

"I like what you've done with the place. It was so dim in here before," the man said. He extended his hand for Gracen to shake it.

"Thank you," Gracen replied. "Blythe Elwood next door really had the vision for it."

"She's a sweet girl," the man's wife said, nodding her head. "This is nice. We've been to Summerstead Isle. That's why we wanted to come here, to see if it reminded us of the shore."

"It's our home away from home," the other lady told him. "Your restaurant really does Summerstead justice. Those posters are wonderful."

The poster prints Blythe ordered had been the perfect finishing touch. She had selected three old family photos to highlight with color-editing software. Bright red, yellow, orange, green, and blue popped out of the crisp black-and-white shots as if coming to life and joining the twenty-first century right in front of the customers.

"Those photos are from the Elwoods. The flapper is Miles's mother, Goldie, and the Gidget girl, as Blythe calls her, is actually Mary Alice," Gracen explained. "And the last one, the little girl, that's Blythe."

The opposite technique had been used on Blythe's photo. She was jumping in the waves sporting a bathing suit covered in bright colored polka dots. The waves were transformed into muted shades of gray so she could shine in her girlhood glory. Gracen guessed she was about eight in the photo and she looked completely free. He'd never felt that way in the ocean. The photo of Blythe was his favorite; something about it gave him pause for thought.

"Can't go wrong with three generations of Elwood girls," the man grinned. Gracen nodded and shook the man's hand again.

"Your food will be right up. Thanks for giving us a chance."

"If the food is half as good as it is on Summerstead, we'll be back," the man's wife promised him. As Gracen turned to leave the table, Lily brought a tray of pizza. The man took a bite, smiled, and gave Gracen a thumbs-up. They'd be back.

* * *

Iridescent bubbles drifted on the breeze fluttering the leaves in the Elwoods' backyard. Viola blew bubbles, giggling as Teddy popped them. Liam fired up his beloved grill to throw some hamburgers and hot dogs on. One bubble made it all the way to him before popping suddenly. Teddy yelled at Bandit, who was chomping at the bubbles wildly and barking madly. Teddy liked to yell at anything further down the totem pole than he was. Teddy liked to yell, period.

"Lunch is almost ready," Liam announced. "Go in and wash your hands."

"NO!" Teddy declared. "No!"

"Here we go," Viola muttered, sounding very much like her often worn-out mother.

"Teddy, do you want to go inside and put some food in Bandit's bowl?" Liam suggested. Every now and then he was hit with a stroke of genius.

Just as Teddy had become entirely red-faced and worked himself up into a proper tizzy, he stopped short and an eager grin spread across his little round face.

"Yeth!" he squealed. "Yeth, I do!"

With long strides, Teddy marched towards the back door and reached for the handle. He couldn't quite work it right to open it, but Viola helped him and he hustled to Bandit's bowls. It took Liam a minute to catch up, but Teddy waited, hopping from one foot to the other.

"Feed dog. Feed Ban-it! Feed dog. Yeth do!" he announced proudly.

"Yes, you're going to feed Bandit, and that will be so helpful," Liam nodded as he lowered the tin can of dog food to the floor so Teddy could scoop. He realized that there were ten-to-one odds that Teddy would spill the food all over the floor, but he figured it was worth it if it got him inside without any fits. Teddy was notorious for his 'coming inside' tantrums.

"Oop! Methy! Methy!" Teddy shouted as kibble dropped from the tilted scoop and scattered across the linoleum.

"Oh, Bandit will get it. It's okay," Liam assured him. Right on cue, Bandit bounded in the door under Liam's feet. His nose and curiosity led him directly to his bowls, wondering what the small person was doing with his food. Bandit wasn't entirely sure about Teddy. He yelled an awful lot and sometimes he pulled his tail. He was much louder than the girl. But there were a lot of snacks with the small one. And this time there was dog food all over the floor.

"Ban-it!" Teddy chirped as the dog's cold nose nudged the little boy's chubby leg. Teddy was standing on a delicious piece of kibble.

"Come on, Teddy, let's wash our hands so we can eat lunch," Liam said. No longer annoyed with having to get washed up, Teddy shrieked with unfiltered joy as he took off for the bathroom sink where a stool was waiting to make him tall enough to reach. He turned both handles on full blast. Then reached for the pump bottle of soap and got a big glob on his hands. Without rubbing it in he put his hands directly under the stream of water and washed the soap right off leaving plenty of dirt and germs on his hands.

"Here let me help you," Liam said. He stood behind the boy, put soap on his own hands and washed Teddy's hands inside of them. Teddy splashed gleefully in the water and bubbles for just a minute.

"Babas!" he exclaimed.

"Yup, bubbles," Liam said as he took the hand towel off the rack.

"All done!" Teddy declared. "Dry now!"

Obediently Liam dried off Teddy's wiggling hands and then helped him jump off the stool. Teddy took off in a flash for his high chair, far too excited about his hot dog and "chup". Keeping up with Teddy was exhausting and Liam was ready for nap time.

\* \* \*

Time raced by unnoticed along the river. Festival-goers were only interested in getting the summer started right and the festival workers were only interested in keeping up with the demand. The crowd thinned in mid-afternoon so Gracen insisted that his staff alternate breaks and eat. Ginnie sat with Sawyer, Ella, and Lily, slumped into extra chairs from the dining area devouring pizza and exchanging funny moments from the day. Busyness kept Gracen's mind occupied, so he continued working behind the counter.

A young man of average height with a thatch of nearly black hair entered. He surveyed the shop, clearly looking for someone specific.

"Can I help you?" Gracen asked. The appearance of a customer grabbed Lily and Ella's attention, and they turned to look. A bright smile filled Lily's face as she stood.

"Brady! You said you wouldn't be able to come."

"I got the afternoon off, just for you," he said, slipping his thumbs into her belt loops and kissing her. Lily tucked her hand into Brady's and turned to face them.

"This is Brady Carmichael, and this is my boss Gracen Hall. You know Ella and Sawyer. And this is Ginnie Elwood. I babysat for them at The

Gala, remember?"

Brady eyed them and placed a possessive hand on Lily's waist. "So can you take a break, go for a walk with me? I'll buy you lunch."

Oblivious to the tension mounting in the room, Gracen answered for Lily, "You have time before the dinner rush. You've earned it."

"I don't want to leave you in a lurch," she said shaking her head.

"I think we'll be fine. It's slowed down now."

"Thanks, Gracen," she said, untying her apron and smoothing her hair. She stashed the apron behind the counter before leaving with Brady. As she left, Sawyer and Ella looked at each other with grave faces. Neither one of them trusted Brady any further than they could throw him.

"Not what I expected you to do," Ella said simply.

"What did I do?" Gracen asked. He took out another finished pizza and slid in the one waiting on the counter.

"You just sent Little Red Riding Hood out with the Big Bad Wolf."

* * *

Little puffs of air escaped Teddy's pursed lips so he purred like a kitten as he napped. Viola was too old for naps so she curled up on the couch with a stack of vintage picture books. The window air conditioner hummed in the dining room window, cooling most of the downstairs.

Liam's phone buzzed, Ginnie was calling on her break.

"How are you holding up?"

"Teddy is down for his nap. Thank the Lord. How long will he sleep?"

"At least an hour, two if we're lucky, three if we're really lucky. Any longer than that and you've bypassed lucky and gone straight back to doomed."

"Do not pass go, do not collect two-hundred dollars?"

"Something like that."

"I don't know how you do it, Gin. Day in and day out. I'm exhausted."

"It's your first day, rookie."

"I've had other summers off."

"Not with Teddy as a two-year-old. And believe me, Viola has her moments. She can be quite a diva when she wants to be."

"She gets that from her aunt."

"She gets that from her father."

"Excuse me?"

"You know you have your moments, dear."

"I thought after nap time I'd bring the kids to get pizza for dinner?"

"They'll love it. It's really good pizza. Just like the beach."

"That's what Blythe said."

"She did a good job with the place. People are loving it."

"And you? How are you holding up?"

66

"My feet are killing me but the work is good. I like feeling useful."

"You are useful."

"It's different."

Viola curled up next to Liam with a chapter book. Someday she would be a voracious reader, but it was hard when the words were still too big.

"We'll see you later, okay? Viola wants me to read."

"Give her a kiss for me, I miss her."

* * *

The dinner crowd stuffed Summerstead Isle Pizza to the gills. Around seven or so it started to thin out. This was when Liam led his family through the front door. It had taken them an absurd amount of time to get ready and out the door after Teddy woke up from his nap.

At the sight of his mother, Teddy bolted and tried to shimmy up her leg. She laughed as she picked him up to squeeze him tight. Liam grabbed a high chair and wrestled his son into it as Ginnie snatched coloring pages and crayons for the kids. Gracen told her to take a break and eat with her family. She had certainly earned it.

With the kids settled, Liam sighed, "Well, give us the house special."

"Coming right up," Gracen nodded, turning back to the counter. He tapped the order into the register as Sawyer slipped in another pizza. It wouldn't be long until the Elwoods' order was ready, which was a good thing. Teddy was already rocking in his highchair, demanding to get down and go home. Even Viola was starting to fray around the edges as Teddy kept throwing her crayons on the floor.

"Order up!" Sawyer called as he plated the slices of pizza for the Elwoods. Ella brought the pizza out just in time to prevent a fierce Teddy meltdown. Pizza was a main food group for Teddy so he gobbled up an entire oversized slice by himself before proudly announcing he was all done. In a much more demure fashion, Viola ate most of her piece, all the while keeping a dainty eye on Gracen. When he smiled at Viola, her young heart fluttered. When Teddy started to get restless again Gracen came over to the table to work damage control.

He took one of the coloring pages and flipped it over to the blank side where he began to sketch Bandit which Teddy immediately identified. He added a tree, then drew bones on the tree as if bones could grow on a tree. This made Viola giggle.

"You think that's funny?" he asked her. She nodded shyly. Gracen added grass for Bandit to sit on and on either side of him flowers shaped like bones. Then he drew puffy bone-shaped clouds in the sky, Viola smothering laughter all the time.

"Ban-it! Bone! Mommy, wook! Mommy, wook!" Teddy insisted, tugging on Ginnie's arm as she popped her last bit of pizza in her mouth.

"I see it, darling, it's very funny."

"Funny!" Teddy repeated. "Daddy, wook!"

Liam nodded slowly. He knew that he should be grateful for Gracen stepping in to entertain the kids so they could finish a meal peacefully, which was no small thing. But Liam didn't enjoy the way Viola looked at him. She was much too young for this. Then again, Blythe had always been boy crazy. And look where that got her, Liam thought grimly as he handed his debit card to Gracen.

When the Elwoods finally rounded up their pieces and parts and wrangled Teddy out the door, the restaurant was nearly void of customers. Gracen insisted that Ginnie go home with her family. She had put in a long hard day's work, and she'd be needed again the next afternoon.

"I think your grand opening was a success," she said as she clocked out.

"You know, I think it was too."

"Surprised?"

"Floored."

* * *

Ginnie knew that babies are supposed to give up their bottles around the one-year mark. If they even take bottles, to begin with. But Teddy had such a difficult time sleeping that she just couldn't bring herself to do it. She also knew that most people put great stock in sleep training and that Teddy would've been left alone to sort out his sleep issues by most other parents. But she couldn't bear the thought of her child screaming, scared, alone in the dark night. Perhaps it was her own lingering fear of inky shadows creeping elongated across darkened walls, or maybe it was because he had come into the world in such uncertain terms. In any case, Ginnie simply couldn't just set Teddy in his crib and listen to him cry for her. If it made her weak, then so be it.

Instead, she sat up with him in the worn and faded recliner. She read him stories, said prayers, and sang him songs, then she rocked until sleep finally overcame him. On rare occasions, Teddy fell asleep before the songs were over, but most nights, it was another thirty minutes of rocking. He simply had more energy than he could use up in his waking hours, and it took time for his little body to unwind and his spirits to settle. Ginnie rocked him in the dark, holding his dimpled hand in hers, gazing into his dark eyes. There was love in those eyes and trust. No one on earth trusted Ginnie as much as Teddy. Not even Viola.

The simple fact was that Ginnie needed these quiet moments just as much as Teddy. Maybe even more than Teddy. Her life was unrecognizable from the one she once imagined, but in the stillness of the night, listening to Teddy's hushed breathing as he snuggled in her arms, she had more than she could have ever imagined.

# Chapter 11

At ten Gracen closed his doors. Customers finished trickling out around nine, and he'd sent the rest of his staff home shortly after that. By eleven o'clock the last of the dishes were washed, the dining area was cleaned, and the kitchen was prepped for the next day. He left SIP through the front door into the cool June night and the quiet plaza. In The Yellow Bowl, he could see Finn tidying up and doing closing work, while Blythe filed receipts and made notes in a ledger behind the counter. Finn said something that made her laugh. Her hair was disheveled, her apron was smudged with stains, but when she smiled at Finn she was radiant.

Gracen considered going in to talk with them, have a cup of tea or help clean up. However, he needed to run more than he needed to chit-chat. Running in cargo shorts wasn't ideal, but he didn't want to waste time going upstairs just to change. So he stretched his calves against the brick, jogged past The Yellow Bowl and headed to the boardwalk.

As he ran, he assessed the day. All in all, it had been a solid start. If every festival weekend was like this one, Gracen figured he had a shot of making it. Looking ahead to winter, he knew he'd have to make some adjustments to stay lucrative. His brain cycled through some ideas, and he found himself wishing he could just call up Uncle Harry and ask for his insights. More than anything, he wished he could just ask him if he was doing the right thing and making him proud at all.

The pylons were getting closer as Gracen jogged, but he saw something that made him stop his approach. Perched on the pylons was a pair of teenagers really getting to know each other. He smirked to himself. Figuring he wouldn't interrupt this heavy make-out session, he turned to head back to his apartment. Then, he realized he recognized the clothes the girl was wearing. It was the uniform for his own restaurant. The girl's blonde hair had been released from its ponytail, so while Gracen couldn't see her face, he knew it was Lily Morgan.

"Little Red Riding Hood and the Big Bad Wolf," he repeated to himself. Still, he wasn't her father. It made little difference to him what Lily did with her spare time. If this Brady guy was bad news, Gracen didn't really care to get involved. He was sure Ella would make her opinions known and hopefully Lily would listen.

His jog back was peppered with memories of his own youthful indiscretions. His conscience nagged him about Lily. Finn had told him that Lily's home life was lonely. Gracen started to wonder if she was hoping to fill that void with this boyfriend, and then he wondered what particular itch Brady was hoping to scratch with Lily.

"Hey!"

Her voice startled Gracen, and he tripped, nearly falling. He looked up at the balcony outside his apartment and saw Blythe sitting on her half. He replied, "Hi there."

"Are you finished running?"

"For tonight."

Gracen was ready now to just shower and relax before bed. He had a feeling Blythe was going to invite him over. Oddly enough, he wasn't trying to think of an excuse to get out of that.

"I'll be out here for a while if you want to come over," she said casually.

He nodded before he darted up the stairs and out of view. After his much-appreciated shower, he stood in front of his closet feeling dumb for wondering what to wear. It was much more like his brother JJ to stand helplessly in front of a full wardrobe and actually put thought into what he put on. He settled on his favorite pair of jeans which were soft from wear, and a gray t-shirt with "Summerstead Isle" branded on the chest. Gray was a good color for him. He picked his glasses up off the nightstand. Contacts were a more logical choice this morning, but now his eyes needed a break.

Leaving his bedroom, he crossed through the living room and out to the balcony. He slung his long legs over the railing that split the balcony in half so he could join Blythe on her side. She had disappeared, so he took a step inside her balcony door and found her in the kitchen brewing tea. Of course.

Her apartment was almost startlingly different from his. The bones were the same—exposed brick, retro lighting, and so on—but Blythe's space was filled with colors, patterns, and textures. Her style was decidedly shabby chic so everything looked loved and worn-in. Every wall had something on it—a poster, a picture, a mirror, a painting. As Gracen's eyes drank it all in he was sure that if he wanted to he could stay in here for weeks asking her about her collections and they wouldn't run out of things to talk about. Even her knick-knacks had stories.

She pulled a couple of teacups and saucers from her cupboard and poured piping hot tea from a floral teapot.

"Honey? Or sugar?" she asked.

"What are we having?"

"Chamomile, it's supposed to be relaxing. I've been meaning to tell Ginnie she should try it with Teddy. That boy is wound tight."

"He's a good kid though. And Viola is sweet."

"I think she's sweet on you," Blythe said, putting a dollop of honey in her cup. "Ginnie texted and said Viola talked about you all night."

Gracen shook his head, "I'm just new. I'll wear off."

"I doubt it. My goddaughter has very discerning taste, even at five."

"Then I'm certain it'll wear off," he insisted. He took the honey bear bottle from Blythe and squeezed some into his teacup. "I'm still getting used to your tea parties."

"This is not a tea party. We are not wearing hats," she replied with a nearly straight face. "Teddy insists you must wear hats at a tea party. Viola insists that he is ridiculous."

"I could go get a hat. Or does it have to be a special hat?"

"I really have no idea, but I look terrible in all hats, so we'll just skip it."

"I bet you could pull off the oversized Holly Golightly hat," Gracen said before he took a careful sip from his steaming cup. A vague memory came to the surface; he swallowed it with the tea. He'd had this tea before, with his mother. She used to drink it for her nerves.

Gracen followed Blythe to the balcony where two deck chairs and a small table made from reclaimed wood pallets waited for them. She stretched her legs to rest her feet on the balcony railing; she was wearing bright floral leggings and a long plain pink t-shirt.

"So how was your grand opening?"

"People seemed to like it. I got a lot of compliments on the decor."

"I told you people would like it. I mean, who doesn't want to be at the beach?" Blythe added, "Other than you."

"I don't mind the beach."

"Just Summerstead."

"That really intrigues you, doesn't it?"

"It bothers me, I guess," she answered thoughtfully. "For me, Summerstead was one of my safe places where things were right and people were happy. And it bothers me that it seems to have been the polar opposite for you."

"Maybe not the *polar* opposite."

"Okay, so the Greenland opposite."

"Sure, yes, the Greenland opposite," he chuckled.

"Is there a reason you're so evasive about why you're here?" she asked with a sudden burst of boldness.

He paused as he brought his cup to his lips, taken aback by her question.

"Yes," he answered honestly, "but it's complicated."

"I get complicated. We Elwoods appear normal, but we're actually a mess. I mean, haven't you noticed there's a generation missing here?"

"Come to mention it, I have wondered about your parents and why you are so freakishly close to your grandparents."

"Freakishly?" she sputtered with laughter. "Yet another Greenland opposite?"

"No, this one would be polar."

"I'm even more bothered by that, Gracen Hall. Everyone should be blessed with grandparents like mine. Everyone. Period. They're the best."

"I concur."

"But to answer your question, I'm freakishly close to them because I actually lived with them for a while. They had a big hand in raising me."

"So what about your parents? I've gathered that they're divorced."

"See, Princeton, I knew you were clever enough to piece together some of the story," she teased. "They divorced when I was fourteen. About a year and a half later, my father moved to Las Vegas."

"That's random."

"He's a general contractor."

"Ah, yes, that makes more sense."

"And he enjoys gambling."

"Even more sense. And your mother?"

"Mom is from Michigan originally, and she reconnected with a high school flame. When I was fifteen, she wanted to move back to be with Doug. Silas and I were given the choice of staying here in Sayen Falls with Grammy and PapPap or going with Mom."

"Not Liam?"

"He was eighteen by then and already at Ohio State for school. So, anyway, I decided to stay and Silas decided to go."

"So, by the time you turned sixteen, your nuclear family had atomized. Dad in Vegas, Mom and little brother in Michigan, big brother away at school. You with your grandparents," Gracen summarized.

"Exactly, quite a fitting analogy, Princeton."

"You know, if you're going to keep calling me that, I'll have to nickname you."

"I enjoy nicknames."

"That really doesn't surprise me." He studied her face for a minute and noticed how flushed she'd become talking about her family. "I didn't mean to lead us to such heavy conversation."

"Oh, it's all right. I've had some of my heaviest conversations on this balcony after a festival, usually over a box of donuts and cups of tea. Jesse used to live over top of Beckwith's Donuts, and on occasion, Finn stays for a long talk, or my brothers come up for a chat."

"So I'm just another boy on the balcony?"

Her face flushed differently, "Yes, just another boy on the balcony."

"But your family, that's why you idolize Summerstead so much. The drama never followed you to the shore?" he asked, genuinely interested in this bit of her life story, but also focusing the conversation on anything that wasn't his own narrative.

"Never," she replied, shaking her head.

"Well, I hate to break it to you but it takes more than ocean air and saltwater taffy to be happy."

"Don't burst my bubble, Gracen."

"I think you already knew that."

"Yeah, I think I did too. But you actually said it out loud," she said with a smile, but her voice was sad and rather far away. "I thought Summerstead was the answer to all my problems. So much so that I planned on going there on my honeymoon."

Now this one really gave Gracen pause. He leaned forward in his seat, "Honeymoon? Theoretical or were you really engaged?"

"Engaged. I told you I know complicated."

"You sure play that close to the vest."

"You're one to talk," she said flippantly. "I used to talk about it all the time, but this year is supposed to be different."

"Different how?"

"I'm supposed to be focusing on the here and now and not dwelling on the past. Living in the moment. Or something. I don't really know. I had a weird Christmas and made a resolution."

"You know, most people don't keep their resolutions."

"Most people don't have Jesse Beckwith in their back pocket."

"Come again?"

"He leaves the most annoying voicemails about the world being more than tea and books."

"Then clearly he has not read the right books or drunk the right teas," Gracen retorted. He wasn't sure why that had bristled him, but it did.

"Clearly," she laughed, grateful for the break in the tension. She didn't really mind heavy conversations, but it was important to keep some levity in the midst of it.

"Well, I certainly concede that you understand complicated."

"So your family," she said pointedly. "Are your parents divorced?"

"No," he said with a sigh. He had truly hoped to avoid having to talk about his parents. Gracen pursed his lips, then took a drink of tea. He didn't want it to look like he was hesitating. Finally, he figured a way to say it. Clearing his throat, he answered, "My mother's first husband, Robert Hall, died before I was born. I never knew him."

Blythe frowned, "You don't call him your father?"

"I never knew him."

"I'm sorry. That must've been very hard growing up."

He set down the teacup, "It's all I know. My stepdad is an alright guy though."

"You have siblings, right? You've mentioned them in passing a couple times," Blythe continued.

He sighed a little, "Three. My older sister Michelle, and my younger siblings are twins, Josselyn and JJ, um, Jerry Junior. He was named after my stepdad."

"So, I assume your mother is a Wallace? Your grandfather's daughter?"

"Yes, first she was Chrissy Wallace, then Chrissy Hall, and now Chrissy Shepherd," he explained. "Do you want me to write this down? It can get confusing."

"I studied Shakespeare and English history, I'm good."

"Right, I forgot who I was talking to for a minute."

They shared a laugh, but Blythe noticed his left foot was starting to tap. He ran his fingers through his hair, then leaned forward in his chair as if to make a study of the parking lot.

"Aunt Grace and Uncle Harry were good to you though?" she asked gently. All of his signals told her to let it go. Talking about his family was obviously not easy, and yet, he was rattling off answers. Most of the time Gracen was a steel trap, so she didn't want to give up this thread just yet.

"They were very good to me," he nodded. "Without them, I wouldn't be me."

"Then, I'm grateful for them."

He looked at her curiously before smiling. "Uncle Harry would've liked you. He would've wanted you for one of his shows."

"His shows?"

"Didn't I tell you? Uncle Harry was the lead director of Summerstead Isle Playhouse."

"The community theater on the island?"

"That's the one. It was his real passion."

"Were you ever in any of Uncle Harry's plays?"

He laughed, "No. I couldn't do it."

"Why not? Why was that funny?"

It seemed so strange to be forthcoming, but Gracen felt like he owed her after she'd divulged so much about her background. He decided to act like it was not a big deal.

"All of my siblings and myself have a bit of our mom's anxiety. Well, Michelle, it's more like depression," Gracen paused as he thought of his sister. She had married a plastic surgeon who wrote prescriptions for drugs he had no business prescribing. "When I was a kid I could power through my piano recitals and whatnot. It was hard, but I knew I had to do it. But once I was a teenager I started having full-blown panic attacks, and then my mother would have episodes."

"Sounds like dominoes."

"It was a three-ring circus," he said dryly. "But I helped Uncle Harry at the theater. He'd have me record monologues for the cast to listen to so they could memorize, or especially if the character had an accent. I'm surprisingly good at accents. It helped me, too. I'd forgotten about that."

He stared into the sky as if he was seeing a scene unfold. Blythe pushed, "About what?"

"I'd memorize monologues, or even entire scenes of dialogue, and run through them to deal with my anxiety."

"Enter Shakespeare."

"Yes." Gracen looked at her with a wry smile. "Exit, pursued by a bear."

*"The Winter's Tale."*

"Of course you know that."

"It's the only thing I know from that play. Don't get too excited," Blythe said. "You should start that again."

"Start what?"

"Doing the monologues. You can go through them while you run. I'm pretty sure you don't just run because you're a fitness junkie."

"I'm not the only one with coping mechanisms," he replied. "You weren't just out here looking for Ursa Major."

"I was looking for Jupiter; it's easy to see in the summer. But the Pleiades are my real favorite though. I miss it in the summer. I love all that starlight clustered together."

"You would," he grinned, as he stretched his legs out onto the railing. Gracen folded his hands behind his head and gazed up at the sky, "I used to look at the stars through a telescope in my room when I was a kid. I haven't noticed them lately."

"That's the thing about starry nights. They don't really change much."

It occurred to Blythe that was likely why she usually sat on her balcony, drinking in the night sky over a cup of tea. No matter how much changed in her life, in herself, that sky was the same. She could count on the stars in their seasons to be just where they were supposed to be. Just as Gracen could always go back to *Hamlet* and see that the question remained: to be or not to be? Shakespeare and the stars were dependable.

# Chapter 12

"Give me your phone quick! Mine is dead," Liam shouted as he burst through the back door of The Yellow Bowl. The leather band of silver jingle bells rattled wildly as the door opened then violently shut.

It was a Monday afternoon a couple of weeks after Summer Fest. Blythe and the boys, Finn and Gracen, were in the front room working on fresh displays of books for the Irish Festival that coming weekend. Finn had plugged his phone into the sound system and they were listening to the traditional sounds of his homeland. It surprised Gracen how much he enjoyed the fiddles and banjos and concertinas.

"What? Are you okay?" Blythe asked as her brother appeared.

"I need your phone. They're about to ask the question and it's about the Indians."

Blythe and Finn reacted like they knew what that meant, but Gracen remained confused.

"You mean like, Native Americans? First Peoples?"

"No, like baseball, Princeton," Blythe said with a dramatic eye roll. "You're in Northeast Ohio now, remember?"

"Right, Ohio."

The Celtic jigs and reels stopped abruptly as Finn switched the stereo system to a local radio station. He explained for Gracen.

"WQIZ does a trivia question every Monday and they give away tickets to events all over their listening area. Liam has a knack for winning."

"He's a wizard with trivia," Blythe added, as she slapped her phone into her brother's waiting hand. "Don't ever play Trivial Pursuit with him. He's an awful winner."

"It's not my fault you only get three pieces of your pie," Liam retorted.

The radio announcer played three tones on a xylophone to signal that he was about to ask the trivia question. All persons present in The Yellow Bowl instinctively leaned closer to the radio. Liam stood poised with his thumb on the send button, the number set to dial.

The announcer spoke slowly, "Okay, folks, you need to be caller number nine. Got that? Nine! Alright, you ready? This week's question is: Who was the manager the last time the Cleveland Indians won the World Series? If you know, call in now!"

Immediately, Liam's thumb lowered. There was a delay as the phone's signal searched for a cell tower, then it began to ring.

"Why do I feel so nervous?" Finn said to Blythe.

"I do too," she giggled.

And although Gracen didn't admit it out loud, he felt nervous too.

At last, a voice was heard on Liam's end of the phone. "Hello, who are we talking to?"

Liam's face burst into a wide smile. He knew from experience that they only asked that question if he was the right caller.

"Liam Elwood."

Sure enough, his voice came through the radio and into the whole store. Blythe let out a tiny squeal of excitement before Liam shushed her.

"Sounds like you're not alone there, Liam."

"That was my sister. And I'm here with a couple friends too."

"Well, your sister is right to be excited, you are caller number nine. Now, do you know the answer? Who was the manager the last time The Cleveland Indians won the World Series?"

"The year was 1948, they won in six games against the Boston Braves, and the manager was Lou Boudreau."

"Wow, Liam, you're quite a fan. Are you ready to hear what you won?"

"Yes!"

"This very morning WQIZ came into ownership of four pavilion tickets for the Valley Amphitheater's Shakespeare in the Valley production of *Henry the Fifth*. You and three lucky friends will be able to attend the Sunday evening performance. Stay on the line and we'll get your information."

"Thank you," Liam said with a frown so intense he looked just like Teddy. As he was put on hold to be transferred to a back-office person, he muttered, "Last week I was the wrong caller and they gave away four lounge tickets to an Indians game. This week, I'm the right caller and I get tickets to Shakespeare. Bloody Shakespeare."

"It is bloody Shakespeare," Blythe said excitedly. "It's *Henry the Fifth*!"

"I don't know what that means."

She yanked Gracen's arm and pointed, "It's his arm."

"It's a play about Gracen's arm? Sounds riveting," Liam replied with thick sarcasm. A woman's voice came on the line and he turned away from Blythe to complete the phone call.

"I can't believe he won tickets to Shakespeare in the Valley," Blythe gushed.

"That's been on your bucket list for a long time," Finn said, sharing in her enthusiasm.

"What exactly is Shakespeare in the Valley?" Gracen asked.

"There's a big amphitheater in the Sayen Valley that opens out into a grassy hill. Usually, the symphony plays there but a lot of big music artists play the venue, too," Blythe explained. "And for two weekends every year they do a Shakespearean play."

"But that has nothing to do with baseball," Gracen pointed out.

"Oh, the trivia question and the prize don't have to be connected."

"No, they don't," Liam sighed as he handed Blythe's phone back to her. He was nearly whining, "Last week it was a history question for *baseball* tickets."

"What was the question?" Finn asked.

"I don't remember, but the answer was Anne of Cleves."

"Ginnie must've been with you," Blythe surmised. Liam knew a lot of things but English history was Ginnie's specialty.

"Yeah, we were in the car with the kids. Well, my loss is your gain. Obviously, I'm giving the tickets to you."

"Well, that's dumb."

"Excuse me?"

"That is dumb. Your wife has a birthday this same week. Her thirtieth last year was a total dud. You know she'll love this show, it's a history play. Take your wife."

"That means I have to go. Unless you get two more gal pals and make it a girls' night," Liam said optimistically. This was met with a flat stare. "Okay, fine, I'll go. Yay Bill."

"Do not call him Bill," Blythe blanched.

"So that's three tickets accounted for," Finn said.

"Do you want to come?" Liam asked him. "This seems like your scene."

"I would be up for it, except the show is on a Sunday. I'll be at church."

"If he's at church and you're at the play, who will run the store?" Gracen asked.

"Surely you can close The Yellow Bowl for one Sunday night and live a little, Blythe," Liam insisted. "How much business do you really do?"

She was busy thumbing around on her phone checking weekends. "Did they give you tickets for the first or second weekend?"

"The second. It will be the final performance."

"Whew, then we're good. The first weekend is also the Sweet River Festival, which isn't like the biggest one of the summer, but still, tons of food trucks mean tons of people."

Gracen opened his mouth to ask, but Finn preemptively explained, "The word 'sayen' means 'sweet'. Hence, Sweet Street which runs all through town, the Sweet River Café, and the Sweet River Festival."

"Gotcha. Thanks."

"It's a steep learning curve your first summer here. I get it."

"You should come with us," Blythe said to Gracen. "It's *Henry the Fifth*."

"I've seen it," he said as if all productions were one and the same. It was extremely tempting, but he hadn't come here for Shakespeare. He'd have to take a night off, even if it was a Sunday night. And he'd be going with Blythe. Something else he hadn't come here for. He had to remind himself of that more and more often these days.

"You haven't seen this one. And as I understand it, *Henry the Fifth* means a lot to you," Finn persuaded. "You can call it, what's that word, Blythe? An undate."

Liam groaned, "Not this undate stuff again."

"You always were allergic to silly," Blythe said tartly. She explained, "It's a word Jesse and I made up when we were in high school. It's like *Alice in Wonderland* and un-birthdays. An undate is just going out with a member of the opposite sex but it doesn't mean anything."

Gracen couldn't help the wicked smile on his face as he said, "Then I've had a lot of those."

She looked at him flatly, "This isn't one of those experiences, Mr. Hall."

"Duly noted, Miss Elwood."

"I know you wanna go. That tattoo on your arm is telling me you want to go. Don't let me stop you," Blythe said simply.

"Let me think about it," Gracen replied. "I'll have to close my shop, too."

"Well, when you're done punching numbers into your apps, you can let us know," Blythe teased him. She drummed her fingers on the counter, then slapped it, "Jesse said he might come home in August. He'll go if he's here."

"Ginnie can ask him," Liam said. "She seems to talk to him the most."

"She nags him until he responds," Blythe laughed. "I gave up ages ago."

"Well, anyway, I am here to balance the books, so I'll be in your office, probably muttering about Anne of Cleves and Shakespeare and Lou Boudreau."

"I feel like I owe you tickets to a game, but I have no dollars because I run The Yellow Bowl. And you have no dollars because you're a teacher," Blythe said as she followed him down the hall. "Maybe between us, we could scrape enough together for bleacher seats and split a hot dog."

"You're killing me," he sighed. "Maybe next year I'll get tickets to a game and Teddy will be old enough to act almost human."

"That's a good goal to shoot for."

As they faded from earshot, Gracen returned to arranging books for Blythe. It bothered him how much he wanted to accept that ticket. As he moved a volume of W. B. Yeats, he studied the words on his arm. He heard Uncle Harry's hoarse voice reciting them with earnest intensity.

"'Once more unto the breach'," Gracen whispered to himself, "To go or not to go? That is the question."

* * *

On the following Thursday Gracen closed SIP at nine o'clock. Lily and Ella headed next door to help Blythe stock for the festival, and Gracen sent them with the message that he'd be over soon to help. He took about thirty minutes on his laptop to balance figures while the last load of dishes finished in the industrial washer. The quiet was good for his concentration, and he hardly noticed that his legs were bouncing under his desk. His body seemed to hum with surplus energy even when his mind was sharply focused.

When he finished in his office, he stepped into the kitchen and pulled the rack of clean dishes through the other side. He'd let them air dry tonight. Gracen flipped light switches and turned the lock on the front door after exiting outside. Beckwith's Donuts was also closing for the night, which was normal, but the sight of Becky and Miles on the riverfront this late was very abnormal. Miles waved Gracen over his way and the men met under the lamppost.

"Everything okay?" Gracen asked with a frown.

"Just checking on the place, making sure everything is set for the festival tomorrow," Becky explained. Beckwith's was no longer managed by any relatives as Becky's sons and grandchildren had taken opportunities elsewhere. He made a point to stop by and check on things every so often to make sure it was all up to his standards.

"I see The Yellow Bowl is a flurry of activity," Miles observed, nodding his head towards the store.

"That's where I was headed," Gracen told them.

To Miles, Becky said, "I'll get the car and pick you up behind the shop."

As Becky disappeared into the parking deck, Miles sighed, "It's my eyes, can't do the night driving anymore. Although, I don't need this curbside service. I'm not an invalid."

Gracen motioned towards the shop, "Shall we?"

"Actually, you're the reason I'm here," Miles said, staying firmly in place. "I wanted to see how you're doing. It's a pretty big shift from Summerstead Isle."

"It is a change; it's a little slower here," Gracen answered, waiting for the real question.

"My granddaughter seems to like having you around. It's good to have a neighbor."

"I can see how it would be lonely without one."

"She's excited about that Shakespeare thing. I bet you are too."

"If I go," Gracen said, his voice thinning. "I haven't decided."

"What is it she's calling it again?"

"An undate."

"Yes, that's it. It's been ages since I've heard that silly word. Since Jesse packed up and left actually," Miles sighed. "Jesse had questionable intentions for Blythe I think, despite our best hopes."

"I can assure you that I don't have any intentions for her."

"I don't care very much about your intentions. The road to hell is paved with good intentions," Miles stated matter-of-factly.

Words escaped Gracen, "I … I'm afraid I don't follow."

"I'm concerned more about your actions than your intentions," Miles explained. "I don't really mean to give you a hard time. Well, maybe I do, but it's not personal."

"You hardly know me, I don't blame you actually."

"Blythe has been through a lot. She's had her heart broken. I'm not accusing you of anything, I believe you when you say you don't have any ill intentions, but, well, I'm not sure Jesse had ill intentions either," he shook his head. "Ian had nothing but bad intentions. My wife says it's not very Christian of me, but I'd probably strangle that boy for breaking her heart and ending their engagement."

So the former fiancé had a name. Ian. Gracen swallowed hard, trying to think of a reply. "Blythe is a friend, and I'll keep my boundaries. I mean, I respect her. I … she … she's safe with me."

There was a loud crash from inside The Yellow Bowl followed by a couple of girlish shrieks. Immediately Gracen dashed to the shop and threw open the front door. He followed the sound of the high-pitched voices to a bookcase where Lily and Ella were standing over Blythe. She was on the floor with a dozen oversized books collapsed around her. A chair was lying on its side.

"I'm fine," she grunted.

"Let's get you up before we make that judgment call," Finn said as he extended her a hand. Gracen took hold of her other hand and together they lifted her from the floor. Gingerly Blythe put weight on both feet.

"Glad to see she's in good hands," Miles said as he entered the shop. Finn and Gracen remained on either side of Blythe.

"She's in very good hands," Ella giggled. Lily gave her a gentle push.

"PapPap, what are you doing here?" Blythe asked. Gracen looked at Finn, and Finn knew exactly what that look meant. He'd been in Miles's hot seat himself.

"Becky's out back. We were just checking on things before the festival."

"Irish Fest is nothing compared to the Freedom Fest," Blythe said, "but we'll have no time to prep since they're back to back. I told Kyle not to schedule them like that again this year, but he never listens to me."

She limped her way towards Miles and planted a kiss on his soft cheek. His blue eyes gazed at her with such affection, it was nearly palpable. These two adored each other, the best grandfather and granddaughter on earth.

"I'll walk you out. I need to make sure I didn't actually sprain my ankle. Or my handlers over there will never let me live this down."

Finn rolled his eyes as Gracen smirked, "Don't worry, I'll clean this up."

"I told her we'd handle all the top-shelf books, but she's impatient," Finn said as he started picking up books. He lowered his voice, "Miles gave you the 'intentions' talk, didn't he?"

"Yes, I think I passed."

"Ha, you passed the first round."

"There's going to be more, aren't there?"

Looking around and spying the teenage girls, Finn motioned for Gracen to follow him into the stock room. This room was the fragrant epicenter of the shop where teas and books just waited for their chance on the shelves.

Finn continued quietly, "It took them a while to accept that I wasn't going to make a move. That was right after her relationship with Ian ended. Do you know about Ian?"

"She mentioned she had a fiancé and that's all."

"Then she's been doing well at not talking about it," Finn said pensively. It was unclear to him if that was good or bad in this particular case.

Gracen spoke again, "So you did the nice guy, cry on your shoulder routine?"

Finn sighed heavily, "When I moved here, they were still engaged. Then the engagement ended, but the relationship carried on for like two more years in varying stages of commitment and chaos. Jesse was always coming and going, causing more drama. I wasn't going to push in and take advantage of her pain."

"No one needs that drama."

"It was as much for her as it was for me. I've always cared about her too much to add to the insanity."

"So why not now? I assume Ian is officially out of the picture."

"It's been about a year and a half since they finally abandoned that ship. But the timing between Blythe and me has never been right. One of us is always a little off-kilter."

"Well, you're at least a logical choice. You're one of the good guys."

"You have your reasons for leaving Summerstead, I have mine for leaving Limerick. But let me tell you this, the Elwoods will take you in as one of their own. No questions asked."

"I didn't come here for the friends and family package. No offense to anyone. It's just not who I am."

"I didn't come here for that tour package either. Yet here we are. We're friends and they're family. Intentional or not, you belong now. What you do matters." Finn plunked two more large books into Gracen's hands.

As they left the room, Gracen's path joined with Blythe as she returned through the back door. She was barely limping now.

"Are you sure you're okay? You really should've waited and let me put those books away," Gracen told her.

Blythe placed her hand on his arm, "Next time, don't make me wait."

Gracen hoped that Blythe didn't feel the goosebumps on his bare arm. Miles was in his head. Finn was in his head. Blythe was in his head. And he didn't have enough headspace for all these voices.

He broke eye contact with Blythe and stalked into the main room. He'd come over here to help, he couldn't leave just because she touched his arm. That would be insane. Gracen decided he'd just do what she needed him to do then leave as soon as possible.

Blythe turned to Finn with a raised eyebrow, "Was it something I said?"

"Not you. Your grandfather," Finn replied.

"I knew this Shakespeare in the Valley thing would be a catalyst. He hasn't even officially committed to going."

"Honestly, I'm surprised it's taken this long for Miles to start asking questions. Gracen arrived in April, it's nearly July."

"They didn't start on you that early."

"Those circumstances were quite a bit different. You were with Ian, and then you weren't with Ian. And then there was an appropriate gap of time before every member of your well-intentioned family started pushing."

"It's a compliment, Finn. They like you."

"They want you married. And since the first choice is globe-trotting ..."

Blythe rolled her eyes. Finn was referring to Jesse. She scoffed, "At any rate, I don't see why my love life is the only thing anyone talks about. I'm more than my marital status."

"Miles and Mary Alice have been blissfully happy together. And Becky was with Pearl. They want that for all their grandchildren. They mean well."

"Well, the road to hell is paved with good intentions," she declared, sounding exactly like her grandfather. She marched into the stock room, grabbed a box of books, and stomped out to the main room. She unceremoniously dropped the box near the bookshelves where Gracen was finding places for some travel guides.

Tucking her hair behind her ear, she approached him, "I'm sorry about my grandfather. He does this to everyone. They all do it in their comments and glances. It's exhausting."

"Honestly, I don't blame him really for wanting to vet me a little. You're his pride and joy. I assured him I have no intentions."

Hearing Gracen say it out loud struck a strange chord with Blythe. She knew it, but hearing it from his lips was different. The coy little flirt inside of her wanted to change his mind. That was also terrifying, so she immediately silenced it.

"We'll just keep telling them this is strictly Shakespeare. If you go, of course. Jesse is still up in the air, too. Evidently, a night out with me isn't that appealing," she grinned. Apparently, the inner flirt was only mostly silenced.

"I wouldn't put it that way," Gracen replied. His slow smile made her liver quiver.

"Anyway, we're good, right? I mean, after the investigation out there?"

"I don't spook that easy."

The length of his run along the river that night, however, suggested otherwise.

# Chapter 13

The air conditioner unit behind Summerstead Isle Pizza hadn't shut off in days. Beads of sweat trickled down Ginnie's neck. Sayen Falls was in the throes of an Ohio midsummer heatwave with little relief forecasted.

"This is banana balls. I'm so hot," Ella moaned sliding low into a chair by the wall.

"I thought it was hot during Freedom Fest a couple weeks ago, but at least there were like a zillion people and constant orders that justified it," Lily said as she stretched her lithe frame across the front counter. "But this is just hot. This is the worst it's been all summer."

"I don't let the kids talk about it at home," Ginnie said. "My grandmother used to say that if you don't dwell on something awful, then it isn't quite so bad."

"I think that works if we're talking about a papercut but a nine-day heatwave is different," Ella argued. "It's gonna be hot whether or not we talk about it."

"Well, we don't need to *dwell* on it," Ginnie insisted. She crossed behind Lily to the lemonade machine and poured three glasses, "Let's talk about something fun."

Craning her head she peeked in Gracen's office. He looked intensely focused, clacking away on his laptop as indie rock music streamed in the background. Ginnie took the three cups of cool lemonade to the dining area and motioned for the girls to sit down.

"Let's talk about boys," she smiled.

"That is more fun than complaining about the heat," Ella conceded. She looked at her friend pointedly, "How are things with Brady?"

A heavy sigh escaped Lily's lips before she took a drink of her lemonade. She knew Ella didn't like Brady. No one seemed to like him. They didn't know him like she did. They only knew that he liked to get drunk with his cousins and sometimes he got high on the weekends. Lily knew there was more to him than those behaviors. It was just how he dealt with life.

"Things are fine, Ella."

"He doesn't seem to like Sawyer very much," Ella said coolly. "He came in the other day just to tell him to keep some distance."

"I didn't know that," Lily replied. "He can be suspicious. I think his mom cheated on his dad a few years ago."

"He should know you'd never do that since he says he loves you."

"He does. I mean, he just … I don't know," Lily gave up.

As she took a sip of her lemonade, Ginnie knew she needed to course correct this conversation. She wanted to talk to Lily about Brady, but clearly, that couldn't be done with Ella around. Ella put Lily on the defensive, and that was never a good way to change someone's mind.

"Well, I have a question," Ginnie smiled at Ella. "What's the deal with you and Sawyer? It's obvious he likes you."

Grateful for the subject change, a smile burst on Lily's face as she exclaimed, "That's what I'm always saying! He's just intimidated because you're so confident and smart."

"Sawyer and everyone else then," Ella laughed awkwardly. She sounded uncomfortable which was most unusual for the confident sass master.

"He probably thinks you have high standards, which you should, and he's nervous about it," Ginnie said. "Blythe was like you in high school. You know, sassy and smart and talented. No one asked her out on dates."

"That's super good news, Ginnie, thanks," Ella said as she made a face.

"Come on now, hear me out. The guys went for low-hanging fruit—you know, the girls that made it easy, *too* easy. It was hard for Blythe then but looking back, I know she feels like she dodged a lot of potholes."

"Potholes," Ella giggled. "That's one way to put it."

"I think Sawyer will come around. He just needs some time to figure you out," Ginnie said brightly. "Don't change for him. Just be you. And if he's a good one, he'll make the effort."

"I sorta assumed Blythe had a lot of boyfriends in her past," Lily admitted. "I mean, just because she's so great and so pretty."

"No, only one or two really," Ginnie said slowly. She thought the music in Gracen's office had lowered slightly, but it was probably her brain just melting from the heat.

"Well, Jesse Beckwith was one, right?" Ella asked.

"Not exactly," Ginnie answered. "They've always been close, but they insist they're only friends. I do think he got in the way of other guys asking her out though."

"That's rude," Ella snorted.

"So who were the boyfriends?" Lily asked.

"Aside from Jesse, there was almost Linus Huxley in college. He was so nice, very honorable, but he never asked her out. He might have if Ian O'Hare hadn't come along."

"That's it! That was his name!" Ella exclaimed, snapping her fingers. "I've been trying to remember. The fiancé, right? Ian O'Hare. I saw him a few times. He was cute."

"Yes, he was cute. But he was trouble," Ginnie said.

"Yeah, what happened there? I've always wanted to know," Ella asked.

"Of course you have," Lily shook her head.

"Not just for gossip!" Ella insisted. "It was kind of a big deal, but I've never known what was true and what was rumors. I just know that everyone in all the shops talked about it. A lot."

Ginnie sighed, remembering, "That didn't do Blythe any favors. The whole thing was so hard for her. I don't know how much truth was ever in the gossip mill, and I don't really know how much truth Blythe wants out."

"Then let me ask you this," Ella said carefully. "What made Ian 'trouble'?"

"He was a lot of talk and not much to show for it. And I don't mean his career or anything like that. Ian's actually had a pretty impressive career in architecture, from what I've heard. But he made Blythe a lot of promises and never followed through. He was emotionally …," Ginnie trailed off, looking for a word.

"Unavailable?" Lily offered.

"Maybe. But it was more like manipulation. When all was said and done, Ian had Blythe *convinced* that he was the only man who could love her and that without him she'd be completely lost. It was like she was addicted to him. They were together three years before the big break up, but she held on for two more afterward."

"But Blythe is so confident," Lily sounded bewildered.

"Girl, she has had to fight tooth and nail to get every bit of that confidence back from Ian. He stole it and crushed it and crushed her," Ginnie said. The edge in her voice revealed that even sweet Ginnie was capable of open disdain.

"Is that why she's stayed single?" Ella asked quietly. The giggles had rather gone out of her. "I wondered why she and Finn never became a thing."

"You and a whole lot of other people," Ginnie smiled. "It's taken Blythe a long time to come out of that fog. I don't think Finn wanted to make it harder for her. But beyond that, their reasons are known only to them."

"I didn't realize Blythe was so secretive," Lily said.

Ginnie thought for a second, "I think a better word is 'complicated'."

"Then I won't even bother asking about …," Ella jerked her head towards the office.

"That?" Ginnie said, her eyes following suit. "No one knows anything about that."

"No one? Miles was down here asking about his intentions a few weeks ago," whispered Ella. The giggles had returned and she had a huge coy smile on her face.

"Okay, well, yeah, we all know that. On record there are no intentions from either one of them for anything ever," Ginnie nodded.

"But?"

"But all I know is Blythe isn't in a hurry to get involved."

"That's the understatement of the year," Ella scoffed. "Her engagement ended like forever ago and he's been here like four months. She should get over Ian O'He's-Not-Here-Anymore and give Gracen a chance."

"After you get over a relationship, you do things differently," Ginnie explained. "At least, if you're smart you do. Blythe is one of the smartest people I know."

"You sound like you speak from experience," Lily noted, hoping Ginnie would elaborate.

"I do. I've had my heart broken."

"I bet Mr. Elwood wants to kill the guy who did it," Ella said and Lily nodded. Liam and Ginnie were basically couple-goals for the teenagers.

She had to laugh when Ella said this. It was a logical assumption knowing them now, and not half wrong. But not all right either.

"Mr. Elwood has very strong feelings about it. He was the guy."

"He was the guy?" Lily repeated. "But ... you guys are so happy."

"We are now."

"Did you like almost get divorced or separated or something?" Ella asked, wondering how she missed something so big on the riverfront.

"No, not like that. This was before we got married. In fact, I very nearly didn't marry Liam, uh, Mr. Elwood."

"Okay, now *this* is banana balls. I thought the heat was crazy, but this is insane," Ella said, pushing her lemonade away from her in a show of surprise.

"I thought you guys were childhood sweethearts," Lily frowned.

"We were. Growing up, I thought we'd be together forever. No doubt in my mind. But when Liam left for college, things changed. Things here changed—his parents both left, Blythe moved in with Miles and Mary Alice, and Silas went to live with their mother. It was a lot of change for everyone. And Liam sort of steeled himself over. He came home and was very cold and distant. Not just to me, to everyone. He broke up with me that summer. I left that fall for college myself."

"You went to Bowling Green, right? And Mr. Elwood went to OSU?" Lily confirmed.

"That's right. And it was years before Liam really came out of all that cold. We both ended up with teaching jobs back here in Sayen Falls. It took him a while to get the courage to ask me out on a date, let alone to marry him. He had no reason to believe I'd take him back. And he knew I had someone to compare him to then."

"Whoa, hold up, you dated someone else?" Ella asked. "Who? How did I miss all this?"

"Ella, this was a long time ago now. You would've been a little kid," Ginnie smiled. "And yes, I dated someone else. A really great guy actually."

"Did you love him?" Lily asked. "I'm sorry, that's really invasive."

"This whole conversation is invasive, Lily, don't start getting polite now," Ella laughed.

"Yes, I loved him," Ginnie answered. "You can love more than one person in a lifetime, you know. Thank God really. Most of us have at least one mismatch before we get it right. Even Miles Elwood went with a couple other girls before he fell in love with Mary Alice."

Ella rubbed her temples, "This whole conversation is starting to make me think everything I know is a lie."

"Oh, it's not that bad," Ginnie laughed.

"So who was this other guy?" Lily asked.

"Knox Callahan. We dated for about a year. Then, before his senior year, we decided to break up. He was going to graduate as a second lieutenant since he completed the Army ROTC program, and I knew I couldn't be an army wife. I worry too much. It's been hard enough worrying over the years as it is. I can't imagine if I'd married him."

"Wait, so you like, keep in touch?" Lily asked.

"He married my best friend."

"Ginnie Elwood. Stop it right now," Ella groaned.

"At least you're not thinking about how hot it is anymore," Ginnie grinned.

"No, now I'm thinking about how much more complicated life clearly is and there's no hope for any of us of having a nice simple straightforward life. Thanks so much."

"You're so dramatic," Lily said flatly.

"Think about it, Lil, if Ginnie and Liam—Mr. Elwood—don't even have a straightforward love story, how can any of us?"

"Who wants a straightforward love story? That sounds incredibly boring," Ginnie told her. "Those years without Liam were hard. But the time I spent with Knox was wonderful. He taught me how to trust and how to love. I grew up loving Liam; it was simply there like my address and the giant oak tree in my backyard. Being with Knox was different. And letting go of him was different too. Yes, he married my best friend. Audrey was my roommate in college and I actually set them up. They've been really happy together."

"Is he still in the Army?" Lily wanted to know.

"No, he did eight years and left. He's a pastor now."

"So why did you give Mr. Elwood another chance?" Lily needed to know. "How did you know he was a good guy again?"

"I could see it all around him. It wasn't just me. He made amends with all of us. He'd said some really hurtful things to Blythe and Silas in the 'lost years', as we call it. I saw him mending bridges wherever he could. He earned my trust back. We talked all the time. He listened to me. He remembered important things and trivial things. He loved me. And I don't mean that he had feelings for me. I mean it as a verb. He actively loved me."

"That's really beautiful," Lily said quietly. "I don't think I've ever seen that in action."

"You'll see it in action when they go to Shakespeare in the Valley," Ella smiled. "That's an act of love. I know Shakespeare is not his jam."

Ginnie giggled, "Mr. Elwood knows how excited I am and that makes it worth it for him. He'll enjoy being out anyway. We love our kids but date nights are our favorite."

Lily asked, "Do you have a sitter yet?"

"Well, if Gracen decides to go and closes the shop, we'd love to have you. Otherwise, it's my parents and they sugar them up the whole time."

A deep voice cleared his throat, "In that case, I'll go. We don't want the Dennis and Linda Beckwith sugar patrol."

Ginnie's head whirled around to see Gracen leaning in the doorway of his office, arms folded and a smirk on his face.

"How long have you been standing there?"

He shrugged.

"We were tired of being hot," Ella said to him.

He raised an eyebrow but the smirk didn't fade a bit.

"I'll text everyone the good news that they get an evening off," he said, backing into his office. The door remained wide open.

"How much do you think he heard?" Lily whispered.

"I hope he heard all of it and makes his move," Ella grinned. She raised her voice to slightly above normal speaking level, "Ginnie, do you think Ian would have gone with Blythe to Shakespeare in the Valley?"

Ginnie shook her head at Ella, knowing exactly what the girl was trying to do, but she matched the same volume in her voice as she replied, "Not a chance. He was the wrong guy."

# Chapter 14

Ginnie couldn't remember the last time a birthday had been exciting. Her thirtieth last year came and went with little to no fanfare. Such is the life of a suburban homemaker. However, this year more than made up for it—dinner at the fanciest place in town *and* Shakespeare in the Valley. To celebrate, she even treated herself to a new dress with the birthday money from her parents. It'd been ages since she'd had a new dress.

Around four that afternoon, Ginnie started getting ready, taking a long (quiet) shower while Liam kept the kids far from the bathroom. He put *Cinderella* on to keep them occupied while he shaved and showered which gave Ginnie a little more time to style her hair and apply some makeup. He emerged from the master bathroom, towel around his waist, just in time to zip up Ginnie.

"You know I love you in blue," he said, planting a generous kiss on his wife. "You look gorgeous."

"Thanks, babe," she replied, patting his terry-covered behind.

"Are we matching?" he asked as he took a blue shirt from the closet.

"No, I like that green one on you better," she answered. Ginnie opened her jewelry box to select a necklace just right for the dress. She was astonished to find a new necklace hanging on one of the tiny brass hooks. It was dainty and sweet, two hearts linked on a silver chain, a diamond in the center of one heart and a pearl in the center of the other.

"The children's birthstones," she breathed as she slipped the necklace from the hook. Liam's warm hands took the necklace from her and placed it around her neck. He kissed her nape and she sighed, "Thank you. It's beautiful, perfect."

A relieved grin spread across Liam's face. He'd been saving for months to buy that necklace for Ginnie. One real diamond and one real pearl weren't much but it was quite a lot on one income, particularly when that income was a teacher's salary.

"Are you feeling any better about tonight?" she asked as she helped him tie his necktie.

"I'm not nervous. I'm glad Blythe and even Gracen are going. You'll have people to enjoy the experience with, and so you won't be disappointed that I'll be completely lost."

"You won't be lost; we'll give you a good synopsis at dinner."

"Will there be pictures? That might help."

"We're seeing a play, goober, there will be real live people acting it out."

"I'm familiar with live theater," he said ironically.

"I've seen your musicals," she retorted making a sour face.

"I'll remember that the next time you want something from me."

"And what do you mean, 'even Gracen'?"

90

"That was a delayed reaction. I just mean, I don't know what to think of Gracen. I was sorta hoping Jesse would be here."

"Well, Jesse is in Spain and that's where he should be."

"That's unlike you. You always want Jesse to come home when he can."

"I love my cousin, but I do think it's time for him to make up his mind. He can't just come and go, pick her up, and set her down whenever it's convenient for him."

"I'm still Team Jesse. Better the devil you do know than the devil you don't, as my mother would say."

"It's a sad day when you start quoting one of your parents."

"You're telling me," Liam said. He dabbed on some cologne, then checked his hair. He turned to Ginnie and offered a hand to help her up, "But this is not a sad day. It's your birthday. We're going to see Shakespeare. It's going to be great."

"You almost said that without wincing."

"I've been practicing."

\* \* \*

Gracen recited several long portions from *Henry the Fifth* while he showered before the play. As he ran a towel over his head, his curls going wild, he force-stopped his brain to stop quoting. Sometimes he got on autopilot and had to kill the sequence.

He slipped on his shirt, the same midnight blue shirt he had worn to The Gala. A few days earlier, Mae Houser had waved him over to her shop and insisted he take a three-piece gray suit. Now, as he slipped on the pants he wondered how she had guessed his pant size. He buttoned the vest, surprised it wasn't loose on his lean, albeit defined, torso. He decided to forgo a tie, figuring the vest more than made up for it.

As he steeled his nerves, he rapped on Blythe's door and resolved to not be a doofus about the evening. It was dinner with friends, no big deal. They were going to a play, a classic, his favorite. There was no reason to make it a big thing. It was just an evening away from work. Surely, Uncle Harry would approve.

Then Blythe opened the door and his resolve evaporated. She was wearing a red dress from Mae that fit in all the right places, and the sweetheart neckline accentuated her simple strand of pearls.

"I don't know about you," he cleared his throat, "but I'm not up for the parade downstairs."

"That makes two of us."

"How do we get out of here without being seen?"

"The fire escape?" she joked. Gracen shrugged as if that wasn't insane. "No, I'm afraid of heights. And I'm wearing heels."

"I'd catch you."

"Oh, yeah, that'd be a great way to avoid a show," Blythe rolled her eyes. "The best thing to do is wait until Ginnie and Liam get here, and come down so late that Liam freaks out and we have to leave immediately."

"It seems like you've done this before."

"Not on purpose, but my brother can't stand being late."

And so they waited. And after Ginnie and Liam arrived they waited some more. Sure enough, by the time they came down the stairs, Liam was irritated and anxious to leave so there wasn't time for a fuss.

"If you're really worried about being late," Gracen said to Liam, "take the Shelby."

"Me? You want me to drive?" Liam asked as Gracen slipped him the keys. His eyes were huge.

"You know your way around, I don't. Besides I've never sat in the back of the Shelby."

"That's good to know," Blythe teased him. He wrinkled his nose at her. "You should sit behind Ginnie, those legs of yours will barely fit as it is."

"I'm up for the challenge," he said as he climbed in the back passenger. Blythe slipped in behind the driver's seat and had no choice but to cozy close to him. Immediately Gracen wondered if showing off the Shelby to Liam had been a bad idea. His eye caught Aunt Grace's necklace hanging from the rearview mirror. She would've been tickled to see him dressed up and out with a girl on a proper date. No. Stop that. It's not a date.

By the time they arrived at the restaurant Liam was so enamored with the car that he no longer cared that they were almost ten minutes late and on their way to see Shakespeare. He prattled on and on about the powerful engine and the smooth handling as the hostess seated them at their table.

"Gracen, I owe you," Ginnie grinned as she slid into the chair Liam held for her. "You've improved my husband's mood immensely."

"I'm amazed you let other people drive her," Liam said. Gracen pushed Blythe's chair in, an unexpected gesture.

"It's just a car. I have insurance," Gracen said.

"I keep telling him that won't last if he isn't careful," Blythe said.

"And I keep telling you that it's just a car. There are some things in life I refuse to lose sleep over," he replied. Liam slid the keys across the table, but Gracen shoved them back. "You're the driver tonight. No reason Ginnie should be the only one enjoying herself."

"Hopefully we all will," she beamed. "I know Blythe is just as excited as I am for Shakespeare in the Valley."

"I've always wanted to do this," Blythe nodded. "The only live theater I see these days is the high school musical."

"And what's wrong with that?" Liam demanded.

"Absolutely nothing, you do a great job," Blythe said before rolling her eyes at Ginnie.

"I saw that."

"You direct the shows at the high school, right?" Gracen asked.

"Yes, along with the music teacher, Debbie Reitzel."

"Speaking of, have you picked a musical for next year?" Blythe asked.

"Well, it's August and the show is in March, so … no."

"You know Debbie and Russ will already have decided on something. They probably picked it last March," Blythe said.

"Good point. And I really can't face doing anything fluffy again."

"Fluffy?" Gracen asked with amusement.

Scowling, Liam explained, "I've done two shows, *Meet Me in St. Louis* and *Brigadoon*. Not a lot of depth."

"Ouch, I mean, *Brigadoon* isn't maybe so bad … well, no, it is," Gracen laughed.

"He knows musicals?" Ginnie said to Blythe as though he couldn't hear.

"I grew up on them," Gracen replied on Blythe's behalf, "but I can't think of very many that aren't, um, fluffy."

"You know, I've always thought *Henry the Fifth* would be a good musical," Blythe said in complete earnestness. Of course, Gracen had chosen that moment to take a sip of his water which left him sputtering.

"You're serious, aren't you?"

"Entirely. I'm telling you 'once more unto the breach' would make an awesome ballad."

"All those coffee fumes and old book smells have finally cracked you," Liam said.

"First of all, you don't even know what the show is about," Blythe retorted and then using her fingers to count, "Second of all, *Les Misérables*, *Phantom of the Opera*, *The Secret Garden*, *Jane Eyre*, *Jekyll & Hyde*, *West Side Story*. That last one is an adaptation of Shakespeare, in case you didn't know. As is *Kiss Me, Kate*."

"Thank you for clearing that up," Liam said wryly.

"You might have a point," Gracen granted. "With the right composer, it could work. I'm sure *Les Mis* seemed crazy but it's been a massive success."

"*Les Misérables* is my favorite show of all time," Blythe sighed dreamily. "I think you should pitch that idea, Liam."

"Well, it definitely isn't fluffy," Liam conceded.

"Not a single ounce of fluff anywhere," Blythe nodded.

"It has possibilities," said Liam, considering.

"I'm still stuck on *Henry the Fifth* being a musical," Ginnie interjected. "Would you start at the real beginning? I mean, with *Henry the Fourth*?"

"Why would *Henry the Fourth* be the real beginning to *Henry the Fifth*?" Liam asked.

"You really know nothing, don't you?" Blythe sighed.

"Here's that synopsis I promised you," Ginnie grinned.

"It gets a little confusing because everyone is named Henry," Blythe began, "but I promise you it's worth it to start at the beginning. Henry the Fifth started out as wild and unruly Prince Hal in *Henry the Fourth*. His father worries about what will happen to the throne when he dies and Hal is crowned. There are two entire shows dedicated to the evolution of Prince Hal into Henry the Fifth."

"Some really poignant scenes and important characters. One of the most iconic characters Shakespeare ever created is from the *Henry the Fourth* plays," Gracen added. "Falstaff. He's the main negative influence on Prince Hal and the source of the comic relief. But he's banished when Hal is crowned, and he dies at the start of *Henry the Fifth*."

"That's cheerful," Liam remarked.

"Oh, there's a lot of death. Henry goes to war with France," Ginnie explained. "The prince of France challenges him and he decides to claim his right to the French throne. There's a big siege—"

"That's where the 'once more unto the breach' monologue comes in," Blythe said, taking Gracen's arm and pointing. His sleeves were rolled up, as always, and the tattoo was clear.

"Okay, got it, arm tattoo speech, big siege in France."

"The English are successful, but the army suffers losses and sicknesses and it looks pretty grim for the last battle," Blythe continued.

"There's a pretty moving prayer after Henry realizes how scared his men are and how scared he is himself," Gracen said. "And then the famous 'band of brothers' speech."

"The Saint Crispin's Day monologue," Blythe chimed in.

"Right, Rice Crispies Day," Liam said with an exaggerated raise of his eyebrow.

"Don't start that," Blythe giggled. "John is John."

"There aren't any Johns in *Henry the Fifth*," Gracen said with confusion.

"That's a *Les Mis* joke," Blythe said. "It took Liam a while to catch on to the greatness that is *Les Misérables*."

"I still think Hugo could've picked a better name than Jean Valjean," Liam shrugged.

"You are the only one in the world who thinks that."

"I'm sure that's not true."

"Anyway, that gets you almost to the end of the play," Ginnie said before Blythe and Liam could get any more off topic. "Make sense?"

"Sure, wild prince becomes king, goes to war to prove he's worthy, fights some French people, a couple big speeches I probably won't understand but the three of you will geek out over, and then something will happen, it will end, and I'll wake up and drive us home."

"Yup, sounds like he got it," Gracen snickered. "At least you'll be well rested to drive the Shelby home in the dark."

Across the table Ginnie met Blythe's eye, twinkling in a conspiratorial way. Blythe shook her head and looked back at her sternly. There would be no mischievous nods and grins laced with romantic implications here tonight. It was just nice to be out with friends, nothing more. Blythe needed Ginnie to get that.

* * *

Ginnie read the message loud and clear, but that didn't stop her from making sure that Blythe and Gracen sat next to each other. Although it was a logical configuration that Liam and Gracen would be the bookends, so Blythe and Ginnie could sit together and whisper.

The evening air was perfect, just a slight chill as the sun set behind them in the west. The amphitheater was covered with a large roof, but by leaning back and to the left, Blythe could still see the night sky. The sky was so much darker in the valley than it was in Sayen Falls. She missed the nights when she'd come down with friends to sneak into the parks that closed at dusk and count constellations. She craned her neck, scanning the sky.

"I thought the stars would be clearer here," Gracen said. The amphitheater lights flashed twice; the show would be starting imminently.

Keeping her eyes trained on the sky, Blythe replied, "It's too cloudy tonight, but look at the fireflies. The trees glitter."

Gracen strained to look; sure enough, the forest around them was shimmering with the firefly light. He looked back at Blythe, grinning at him, and the firefly light was nothing compared to the radiance in her eyes.

No sooner had the show begun than a flood of recollections washed over Gracen. It was as if he were hearing every word in stereo, once on the stage and once in a memory. He had helped Uncle Harry with this show twice and read it through with him in the hospital. That was the voice most often echoing in his brain. Grief washed over him anew, leaving him shaken and breathless. He could only hope it didn't show, or that Blythe was so invested in the play that she didn't notice.

And she was riveted. She hung on every word, every pause, every step. Her heart soared in the theater, awakening deep longings to be creative and drink up beauty. When King Henry began the 'once more unto the breach' monologue she tapped Gracen's arm. There was a strange look in his eyes when he turned to her. She saw a man who needed hope. As he blinked and looked away from her, he stretched his arm out behind her, resting on her seat where the ink remained visible in her periphery. His arm stayed there until the Saint Crispin's Day monologue much later in the show, just before the final battle.

Gracen leaned forward, spellbound, folding his hands together and resting his elbows on his knees. His legs were bouncing, first, the left up, then the left down, then the right up, then the right down.

"'We band of brothers'," he whispered between his fingers. Uncle Harry's tired but sure voice resounded in his head. Unwittingly, he glanced at Blythe and saw a tear slipping down her cheek as King Henry emboldened his troops with mere words.

As the battle raged on stage in a spectacular display of swordplay and masterful blocking, Gracen settled back into his chair to watch the drama unfold. When King Henry bellowed for the French prisoners to be executed on the spot in a fit of rage, Blythe grasped Gracen's arm. She knew it was coming, but hearing it in person, feeling the intensity of his wrath, she leaped out of her own skin and clung tight to Gracen's arm. He tensed for a moment, then folded his hand over hers.

At last, when the warring was done, Blythe's favorite part began: King Henry's courtship of Katharine. They'd forgotten to tell Liam about this part. There were a lot of plays on words, classic Shakespeare, but the methodical wooing of Katharine gave Blythe tingles. The actor playing King Henry did it well, too. When at last he kissed Katharine, Blythe noticed that her Claddagh ring was spinning on her finger. Looking down, she saw that Gracen was absentmindedly spinning it with his thumb as he held her hand. His legs had stopped bouncing.

During the drive home, Blythe stared pensively at the cloudy sky while Ginnie explained pieces of the show to Liam. He'd understood far more than he expected but some of the rapid-fire dialogue had been too much. The history geek in Ginnie loved every minute of the show and was in her glory reliving the scenes for her husband, who at least feigned genuine interest.

Only Gracen seemed unsettled. Grieving Uncle Harry was hard enough, but he also had unwanted feelings for Blythe hissing in his head. He'd never been out with a girl that he didn't intend to get into his bed at the end of the night. The fact was, he had no idea how the end of this night was supposed to look. They'd climb their mutual staircase and just say good night? His palms sweated at the memory of her hands in his. This was not good. Besides, he couldn't run tonight, she would see him and then she'd know. And he could not let her know.

# Chapter 15

"I think I'd forgotten how much I really love Shakespeare," Blythe sighed contentedly at the top of the stairs. "How is it that after something like four hundred years the Bard still feels so relevant and accessible and important?"

"That's what makes him the Bard, I guess," Gracen said. He put his hand on his doorknob.

"I can't go to bed yet. I get such a high from live theater. Why don't we sit out on the balcony and try to look at stars?"

"Too cloudy remember?" he deflected. It was of no use.

"Balcony in five minutes," she said as she ducked inside her apartment. He shook his head but five minutes later he was on his half of the balcony, vest left behind on his couch, shoes kicked off in the living room.

Blythe appeared shortly with two cups of tea and a plate of donuts undoubtedly from Beckwith's. Her dress clung to her legs as a breeze whipped by the balcony. Gracen noticed she was barefoot.

"Would Uncle Harry approve?" she asked. Gracen looked confused and slightly startled, so she added, "Of the show?"

"He would've loved it. The cast was spectacular. I like how they did the blocking. The battle scenes were always hard for us to block."

"You speak with ownership when you talk about the theater."

"Uncle Harry wanted me to help him with everything. Especially in his last shows at the theater. He knew he was sick then. He was just putting off the diagnosis," Gracen said mechanically. He needed to stop remembering.

"I like when you talk about him. He sounds like a really incredible guy, especially pushing through the sickness to do what he loved."

"He was the most incredible guy," Gracen whispered. He cleared his throat suddenly and confessed, "I thought about him a lot tonight. There's so much I want to talk to him about. I feel like there's something he tried to tell me that I missed. Something I need to know."

"I'm sorry, Gracen. That must be so hard," she said gently. She paused to take a drink of tea, then she asked, "Will you call Aunt Grace?"

"I don't know," he sighed. Talking to her about the play would probably lead to tears. He didn't want to listen to her cry from so far away.

"I think you should call her. If your uncle still has something to tell you, it will come from her lips now," Blythe suggested. As Gracen's head snapped up to meet her eyes, she wished she could just go into her pantry and bring him some hope on a cake plate. Or love or peace, or whatever it was he needed.

"Uncle Harry would be crazy about you," Gracen mumbled. He rubbed his face with his hands, trying to remove the cobwebs of sorrow and memory. Then he took a deep breath and adjusted his voice. "Enough of my grief. Did *you* enjoy the show?"

"Every minute," she bubbled.

"Shakespeare in the Valley really lived up to the hype?"

"I think so. But, objectively, I do tend to get carried away easily."

"You don't say," he teased.

"I do!" she laughed. "But you know, I feel more like me than I have in years. The me that reads and writes and believes in things."

"Easy, girl, we saw *Henry the Fifth*, not *A Midsummer Night's Dream*."

"Can you imagine if we had?" Blythe giggled. "I'd be completely bonkers right now."

This made Gracen laugh and his entire being sighed with relief. The tension eased from his shoulders and slipped out of his fingers and toes.

"What is your favorite play?" he asked with a real smile.

"My favorite play is *Noises Off* because it's hilarious and so on point."

"The classic play about doing a play," Gracen nodded, lifting his teacup to her.

"But my favorite Shakespeare is *Much Ado About Nothing*. It was the first one I saw start to finish, although it was Kenneth Branagh's film and not a live show. I saw it when I was fifteen and I absolutely fell in love."

"It's a beautiful adaptation," he agreed. "Uncle Harry always wanted me to be Benedick."

"I always wanted to be Beatrice," Blythe replied, as Benedick and Beatrice are the central couple. "But I really want to be adored like Hero."

"No, you don't. Claudio abandoned his love for Hero the moment her honor was in question. That's not much of a love story, in my opinion."

"Well, there is that. You really burst my bubbles, you know that?"

Suddenly, her phone started to ring from inside her apartment. Her balcony door was open and the familiar chorus of "Jesse's Girl" came out to greet her.

"That's subtle," Gracen said, raising his eyebrow.

"Jesse's about as subtle as a tow truck—very big and very noisy and I'm always annoyed when I need to call for his help."

"So you're not going to answer it then."

"He's only calling because he's jealous," she said flippantly. Instant regret followed and the tips of her ears burned red. "I didn't mean ... I ... never mind."

"It's okay," he said with a not very careless shrug.

"The fact that I'm letting it go to voicemail will drive him insane. He's going to think something is really happening right now."

"Then he must not know you very well."

"He says I don't know you well enough," she replied carefully.

"You probably don't," he agreed. The phone stopped ringing. He decided that was enough talk of Jesse. He turned to Blythe instead. "So, you who believe in things, you write?"

"I used to write. Back when I believed in things."

"What kind of writing? More Shakespeare analysis?"

There was a long pause. Not only had she stopped writing, she had stopped talking about her writing except in the most dismissive sense.

"I started writing a play when I was in high school. I've fiddled with it off and on ever since, but I haven't touched it in years."

"A play. What's it called?" Gracen asked. He was amused but not in a patronizing way.

"*Ex Libris.*"

"'From the library'," he said translating the Latin. "What a curious title."

"The characters are the classic archetypes—like the brooding romantic, the giddy young girl, the hero, the lover, the beloved, the villain, the anti-hero, et cetera. They all interfere with each other's ability to get what they want. But one by one, everyone succeeds and then they fade to gray until the last part is just the lover and the beloved."

"Because love is elusive, it's the hardest to find."

"Exactly."

"So how does it end?"

"It doesn't have an ending. I can't bring myself to make it end sadly but a 'happily ever after' ending just feels trite."

"Happily ever after isn't always trite. Aunt Grace and Uncle Harry lived happily ever after. Even now. In fact, I think she's even more devoted to him now than when he was alive."

Blythe blinked twice and took a long drink of her tea. It had cooled down too quickly.

"So maybe that's my ending. A widow on the stage alone, then behind the scrim the lover appears, I never would've thought of that myself," she mused. After a beat, she said, "I've been thinking about it for a while, and I think I gave up on my play when I gave up on everything else."

"Everything else?"

"My romantic delusions, too many books, too many old movies. I used to be like Ella, silly and naive and believing in everything. Then I grew up. And I gave up expecting to have what my grandparents have."

"Miles and Mary Alice remind me of Aunt Grace and Uncle Harry."

"They sound very similar," Blythe agreed. She sighed, "I worry about when one of them dies, I don't know how the other one will go on."

"They will, they'll have to," Gracen said. "And not having read it, I think that'd be the perfect ending to your play. You should write it. You shouldn't give up on all your romantic delusions."

"It wasn't really a choice," Blythe said, looking up into the night. The streetlights bounced off the clouds and obscured every star in the heavens. "I just lost it along the way, after my parents divorced, after Ian."

"I overheard Ginnie say that Ian would never have agreed to go to

Shakespeare in the Valley. So is it safe for me to assume that this Ian chump didn't encourage your writing?"

Blythe laughed cynically, "Yeah, that's a safe assumption. He didn't see the point of it. It wasn't like it was ever going to amount to anything."

"Why did you let him tell you that it was a waste of time? And why did you believe him?"

"Because I was in love with him," she said simply. "And I thought he was right. My relationship with Ian wasn't healthy. I believed he was the only one who would tolerate me."

"Tolerate you?" Gracen repeated, his eyes darkening.

"Yeah, I can be high maintenance, clingy. Or at least, I was then. And, I think I was afraid to be alone. I know I was actually. Hard as it was, it was easier to be with Ian than to be alone."

"And has it been harder to be alone?"

She stopped as she thought about the weeks of depression and the Christmas when Finn flushed the antidepressants down the toilet before she could swallow them. She'd been so broken, so frail, so burdened with darkness. Eventually, she continued, "I'm better now. I'm happy now. But it's taken a long time. Ian was like a drug and I went running back every time he called. He finally stopped calling and I finally stopped wanting him to call."

"He really broke your heart, didn't he?"

"Into a million billion zillion little infinitesimal pieces."

"That sounds like carnage."

"It was."

"How long were you together?"

"Five years, more or less. We dated for two, were engaged for one, and then two more years of dating ... sort of. It was messy."

Gracen gulped audibly, "Five years?"

This made Blythe smile, the tension building in her broke like a pebble disrupting a pond. She was grateful for the disturbance, "Yes, five years, Mr. One Night Stand, some of us believe in commitment. Or did."

"Five years. I can't imagine that," he remarked. "Good grief."

"Yes, there was a lot of grief. And poor decisions and even more grief. And then thinking about the grief. I've only recently gathered up my wits and stopped dwelling."

"So have you given up on it?"

"On love? Not entirely. I hope someday to be loved again, and to love again. But I don't look for it, I don't anticipate it. And if it's going to happen, it's got to sweep me off my feet."

"So much for abandoning those romantic delusions."

"It doesn't have to look like the musicals to achieve feet-sweeping status. It's not really moonlight and diamonds and poetry."

"Then what is it?"

Blythe laughed as she shrugged, "Don't ask me. I know what it isn't. Not what it is."

As Gracen stretched his arms he caught sight of his tattoo. The boldly colored medieval lettering was a true piece of artwork. It'd taken several sessions and serious cash to complete. It had been worth it.

"You know why I got this tattoo?"

"You really like Shakespeare?"

"I appreciate Shakespeare. This was advice Uncle Harry gave me. It's the idea of not giving up. You go back one more time, and one more time, and one more time pushing through weariness and exhaustion. And that's how he lived his life, even fighting cancer. So when he died, I had this designed. I didn't want to forget the bravery with which Uncle Harry lived his life and the way he wanted me to live mine. He used to say it wasn't about being fearless but using that fear to propel you towards the right things. Maybe that's why that play meant so much to him. I feel like that's a theme, in a way."

"I can see that," Blythe nodded. "'Imitate the action of the tiger, stiffen the sinews, summon up the blood.' Fake it 'til you make it."

"I've never heard that … translation before," Gracen winked.

"That's because I never finished my play," she retorted. Boldly, but gingerly, she traced the letters on his arm. As a reflex, he stiffened his arm. "What did your family think?"

"Aunt Grace cried and said Uncle Harry would be pleased. Roy had a fit, and everyone followed suit. That's how it works. Roy's way or no way."

"Except for Aunt Grace."

"She's his sister and he doesn't dictate to her."

"So, Aunt Grace, any chance your name comes from her?"

There was a long pause before he answered, "I was named for them both. My full name is Gracen Henry. Harry was a nickname for Henry. They named me and she always said I was a child of grace. Whatever that means."

"Child of grace," she turned the words over slowly in her mouth.

"Beats me. I don't feel like a child of anything."

"I know that feeling. So you're Gracen Henry. Do you know my middle name?"

"I don't think it's ever come up. Is it Grace?"

"Interesting guess but no," she smiled. "It's Katharine. I was named for my Aunt Kate. She died when she was eight years old and my dad wanted to honor her memory."

"Gracen Henry and Blythe Katharine. Like King Henry and Queen Katharine."

"Don't tell Ginnie. She'll think it's a match made in Shakespeare."

"Well, we wouldn't want that, now would we, Kate?"

The struggle to resist quoting the famous love scene they'd just watched was very real. For the moment, Gracen entertained the thought of giving Jesse something to be jealous about. Then, he thought, maybe just a kiss. And, at last, he decided it was better to keep that line firm. He had not come here for this. And she was just gathering her wits about her, as she'd said. It was best to just leave well enough alone.

# Chapter 16

Late the next morning Blythe awoke in her bed feeling cozy and content under her warm crazy quilt. A smile stretched across her face as she rolled over and saw her red dress in a heap on the floor. It had been such a lovely night and she hadn't wasted a minute of her time away from responsibility.

When at last she'd left the balcony, at nearly three a.m., she'd first scribbled down some thoughts about the ending for her play. Then, she'd stripped off her dress, thrown on some PJs, and sunk into bed without even washing her face or brushing her teeth. She was happily exhausted and wanted to sleep before something burst the bubble.

Now awake again, she spent ten lazy minutes simply staring at her ceiling and remembering every detail of *Henry the Fifth*. She hoped to cement the memory so she'd have it for a long time to come. Yet, when she got to the last act and the courtship of Katharine, her mind began to wander.

Gracen. He was probably up and running. Literally.

She knew she'd spooked him when she'd said that Jesse was jealous, and, clearly he'd been deeply affected by the play.

Thinking briefly of Jesse, she remembered his call and finally reached for her phone on the nightstand. There were texts from Ginnie, Ella, and Finn. No big surprise there. Everyone was waiting with baited breath to see if Blythe and Gracen would emerge from the undate as a couple. So sorry to disappoint, but not happening.

And there was a voicemail from Jesse. Preemptively sighing, Blythe lowered her thumb on the voicemail symbol and awaited the connection.

"Hey, um, it's me. I'm in Spain. I'd be more specific but I can't pronounce the name of the town. I should've worked harder at Spanish in high school. Um, anyway, I was just calling to see how it went tonight. You know, the play and all. And that guy you're not supposed to let too close. So, I hope you loved it. And I hope you're not doing anything stupid."

There were a few beats of silence. Then, Jesse continued.

"I read your play. I've been meaning to tell you. I've actually read it twice since you gave it to me. There are some really beautiful moments in there, Blythe. And some really funny bits. I really wish you'd just write again. Anyway, I'm gonna go. I hope you're okay. And sleeping. Oh, and hey, I'm gonna try to come home for Gramps' birthday. Ginnie told me you two are planning a big thing. Of course, Uncle Dennis and Aunt Linda aren't helping. But let's not start on the Beckwith family dysfunction. Okay, well, anyway, I'll talk to you soon, okay?"

The worry and suspicion in his voice made Blythe grin. It was quite fun having Jesse over a barrel for a change. The shoe was on the other foot and she found it terribly amusing. Particularly since nothing had happened.

Amusement quickly yielded to pensive as her thoughts returned to the details of her night. Nothing physical had happened unless they were counting hand holding. But she decided that since they weren't first graders, it didn't count.

Except the butterflies in her tummy were counting it. They were counting it hard.

Holding his hand in that moment of that play in that theater on that cloudy starless night meant something to her, whether she wanted it to or not. They shared something in that moment. And they shared even more in their conversation on the balcony. What was it about that balcony that made Gracen open up? He was so closed off otherwise. Last night, Blythe felt that she'd really seen him. It was that look on his face. Her heart went out to him and evidently, the butterflies found that very thrilling.

"I'm not ready for this," she breathed.

She didn't want these feelings for him. She wanted it to be all about Summerstead and getting her old happy back. The happy from a long time ago, long before Ian and the carnage. But it wasn't anymore. This friendship, her time with Gracen, it wasn't about Summerstead at all anymore. It was Gracen for his own sake, his own troubled enigmatic sake.

Not that it mattered what her reasons were or were not. Even if Gracen found her attractive, his interest wouldn't stretch beyond that. She was inherently messy, a patchwork romantic of broken dreams and insecurities. And he was rigid, a methodical planner with tidy compartments for his every thought, feeling, and relationship. Her mess would wreck him. She didn't need to be someone's wreckage again. She was sure he would keep some distance and that was for the best.

The butterflies stopped fluttering. Tears came to her eyes.

"Stop it," she whispered to herself.

Her mind zeroed in for a quick-study of her heart and realized what it was about Gracen that kept her from being bothered about his past and his secrets. When they talked, even about broken things, he didn't talk to her like *she* was a broken thing. Everyone else around her wanted to fix her with a cup of tea, a bit of inspiration, a perfect date; they all had a solution for her brokenness. Except for Gracen, and Blythe knew it was because he was broken himself. And she didn't mind. She didn't care about his cracks and scars, except for that it all was part of him.

What they shared last night was beautiful. The play, the night, their private conversation brought a little glitter back into her world. Even though their talk was hard, with grief and romantic delusions, there was something so delicately beautiful in sharing those very broken parts with him and having him share with her. She knew it was rare and that also made it beautiful.

Beautiful. The word repeated and repeated until it was lost.

"I knew the bubble would break," she muttered to herself. "Leave it to Jesse to bump into my happy and now beauty is bleeding out on my floor."

That wasn't dramatic at all, her sarcastic subconscious interrupted. Alright. Enough of this. She might be a mess sometimes, but she didn't have to wallow in it.

Taking a deep, sharp breath, Blythe pressed the palms of her hands to her eyes. Blubbering like an idiot at random with hardly just cause was a behavior of the past. It was not something to do today. Today she was going into the woods. Today she wanted to live deliberately. And other Henry David Thoreau and *Dead Poets Society* things.

With new resolve, she slid out of bed and took a giant step over the crumpled dress. She took time to use the fancy face wash and moisturizer Ginnie had given her for her birthday. Then, she put on just enough makeup to not scare anyone who came upon her. She rummaged in her dresser for her favorite pair of comfortable jeans and one of the concert t-shirts from Silas. Slipping on her tennis shoes, she was ready.

She was going to one of the parks in the Sayen Valley to walk the trails. It was the most beautiful place she knew.

Before she knew it, she heard herself saying, "'Once more unto the breach.'"

Then, she went to her desk where she kept index cards and stationery and a few notebooks. She selected a purple notebook and snatched a pen from the Ford coffee mug which kept her writing utensils corralled.

Today she would begin writing again. Not because Jesse said so and not because Gracen thought she should, but because she wanted to. She had felt that longing stir last night before the end of the first act. Writing was in her veins and it was far too long since she'd had a letting.

# Chapter 17

"'Heavy is the head that wears the crown'," Gracen breathed out through his mouth, inhaled fresh oxygen through his nose. He was running up Sweet Street on a new route. He'd taken a new path through town every day since the play. It was time to see more of Sayen Falls, he reasoned.

The light at the intersection turned red and the crosswalk sign blinked to orange. He jogged in place but felt his calves groaning. Time to stretch. He pressed his toes against the base of the crosswalk sign in front of him and leaned back. The muscles pulled with satisfactory tension. If only he could take out his brain and stretch it a bit too. His daily runs weren't helping enough. His brain remained a mess of Shakespeare, Uncle Harry, and Blythe. In fact, every time Gracen closed his eyes it was Shakespeare, Uncle Harry, and Blythe.

He checked the time on his phone—7:27—and noticed a text from Lily Morgan. That was odd. She should be on her way to school.

*We just passed you on Sweet Street. Are you lost?*

He smiled and replied, *No, just expanding my perimeter. And who is we? Better not be Brady. I'll have to ask questions.*

*Relax. It's just Ella and me. No boys allowed this early in the morning.*

*Good girl. See you this afternoon for your shift.*

He shook his head as he slipped his phone back into his pocket. Then he noticed the sign had changed, in fact, it was blinking to warn him that it was about to change again. Quickly, he dashed across the street and resumed his journey up Sweet Street. At the end of the block, he turned right and began navigating through side streets to get back to the riverfront.

Unfortunately, he miscalculated the blocks. It wasn't all his fault. The city blocks in Sayen Falls weren't even and some streets jogged and crossed and made no sense at all. So, when Gracen returned to the riverfront he was a block further west than he wanted to be and he had to run past The Yellow Bowl to get to his place.

"You're an idiot and Uncle Harry would slap you," he muttered to himself. Inwardly, he argued back that he was trying. There was only so much that could be expected. After all, he had fielded the text from Lily well. There was almost brotherly affection growing there for the kid and her mess. And, he hadn't so much as flirted with any of the girls who came into the shop and clearly flirted with him. The old Gracen could've snagged one of them, hook, line, and sinker, but he hadn't. He was even working on having friends. Finn was a friend. Ginnie was a friend. Blythe was a friend.

Blythe. Nope. His brain had gone one step too far and there was Uncle Harry's voice again. Yes, she was a friend, but only an idiot would keep her in the friend zone. Only a fool would run from a woman who thought and felt and emoted like her.

"'A fool doth think he is wise, but the wise man knows himself to be a fool,'" he quoted. "*As You Like It*. Well, I don't like it."

With his head down, he finished his run. Upstairs he showered and dressed then disappeared into his office before the college kids arrived for the lunch shift.

A little before three that afternoon, Ella, Sawyer, and Lily arrived for their shift. They brought with them their usual cloud of energy and enthusiasm. When Gracen didn't come out of his office to greet them, Lily, ever unsure, stepped into his office to speak with him.

"Hey Gracen," she began timidly. He was clicking on his laptop with an intense frown, deep lines creased into his forehead. His eyes flicked around the screen for a few seconds, there were more clicks, then he looked at Lily and his face softened with a smile.

"I didn't hear you come in. Any of you, I mean. Is it three already?"

"You must be hard at work. Ella is louder than usual today."

There was a peel of laughter in the kitchen as Lily said this. Gracen nodded. "Ah, yes, I hear her now. So, what's up?"

"I was hoping I could have next Friday off. Brady has concert tickets."

"That shouldn't be a problem," Gracen said slowly as he pulled up the schedule on his laptop. It was only Tuesday, and looking ahead to the next week he didn't see any other requests. He did, however, notice the note to RSVP to Becky's birthday party. Ginnie and Blythe had been planning it for a month and it was now just about a week away. "Yeah, that's fine. I'll get that in right now and figure out who to put in your place. Is anyone else going to this concert? Ella? Sawyer?"

"No, just Brady and me."

Gracen leaned back in his desk chair as he regarded Lily in all her insecurity. She was a natural beauty, but she'd been diminished with uncertainty and loneliness. The hunger for love and attention could be seen in her eyes. Lily looked at everyone with big blue eyes hoping that they'd like her and take her in. It took Gracen a minute to remember where he'd seen eyes just like that before. His sister Michelle. His mother. He had grown up around eyes just like that.

"You know you could do better, right? I know it's good to be liked but, I've heard him talk when he's here. There's nothing there. No plan, no ambition. Just partying. Which I can understand, I've done my fair share of partying and bad decisions."

"There's more to him than that."

"I'm sure there is. There was more to me. But what I'm telling you is, I've been a version of Brady. And you could do better."

"That's unlikely. It's not exactly like they're lining up behind him."

"You'll never know who is walking away from you since you're unavailable dating him."

"Ginnie said the same thing to me a few days ago."

"We didn't plan this," Gracen said with a reassuring grin. "It's not like me to do this. Ginnie, on the other hand, is the den mother of Sayen Falls."

"I told her and I'll tell you, Brady's not a bad guy. I promise. He's trying to get his life together. And, I think it's better than being alone."

He snorted, "You should talk to Blythe about that theory."

A curious smile twitched on Lily's lips, and Gracen demanded, "What? Why is that amusing?"

"It's only amusing coming from you. You haven't talked to Blythe in over a week."

"I was unaware that my activity was being that closely monitored."

"Not so much monitored as talked about," Lily explained. "You have to know there was hype about the play. Everyone's been comparing notes. I don't say much, but I can't help what I hear. And I have noticed that you don't seem like yourself."

It was a strange assessment. In reality, Gracen was probably more like himself than he had been right before Shakespeare in the Valley. This guy was fully dialed in with no distractions. But this Gracen was also a knot of grief and guilt. Every time he ran away from The Yellow Bowl he felt wrong. Every night when he went to bed and every morning when he woke up he felt wrong. Shakespeare, Uncle Harry, and Blythe.

"I'm okay. Just a lot on my mind, crunching numbers and running projections. Nothing happened between Blythe and me. You can tell them all that with the utmost authority. Nothing happened," he stressed. "I enjoyed the play, but I'm a workaholic at heart. One night away, and I've been going crazy feeling like I need to catch up."

Yeah, that sounds good. Go with that. He continued, "And I don't know what's going on with Blythe. I guess I haven't really seen her since the play. I hadn't thought about it."

Well, that was a boldfaced lie. He'd done nothing but think about it. About her. He kept talking, "Now that you mention it, I should go over there and be more neighborly. I've been so lost in my work."

"She's not in the shop right now," Lily told him. "She has a migraine. Ella wanted a coffee before work, so we stopped there real quick and Finn told us Blythe was laying down. He said that's the second one this week."

"I didn't know she got migraines," he murmured. Obviously, he wouldn't know. He'd been avoiding the place like a medieval quarantine.

Suddenly, Ella appeared in the doorway behind Lily and poked her hard. She put her hands on her hips and said to Gracen, "I hope you didn't give her the night off next Friday."

"I didn't have a reason not to."

"Yes, you do! Brady's not good enough for our Lily. C'mon, Gracen, we were counting on you to cut the head off that one."

"You want me to decapitate a twenty-year-old boy?" Gracen teased.

"No, just the concert," Ella sighed. "I hope you drive, Lily. You know Brady is going to get stoned at that concert with his idiot cousins."

"You don't know that," Lily snapped. She looked nervously from her friend to her boss, wondering if Gracen would make her work instead.

"Listen to me, Lily Morgan," he said gravely, "I don't know what your parents think about this guy but I gave you my opinion, so did Ginnie, and I know Ella is vocal. But you're seventeen years old and I know that you'll do what you want to do. God knows I did. *However*, if you get into a situation where you aren't safe, or that clown puts you in a situation where you aren't safe, you call me immediately."

"Gracen, I—"

"I mean it. I have a little sister. Well, she's twenty-three now. But she never asked for help when she got in trouble. Don't be stupid like Josselyn," Gracen said sternly. He looked at Ella, "That goes for you too, just for the record. Although, I think Sawyer would beat me to the punch."

Ella blushed for a second at the mention of Sawyer, "Thank you, boss."

She grabbed Lily around the waist and dragged her away from the office into the kitchen. Out of earshot, she whispered, "I can't believe he just said that. I can't figure him out. He's so closed off one second, clearly avoiding Blythe, and yet totally willing to kick Brady's butt if he hurts you."

"I don't know," Lily said simply. "I'm not sure he knows either."

# Chapter 18

A week later Blythe was working solo at The Yellow Bowl when a pair of customers ordered an iced fruity oolong tea and an iced green tea with peach-infused honey. She had made these drinks a million times, the green tea concoction was a house special she had crafted herself. And yet, on this particular Tuesday afternoon in September, she was on the struggle bus.

First, she measured too much of the green tea leaves into the diffuser. She knew the color was wrong as soon as she poured it into the cup of crushed ice so she tossed it in the sink. She reached for the tea leaves but realized the oolong tea would be getting bitter from being steeped too long. So, she pulled the diffuser with the oolong and sniffed the tea. Bitter.

After a deep breath, she forced herself to think. She put all her attention on the green tea, carefully measuring the right amount of tea leaves into the diffuser. Then she set a timer. It had been ages since she'd used one of the timers she kept under the counter for her seasonal staff. Next, she focused on the oolong. Neatly measuring into another diffuser, she plopped it into the water and set another timer.

"I'm so sorry about that," she told her waiting customers. "Every now and then my rhythm gets off and I mess things up."

They assured her it was okay and they didn't mind waiting. In fact, they found a couple of interesting books while they lingered. Looks like her mistakes weren't a total loss after all. The timers went off and Blythe set to work finishing the drinks. She garnished each with a straw and a mint leaf.

When she started to ring up their orders and their book selections, she did it again. It was an old register instead of a computer point of sales, and her fingers punched the wrong keys. She cleared the sale, crumpled the receipt, and started over. Mercifully, both women paid with debit cards so there was no change to count.

At last, when the transactions were complete, Blythe profusely thanked them for their business and their patience. As the women meandered to a table in the back to enjoy the fruits of Blythe's labor, Finn approached.

"That was painful."

"I didn't hear you come in or I would've let you do it," she groaned.

"Is it your head again?"

"The trouble is I don't realize I even have a headache until it's trying to tear my brain in half from the inside out."

She moved to start dealing with the dirty cups and diffusers then stopped suddenly. The room was spinning before her eyes. Immediately, she jerked her eyes shut. That shifted the whirling feeling down into her knees. As she gripped the counter, she could hear Finn rushing to her then she felt his hand on her waist.

"You need to lie down. I can handle the shop."

"I can't just go lie down every time my head hurts."

"Blythe, if you don't go now, it will turn into another migraine. Do you really want to throw up again?"

"It's not that bad," she insisted. She rummaged under the counter for a bottle of ibuprofen, then counted out three pills and washed them down with some cool water. "There, see? I took some medicine and I'll be fine."

"Sounds made up," he said, clearly unconvinced.

Determined to prove that she was fine, Blythe continued clearing the dirty dishes. She loaded what she could into the dishwasher, then filled a sink with soapy water to hand-wash the rest.

"Silas called yesterday," she said. She winced. Talking hurt. Thankfully her back was to Finn so he didn't notice unless her voice betrayed her. "He's coming today. He needs to get out of Ann Arbor, I guess."

"I spoke to him, too, on my way here actually. He sounds so defeated. He told me he's been fighting like hell. I hated to break it to him, but hell is fighting a losing battle."

"That's encouraging," she said dryly. She turned her head to look at him and instantly regretted it. Her head was still swimming in pain. Those pills weren't working at all yet.

"Hey, we've had some good talks," Finn assured her. "I have to say hard words to people sometimes, but we've talked a lot about grace and what God wants for Silas. I admire his tenacity to honor his vows and do what he can to make it work."

"If only Mindy would do the same."

"I really don't think it will work. I think something will happen that will cause Silas to agree to the divorce. I'm not sure what I think of all of that biblically. I guess I think God's law is God's law, but we live here in this fallen ugly world, and we can't control what the people around us do. She's torturing him, Blythe."

"I know she is. And I know that my thoughts and feelings for Mindy aren't the least bit Christian so I won't burden your ears with them."

"I know how fiercely you love both of your brothers."

"Silas is still my baby brother in my eyes. It kills me to know he's in pain. And on top of this mess with Mindy, the theater is shutting down? I don't know how he hasn't snapped."

"The deposition for that is today. He was on his way to meet with the lawyers when we were on the phone. I prayed with him. I know he'll tell the truth, he has nothing to hide. But it's still hard on him. I mean, he's losing his job and he was friends with the guy who embezzled the money."

"I have a feeling that Silas's friends are actually his worst enemies," Blythe said grimly, picking up a towel to dry the things she'd just washed.

Overhead the music changed from Coldplay's song "Yellow" to the Dave Matthews Band's song "Ants Marching". Both of these songs were on the playlist called 'Blythe's Old School Favorites' but the blast of brass instruments was sharply jarring. Her whole body startled as her brain screamed. The tea diffuser slipped from her hand and rattled as it rolled across the floor. Then, she realized that her stomach was churning. The pain had redirected to her stomach as Finn had predicted. The headache was officially a migraine.

"Go upstairs now," he said firmly.

"This is getting ridiculous," she breathed.

"You should see a doctor. You haven't had migraines like this in well over a year. And now you've had three in the last two weeks."

"I know what's causing it. I'm not sleeping enough. But I did finish *The Great Gatsby* in two days."

Finn stared at her, "But you just read *The Awakening* and *Persuasion*."

"They're my favorites."

"And they're not going anywhere. These books are enduring classics."

"I know that, but … I don't know," she said, squeezing her eyes tight again. He took a glance around the shop and their handful of customers looked content with their tea and books. So, he took Blythe by her stubborn hand and led her to the back of the shop.

"Blythe, I don't know what's going on. This feels so frantic."

"I don't want to lose it, Finn."

"Lose what?"

"This feeling. The inspiration. I don't know. I can't explain it," her voice broke and she winced again as a new wave of pain emanated in her brain. The lights were hurting now. She felt Finn's firm but gentle hands on her shoulders. His soft Irish accent fell lightly on her ears.

"You don't need to explain anything to me. But I'm not going to watch you self-destruct in a new way. You need to sleep, drink water, take care of yourself. No amount of inspiration is worth this. We'll figure it out when your head isn't trying to kill you."

Without another word, Blythe accepted defeat and went upstairs to her apartment. She closed all the curtains and kept the lights off so her eyeballs would stop stabbing her brain with tiny knives. She got a washcloth out of the linen closet and soaked it with cold water. Then she filled a gallon-sized freezer bag with ice cubes and took the cloth and the bag to her bedroom. She slipped into bed, sank her head onto the pillow, and lightly put the cold cloth over her forehead. She put the bag of ice on the top of her head.

On her night table sat *The Great Gatsby* and *Wuthering Heights*. It had been her plan to start Emily Bronte's book after work. The funny thing was she didn't even like *Wuthering Heights*. The narration annoyed her and so did Catherine and Heathcliff when she got right down to it.

Sleep soon overcame her. She was utterly exhausted. Her being was exhausted as well as her body and her brain. It had been eleven days since the play. The inspiration of that night had launched her into an almost manic quest to gobble up more inspiration and more beauty and more drama and regurgitate it in writer-words of her own. Her room was strewn with sheets and sheets of paper torn from her spiral notebook. Most were crumpled, a few had notes scribbled across them, some were paperclipped together as if she would come back to them later. Yet Blythe felt deep down that this frenzied pace wouldn't last and the inspiration would evaporate. The books would go unread, the words would stay unwritten. Her play would never end. The moment would pass and be gone again.

When she stirred from sleep she discovered that nearly two hours had passed, her headache had downgraded considerably, and her brother had arrived. He sat at the foot of her bed reading some of her notebook pages.

"You're so good. You're all over the place with this. But the words are good," he informed her. He plopped the pages down, then ran a hand over his scruff of a beard. The beard aged his baby face, but nothing could diminish his bright blue eyes.

"You know words. You just set them to music whereas I try to put them in the mouths of people that do not exist."

"They exist to you. They exist on your page. They'd exist to the rest of us if you ever shared it."

"I have to finish it first. I thought I had an ending. But I can't make it work. The rest of the play feels hollow now."

"That's because you're trying to take something from your past and make it fit into your present."

"I'm not sure we're just talking about my play anymore."

"I'm not sure we're just talking about you anymore."

"Silas, I'm so sorry all of this is happening to you. You're the best guy in the world. Mindy is a fool. And this thing with the theater. What a nightmare."

"At least that's behind me now. They said I should get some kind of severance or settlement or something. I'm not holding my breath though."

Blythe shifted her body weight so she could sit up to talk to him. Her stomach stayed in place and she breathed a sigh of relief.

"What can I get you?" Silas asked. He pointed to her nightstand, "I brought in an ice water. You need to stay hydrated."

"I could use another cold washcloth," she said sliding the damp cloth from her head. Her brother took it to the bathroom and got it cold again. "Thanks. I take it you talked to Finn?"

Silas nodded, "He's worried about you, but he won't admit it. I don't think he wants anyone to start panicking that you're going into the dark place again."

"I'm not, Si. I promise this isn't like that. It's more like I'm chasing the light."

"I get that. Maybe that's why I'm here. You know, other than the advice of counsel to be out of town until things are settled."

"Which counsel and which things?"

"All of them really. I'll be here for about a week or so, and by then they'll have finished taking all the testimony from anyone at the theater," Silas sighed heavily. "I'm also expecting to find my apartment fairly bare."

"Mindy is moving out?"

"She really doesn't live there already, but she'll have time now to get anything she wants."

"What about the things that are yours?"

"She can have it, Blythe. I don't care anymore."

"What will it take for you to sign the papers and be done with her?"

"I don't know. I don't want to end my marriage in anger. I know that sounds stupid, but there needs to be a better reason for me. I still believe God can fix us."

"I think God can heal any marriage, no matter how messed up and ugly it's gotten. But I think both parties have to want that. And I just don't see Mindy humbling herself before God and getting the help," Blythe said. It was hard but she had to be honest.

"I can't give up on her yet," he shrugged helplessly. "I know everyone else has. I don't blame you or anyone. But I can't yet. I'm waiting for God to move."

"I don't think I've ever had that kind of faith."

"Maybe you should. Maybe that's the light you're chasing. It's not what's in these books," he said, picking up *Wuthering Heights*. He looked her in the eye and added, "And it's not in the guy you're avoiding either."

"Finn talks too much."

"That one was Ginnie."

"Of course. I love her but she is the town crier."

"She is, but she has nothing but good things to say about Gracen."

"Same here."

"So what gives? You know you can't exchange one method of avoidance for another. You can't hide from life in the Yellow Bowl or in reading and writing yourself into migraines. I want you to read books you love and write words you believe in. But I want you to live your life too. You're my big sister and you've been hiding a long time now."

"And I want you to be happy. I want you to be okay. I want you to thrive, Silas. And you're trapped. Everything is draining you."

"If only we were like Liam," Silas said with a wry laugh.

"Don't let the white picket fence fool you."

"I don't. Look, there's no such thing as a perfect life. You and me? We're both romantics and that's what we're looking for. It's what Mom and Dad were looking for too and they messed it up because they couldn't learn to love each other in the mess. I'm treading in mess right now, and I don't know how it's gonna end, but I know one way or another that on the other side of this, I'm going to love better. And you waded through your mess already. But if you're gonna love better and live better, then you gotta do it."

"You're saying a lot of words to me and I have a headache," Blythe said, obviously deflecting from his truth.

"You can handle it. You're a master of words." He picked up the stack of papers, "You just gotta get your feet under you *and* remember they're there."

"Silas, I'm really glad you're home and you're going to be here for Becky's party. I don't think I could do it alone. They're all gonna ask why I'm single."

"They'll ask me about Mindy."

"I'll have your back."

"And I'll have yours. It's what we do."

# Chapter 19

For the grand occasion of Becky's birthday, Ginnie and Blythe planned a large gathering with all the people and things he loved. Blythe handpicked the music selections, Ginnie carefully chose delicious hors d'ouevres (paid for by Alex), and together the girls decorated the banquet hall on the riverfront. From a distance, Jesse had paid for the open bar. He'd electronically transferred an absurd amount of money to cover it.

The guest list included guys he used to work with, folks from his church, friends from childhood, and of course, the gang from the riverfront. All of the Elwoods were there, naturally. Becky's oldest son (and Ginnie's father) Dennis came with his wife Linda. The lingering question was whether or not Becky's younger son, Donald, or either of his grandsons would appear.

Twenty minutes after the party began Blythe skidded in looking slightly frazzled but impeccably stylish. She was wearing a pale blue seersucker dress, white peep-toe heels, and her string of pearls.

"I am so sorry," she said, clutching Ginnie's arm as soon as she found her. Ginnie was over by the bar getting an amaretto sour for herself. When Blythe walked up, Ginnie told the bartender to make another one.

"Only you would be late to a party you helped plan," Ginnie laughed with a reassuring hug. "You haven't missed much. I do think you're the last to arrive though."

Taking a sip of her drink, Blythe cast a glance around the room to assess who had followed through with their RSVP. She was pleased to see how tickled Becky was to have a room full of friends just there for him. He'd been so lonely ever since Pearl died.

Then her eyes rested on Gracen. He was wearing the same vest and pants that he'd worn to the play, but the shirt was different. It was a light orchid color which popped next to the gray. She noticed he had opted to wear his glasses too. Of greater interest, however, was his company. On his shoulders sat Teddy who was chattering about cake. To Gracen's left was Liam and to his right was Silas. They were talking freely like they were all good friends, which slightly irritated Blythe. In fact, Silas had gone out of his way in the last few days to befriend Gracen in an effort to get under her skin. It was his strange little brother way of trying to motivate her to be normal.

"It's a good turn out," she said distractedly. Her tone prompted Ginnie to follow her gaze.

"I think so too," Ginnie said slowly. "Blythe, it's okay that he's here, right? I mean, nothing's happened between you two? You've been a little off ever since the play."

"Nothing's happened at all. I don't think we've even talked since then."

Blythe knew darn well they hadn't talked. They hadn't even been in the same room.

"I know. And that's a little strange. You guys were getting close, I thought."

"Not close. Just friendly. It's fine, Ginnie."

"Hello? I'm a woman and I know that 'fine' never means fine."

"I've been trying to focus on other things. Reading and my writing."

"I am glad you're writing again."

"You don't sound glad."

"I just don't think working on your play should include ignoring Gracen."

"I'm not ignoring him. I just needed a little space. I don't want to get carried away."

"But I don't understand why. I promise I'm not trying to be dense," Ginnie sighed, "I just want you to be happy. You're like my real sister. You always have been. And I don't understand what you mean that you shouldn't get carried away."

"I'm not exactly his type, Gin."

"He can't take his eyes off you whenever you're in the room."

"That doesn't mean anything in the long run," Blythe took another gulp of her drink. "Trust me here. I'm not what he's looking for. I'm a lot of work and a lot of mess. And the only work Gracen is interested in makes him money."

Ginnie had a reply but unfortunately was cut off by Lou Harper who ran the hobby shop at the end of the plaza.

"This is a great party, girls. Pearl would be proud of what you've put together for Becky."

"Thanks, Lou. That means a lot," Ginnie said with a gracious smile.

"Blythe, you look lovely this evening, as always," Lou said. "Can't believe you're still single. I thought someone would've snapped you up years ago."

"Well, there's no accounting for taste," she shrugged with a big false smile. "I'm going to check in with my grandparents."

She handed her drink to Ginnie then made her way over to Miles and Mary Alice who were sitting at a table near the cake. Conversation with them would be easier. And it might have been except that before too long Jimbo and Millie Watkins joined them. Jimbo had worked at the paper mill with Becky and Miles and had about as much tact as a hyena.

"So Miles, haven't married her off yet. Can't get her off your hands?"

"Waiting for the best guy in the world," Miles retorted. "Haven't found him yet."

"You're too picky, Miles. Blythe can't stay on the market forever. No one likes an old maid," Jimbo said with a hearty laugh.

"Finn is a nice boy," Millie said suggestively.

The amount of willpower it took to not roll her eyes was staggering. Instead, Blythe mustered a very sweet smile as she said, "Speaking of Finn, looks like he's talking to the birthday boy and I haven't even given Becky a kiss yet. It was nice talking to you."

On her way to speak to Finn and Becky, Liam intercepted her and handed her a cocktail that was roughly the same color as Gracen's shirt.

"I remembered why I don't drink this stuff. It's so sweet," he said blanching. Teddy, who had been holding his father's hand, threw himself around Blythe's legs in the type of reckless enthusiasm only toddlers have. She knelt to give him a hug, careful to not slosh the colorful cocktail on Teddy's party clothes.

"Are you having fun, Teddy Bear?"

"Cake!"

"Soon, baby, I promise. We just need to sing 'Happy Birthday' to Gramps first."

"If you get that underway you'll be Teddy's favorite aunt," Liam said.

"I'm his only aunt."

"We don't count Mindy?"

"I'm not even going to dignify that with a response," Blythe said as she straightened up. She took a sip of the mixed drink and shivered. Whatever it was had vodka in it. "I will collect Becky now so we can cut the cake."

However, by the time she reached Becky, he and Finn had been joined by Mick Rhinehart. Mick went to church with Becky and could remember when Jesse and Alex were altar boys.

"Are your grandsons coming, Beck?"

"Blythe here has been talking to Jesse quite a bit. The boy said he'd try to come," Becky replied with much optimism.

"Ah, yes, Blythe and Jesse. Quite a pair," Mick chuckled warmly. "When are you two ever gonna settle down?"

"Is Becky still spreading that rumor?" Blythe said coyly. She wrapped an arm around Becky as she gave him an affectionate kiss on his cheek. "Your great-grandson would surely appreciate it if we cut your birthday cake. Are you up for some singing?"

"Oh I hate all that 'Happy Birthday' hooey," Becky scowled, but then his eyes lit up, "But I'd love it if you sang for me. Silas is here, and he could play that piano over there."

"Becky, I planned you this party. I've talked to Jesse four times in the last week on your behalf. And now you want a song?"

"You bet I do. I don't get to hear you sing often enough anymore."

When Blythe had been in high school and singing all the time Becky often told her how much he loved listening to her. Sometimes she and Jesse would go over just to sing some duets for Becky and Pearl. They requested their favorite songs, mostly hits from the Rat Pack and The Beatles with occasional Hank Williams or other country-western hits thrown in. Those days felt like a lifetime ago now.

"Alright, fine. One song," she conceded. "*After* we sing 'Happy Birthday'."

"Deal."

"You handled that well," Finn whispered as they walked away together to find Silas. She handed him the purple drink.

"This is awful. Liam gave it to me."

"Why did he have it?"

"I have no idea. It's like vodka-infused grape cotton candy. Or something. It's not right."

As they passed the bar, Finn slid the drink on top of the counter. He picked up a glass of wine instead.

"I know you're not much of a wine drinker, but just a sip," he said, "I'll finish the rest."

"Don't let Reverend Smith see you," she teased.

"I'm just an intern. Besides Eddie himself drinks a glass of red wine a couple nights a week."

"That's probably for his heart or something."

"Well, then, let's drink to our hearts. May they never break and always love," Finn said as he took a drink from the glass. He offered it to Blythe. She rolled her eyes but accepted it. It was a full-bodied sweet wine, not dry at all, and a hundred times better than that purple thing.

"Sometimes your Irishness just drips off of you," she grinned.

"Is it true you agreed to sing if I played the piano?" Silas demanded as he approached.

"Oh, please, you're a musician. You should love performing."

"This isn't exactly what I do."

"You technically don't do much of anything these days."

"That's harsh. Albeit true, but harsh."

"It's okay, I don't do much of anything either." Blythe put on a fake girly voice, "And have you heard that I'm still single?"

"I have," Silas replied with a similar mocking tone. "Did you hear that I'm getting divorced?"

"True story."

"This is why I don't come back here more often," Silas grunted.

"Come on. It's just one song. We can muster up one song."

As word spread that they were going to sing the guests gathered around the piano. Becky sat on the bench with Silas and Blythe stood in the bend of the baby grand. Looking at that crowd of smiling faces the performer in her surfaced. They hadn't planned this so there wasn't a microphone to use. Still, it was a small enough crowd for her lungs to handle.

"First, I want to thank all of you for coming out tonight to celebrate

Becky's birthday. And let's give a hand to Ginnie for making so many of the arrangements."

The partygoers gave a polite round of applause for both the guest of honor and his treasured granddaughter. On cue, Ginnie came forward with the cake with Viola helping to carry one end. Liam followed behind with a ravenous Teddy cheering. Silas began playing "Happy Birthday" as the guests sang along more or less on key, and with great affection. Just as Becky blew out his candles, the door to the banquet center shut with a remarkable clang. All heads turned to see who had joined them a full hour late. Because Blythe was in the middle of the gathering she couldn't see, but she deduced quickly from the murmur of the crowd it was one of the Beckwith boys. Jesse was famous for his late entrances.

As people began to shuffle aside to let the latecomer through to the guest of honor, Blythe saw that it was not Jesse. It was Alex. Her eyes shifted to her feet as though her toes were suddenly extremely fascinating. Pushing a strand of dark hair from her eyes, she swallowed hard. Not again. Her emotions had been so unwieldy ever since the play. It was getting rather old. It should be great to see Alex; he hadn't been home in ages.

Finding a smile, Blythe looked up to see Alex embracing his grandfather in a warm hug. There were tears in Becky's eyes. She scanned the crowd to find Gracen, wondering if he had known Alex was coming. There was a distinct look of surprise on his face. Surprise and something else. Skepticism maybe.

Suddenly, he looked at her and their eyes met for the first time in two weeks. The look in his eyes shifted when he realized she was looking at him. That was a look she couldn't name. But she felt quite certain her face conveyed something similar. Breaking away, she turned to Silas who was watching the whole thing. He raised an eyebrow and she gave a threatening glance. This made him grin quite devilishly, but he tinkered a few chords on the piano to get the crowd's attention again.

"We promised you a song before Alex joined us. Welcome, Alex," Silas said. "So if you don't mind, Blythe and I would like to get this over with so we can enjoy ourselves again."

"I appreciate the sacrifice," Becky smirked.

"Pick your poison, Becky. What are we singing?" Silas asked. "Bear in mind, I'm rusty."

"Then how about one that I know you know? 'When I Fall in Love'."

It had been one of Pearl and Becky's favorite songs. In fact, Silas, Blythe, Liam, and Jesse had performed a version of it at their anniversary party, shortly before Pearl passed. And being the old romantic that he was, it was the song Becky wanted most to hear. It was also one of the harder ones for Blythe and Silas to do with smiles on their faces.

They shared a look, just between them, before Silas began to play. For an impromptu performance at an old man's birthday party, it went quite well. Blythe sang all of it, and Silas harmonized in the choruses. Most guests present thought it was a very lovely song all in all. Yet, a few guests were aware of the strain in Blythe's voice. And one was acutely aware of the fact that her eyes never moved away from the end of the piano.

After the song, there was happy applause and pleas for another one, but Silas insisted they were done. Becky affirmed that they had only agreed to one, so the crowd broke up and began mingling again. Some folks danced to the oldies music Blythe had selected for background noise.

Finished with his obligation to play, Silas stalked away from the piano and ran into Gracen at the bar. Gracen was simply lingering there, observing. Silas ordered a beer. He liked Gracen. More than likely, he had made this decision before meeting him. He'd heard all about the guy from his grandparents, his brother, his sister-in-law, and Finn. He was also pretty sure Blythe was just a few yards away from a first down in love with him.

He took a couple of swallows of his beer and started talking, "Well, that was painful."

"I thought it was pretty good, particularly off the cuff like that."

"I don't mean how we sounded. Blythe is always great and I'm a good musician. I mean the actual song."

Gracen had heard some of the other guests discussing Silas's private life amongst themselves. He said carefully, "Because of the divorce?"

"We're not divorced yet," Silas pointed out. "But at least you're up to speed, thanks to our chatty guests, no doubt."

"I'm sorry."

"It's okay. I knew it would happen. Just like Blythe knew they'd all ask her why she's still single. These people, nice as they are, never want to talk about us like we're people. They talk about Liam's kids, my divorce, and Blythe's naked left hand. That's it. And the funny thing is, if Blythe got married tomorrow, they'd immediately start asking when she's having a kid. Then if she had a kid, they'd start asking when the next one is coming. That's how it is."

"Can I be as blunt as you for a second?" Gracen asked. Silas gave a nod as he took another sip of his drink. "You're cynical for an Elwood."

Silas laughed, "Liam is supposed to be the cynical one. I've gone and messed it up."

"No, he's definitely on the cynical side. I don't think he's my biggest fan either."

"He thinks you're alright. He's just uptight because of what Ian did to Blythe," Silas said off-handedly, "and because Viola is nuts about you."

"Then I hope her taste improves with age," Gracen replied. He spied Viola halfway across the room sitting head to head with Blythe in a giggling conversation. "Who really asked why she was still single?"

"No one of any real consequence. No one whose opinion matters to her, I mean. But what is she supposed to say to that?" Silas seethed. "The only guy who did ask her to marry him turned out to be a lying cheating bucket of scum."

That was fresh information. Learning that Ian had cheated on her gave Gracen angry, jealous feelings that were brand new to his being.

"He cheated on her?"

"She didn't tell you?"

"No, she hasn't said much to me about Ian at all."

"Then you didn't hear it from me."

"So that song really was a hard one to sing."

"I think tonight any song would've been hard," Silas answered. He finished his beer and pushed the bottle away. "For what it's worth, and I can't imagine it's worth much, I'm okay with you living across the hall from my sister."

They both turned to look again at Blythe. Viola had left the table. In her place was another old timer from the mill. He was holding Blythe's left hand and she was feigning laughter.

"Another one," Silas shook his head. "I'll go rescue her."

He ordered a beer for the old timer and a whiskey sour for Blythe. Gracen opened his mouth to say that he'd seen Blythe with three drinks already, but he stopped. That sounded a little creepy in his head, let alone out loud.

As Silas handled the situation with Blythe, Gracen directed his attention elsewhere. About ten feet away he heard Ginnie telling her children that they were leaving in fifteen minutes. It was not in Viola's nature to make a big stink, but it was very evident by her face that this was disappointing news. She looked so pressed and perfect in her party dress. It seemed a shame that she'd get all dolled up and have so little to say for her evening. Gracen decided to ask her for a dance.

"Hello there, Viola," he said, sitting in a chair next to her.

"Hi," she replied in her usual shy manner.

"You know, I haven't had a dance all evening. And this is a great song."

"It's Louis Armstrong," Viola told him. "Gramps plays this record for me when we come over. I like this one a lot."

"You have very refined taste. Louis is one of the best. Would you care to dance with me?"

Her eyes doubled in size as she considered his offer, then she nodded with great joy. Taking her small hand, Gracen said to Ginnie, "Just one dance with your daughter."

"Just one dance or her father will have something to say," Ginnie teased.

The song was "What a Wonderful World" and idly Gracen hummed along while he danced with Viola. Then he said, "You look very pretty in your party dress."

"Thank you. It's my Easter dress. Daddy said it was good to get more use out of it."

"He's right. It's quite a lovely dress."

"I like Aunt Blythe's dress. She always looks so beautiful at parties. She's so elegant."

"She is a very classy lady."

"You should ask her to dance," Viola said innocently.

With a friendly frown, Gracen replied, "You think so? I'm not sure she'd say yes."

"I think she would. She likes you. And if she said no, then you could talk to her and find out why she's sad tonight."

"Did she tell you she was sad?"

"I can tell. I asked her and she said that grown-ups are silly."

"And she's right. Grown-ups are rather silly."

"I think she'd be happy if she danced with you."

"Are you having fun?"

Again, Viola nodded vigorously. Gracen laughed. He'd never had a girl like Viola in his life; someone young and sweet who was capable of thinking the world of someone so unworthy. When the song ended, he delivered Viola back to her mother—as promised. But he knelt to kiss her hand, just as Prince Charming would have.

"You have a very special girl here, Ginnie," he said as he stood up.

"I know," Ginnie said purposefully. "She's just like her aunt."

The intimation was not lost on him. Thankfully, for him, there was no time for further discussion of the matter. Teddy had started to cry, a tired cry from too much party and a bedtime missed by nearly an hour.

For the remainder of his evening, Gracen kept one eye on Blythe while he mingled with the guests he knew. By the time she'd finished a drink from Becky, he knew she'd had enough, if not too much. He waited for someone else to notice how loose she seemed all over. But the others had either left, were leaving, or were engrossed in deep conversation. It fell to him to do something to make sure she didn't get sick. Or worse.

Finally, he approached her, "Hey Blythe, I just realized I'm locked out of my place. Would you mind walking back with me? I can get in through my balcony."

She turned to look at him. Her eyes narrowed, but she grinned, "You could climb the fire escape. But those aren't probably the right shoes for climbing. No traction. They'd be terrible for running too."

"That's why I'm hoping you'll bail me out," he replied. His eyes locked into hers. She was aware that his keys were in his pocket.

"I'll go home with you. Don't worry," she said. She turned to Becky and gave him another kiss on his wrinkled cheek, "I hope you had a good party.

I am sorry Jesse didn't turn up. I guess neither of us was worth it."

"Oh, you know Jesse. That boy. At least Alex is here," Becky said. After a pause, he redirected his attention to Gracen, "It was good to see more of you. My buddies were impressed by the Shelby, too."

"Stop by sometime and I'll let you take her for a spin."

"An old man like me?"

"Only as old as you feel. I know she'd be in good hands with a car guy like you," Gracen said, patting him on the back. He looked at Blythe, "You ready to go?"

"Just waiting on you."

As they left, Gracen thought he heard Becky mumble something about her being in good hands too, but he wasn't quite sure.

# Chapter 20

"So you're locked out of your apartment," Blythe said with a cool smile once they were outside. The air was brisk, but after all, it was early September. Up above, the sky was crystal clear and the moon was waning.

"I was getting worried about you."

"That's interesting. Seeing as we stopped talking to each other two weeks ago."

"Like I said, I was just worried about you," he shrugged. He was trying to do the right thing here, but he did not want to discuss the last couple of weeks. He didn't have a good excuse for his behavior, and he wasn't sure he wanted to hear her excuses either.

They walked in silence for a few paces before she admitted, "I was surprised you came."

"Ginnie told me I should come."

"Ginnie likes you. Silas likes you too. You're even growing on Liam."

"Like a fungus."

"And why not? You're a *fun guy*."

She was being quippy, but the tone was biting. They reached their building as it was only a stone's throw away from the banquet center. Inebriated or not, she hadn't needed an escort. They both knew that.

Instead of walking to the door, Blythe wandered to the middle of the plaza until she was under the street lamp. She crossed her arms and looked up at the sky.

"It's okay, you know, that you've been avoiding me. I've been avoiding you too. Maybe if Jesse knew that he'd stop calling me every few days. It's annoying. I think I'd rather have you."

She was saying a lot. Most of it was candid and unexpected, particularly after two weeks of radio silence. Gracen combed his fingers through his hair, gripping the slightly curled ends tightly. He adjusted his glasses. His left leg began to bounce; he needed to run. Blythe watched his movements. Then without a word, came to his side, took his hand, and began walking towards the riverwalk.

"What are you doing?"

"We're going for a walk. I know your tells, Gracen."

"My tells?"

"Your leg. You get twitchy when you're tense because you need to run."

It disturbed Gracen that she had noticed. He rerouted the conversation, "Blythe, it's late, you've had too much to drink."

"I'm not drunk. It's been a while though so I've lost any semblance of tolerance."

"The fact you're still using words like 'semblance' and I can understand you says a lot for your state of intoxication," Gracen admitted.

Again quietness overtook them. They came to the boardwalk and the dark river bubbled past them on a mission of its own.

"I saw you dancing with Viola," she said suddenly.

"She told me I should ask you to dance."

"Why didn't you?"

"I thought you'd say no. She told me that if you said no, I could ask you why you're sad."

"That girl," she said tenderly. "She's too insightful for her own good. She sees people, but she doesn't understand how the world works. She's so trusting. She's never been hurt."

Abruptly, he confessed, "I am sorry for the last couple of weeks. I—"

"I told you, Gracen. It's okay. Really. I get it. I'm a lot to take in. I'm a mess of emotions and other messes. You wouldn't be the first person to find me overwhelming or difficult," she explained. Her voice cracked. Resolutely, she looked up at the sky. Only the moon above, still waning. She dropped his hand to cross her arms again.

"Is that what you think?"

"It's what I've been told and there's a lot of evidence to support it."

"More Ian," he said crossly.

"Yes, Ian. It's all I have to go on," she retorted. Her green eyes narrowed again.

"Well, his opinion shouldn't count. He cheated on you!" Gracen blurted out.

"I never told you that." She thought for a moment, "Ginnie? Finn?"

"Silas. We were talking about the questions you kept getting tonight."

"You mean all the questions about why I'm still single? What am I supposed to say to that?" she demanded. The pylons were just a few yards ahead of them. When they reached the cement pillars, she plopped onto one with a heavy sigh, "I don't have an answer other than what Ian told me."

"Ian is an idiot," Gracen snapped. He sat on the pillar closest to Blythe. His fingers brushed his hair again as he sighed, "I don't have an answer either. It beats me why Finn has never made a move."

"Everyone's favorite bachelor. I know all about Finn and his reasons. They're good ones. Finn is not the problem."

"I really have no idea why Jesse doesn't give the people what they want," he said dryly.

"Jesse. Jesse. All my life it's been Jesse. He's the boy who won't grow up. He's Peter Pan. And I am Wendy, left at home with his shadow. Jesse isn't the one. I've known that for years. It's just taking the rest of the community a while to come to grips with it."

That knocked out the obvious choices, other than himself. He swallowed, unsure what to say. She saved him from having to figure it out.

"I know why I'm single. Ian was right, idiot or not. I'm spectacularly difficult to love once you get started," she scoffed. "Everyone who should've stayed didn't. Says a lot about me, don't you think?"

"No, that says a lot about them," Gracen said firmly. His eyes considered her with great intensity. He barely recognized this woman in front of him. This was not the Blythe Elwood he had met at The Gala. This was not the stunning woman he had sat next to at the play.

"I don't understand what's happening here. At the party, I watched you sing. You were charming, you held that room in your hand. I know that you're witty and very perceptive. Some of our conversations about literature are better than I had at Princeton. But now, all of a sudden, it's like I'm looking at you and you've completely withered. Right here before my eyes, the woman I know is gone, and this shell is here. This shell who thinks that she has nothing to offer anyone and is completely unlovable. And I just don't get it. I don't get how that happens."

Blythe pushed herself off the pillar as she began to rant.

"It happens because my father and mother both left when I was fifteen. It happens because my fiancé slept with someone else for a really long time and convinced me it was *my* fault so I'd take him back. It happens because everyone in Sayen Falls thinks that I'm defective because I'm single. Which is outrageous in the twenty-first century, but Sayen Falls tends to lag behind the times. So here I am, just trying to live my life and figure out if there's even a point to what I'm doing here with my tea and books. I've even been trying to write and I'm coming up pretty empty on the purpose meter. That's how it happens."

"That's not why I've been avoiding you at all," he declared as he stood.

"Then why? What's your big fat reason?"

"Because I'm afraid that I'm falling in love with you and I have no idea how to love anyone!" he exclaimed. "Let alone someone as incredible as you. Someone with a heart as big as yours. Good grief, I come up pretty empty compared to you."

His words hung in the air, suspended by moonbeams and the rustling river water. As they resonated in Blythe's ears and finally registered in her brain, her mouth parted slightly.

"What?" she breathed.

"I think you heard me," he said quietly. His heart pounded in his head; his eyes filled only with her. For a moment he thought she looked relieved. Then, her eyes changed again and that withered look returned.

"You don't need to be afraid of falling in love with me. Even if you did, you'd soon find out that you can't maintain it."

A tether snapped inside Gracen. "That's what you have to say?"

"What do you want me to say? That I'm falling in love with you too?" Her voice was a little shrill with emotion. "Gracen, that's why I've been avoiding you. So I won't fall in love with you. I know I'm not your type. I know my mess doesn't fit into your method."

"I don't see a mess when I look at you. I've never felt this way in my life. Right now I could murder a man I've never met because he's taken that lovely brain of yours and turned it inside out. And quite honestly, I could do some damage to Jesse because it seems to me he keeps digging in," Gracen grunted. "For that matter, I'm angry with myself because I played right into this. If I'd had any idea what was going on inside your head—"

"What would you have done?"

"I don't know. I don't know! I don't know what I'm doing right now. I just ..." He took a deep breath. A second was needed to collect his thoughts. "You know what? You're stronger than this and you're better than this. I *know* you are. And that's why if I ever make you feel that way again, I want you to slap me."

"You want me to slap you?"

"Yes, I want you to just haul off and slap me if I ever am part of making you feel even for a second that your worth is of question."

"I would never do that. Don't you get it?" Blythe shook her head. "I never even told Ian off for what he did. He told me it was my fault and I went along with that. For two more years, I went along with it. I never slapped him. I'm a nice girl. And I would never slap you."

She was clinging desperately to her broken pieces, yet Gracen was resolute. His eyes darkened, but not with anger. Taking a step towards her, he lowered his voice.

"Yes, you will if I ever deserve it. Because you will remember this night and this conversation. You will remember how I looked you in the eye and told you that you are strong, and you are dazzling, and no one, especially me, should ever get to take away that fire God gave you."

"Gracen," she inhaled.

He slipped his hand into her dark hair, her lips parted, and Gracen pressed his mouth to hers. The dam holding back his emotions broke, leaving him breathless and momentarily lightheaded. To steady himself, he leaned further into her. Then he felt her hands slip around his neck, her fingers in his hair. Gracen had known physical passion before, but not the moment when two hearts connect. It was a strange sensation. He simultaneously realized how hollow his heart was and that he could learn to fill it up by loving other people.

But even first kisses must come to an end. After all, hearts need oxygen to beat. Her fingers linked around the back of his neck and their foreheads rested on one another. She whispered, "I think I'll remember that."

"I know I will," he replied with a throaty chuckle.

At last, she smiled. A giddy smile that softened her whole face. There she was. Blythe Elwood. The woman he knew.

"I don't know how I've avoided you for two weeks," he confessed.

"There seemed to be a lot of running."

"And you seemed to be deep in your books, from what I've heard."

"It wasn't easy staying away from you either," she admitted.

"Come on," he said, taking her hand. "Let's go home."

The silence now was easy, comfortable. The thoughts tumbling about in their brains were far less jagged and raw. Their scared hearts had started the slow turn back toward each other.

At the top of the staircase, she looked at him exactly the same way she had the night of The Gala. She stood with one foot on pointe behind the other and a hand on her hip. Gracen had no idea what the consequences of these actions would ultimately be, but he was tired of calculating and predicting. He wrapped his arm around her waist and kissed her again.

"Just to be sure you always remember."

"I'll always remember this night in September," she giggled. Her fingers traced his jawline as she drank in his eyes. "Good night, Gracen. Thank you for walking me home."

"Just trying to be a good neighbor," he answered. And when she disappeared into her apartment, a great feeling of dread came over him. He had no idea what to do next, what any of it meant, or what she was thinking. But one thing was sure—he couldn't run away from her again. The hollowness in his chest demanded a cure.

# Chapter 21

Around five-thirty the next morning Gracen finally put himself out of his misery by getting out of bed for a run. One glance at his running shoes and he realized that he didn't feel like running. It wouldn't help. He didn't want to rid himself of what he was feeling. He wanted to understand it.

Few moments in his history had prepared him for these normal human emotions. Vaguely, he remembered having crushes on girls in middle school and high school. But he had always been handsome, so it wasn't too long after puberty hit that Gracen figured out how to be the one wanted instead of the one wanting. Besides, there was something more instinctual about the longing he had now. There was romantic desire, but almost more than that, the innate programming to turn towards someone who offers love and security. In that regard, Blythe was just one piece of the puzzle.

As he padded through his apartment, barefoot and in deep thought, he recognized that the entire night had ministered to his empty spirit. He was welcomed by the Beckwiths and wanted by all the Elwoods. They treated him as an old friend and he, in turn, was genuinely friendly and happy to be with them. He stopped short, suddenly sure Uncle Harry was proud of him.

"People," Gracen said aloud. It was as though he saw his own kind for the first time in a long, long time. His subconscious nagged at him, wanting to jump down the rabbit hole to find the bunny that would explain to him how this had happened in the first place. What had made him so empty and closed off? And was there any wisdom to this undoing? But he refused to chase the bunny. Not today. There was no running today.

Then, all at once his web of thought bubbles popped simultaneously as his phone rang. A glance at the ID told him it was Alex.

"Hello?"

"Good, you're up. I thought maybe being here made you lazy. Is this a good time to talk?"

"Alex, it's like barely six in the morning."

"I know, but I need to head to Cleveland for some important meetings. I wanted to catch up with you first. You disappeared last night, you know."

"Come on up when you get here."

"I just parked. Be up in a minute."

Presently there was a knock on the door, and Gracen let him in, gesturing to the couch. "Good work, by the way, on the couch and everything."

"You're not having buyer's remorse? I thought Sayen Falls might be a little too Midwestern for your blood."

"So far, so good."

"Glad to hear it. Is it okay being next to Blythe? I've wondered if I made the right call."

"Everything is fine with Blythe."

"I was surprised to hear you closed the shop for that play. How was that, by the way?"

"It was good," Gracen replied. Alex was asking a lot of questions, standard procedure for a lawyer sniffing for something. "It was *Henry the Fifth*. He came, he saw, he conquered, he got the girl, and—spoiler alert—he died of dysentery."

"Thanks for the review. Now I don't have to see that one."

"As if you would."

"I might. Probably not though. And you? Did you get the girl?"

"Seriously? Is that why you wanted to talk to me? To make sure I'm not messing around with the girl next door."

"I'm not the only one who noticed you left together last night."

"She had a couple drinks. I made sure she got home alright. That's all," he gritted his teeth as he lied. "How stupid do you think I am?"

"I've seen you be pretty stupid."

"Then let me assure you nothing happened. Not after the play, not last night. It just so happens I'm more interested in what's between her ears than what's between her legs."

Alex raised his eyebrows. "That's a relief, albeit a bit surprising. When Ginnie told me about the show, I wasn't sure how it would play out. Blythe can be clingy."

"I've not seen that side of her."

"Well, keep your distance and hopefully you never will. Don't get me wrong. I like her. She can just be intense. Emotionally."

It was strange to hear echoes of her own words coming from Alex's mouth. Gracen didn't want to dwell on the notion that there might be something to her claims.

"So is Blythe the only reason you're here?" he sighed.

"No," came the cautious reply, "I spoke with Roy before I came to the Falls. He wants to give you more money. Beyond the agreement."

"I don't want his money," Gracen immediately snapped. "Wait, more money?"

In one of the diatribes before his departure, Roy had made it clear in no uncertain terms that Gracen would not be receiving any more of his money than they had agreed upon. And Gracen had made it abundantly clear that he was just fine with that.

"He's concerned about the off-season. He asked for my honest thoughts about your place staying viable on the riverfront. I have to say, sometimes I think I should've worked a little harder and gotten you set up closer to campus. Drunk college kids will always get pizza."

"I'm not that concerned about the off-season. I'm not interested in Roy's money. And I'm happy here on the river. It's a good spot."

"You say that now, but it could be a lean winter."

"I'm not a bear. I can economize and figure it out."

"Says the man who's never had to budget in his life."

"You're one to talk. How much are the payments on that Tesla you're driving?" Gracen retorted. "And Roy, of all people, knows how efficient I am with a budget. My penny pinching made him an impressive amount of extra profit."

"Hey, don't shoot the messenger. I told him you'd say no, but I felt obligated to tell you anyway. I thought it might at least be gratifying to know he was concerned."

"He wants me to come crawling back. That's not happening."

"You're really happy here?" Alex sounded skeptical.

"You're the one who assured me the people are great and that Sayen Falls was laid back. Why are you so shocked to discover it's working out?"

"Because you don't do people and you don't do laid back."

"I'm evolving. I can think away from all that salt in the air."

"Just don't think too much," Alex advised. "I know how that brain of yours likes to beat you to death."

* * *

The beaters in the bowl whirled away at top speed as Blythe carefully sifted in the dry ingredients to the wet. She used to over-mix things and end up with rock-hard baked goods. Mary Alice had coached her on some of the finer points of baking and most of the time there were excellent results.

Today, however, Blythe was bordering on the edge of over-mixing again. Her eyes glazed over as she stared into the bowl. Inside her brain, her thoughts insisted that they felt exactly like those ingredients getting beaten and swirled in the bowl. A second later her thoughts changed their collective mind and said that instead, they felt like the beaters, churning at top speed and making a lot of noise and commotion. She was inclined to agree with the second claim.

"Blythe, that's probably enough," Mary Alice said gently.

Blythe blinked her eyes as she startled from her near-hypnosis. She briefly hit the 'burst' button so the beaters would spin even faster and throw off the excess dough. As the mixer nearly screamed at the demand to spin faster, she decided she identified completely with a kitchen appliance.

They were making raisin-filled cookies, a classic recipe in any Elwood kitchen. Mary Alice was able to help spoon out the dough and put in the raisin filling as she sat at the kitchen table. Soon after they began, she sensed Blythe's mind wandering again.

"Is everything okay, dear?"

"Huh?" Blythe asked, coming into focus again. "Oh, I'm fine. Just tired."

"I was a little surprised you came over today actually, after last night."

"I figured I'd take advantage of Silas being around while he's here," Blythe explained.

"I'm always glad to have you," Mary Alice smiled. "And, I'm glad you're out of the shop for a little bit."

The Elwood homestead was just a few short blocks away from the riverfront plaza but it was the necessary distance Blythe needed today. When Gracen hadn't appeared for his run or come over for a cup of tea, her feelings of insecurity started fighting with her feelings of romantic delusion. It occurred to her that she could leave the shop in Silas and Finn's care, and escape to make cookies with her grandmother.

"You're sure everything is okay?" Mary Alice asked again.

Don't say anything. Do not say a word about last night. Blythe had intended on keeping the words that had been said and the kisses that had been exchanged a secret known only to herself and to Gracen. There was no need to get every Elwood and Beckwith all up in arms about it, and with the wonders of cell phones and speed dial, they'd all know by noon.

But when her mouth opened, she heard herself saying, "Gracen and I talked last night."

"What did you talk about?" To her credit Mary Alice almost sounded disinterested.

"He said he thought he had feelings for me," Blythe confessed.

"So that's why you're here," Mary Alice nodded.

"I'm not avoiding him. Well, maybe I am. But he didn't come in this morning. And I don't know what I would've said to him if he had."

"Well, how do you feel about him?"

"I don't know. I really don't know. I'd be lying if I said I didn't feel things for him too. But, come on, let's be real, I've always been boy crazy. And I don't have the best judgment, clearly. So I don't know."

"That's a lot of 'don't knows' and I know you well enough to know that you usually do know when you say you don't."

"I might need you to write that down."

"Blythe."

"Alright, alright," she said, tossing her spoon back into the bowl of cookie dough. "I'm scared. That's it. I'm scared that I'll do it again."

"Do what exactly?"

"Completely lose myself in another relationship. Or put too much on him. I know that Ian did some terrible things, I don't try to justify that anymore. But objectively, we all have to admit that I was a nightmare."

"A nightmare is a bit harsh, dear. But you were … desperate, as much as it pains me to say it. But I don't see that in you anymore."

"I feel like I've just come back into daylight."

Mary Alice finished scooping out enough cookies to fill the tray sitting

133

in front of her. She motioned for Blythe to put it in the oven and when her granddaughter returned to the table, she asked, "Do you want an old woman's advice?"

"I'll take yours."

"I've lived enough years to know that sometimes life can feel very long. I've spent decades now waiting for my reunion with Kate and Bill and to tell them how much I still love them," Mary Alice began. She paused a moment to collect herself; the grief of losing two children was always just there under the surface. She went on, "But I can also assure you that life is short. People can be taken from you in the blink of an eye. Now, I don't think some other girl will come along and snag Gracen away from you. It's clear to me that he only has eyes for you. But, sweetheart, you can just never be sure that life won't interrupt you and rob you of opportunities."

"Jesse keeps saying that I don't really know Gracen."

"Oh, darn that Jesse Beckwith. He just doesn't want anyone else to have you until he's made up his mind. Don't you listen to him."

"I've never heard you say anything like that about Jesse," Blythe gasped.

"I love that boy, love him to pieces. But where you're concerned, my loyalty is to you. Besides, you've always insisted there's nothing there. Right?"

"Right," she replied vaguely. "So what do I do?"

"You're the only one who knows your heart. If you think you could love him then take the next opportunity that comes along to see what's there. But if he's just a handsome man with interesting things to say then enjoy his company. There's no harm in that. You can add him to your collection."

"My collection?" Blythe scoffed. The oven timer went off and she stood up to retrieve the first tray of finished cookies.

"Yes, your collection. Finnian McCartney, Jesse Beckwith, and now Gracen Hall. Quite a trio of handsome interesting men, I should think."

"No wonder everyone kept asking me why I'm still single," Blythe said with dry disdain.

"Those old dopes. You don't pay them any mind either. They just gossip because they have no imagination."

\* \* \*

Blythe no sooner pulled into a parking space behind her shop than Silas emerged from the back door with his duffle bag over his shoulder. He was on the phone and looking very somber. Mostly replying with "uh-huh" and "yeah" he crossed past his sister to throw his bag into the hatch of his SUV. When the call ended he slammed the glass door so hard she was surprised it didn't shatter on impact.

"You're leaving."

"That was my lawyer. There are papers to go over."

"Which lawyer?"

His look told her everything. Silently, she wrapped her arms around her little brother and hugged him tightly. The smallest hint of a sob escaped him before he swallowed hard.

"I know it's stupid that I'm fighting this so much. I don't know if it's because I still love her or I just can't face that I was wrong. Sometimes I'm not sure we were ever in love the way we needed to be."

"I'm sorry this is happening," Blythe whispered. "You deserve to be loved so much more than you are. I could wring her neck."

"Now you know how I felt about Ian. And I think I know how you felt about Ian."

"Silas, I'm here for you whichever way this pans out. I'll stay hopeful for your sake."

"You know what else you can do for me? Keep getting back to being you. You're more like you than you've been in ages. Keep writing, even if it feels like nonsense. Someday you'll scribble down just the right thing. That's how it works with words."

"I'll do my best."

Silas looked her dead in the eye as he went on, "And keep big fat believing in people and love and impossible things. You have no idea how important it is to the rest of us."

Blythe broke eye contact as she mumbled, "I'll try."

"I mean it, Blythe. Don't hide in the shop. Don't hide in your books. Don't hide in your head. We need you out here in the real world. You help bolster the rest of us."

"The real world," she mused.

The backdoor of Summerstead Isle Pizza opened and Gracen appeared with a sizable stack of collapsed boxes. He tossed them in the dumpster designated for recycling cardboard, then turned his head towards Blythe and Silas.

"Silas is leaving," Blythe told him. "His lawyer called."

Gracen came to shake his hand. "If there's anything I can help with, don't hesitate to give me a call. I have no idea how I could help, but—"

"I appreciate the offer," Silas assured him. "I don't have many friends left in Ann Arbor."

"You know you have family here," Blythe said. She opened the front door of her jeep and retrieved three bags of raisin-filled cookies. "Take one for the road."

"And I'll call you when I get there," Silas smirked as he opened a bag and took a bite of a cookie. "Pretty good."

"You don't have to call when you get there, punk, but let me know how things are going. Do that for me, okay?"

"Fair enough," he agreed. He climbed into his car and said one last thing, "Remember what I said. The real world needs the real you."

Her cheeks flushed. Blythe and Gracen were quiet as Silas backed out and then left the parking lot. He wanted to ask what that meant but knew better than to do so. When the quiet became awkward, Blythe finally spoke.

"Gracen, about last night."

"I'm s—"

"No, hear me out. Gracen, I can't deny that I have some strong feelings for you. And that kiss, quite honestly, keeps making me weak in the knees."

A grin pulled at his lips.

Blythe continued, "The trouble is I tend to define myself by the men around me which isn't very fair or pleasant for them. Now, I'm not berating myself like I was last night, believe me. I just … I don't want to do that to you. I don't want to make you tell me who I am every day. That's not why you came here."

"So what you're saying is 'it's not you, it's me'?" Gracen asked, still grinning ever so slightly. The grin served as a mask.

"Not exactly," she turned to face him directly. "I think what I'm saying is give me a little time to make sure my head is on straight before I fall completely head over heels for you."

"With your head on straight you may find that I'm not the guy worth falling for," he cautioned her. "So I can only support this decision. I don't want to hurt you. And I'm sorry if I overstepped last night."

"You did not," she assured him. "You were quite a gentleman, really."

"Well, that's a first."

"How does it feel?"

"Pretty good actually."

"Good," she smiled. "And we're okay? You're good? You're not going to avoid me and I'm not going to avoid you and we're just going to see how this plays out? Seeing as we're both so self-deprecating, we could just go in circles forever."

"I'm fine. I didn't come in this morning because I was dealing with some stuff Alex told me," Gracen revealed. "And frankly, I don't know how I stayed away for two weeks. My monologues were really letting me down in the conversation department."

"Not a lot to say back?"

"Nothing new anyway."

# Chapter 22

Only Mary Alice had confirmation that something had transpired between the riverfront's most fascinating duo. Both Blythe and Gracen were careful to appear extraordinarily normal and casual together. Routine cups of tea, regular slices of pizza, insert a literature joke here, a line of Shakespeare there. They staunchly refused to acknowledge any of the gossip circulating among their respective staff members. If they didn't dignify it with a response, eventually it would go away.

And sure enough, the high school homecoming dance provided just the necessary distraction. All discussion soon turned to dresses and shoes, dates and dinners, and away from Gracen and Blythe. After Sawyer asked Ella to be not only his date but also his girlfriend, even she abandoned the rumor mill. Although she didn't approve of Lily going with Brady, Ella couldn't resist discussing all the painstaking details of their plans.

Lily had never attended a school formal before. She hadn't been asked, and going with a group of loud girls who are adept at being carefree and fun intimidated her. This year she had a boyfriend, and to her surprise, Brady agreed to go. School dances weren't exactly his favorite thing, but he did care for Lily. He could tell she really wanted to go. After all, it was her senior year. There was some concern over his age, seeing as he was twenty years old, but the teachers taking tickets didn't ask. None of the chaperones questioned his presence.

In fact, the only ones who seemed to notice them at all were the Elwoods.

"I love your dress, Lily. That blue is such a good color with your skin tone and your blonde hair and blue eyes," Ginnie raved as she gave Lily a gentle hug. She took her hand to examine the corsage. "These flowers are beautiful, Brady. You did a good job."

"They reminded me of Lily. They have a weird name though," Brady replied, with an unusually bashful smile. It was a credit to Ginnie's kindness.

"Dahlias," Ginnie said. "I wanted them in my wedding bouquet but they were out of season. I had lilies and daisies instead."

"I should've gotten you a corsage tonight," Liam said to his wife. "I don't know why I didn't think of it. Blythe should've reminded me."

"I feel like she's had other things on her mind," Ginnie replied with a mischievous smile.

"You're not the only one. Ella analyzes their every move," Lily laughed. "She's been a little less obsessive lately though."

"Ella should worry less about other people," Brady grunted. Although he agreed to the dance, he refused to come with any of Lily's friends, especially Ella and Sawyer. It was weird enough coming to a high school dance; he didn't want to spend the evening in the company of teenagers who didn't think he was good enough for their friend.

"Well, don't let us keep you," Liam said. "You came here to dance, not to talk to the old people holding up the walls."

"Excuse me? We're not going to be wallflowers ourselves, Mr. Elwood," Ginnie informed her husband. "I forgive you for the corsage, but I demand dancing."

"Then we'll see you out there," Liam winked at Lily. She gave a small wave goodbye before slipping her hand into Brady's and following him into the center of the gym floor.

The decorations, the lights, and the DJ did much to help Lily forget she was in a gym, but it was Brady that kept her spellbound. He looked quite handsome all polished up in his suit and tie. Her dress was a tea-length midnight blue, and she had helped him find a dark gray suit with a navy blue tie. They looked well together. And they looked in love.

And they were in love. Lily was sure of it. Brady was too. Life had been lonely before their paths crossed. Then, when they found each other that loneliness went away.

"I'm so happy I'm with you tonight," she whispered as she linked her fingers behind his neck. His hands wrapped around her waist and they began to dance to the music.

"I'm just happy I was working the day you came in to get your oil changed. I was thinking about that at work yesterday. I might've missed you completely."

"See? It's meant to be."

"Do you tell your friends that?"

"Brady."

"I'm not trying to be difficult here, but they need to know that this is for real. I love you, Lily. I might not be this clean-cut perfect guy, but I mean what I say."

"I know that. And that's all that matters. I've talked to Ella and Sawyer," Lily said dismissively. "If we all hung out, I think they'd see you like I do."

"I already don't see you enough as it is. You're either at work or you have homework."

"You can always come to the shop."

"I'm not sure your boss likes me any more than Ella does," he grunted.

"They don't *know* you. They just see the older guy dating the seventeen-year-old. You and I know the truth. That's what matters," she insisted and sealed it with a kiss. "I know that this year is different for me. It's my senior year and I finally feel like I own it. I have a job that I like, I'm doing well at school, and I have *you*. I almost don't care anymore where I fall in my parents' spectrum of caring."

"Ha, I know they don't like me," Brady said with a sly smile. "I am not

138

what your dad ever pictured for his daughter."

"And yet, he says nothing. If he has an opinion, I haven't heard it."

"He looks at me like I'm a disease."

"That's just his face," Lily giggled. "I'm not sure I've seen him really smile in years. Oh, good grief, that's sad. Isn't it? It is. That's sad."

"It is pretty sad. But that's why you need to get away from your parents and live your life. That's the only reason I think this SIP job is a good idea. You're earning your own money and you'll be able to do whatever you want when you graduate."

"I'll have to go to college."

"Says who? I haven't gone to school."

"But you want to. You're always talking about going to flight school."

He shrugged, "Things are going well at Anderton's. I'm learning a lot at the garage. And I'm doing alright."

"And you're going to live with your cousins forever?"

"Not forever. But I can save money living with them and someday get a nice place of my own. Maybe share it with the girl of my dreams," he winked.

This statement was theoretically true. However, he wasn't actually saving anything. His money seemed to disappear every Friday and Saturday night when he shelled out his fair share for the beers and other recreational products that helped them blow off steam. Lily knew he liked to get high sometimes, but he never did it around her or pressured her to try it. It was just his thing. And she often thought about what Ginnie had said about Liam. Even he had hit a rough patch. Poor Brady's whole life had been a rough patch and so it stood to reason that if she could just be supportive and loving, he'd find his way eventually.

"Anything is possible, Brady," she replied. Her voice was hushed but her smile beamed.

"Just so long as no one takes you away from me or talks you out of loving me," he said, suddenly turning a little dark. He was staring past her. Lily glanced over her shoulder and spied Sawyer.

"I told you before, no one could steal me away. No one is even trying."

"You're too naïve to realize you're the most beautiful girl in the room tonight and everyone here knows it."

"Oh please, I am not."

"Oh, but you are. And I assure you I'm not the only one who has noticed you."

"I don't care about anyone else. I only want to be beautiful for you."

"Mission accomplished."

"Besides, you know that Sawyer and Ella are a thing now. It's not like I would ever really be attracted to him anyway, but that should put your mind at ease that absolutely nothing is happening there," Lily said carefully. There had been more than one lengthy discussion about her friendship with Sawyer Charles.

Brady raised an eyebrow. "That doesn't mean much to me. People cheat all the time."

"I don't."

"You know better."

Infidelity was one of the demons that had haunted Brady ever since his mother had abandoned her family to have an affair. It left him deeply suspicious and gave him a controlling streak. This was another wound that Lily believed she could heal by pouring enough of herself into it. She could bring him peace, and in that, she could find her purpose.

Wanting no more discussion of Sawyer or Ella, Brady drew Lily even closer to him and whispered into her ear, "I'm glad you decided to stay at my place tonight."

Instantly, Lily's face flushed and the heat rushed the entire way through her body into her very tippy toes. They'd been dating for five months and three days, and Brady really wanted her to stay the night with him. Although she was uncertain, she'd agreed. Getting it past her parents proved to be easy—she just told them she was staying with Ella, and they didn't bother to check.

"I didn't tell anyone," she breathed. "I feel like we have our own little world."

They both knew the real reason Lily hadn't told anyone. There wasn't anyone who would approve. Lily was going into this alone.

When the dance was over, she slid into Brady's car knowing that he was not taking her home but to his apartment. At that moment, Gracen's insistence that she call him if she ever needed him echoed in her brain. This was really happening. She was going to Brady's apartment to stay with him all night. A strange feeling came over her, a nauseating blend of adrenaline and anxiety. Part of her wanted to do this very common, very adult thing and stay the night at her boyfriend's apartment. That feeling was only surface deep. Below the surface, all the rest of Lily did not want this at all. She was scared to follow through with Brady and scared to tell him no. She was worried it would hurt or she would do it wrong. She was concerned that once they had sex, that's all there would be between them anymore. That seemed to be what happened to the couples all around her at school.

She pulled out her phone and cycled through social media apps, going through the motions. The compulsion to reach out to Gracen would not go away. She decided to text him something simple.

*Just wanted to let you know that Brady is bringing me to work tomorrow.*

Her phone buzzed with a reply: *Does that mean what I think it means?*

"Who is that?" Brady asked, trying to steal sideways look.

"Gracen," Lily said casually.

"He's checking up on you?"

"No, I just remembered I need to tell him I can't work next Sunday," she lied. Then she tapped a response to Gracen's question, *Yes.*

Two minutes passed before her phone vibrated again. As nonchalantly as possible she hid the screen entirely from Brady's view and read: *I'm trying to not be a judgy adult, so hear me out. I think you'll regret that. I can come to get you if you need a ride. Or Blythe can come.*

Her heart came to an abrupt stop. Her face flushed then became cold as the color drained from her face. Gracen was right. She knew he was right. This was a mistake.

"Brady," she said slowly, her voice shaking, "can you take me home?"

His head snapped in her direction, "What?"

"I'm not ready. I thought I was, but I'm not."

"Lily, you're just spending the night. We're not having an orgy."

"I know. I just … I'm really tired and I do have to work tomorrow."

"This is because of Gracen."

"It's not. I promise it's not."

"I'm telling you, I don't like that guy. I don't like how he looks at you."

"He's my boss, that's all. And my friend."

"You have a lot of guy friends."

"Brady, please, not that again. I told you I would never cheat on you."

"And you also told me you'd come to my place tonight."

"I'm just not ready for that."

"It's been five months. No one else would wait that long."

She swallowed hard as she felt that familiar lump of tears in her throat. The night suddenly felt like such a cliché, she felt like a cliché, and just minutes ago everything had been perfect.

"I'm sorry. I know I'm ruining everything, but I figured it'd be better to tell you here in your car than at your place."

"I don't get you," he sighed angrily. He flipped the blinker on his car to the right and Lily knew he was taking her home. Not another word was spoken between them. He pulled into her driveway and when she slipped out of his car, the tears finally spilled down her cheeks. Her parents were both in bed. A single light was on in the kitchen for her. In her room, she dropped onto her bed where she cried and cried, still in her tea-length midnight blue dress.

And on the riverfront, Gracen burst into The Yellow Bowl and shoved his phone at Blythe to read. She scanned the texts, her eyes growing wide.

"Please tell me I did the right thing," he pleaded. "I am really not the guy for this. Where's Finn when you need him?"

"Evidently you are the guy for this. She reached out to you."

"It's not really my business. She's just a kid who works for me, but I had to say something. I have regrets of my own; I know how this ends."

"So do I."

"I don't want that for Lily."

Blythe smiled at him fondly, "Aw, Princeton, who knew you could care so much?"

His face relaxed at her teasing. "Listen, Kate, this is very unsettling for me. I turned this part of me off. My sister had a bad boyfriend that I got fired. As far as I know, I'm still not forgiven. I said I'd never bother again. No one wants to be saved from their bad choices."

His phone beeped with a new text: *I had Brady take me home. You're right about regrets.*

A wave of relief washed over his face and he showed the text to Blythe. She shared in his relief and said to him, "You might want to check that switch. Clearly, the do-the-right-thing part of you is on and working. You did the right thing, Gracen, reaching out to Lily and being honest with her tonight."

"I don't want what happened to you to happen to her. Being committed to the wrong guy and all that," he replied. "And for that matter, I don't want her to turn into me and think that sex is somehow an answer for something. She's looking for meaning with Brady. She won't find it there."

Uncle Harry had told him that time and again. Stop looking for your answers in bed, boy. It had taken his uncle's death and a move of almost five hundred miles for Gracen to listen. It was too late now to ask Uncle Harry for more advice. Yet, when he thought about it, he knew exactly what his uncle would tell him. Pray. Get your heart right. Then do what it tells you. And if all else fails, 'once more unto the breach'. Or something to that effect.

## Chapter 23

The monotony of folding laundry made Blythe so itchy with boredom she actually wondered if she was allergic. She did all her laundry on Mondays, and she skipped a week whenever she could. It was a shameful system that would horrify her mother. On top of the shame, it left Blythe with a mountain of laundry to deal with sorting and folding and putting away. To help with the tedium, she binge-watched favorite shows or caught up on films she'd been meaning to see. Currently, she was deep into *Downton Abbey*, sitting on her bed matching socks and talking the characters through their immense drama.

The theme song had just started for the third time that evening when her phone rang. It wasn't Jesse's signature ringtone, and there was no photo ID as she grabbed her phone from the nightstand. In fact, it was an unknown number, but an app told her the call was coming from Las Vegas, Nevada.

"Hello?" she asked cautiously as she paused her show.

"This is Blythe Elwood, right? Nick's girl?" said a deep male voice that sounded nervous.

"Yes, this is Blythe. Who is this? Is he okay?" she asked. Her heart jumped and she felt it beating all over the place. Like her grandfather, she could worry in a hurry if prompted.

"This is Luke Hannigan. I work for your dad. He didn't want me to tell any of you, but that just doesn't feel right to me."

"Tell me what, Luke?" Blythe demanded. Her tone wasn't harsh, just urgent. She only knew of Luke, as they had never met. He was the lead foreman in her father's construction business, essentially his right-hand man and the closest thing to a friend he had.

"Nick had a heart attack today," Luke told her, then hastened to add, "He's alright now. We called an ambulance right away and they came pretty quick. I'm at the hospital with him. He's stabilized now, but a cardiologist just left. His heart is apparently in bad shape."

"Oh no," Blythe gasped.

"He is stable now," Luke repeated. "I hope you don't mind me calling you. I tried Liam but he didn't answer. I had to go through your dad's phone. Nick doesn't know I have it," he chuckled uneasily. "It was on his desk and I swiped it when the ambulance came."

Blythe glanced at the clock by the TV and knew that Liam was probably heading up bath time before getting the kids settled into bed.

"I'm thankful you called," she assured him. "Grabbing his phone was quick thinking."

"I had no idea what paperwork might need to be filled out and I don't have all his information," Luke explained. He sounded helpless and Blythe felt sorry for him. "Nick wanted me listed for his emergency contact. For that matter, I'm probably violating the health privacy laws."

"Don't worry, Luke, I think you did the right thing. He's our dad. We should know. It shouldn't be on you."

"Well, there's more. I thought you kids needed to know that they're saying Nick needs surgery. They want to put a defibrillator or something in his chest."

There was some sort of great-uncle in the family that had one of those little boxes in his chest. Blythe was vaguely aware of how it worked, but she knew it was a big deal to have one.

"But he can't have that kind of surgery out there. I'm sure the recovery time is ridiculous," she murmured. Heart attack. Surgery. Defibrillator. It was too much for her brain. No, too much for her heart. It was still thumping around wherever it wanted to and not at all in her chest.

Mechanically, she slipped from the bed and padded to the window. The Shelby was in the parking lot. Gracen was home.

"The doctors said recovery is twelve weeks," Luke informed her. "And Nick says he'll hire nurses or go to a rehab facility or whatever it takes. But I don't think that's realistic."

"Twelve weeks," she repeated. She left her bedroom and traveled across her apartment to her door. She opened it and went through it. Then, she knocked on Gracen's door. She needed to see his face. That's all she knew. She needed his face.

"I guess there will be some time before they schedule it and all that. It's not like it's happening tomorrow," Luke continued.

Gracen opened the door and found Blythe white as a ghost and eyes as wide as saucers. Without a word, he ushered her in. He went immediately to the kitchen to get her a glass of ice water. She followed.

"Right, yeah, it will take time, I'm sure. He'll need to have a follow-up with the cardiologist," Blythe said to Luke. It occurred to her how little she really knew of her father's health and for all she knew he had specialists out the wazoo.

"Well, I don't know how you kids will bring it up to him since you're not supposed to know, but I thought you had a right *to* know and come up with a plan together. I'll help him however I can, but my skill set is really best suited for building sites, you know?" Luke said.

"Of course, I know you're the best guy my dad has. And I really appreciate your willingness to help. I'm sure he does too," she said. She felt so unwieldy but wanted very much to reassure this kind man she had never met. "I'll talk to my brothers and we'll figure out what to do."

"I didn't leave a message or anything for Liam. I didn't know what to say in a voicemail that wouldn't be alarming."

"He'll probably assume it was a junk call then, don't worry about it. I'll call him in a little bit. He's probably getting his little ones into bed now," Blythe said. She knew she was starting to ramble. It was her nerves. They were going haywire. It would help if her heart would return to its assigned seat and behave itself.

"Don't hesitate to call me if there's anything you think I can do."

"I appreciate that. And thank you for calling. And for being there with him," now her voice was starting to break. Her father might have died without Luke being there to help. She stared at Gracen who was waiting to offer her the ice water. Concern was etched all over his face. She focused only on his eyes, those eyes that went on forever.

"Of course. He's not just my boss, you know. That's why I'm really trying to do the right thing and not just what Nick thinks he wants. Anyway, I'll let you get back to your evening."

"Thank you again, Luke. Goodbye," she said. Gracen extended the glass of water.

"I'm sorry I don't have any tea," he said gently. "I get all my tea from this girl I know."

His little joke broke the tension inside her like a chisel hitting an icy pond. She smiled but cracking that smile actually opened her up for all the feelings to surface. Tears began slipping down her cheeks. Without hesitation, Gracen removed the glass from her hand, set it on the counter, and enveloped her in a bear hug. She clung to him and said nothing until she thought her voice could be trusted.

As she recapped the call, her voice broke every now and again, and she took many grateful sips of that ice water to keep her throat clear of any clogs of tears.

"So your dad had a heart attack and doesn't want any of you to know?" Gracen summarized.

"Evidently not. And I have no idea how to go about talking to him since we're not supposed to know. Luke actually broke the law calling me, thanks to HIPAA."

"Yeah, that's no small thing. We ran into HIPAA laws with Uncle Harry," he recalled. "I was threatened with a sizable fine for getting private information about Uncle Harry's health that I wasn't supposed to have until Aunt Grace got it all squared away with the paperwork."

"Your evil grandfather again?" Blythe asked.

"Yes, it's a long story all about legalities, control, and power. The usual for him. Anyway, this isn't about me. This is about you and your dad," Gracen said. He took Blythe's hand. His fingers rested on her wrist. "Your pulse is racing."

"You just took my pulse?" she said incredulously. "That's so weird."

"It's an anxiety trick. You need to sit down." He guided her to the couch, carrying the glass of ice water. "Do you want a cup of tea? I can go

145

over to your place real quick or something. Or I can call Finn. He's kind of the master of both tea and disasters."

"No, that's fine. I'm okay. I don't need Finn. I just need to talk a little bit before I call my brothers. And, I don't know, I was on the phone with Luke and I started panicking and my brain just led me over here to you. I hope that's okay."

"Blythe," Gracen said, taking her hand again. This time he locked her fingers with his. "It's okay. I'm glad you did. I want to help. You can talk as much as you need to."

"I'm trying to not over-react. I mean, he isn't dead." She gasped and her hand flew to her mouth, "I'm so sorry. I didn't mean to say it like that."

"It's alright," he assured her, "I know you wouldn't be insensitive. And like I told you, I don't think of Robert Hall as my 'dad'. I didn't know him."

"I suppose it's better having a dad who doesn't want me to know anything about his life or health conditions, than having no dad at all," Blythe said softly.

"I don't know. Both scenarios seem pretty messed up."

"I have sometimes thought about something like this happening. I wondered how we would find out and how we'd handle it. But I never came up with a good plan of action. I really have no idea what to do. I'll have to call my brothers. And I have to decide if we tell Grammy and PapPap."

"With the way Miles worries, I'm not sure it's helpful for him to know."

"You're probably right. And, on top of that, we'll have to keep our knowledge of it a secret from Dad until we have a good plan. That won't happen if they know. They won't be able to help themselves." Blythe sighed, "They've lost two kids already."

"I'm sorry, *two* kids?" he exclaimed. "I knew about your aunt because of your name. But there was another one?"

"My Uncle Bill."

"Was Liam named after him? His real name is William, isn't it?"

"It is and yes he was. I suppose I should give you the abridged version of those stories. It really explains a lot about all of us when you know," Blythe said. She took a sip of water and composed her thoughts. Then she started,

"When Kate was eight years old she contracted a mysterious illness. They thought it was one thing and then another, but none of the treatments worked. She was recuperating at home when she spiked a very high fever. There are some complicated details about what the delay was, but Grammy and PapPap weren't able to get her to the hospital in time to bring the fever down. The doctors tried, but ultimately, the fever and the mystery illness took her life."

"That's absolutely horrific," Gracen breathed. "And Bill?"

146

"Bill was the oldest of the kids. It went Bill, Kate, and then my dad. So Kate died when she was eight, and then eight years later, Bill died in a motorcycle crash. He was eighteen and had just graduated high school. He was riding his buddy's motorcycle in a little act of rebellion because Grammy and PapPap were really protective of the boys after Kate died. But he lost control and crashed. Dad was fourteen. It really traumatized him."

"I can't imagine. Losing both his brother and his sister. And your grandparents, losing two children." Gracen ran his fingers through his hair as he exhaled. "No wonder Miles is a worrier. And Mary Alice has this air of, I don't know, regret or something. She's so sweet and kind, but I can sense this ... longing."

"Longing is the word. She still mourns the loss. I mean, she's amazing and so strong. She's lived a good life that Kate and Bill would be proud of, but she's never stopped grieving."

"I think grief isn't something that stops. It's something you live with."

"From what I've seen, I'm inclined to agree."

"Unless your brothers really feel differently, I don't think you should tell Miles and Mary Alice that their son had a heart attack and needs a device implanted in his chest. That's a lot for a parent to process and they're already walking around with a full load."

"It's a lot for me to process," Blythe said. Her lip quivered. Gracen wanted so badly to kiss her but he knew he shouldn't. He squeezed her hand a little tighter instead. "I don't even know how to tell my brothers. Liam won't be so hard. He's so rational. But Silas? Silas is like me. He's emotional. And most things about our dad make him angry."

"I can call Silas if you want," Gracen offered.

"Do you have his number?" Blythe asked with a surprised look on her face. When Gracen nodded, she couldn't help the grin, "I knew it. You guys have like a bromance. You and Finn and Silas."

"I wouldn't go that far. We text a little. I mean, it's not a big deal."

"Has he talked to you about Mindy?"

"Yes."

"Then it's a big deal. He doesn't talk about that hot mess express with very many people."

"It's easier because I'm an outsider. Like Finn."

"Like I said, you and Finn and Silas. Silas considers himself the Elwood outsider. He says he's not like the rest of us. And he isn't. He left and thus far, has not returned."

"It's not always easy to come back. I know nothing could induce me to move back to Summerstead Isle."

"Nothing? Not even if life here completely imploded?"

"Maybe if I lost absolutely everything."

"Well, Silas has. Or he's about to. And he should come home when that

147

bomb finally drops," she insisted. "Ugh, which brings me back to my dad and his heart attack."

"Let me call Silas to help you out. I know you usually love talking to your little brother, but this is different. If it's gonna be a trigger, I don't want you near it. You don't need more stress," Gracen asserted. "I'll have to make you start running with me to deal."

"I don't run," she said flatly. "Only if I'm being chased."

"I really don't want to have to chase you around the riverfront to help with your stress levels, but I will if I have to. I really think it will be easier if I call Silas and you call Liam. And then once the boys know, you can take some time to figure out how to confront Nick."

A laugh bubbled up inside Blythe but the tears had made snot so the laugh got stuck in her throat and she snorted. This made her laugh a little harder so tears came to her eyes.

"I'm such a mess," she breathed. "I told you, Gracen. I'm such a mess."

"I still don't see it," he told her. He lifted the hand he was holding to his lips and gently kissed it. An intense shiver rippled through her body and she feared her heart would go bananas again. It had just settled down. Seeing her shiver, he said, "That reminds me. I have something for you. A package came today from Aunt Grace."

He stood up but didn't let go of her hand, so she stood as well and followed as he went to the kitchen. A medium-sized packing box was sitting on his counter. Blythe wondered how she had missed it before, then remembered, she had basically been in a state of mild shock.

"I haven't actually opened the box," he confessed. "I just read the card taped on the outside."

Now he had to let go of her hand so he could retrieve a knife and carefully open the box. Another brief note on rose-scented paper was at the top, then underneath, wrapped in pink tissue paper, were Gracen's Summerstead Isle sweatshirts. He removed a gray Henley hoodie with an anchor decal and breathed in the smell of Summerstead Isle. Every package that came from Aunt Grace contained just a breath of salty sea air. Gracen handed the shirt to Blythe. She held it up, then eyed him suspiciously.

"You don't seem the tourist trap t-shirt type."

"Family Christmas card, every year a new sweatshirt," he shrugged.

"That's cute."

"You have no idea," Gracen said grimly. He was only a real member of the family when it suited Roy.

"How many are there?" Blythe asked as she dug into the box.

"I really have no idea. Looks like some of my Princeton sweatshirts, and the Summerstead Isle shirts." He pushed the box toward Blythe. "All yours."

"Mine?"

"I'm not going to wear them. Well, there might be a couple I could consider wearing, but like you said, it's not really my thing. And you're always cold anyway."

"Not always."

"You just shivered," he pointed out.

She shot him a look and he couldn't stop a wicked grin from exploding on his face. Rolling her eyes, she pulled the sweatshirt over her head. It was a bit big, which was to be expected, but cozy. She snuggled into the sleeves with a smile.

"Perfect fit, and it looks better on you anyway," Gracen pronounced.

"Well, it is good timing," Blythe said as she stuffed the sweatshirts back into the box. "October was made for hoodies."

"I will let Aunt Grace know that the package is being put to good use. And I will call your brother right now."

"I should call Liam. The kids will be tucked in by now." She sighed, glancing at the time on Gracen's microwave. She started to pick up the box of sweatshirts, then stopped. Gracen already had his phone out but he paused in mid-motion when he saw her staring.

"What?"

Silently, she wrapped her arms around him again. This was a hug of gratitude, and one more helping of respite before she had to call her brother. Slowly, Gracen returned the gesture. He patted her back tenderly.

"Thank you," she murmured. "I'm really glad I wasn't alone on the riverfront tonight."

He walked her to the door, then opened her own door so she wouldn't have to juggle the box. She saw him pick up his phone to call Silas. It meant a lot to her that he wanted to help. In most other conversations, Silas could pull her out of an emotional fog, or she could navigate him to clear thinking. When it came to their dad they fed each other's angst and frustration. And this specific conversation would be emotionally charged. Their dad could've died and there would've been too much left unsaid and unsettled. That didn't sit right with Blythe at all. She hoped Liam would be able to think of a good way to handle this. And she really hoped Nick would finally see the light and come back to Sayen Falls. This was where he needed to be. They could build new relationships; they could help him through surgery and recovery. Maybe they could even have something that looked a little like a normal family.

As Blythe pulled up Liam's number on her phone, she thought again of Silas. Maybe she and Liam could figure out how to get their baby brother home too. Once Mindy was done depleting him of all she could.

# Chapter 24

"So I meant to tell you. Liam talked to Nick again this afternoon," Ginnie informed Gracen. She stood in the doorway of his office retying her apron. It was nearly closing time so he was starting to run numbers for the day. Ginnie just worked Friday and Saturday nights now. But this worked out well for Gracen's young staff. They could rotate through weekends off and maintain their social lives.

"Any luck this time?" Gracen replied.

"I told Liam that Nick is going to get suspicious calling so often, but so far the man has said nothing about his heart attack or any surgeries."

"I bet Liam is super happy about that."

"Oh yeah, it's all rainbows and unicorns at our place when we talk about his dad," Ginnie said dryly. "Liam also talked to Luke last week, but he didn't have any updates."

"Maybe Nick needs time to come to grips with his mortality before he talks about what happened. It's only been a couple weeks," Gracen suggested. Ginnie raised her eyebrow.

"Sure, we'll go with that." She pulled on her ponytail to tighten it. "Anyway, business was pretty good tonight. I don't think I've ever seen so many people in the plaza this time of year."

"Yeah, we're doing alright. Numbers are down a little more than I had hoped, but not beyond my projections. I made my calculations on the pessimistic side. I plan on eating a lot of noodles and rice this winter."

"That's dumb. You could eat pizza."

Gracen started to fire a witty comeback but was halted by incoherent shouting in the dining room. Immediately, he jumped to his feet. Ginnie rushed slightly ahead of him to the front counter.

They discovered that Brady Carmichael was the source of the shouting. More accurately, he was shouting at Sawyer and Sawyer was shouting back. Ella had also decided to throw her two cents in. The rest of the crew had scattered like cockroaches. Smart cockroaches.

For the moment, Gracen decided to observe so he could assess the situation. He didn't like the look in Brady's eyes. He didn't look lucid. Recently Lily had let it slip that she worried Brady was dabbling into harder drugs than the weed he routinely smoked to relax.

"I'm glad I'm not the only grown-up here tonight," Gracen sighed to Ginnie. "Can you go see if Finn is still next door? He tends to be a calming influence. This guy is loaded."

Ginnie had also noted Brady's strange demeanor. She nodded silently before disappearing out the back door to get help.

"Where's Lily?" Brady demanded when he saw Gracen.

"We told you," Sawyer said hotly. "She's not working tonight."

"She's not answering her phone. And she's not at home. I just checked," Brady fired back. "And there's nowhere else she could be!"

"Well, she's not here. Maybe she's with her parents," Ella suggested.

Brady's laugh was cold, "Yeah. Right. Or maybe she ran away and joined the circus. You've gotta be lying. You're her best friend so you'd cover for her. You all have reason to lie."

"You're insane," Ella retorted.

"We don't know where Lily is. It's her night off," Gracen said simply.

"You don't start with me. I saw your text messages to her. You want her for yourself and that's why she won't put out."

"Brady, I'm not sure what you think goes on here, but this is a place of business. Nothing else," Gracen replied. His tone remained even; inside he was relieved to hear Lily still hadn't slept with Brady.

"There's more going on here than just business. You're like her hero. And don't get me started on you, Sawyer. I know there's something going on. Ella or no Ella. There's no way you haven't—"

"I haven't what?" Sawyer barked, as his fists doubled. Brady moved towards the open space between the counter and the wall, and Sawyer met him, ready to fight. Gracen put a firm hand on the boy's shoulder.

"Sawyer, go in the back," he directed coolly.

"Gracen, c'mon, you've gotta be kidding."

"I've got work for you back there," he told him. In disgust and frustration, Sawyer punched the wall as he disappeared into the back room. At the same time, Finn and Ginnie came through the front door.

"There is nothing going on between Lily and Sawyer, or Lily and me. I'm her boss, nothing else."

"Brady, I'm sure she's okay and everything is fine," Finn said. His voice was as tranquil as a pond on a summer day. One could almost hear butterflies drifting on his accent.

"Great, Father Finn is here. Everything is fine," Brady mocked, his voice dripping with vitriol. "Sent for backup? Or is he the distraction while Blythe warns Lily that I'm here?"

"I just want to talk. I want to get this figured out," Gracen said, looking at Finn. Ginnie made her way around Brady and back to where Ella was standing. She was stubbornly holding her ground, refusing to be banished to the backroom with Sawyer.

"No, you want Lily to get rid of me. Everyone does. I'm not good enough for the princess," Brady hissed.

"No one is saying that," Gracen said, shaking his head.

"Her parents act like I don't even exist. They look right through me!"

Everyone there knew that Julian and Karen Morgan looked right through their own daughter, so it was no surprise that they also completely disregarded her boyfriend. Lily was pouring herself out to make this boy feel whole, but it wasn't enough. He was throwing whatever he could find into the void in his life—Lily, booze, drugs—but none of it helped.

"All I've tried to do is love her. Is it my fault I don't do it right?"

"I can see that you care a lot," Finn said gently.

"You don't see anything; you're as bad as he is," Brady said icily, staring at Gracen. "You honestly expect me to believe that you're on my side?"

"It's not about sides. This is about everyone being okay tonight," Finn said.

"Everything is fine!" Brady raged. "Or it would be if someone would just tell me where my girlfriend is!"

"Brady, you need to get some help," Ella interjected.

"I don't have a problem! If Lily was with me like she's supposed to be then I wouldn't get myself into trouble," Brady exploded. "I need her!"

"And was she supposed to snort the coke with you the other night too?" Ella cried. Instantly, her hand flew to her mouth as she realized what she had blurted out. Ginnie's head snapped to look at her. Gracen remained impassive. Finn stifled a groan.

"She told you that? Of course, she did. That way she doesn't have to tell you that she's screwing your boyfriend," Brady snarled. "And I wouldn't have done the coke if she had been with me. Don't you get that?"

"What's she supposed to do? Drop out of school, be with you all the time? She has a life."

"And I'm a deadbeat, I get it!"

"No, she's seventeen! Her life is school, work, and friends. There's room for you too, but you take too much. You expect her to give you everything and then some!" Ella had lost complete control over her words and emotions. She was spewing sentences and tears were streaming down her cheeks. She had been so worried for so long about her friend because of this guy, and he was here now saying the most insane things. She couldn't take it anymore.

"Listen, we need to all calm down," Gracen said, raising his voice.

"Just tell me where she is, man. You've gotta know. I know you know. She tells you everything. You have her wrapped around your little finger," Brady said desperately.

"I don't know where Lily is," Gracen repeated, carefully placing his hand on Brady's shoulder. He was hoping to turn him towards the door, perhaps diffuse this bizarre situation, and with any luck get this lunatic out of his store as quickly as possible. None of those hopes came to fruition.

In a split second, Brady batted Gracen's hand away, doubled his fist and socked him square in the jaw. Gracen spun on his heel, just managing to grab the counter before he fell into it. Pain seared through his jaw and set his whole head on fire. Ella screamed. Finn jumped into action to quickly pin Brady's arms behind his back. There was a flurry of activity behind the counter as Sawyer reappeared along with the two college students on staff that night who had been smart enough to stay out of it.

All of a sudden, two police officers rushed through the back door and into the dining area. Blythe followed behind, making sure to stay out of their way.

"How in the world did cops get here so fast?" Sawyer shouted.

"I called the non-emergency number," Blythe explained. "Not the first time I've called the police to let them know someone stupid is doing something stupid here on the river."

She pushed past Sawyer and gasped at the sight of Gracen. He leaned on the counter with his head in his hands, blood pooling beneath his chin. He raised his head at the sound of her voice. Inhaling sharply he could feel that his lip was split, and judging by the look on her face, it wasn't pretty.

The officers escorted Brady outside and sat him down on the bench under the lamppost. Quietly, Ginnie and Finn ushered the staff into the backroom to await further instructions. Only Blythe remained in the front with Gracen.

"Some people need a permit to interact with the rest of humanity," Blythe muttered, reaching to touch Gracen's chin tenderly. Instinctively he withdrew from her touch but it was soft, gentle, so he leaned into it instead.

"I knew he was rolling on something, but he surprised me." Gracen dropped his voice and Blythe leaned in closer. "He said she won't sleep with him. He thinks it's my fault."

"It kinda is. You told her not to."

"Yeah, he thinks I told her not to so I could have her for myself."

"Well, that's bananas."

"He's not exactly winning awards for Most Likely To Be Sane."

While Gracen talked, Blythe took a clean dish towel from the counter where he stored them and filled it with ice cubes for his lip. Pressing it to his face, she cringed when he winced.

One of the officers came inside. "It's a good thing you called, Blythe."

"I don't think I want to press charges," Gracen said. He straightened up and immediately regretted it. With a deep breath, he stuffed the pain into a corner to be dealt with later and focused on the officer in front of him.

"It may not be your call, um, Mr. Hall, right?"

"Right, Gracen Hall. I rent this building. I'm the boss of that guy's girlfriend."

"Yeah, we gathered that from Mr. Carmichael. You see, this isn't the first time we've had to deal with Brady. Usually, his cousins are the instigators. In fact, you're lucky he came alone tonight or you'd have more than a busted lip to deal with," the officer sighed.

"I had no idea," Blythe breathed. "I wonder if Lily knows that."

"Some people are good at hiding their ugly," Gracen said.

"And some people are good at believing illusions," she added.

"I have a feeling it's a little bit of both," Ginnie commented as she joined them. "Will you need to speak to the staff?"

"Yes, I need it all for the record," the officer nodded.

"Two of them are underage. They're high school students," Gracen said.

"Then, I'd like to have parents here if at all possible," the officer replied. "But we need to start with you, Mr. Hall. You are the chief witness. I'll let you get cleaned up first though. He really split your lip. Do you want us to call an ambulance?"

"No, no, that's fine. And go ahead and use my office to talk to everyone. The kids will be more comfortable in there," Gracen said, pointing to the open door. The officer nodded and went in to get himself situated. Meanwhile, Ginnie reported back to the others that they were going to be official witnesses and needed to stick around. Finn made himself useful calling Ella's and Sawyer's parents. Once the staff was settled, Ginnie stepped outside to phone Lily and Finn tried to get ahold of her parents, but had to leave messages on voicemail for each of them.

Gracen was now holding a blood-soaked towel full of melting ice to his lip. He lowered the makeshift ice pack and felt his lip gingerly, wondering if it would need stitches

"Man, that smarts," he winced. "Maybe I should've said yes to the ambulance."

"Let me see," Blythe said, pulling Gracen towards her. He leaned down so she could ever so carefully touch his lip and examine the split. "It'll bleed a bit, but I don't think you'll need stitches. I was dropped on my face once in a rehearsal; my teeth went through my lips. This doesn't look as bad."

"You were dropped on your face?" he asked, trying to not grin and save himself the pain.

"I was a little too fearless for my own good and let a skinny guy practice a lift. It didn't end well for my face," she shrugged. "We can compare scars once you're healed."

"You know, I used to know how to take a hit," he said, as she handed him a clean towel with ice, "but it's been a while."

"You were a brawler?"

"No, my brother is. And I had a way of making people want to hit me."

"That's a story I need to hear," she winked. "Alright, champ, I'll help Ginnie and Finn get things squared away. You go talk to the nice officer."

# Chapter 25

It took about an hour for the officers to get all the details sorted and everyone's perspectives taken down. The staff left one by one as they finished. Gracen took time to chat with both Sawyer's and Ella's parents before they left. Ginnie and Finn were the last to go, wanting to make sure that Gracen was really okay and there was nothing more they could do.

But, truly thanks to them, it was all done. The only thing left was to balance the books and no one but Gracen dared even try. He insisted that they didn't need to do all this and that he wasn't an invalid just because his lip was busted.

"At least let me help at The Yellow Bowl," Gracen said to Blythe when Finn and Ginnie had finally given up the ghost. He turned off the lights in SIP and together they went outside to their front stairwell.

"It's done. Finn and I made short work of it while you were talking to the officer. You were in there awhile."

"He had a lot of questions. I'm not sure if all of it was on the record. I think he knows the Morgans, he seemed particularly concerned about Lily."

"We're all particularly concerned about Lily," Blythe sighed as she headed up the stairs. On the landing, she waved Gracen close to analyze his lip again. "It's stopped bleeding, I think, but it really looks swollen."

"It feels swollen," he said, patting it gently with the back of his hand.

"Come in. I have just the thing," she said with the bright look of someone who had just thought of a good idea. Dutifully, Gracen followed her inside.

"If you have a magical tea for healing split lips I'm officially done with this place."

"No. Not tea. And it won't heal it, but it will make you feel better," she grinned. She rummaged in her freezer for just a moment then pulled out a handful of freezer pops in assorted colors. "Or I'm done with you."

"Popsicles?" he asked dubiously.

"Plastic tubes of frozen sugary happiness more accurately. Which color do you want?"

"Don't you mean flavor?"

"Princeton, I said color and I mean color. Freezer pops are always selected by color. Duh."

"Be nice to me. My face is broken. And give me blue."

"Blue is my favorite, but I will share with you," she said, snapping apart the tubes until blue was free. She selected green for herself and then cut the tops off with her kitchen shears.

While she fiddled around with popsicles, Gracen noticed a stack of tea-stained papers on her counter. Upon further examination, it was a script she had printed off and was hand-writing notes all over. After he read a few lines, he was sure it was her play.

"You started this play in high school?"

"What?" she asked confused. Then she followed his gaze to her messy stash of papers. "Oh. No, actually, I scrapped that play. And just started this one after Becky's party."

"Really? After Becky's party?" Gracen repeated. Their eyes met, they shared the memory for a heartbeat or two. Then Gracen returned to the present. "This is really good."

"That draft is so rough it will give you splinters."

"Okay, it's a rough draft. But just in the few lines I read, I can tell it has a soul. Why'd you scrap the other one?"

"The ending didn't fit. It was too deep for those characters so I started over. Turns out I have more to say now anyway, but I can't quite figure out the structure."

"How do you mean?"

With a sigh, Blythe picked up the papers and shoved them at Gracen. Then she headed towards her living room where she plopped down on the couch, green popsicle between her teeth. Gracen joined her, leaving a respectable distance between them on the couch.

"You might as well read it if you want to. Maybe you can figure it out. I feel like I have the characters, but I don't know what to do with them. I want it to be more than just another love story, something different than just boy meets girl and insert formula here."

"Formulas are boring. You're better than that," Gracen mused. He flipped through more of the pages, scanning and reading. "Uncle Harry would've liked this. He'd say it has a heartbeat."

"A heart and a soul. Could you be any more of a romantic at heart, Gracen Hall?"

"No one has ever called me that before," he laughed.

"You have Shakespeare tattooed on your arm and you just told me that my smattering of scenes and characters whose names keep changing has a soul. I'd call that romantic."

"Alright, fine, maybe I am deep down. Very deep. But you're talented."

She eyed him skeptically. "You took a punch to the head tonight."

"It was my lip, thank you very much, not my head."

"Well, where do you keep your lips if not on your head?"

"You're being difficult, Kate. Why don't you think I know what I'm talking about?"

"It's not you, it's me."

"Not that again, please."

"I didn't mean—I just, I don't know. Never mind. Eat your popsicle," she commanded. Obediently, he stuck the popsicle back into his mouth but closing his lips all the way around it hurt. He grimaced and she immediately felt bad. Reflexively, she put her hand on his shoulder and drew herself nearer to him, "I'm sorry."

"I'm okay. I'll heal."

Their knees were touching now. Gracen resisted the urge to shift away from her. Sometimes he needed space to keep everything in its place where it belonged.

"What's good about my writing?" she asked softly. "I know why writing makes me happy, but I don't have any idea why anyone thinks it's good."

"These characters are talking to each other like real people, but it still feels like poetry to me. Or music. Or something. I haven't had time for a real literary analysis, Kate," he said, again using her nickname, "I just know how I felt reading it. And I can imagine how I would feel hearing it and seeing it performed."

"How would you feel?"

"Proud of you. And connected with something really beautiful." He turned his head to look at her lovely face. Her eyes were shining at him. "Someone really beautiful."

The next thing he knew, her mouth was fused to his and he was kissing her back. The pain in his lip was nothing compared to the network of emotions exploding within his being. All of his carefully organized thoughts and feelings were being recklessly dumped out and kicked over by endorphins having a rave. And he didn't care. He didn't want to be so compartmentalized and closed off. Not with Blythe. He wanted this with Blythe. Kissing and connection and something really beautiful.

When at last he broke from their embrace, he studied her face again but Blythe was completely unreadable to him. Some of the poets believed that love brought clarity, but the adage that love is blind was frustratingly true for Gracen. Blythe looked up into his eyes, blinking slowly, then she touched her fingers to his lips.

"I'm sorry. Are you okay?" she asked.

Gracen was dumbfounded. "Blythe, I don't understand."

"Neither do I, I just know there's no point in pretending anymore. Every day with you has made me question myself."

"You've hidden it well."

"That's what I do, Gracen. My statement holds true, I'm still a mess. But things seem so different with you. Like you don't want to change me or fix me. Like you see me and you're okay with what you see."

"I wish you could see what I do," he said softly, running his finger along the side of her face. "Blythe, I have to warn you. I have no idea what I'm doing. I've never had more than maybe second or third dates with anyone, let alone anything more emotionally. You're not the only one on this sofa who is a mess of a person," he confessed. "If I had known you were in my future, I would've been a better man."

"I don't want you to be anything other than what you are," she assured him, slipping her hand around his cheek again and meeting his eyes. "So is this a thing? Are we a thing now?"

Gracen nodded as he kissed her again. The pain in his lip gave up being heard over the cacophony of other voices in his head. Each voice muffled and faded away as he gazed at her. He had waited for her. He'd never waited for anyone, or much of anything, in his life but he was glad for the waiting. It made what they shared better, richer, deeper. And now that it had started, Gracen did not want it to end badly on his account. Keenly aware that he would be his own worst enemy, he resolved to be different. A word came to him—honor. He would honor her.

# Chapter 26

Honor. Right. Like you even know what that means, let alone how to do it.

The thoughts pushing Gracen down the riverwalk were accusatory and cynical. His own brain didn't think he had the decency to be a real boyfriend to somebody. Boyfriend. The word sounded so juvenile. They were full-fledged adults. There should be another word for grown-ups.

But thinking of teenagers and boyfriends brought his thoughts to Lily. He reached the pylons and stretched his legs against the odd cement pillars. There were several people in the Lily situation that he wanted to strangle. Her parents, Brady, her parents again, Brady again. Alright, so it seemed to be the same three people he repeatedly wanted to bodily harm. What kind of parents are that oblivious to such a train wreck?

Gracen knew exactly what kind of parents. Wiping the beads of sweat from his forehead, he could feel his hair curling with the dampness. He resumed running. If the Morgans weren't going to be interested, then someone needed to be. Maybe he could schedule her more at the store. Shorter hours but more days, something like that. There were minor labor laws to work around, but she needed a place to be, and people who could invest in her.

His flittering thoughts considered for a moment if a similar line of reasoning had prompted Uncle Harry to give Gracen work at Louie & Lucy's. He'd been seventeen, just like Lily. The previous summer Gracen had worked at Wallace's Wonderland, their amusement park. But Roy felt that Gracen wasn't a good fit for the Wallace image. It was always about image. Uncle Harry offered him a job instead. And it turned out that was the best thing that could've happened to Gracen. It gave him the skills and the knowledge to start over, fifteen years later.

This brought him back round to Blythe. He had skills and knowledge suited for running a pizza shop. He had no skills or knowledge for Blythe. Not decent ones anyway. In the interim of those fifteen years, Gracen had learned as much about sex as he had about business. Yet it seemed to him those skills were the last thing he needed right now. Seducing her didn't feel right, even if it would feel good for the moment.

Honor her. What does that even mean? Opening doors, pulling out chairs, ladies before gentlemen? Those were just the signs and signifiers of honor, Cary Grant tips and tricks.

"Hey!"

Her voice caused him to stumble as he crossed through the parking lot. Gracen looked up on the balcony, confused for a minute. Then he remembered, it was Sunday and she opened the shop late on Sundays. Blythe was wearing sweatpants and one of the Summerstead sweatshirts he'd given her. Her hair was in a messy ponytail, but her makeup was done.

"You okay there, Forrest?"

"I'm surprised it's taken you this long to make the *Forrest Gump* joke."

She rolled her eyes. "Shower and get dressed, then come over. I'll make you breakfast."

Breakfast? This felt very domestic and new. Gracen never ate breakfast, beyond a donut and a cup of Earl Grey. He was used to slim pickings since he'd grown up in a fend-for-yourself kind of family. Although he recalled, Aunt Grace used to make him eggs, sunny side up, when he stayed there. He'd always liked that.

After his shower, Gracen opened the medicine cabinet for his deodorant and some sweet-smelling cologne. For the first time in a very long time, Gracen wished he had his old script for his anti-anxiety meds. He'd started taking them when he was about sixteen and cycled through several brands and doses for years. It did curb some of the anxious thoughts, but the side effects were draining. When he turned thirty Gracen weaned himself off, replacing the drugs with running. Anxiety made him feel like running, so he ran and it worked most of the time. Coming off the chemicals was messy at first. He had to run for hours a day to keep his mind occupied. Thoughts of suicide flooded him. He toyed with ocean storms, running into the waves, swimming into the deep, playing with currents and rip tides. Then, as the detox began to even out, Gracen ran along the bay where it was safer and quieter. He learned to categorize his thoughts and feelings into manageable objects that could be shelved and stored and silenced. He didn't have to feel. He didn't have to overthink. He didn't have to deal with any of it if he could just run it into the ground.

Back in the present, Gracen shut the cabinet door. It was probably for the best. No need to go down that rabbit hole. He could manage this. She was just a girl. She was just a person. They were all just people. Surely, he could handle people. He could be a person too. Without the drugs. He wasn't sure he'd been a person on them anyway.

To tame his curls, he combed light gel through his hair. Then, he slid into a pair of dark jeans and pulled on an undershirt and a flannel button-up. When he finished, Gracen left his apartment and stood at the threshold of Blythe's door, knowing it was unlocked, knowing she expected him to just come in. But what should he do when he did? Hug her? Kiss her? On the lips, on the cheek? On her hand?

Oh, good grief, on the hand. You're *not* Cary Grant. Stop thinking. Open the door.

The smell of fried eggs and sausage wafted over to greet him. It smelled just like waking up at Aunt Grace's. He followed the aroma into the kitchen. Blythe had gotten properly dressed, a pair of dark skinny jeans and a soft pink Oxford shirt, over which she wore an apron covered in a cherry print with a sweetheart neckline.

"Perfect timing!" she chirped, plating a couple of eggs next to just-buttered toast and a few sausage links. Blythe motioned for Gracen to sit at her table, and she set the plate in front of him. Before she turned back to the stove she lingered just long enough to give him a soft kiss.

For a minute Gracen's brain paused. His thoughts settled. She knew what to do. Maybe he could just follow her lead for the first few days until his own instincts sorted themselves out.

"So what were you running about?" she asked as she plated her own food. She brought over the teapot already filled with Earl Grey.

"Lily mostly."

Blythe nodded, chewing a bite of perfect dippy eggs slowly. She attempted a drink of her tea, still too hot. She wondered if he had been running about them as well. Well, it was hardly wondering, she was seventy-six percent certain he had been. Not that she could blame him. When she awoke at her regular time, she tried to roll over and sleep until the Sunday alarm went off. But she couldn't. Her mind vacillated between reliving the feel of his kisses and the warmth of his voice or being completely terrified of what a relationship could mean—for her, for him, for them. Relationships are dicey, a complete crapshoot of emotions. A few bad rolls and it could all fall apart. And Blythe seemed to have a knack for bad rolls.

"I figured as much."

"I hope we've seen the last of Brady Carmichael," he said, stabbing the dippy egg with his toast with more aggression than necessary.

"I hope she breaks up with him, but I won't be surprised if she doesn't. First loves are like any other addiction. It keeps a hold on you," Blythe sighed. She took a sip of tea, cool enough now but it needed more sugar. She remedied her tea as she said thoughtfully, "I think I'll ask Lily if she wants to come in on Monday to work for me a little bit. In October we weed through books that have been sitting for a long time, mark things down, and start to prep for holiday sales."

"This is why I'm glad I don't do retail."

"Right, because food service is always so easy and happy. I do both, remember?"

"You're an overachiever."

"My grandfather is an overachiever. I'm the poor sap that inherited it."

"You love it."

"I do," Blythe admitted. "It's a far cry from the life I imagined for myself, once upon a time, but I can't really picture anything else now."

Her hand rested on the table. He wanted to reach out and hold it, but he didn't dare. Gracen cleared his throat with a swallow of tea. "So when do we break the news?"

"I think we just let them figure it out on their own. They've all been such a nosy bunch of know-it-alls. They'll think they were right."

161

"Weren't they?"

"No," Blythe laughed. "They have no idea how stupendously difficult it was getting here. Wherever and whatever here is."

"Here," Gracen said, finally covering her hand with his, "is whatever we want it to be."

He had no idea where that line came from, but it sounded good. Blythe's eyes relaxed. Gracen hadn't noticed how worried they had looked, but now they smiled. He took her hand fully into his to pull her closer, then pressed his lips to hers.

"Thank you for breakfast," he said.

"Don't get too used to it," she teased.

* * *

Lily parked her car in the lowest level of the parking garage, then practically tiptoed across the cobbled plaza to The Yellow Bowl. Blythe had asked her to come, but it was a Monday and they were closed so Lily felt silly. She knew Blythe was only offering her the work so she wouldn't have to go home. However, she didn't feel silly enough to decline. She hesitated outside the door, then knocked because she assumed it would be locked.

A few seconds later Finn appeared from the storage room, sleeves rolled up, a pen in his teeth. He was grinning as he opened the door.

"Sorry, I should've left it unlocked for you, force of habit."

"It's okay."

"Blythe just got a call from Kyle Farriss—do you know Kyle?"

"He's the community developer for the riverfront, right?"

"Yeah, that's him. He just decided to get as many of the owners together as he can right now to talk about the winter season."

"Shouldn't that meeting have been planned ahead of time?"

"One would think, but this is the riverfront," Finn shrugged. "Anyway, I think I'll have you do the basic restocking while I start to sort through books to remove. You have no idea how much this helps, especially since Blythe just left for that meeting."

The work was simple so Finn didn't have to explain very much to Lily, mostly just where to find things. And they worked easily enough together. After twenty minutes or so, when Lily had found her rhythm, Finn decided to ask the obvious question.

"So why give up your Monday afternoon to stock The Yellow Bowl?"

Smothering a sigh, Lily answered honestly, "Better than being at home."

"Believe it or not, that I understand. I used to help my granddad clean the church—even if it didn't need it—so I wouldn't have to go home."

"Your grandfather was a preacher?"

"My father and grandfather and great-grandfather, many times back. There's been a McCartney in the pulpit for generations."

162

"Is that why you want to be a preacher?"

"That's why I didn't want to be a preacher," Finn clarified. "But it's really more of a calling. I couldn't resist it in the end."

"A calling?"

"Are you a skeptic?"

"Not officially," Lily shrugged. "I've never been to church much. Here and there to youth group with a friend or something. My parents don't go."

"Did your parents have much to say about Brady?"

"No. They argued with each other about it, but no one said much to me. I gathered they think he's an idiot and a grease ball."

"And you?" Finn asked gently. "How are you holding up? Am I right in assuming not very well since, you know, you're here on your day off?"

"You would be right," Lily sighed, her shoulders slumped. She leaned over the counter, scooping coffee beans into plastic canisters, and she looked like a crumpled piece of forgotten paper. "I broke up with him. I told him as much as I love him, I can't enable him. I know Ella blurted out the thing about the cocaine."

"Yeah, that's a bit of a big deal."

"I know. He told me it was my fault."

"He sounds a lot like Ian O'Hare."

"Well, that's just great," Lily said with a sarcastic laugh. "I guess I already knew that. I convinced myself he was more like Mr. Elwood going through a dark patch."

"So Ginnie told you about 'the lost years'. I'm not sure that was the moral of that story."

"I wanted it to be. I'm an idiot."

"You're not an idiot."

"Yes, I am. Because I miss him." Lily groaned, "Ugh, I feel stupid even saying that. Forget I said it."

"I don't think that's stupid. I think it's natural. He's been an important part of your life."

"Everyone keeps saying he's such a loser and I'm better without him. I guess that's true, but it's just not that easy for me to turn the page."

"Of course it isn't, you care about Brady in a way no one else does. And it shows you have a good heart." Finn wanted so much to be reassuring.

"I think it makes me an idiot."

"Enough of that. You'd be an idiot if you held on, but you did the hard thing. You let him go and you set a boundary for yourself. I daresay, you're setting a standard for yourself and that will serve you well in the long run."

"I guess you're right. I don't think I'll fall in love so fast the next time. I'll try to use my brain more and trust my gut when something isn't right."

"See? Not the words of an idiot." Finn added, "I actually think all of this needed to happen. I'm pretty sure I've accidentally been praying for it."

163

"You've been praying for Brady to punch Gracen in the mouth?"

"Not specifically. I've been praying for a catalyst, for something to come along and propel all of us forward. The fact is, I've been feeling like everyone, everything is stagnant here on the river. And we needed something to jar us loose."

"Us? How did Brady going off the deep end propel everyone forward?" Lily questioned. "It seems to me it only propelled him into a three-day rehab program."

"We're all connected. Just look at the evidence. Brady goes mad as a box of frogs so you realize you deserve better. Gracen steps up to protect his staff and your honor, for that matter. Your parents get a wake-up call."

"They hit the snooze button," Lily scoffed.

"That may be, but it's just one domino in a chain reaction. God's not done with them."

Lily eyed Finn carefully, not sure if he was really onto something or really nuts. He set a couple of dusty history books on top of his pile as he continued.

"And just look at Blythe and Gracen. They finally got together over a couple of popsicles to nurse a split lip. And now they're happy. Together. That means that somewhere on this globe, wherever he is, Jesse is forced to consider his actions."

"All the way out in Timbuktu."

"Or wherever he is," Finn nodded. "So you see, we're all connected."

"What about you?" Lily asked. "You have everyone else sized up, what about you?"

"Me? I was forced to make a decision. I've been putting off applying for jobs after seminary, not sure if I should try to stay local, or go somewhere else. Even back to Ireland. But I know now my work here isn't done. I'm supposed to stay."

"You just know that now? Is it because you look out for Blythe?"

"That's part of it," Finn admitted, "but it's more than that. I can't explain it. And I know I sound crazy."

"Not crazy, not exactly. Maybe a little too optimistic, given that all hell recently broke loose." She covered her mouth, "Can I say that?"

Finn laughed. "You can say whatever you want. I suppose I am optimistic, that's my nature. But I also believe in hope. I believe it'll all be worked out, and we'll see goodness in the land of the living. To quote one of my favorite verses."

"You don't do that very often," Lily said, furrowing her eyebrows. "Quote scripture. Or get all preachy or anything."

"And I hope that you don't think I've been preachy today. I guess I just got on a roll."

"No, not at all. This is just classic Finn."

"Classic Finn? Is that like Father Finn?"

"I know you hate that, but that's probably what they mean. You have a way of seeing things differently. That's why everyone comes to you for advice," Lily said. Suddenly she wondered if she'd been set up and if there even was a meeting with Kyle Farriss at all.

"I guess I'm more of a bartender than a preacher these days. Which makes sense since God really chased me down while I was working at a pub in Dublin," Finn recollected. Then he shrugged, "I guess I found my place behind a coffee counter instead of a pulpit."

"Coffee shop preacher," Lily said. "I think they could make a cheesy movie about that."

"Great, something to look forward to," Finn said with an eye-roll.

"For the record, I like your version of things better than anyone else's," Lily confessed. "At least in your version all of this pain has a purpose."

"Pain always has a purpose, Lily. Remember that. I know it seems like all I do is talk, but some things I know from experience."

Lily wasn't the only member of the walking wounded in the riverfront. The cast of characters were all pockmarked with pain, some inflicted upon them, and some self-inflicted. Finn was no exception.

"Looks like I'm not the only quiet one," Lily said. Finn smiled.

"You're definitely not. The Elwoods have the unfortunate circumstance of having their personal lives dragged out in the street for open debate."

"I guess that's why the other brother doesn't come home more."

"Silas? Yeah, that's one reason," Finn nodded. "We can drop it after this and just go back to working quietly if you like, or we can talk about books or movies or you can fill me in on gossip like Ella," Finn offered, "but for what it's worth, you're not alone. Blythe gets destructive relationships and bad parenting, too. If you ever want to talk, or just want a place to be—"

"I know. I can come here. I mean, I'm here now, right? And it sounds really lame out loud, but I sorta feel like I have family here."

"That's not lame. I feel that way. I think Gracen does too. We're all outsiders and orphans of a sort. And the Elwoods have taken us in. It's what they do."

The silver bell on the front door jingled as Blythe stuck her key in the door and shoved it open. "That thing is starting to stick. We'll have to grease it again."

Gracen followed her into the shop and greeted Lily and Finn. His lip was still a bit swollen and the split in it had an ugly scab.

"Oh, my gosh, I am so sorry," Lily gasped when she saw him.

"I forgot that you hadn't actually seen the damage," Gracen said, patting his lip. "It's okay. It'll be all healed soon enough."

"It's really not okay," Lily argued, feeling like a prize idiot again. It was her fault any of this had happened. So much for seeing those silver linings.

165

"Hey, better me than you. If he had laid so much as a finger on you, I'd probably be in jail," Gracen grunted.

"It's over now. I promise. I broke up with him and we're done. He needs more help than I can give him."

"Lily, let me tell you something I learned the hard way," Blythe said. "You can't save anyone. And you can't expect anyone to save you. You need to know yourself and be good with yourself before you can really love anyone else. But when you get that figured out, and you find someone who doesn't expect more than you can give, that's the sweet spot."

# Chapter 27

October's crisp blue skies were soon crowded out by gray November days. Colder temperatures meant even fewer customers at the shops along the river. Summerstead Isle Pizza still thrived, predominantly carry-out orders, but a sale was a sale in Gracen's book. Blythe benefitted some from his continued busyness. People would come over to The Yellow Bowl, browse the books or pick up a piping hot drink to go while they waited for their order to be ready. It wasn't much, but every sale counts in the lean months.

To save his wife's sanity, Liam picked up a pizza once a week. He left the day up to Ginnie, and typically it depended on when Teddy's tantrums peaked. On this particular week, it was a Tuesday, and the tantrum count was approaching double digits.

"It'll be a couple more minutes," Gracen said as he checked the pizza with his long-handled fork. "I know Teddy likes the crust crunchier than most of my customers."

"Spoiled little dictator," Liam grumbled with a smirk. "I need to talk to Blythe anyway."

"She's in my office."

"You keep her on hand now?"

"Those thirty-seven seconds it takes to walk next door really add up," Gracen shrugged. "Her printer is out of ink, she's using mine to catch up on paperwork."

"Right. Paperwork. That's what the kids are calling it these days."

"Oh, ease up, would you?" Blythe grinned as she appeared from the office. "I thought I recognized the distinctive sound of you giving Gracen a hard time."

She took a couple of boxes from the shelf to help Gracen box the order when it was done. Crossing behind him she grabbed the black marker they used to label the orders and jotted a message on each box for Viola.

"There are some sight words for my goddaughter," Blythe said as she capped the marker. "Now what is it you wanted with me?"

"I got a call from Dad today."

"Our dad?" Blythe asked, her eyebrow arched.

"No, Daddy Warbucks."

"That's like the inverse of our dad."

"He says he's coming for Thanksgiving."

Listening closely, mostly for nuances than for literal words, Gracen removed the pizza from the oven, sliced it, and boxed it for Liam. There was an odd expression on Blythe's face like several feelings were elbowing each other out of the way for distinction.

"And still no mention of his heart attack."

"Nope. Not one. Maybe he's going to bring it up in person."

"Have you told Silas that Dad is coming here?" Blythe asked. Liam shook his head. "Well, I'll call him. I doubt he'll change his plans since he always has Thanksgiving with Mom, but I'll let him know."

"I know I wouldn't bother changing plans. There's an eighty-three percent chance that this will be a disaster."

"Is that an exact figure?" Gracen interjected as he handed the boxes over to Liam.

"I have a formula for figuring it out," Liam replied.

"So do I," Blythe snorted. "It's easy. A major holiday plus our dad minus whatever he's hiding divided by pi."

"Clever," Gracen said. When she looked at him, her body language shifted. Her shoulders relaxed, her hands unclenched. As she rested her hand on his arm, her Claddagh ring shimmered over his tattoo.

"Let me know how it goes with Silas," Liam said heavily.

"He may not even care. He has other more pressing issues."

"Yeah, have you gotten to the bottom of the Mindy saga?"

Blythe shook her head, "Not yet."

"I didn't think Silas kept things from you," Liam frowned.

"Mindy changed all that. She drove a wedge between us, between Silas and a lot of people and things he loved. And now, even though the wedge is gone—"

"I thought you said 'wench' for a second there," Gracen grinned.

"If the shoe fits, she should wear it," Blythe scoffed. "Anyway, she's gone but he's not back. If that makes any sense at all."

"Yeah, it's like you and Ian all over again," Liam grunted.

"I'm sorry, but there's a rule in this establishment, you say that name and a quarter goes in the tip jar," Gracen told Liam, completely deadpan.

"It's like a swear jar," Blythe nodded gravely, "and that's a dirty word. So is the name Brady."

"Fresh out of quarters," Liam said rolling his eyes. "But on that note, I should go. I'm sure my kid is starving and taking it out on his mother."

"Have fun with that," Blythe called as her brother left for home.

As Gracen looped his arms around her, Blythe sank into his embrace and breathed in the safe, familiar scent of him—one part sweet-smelling cologne and two parts pizza.

"You are coming to Thanksgiving dinner with my family, right? We haven't really talked about holidays or anything," she asked him.

It went without saying that Gracen had yet to share a holiday with a girl and her family. However, this was different. This was his home, too, and these had become his people.

"There's nowhere else I'd rather be. Insufferable fathers and all."

"Easy for you to say, you haven't met him."

"I won't be there for him. I'm there for you."

Blythe turned her face towards his and kissed his lips. It was so wonderful to be able to reach out and kiss him whenever she wanted.

"That's worth more than you know," Blythe said. "Hey, be available tonight after I talk to my brother, okay? I doubt Silas will freak out or anything, but lately, it's like I have to decompress my own self after talking to him. He's so brooding."

"He's in pain. And everyone wants him to talk about it."

"Yeah, I hate myself every time I ask, and yet I can't help it."

"At least he knows you care."

★ ★ ★

Silas knelt on the floor by his bed, looking for the battery that had popped out of his phone when it crashed full-force into the wall. Ordinarily he'd be using his cell phone as a flashlight but obviously, that wasn't an option so he was groping in the darkness. At last his fingers grasped the plastic-encased battery pack. It was a minor miracle that his screen hadn't shattered. The phone powered on after he shoved the battery in place; a few moments later the apps on his homepage appeared.

His fingers itched to delete the texts. They weren't for him anyway. Mindy meant to send them to Scott. His best friend and the guy she'd been sleeping with for the last year. The guy she moved in with after leaving Silas. The guy who had stood up next to Silas on his wedding day. Everyone said he should've asked Liam to be his best man. Guess he should've listened.

His lawyer had told him not to delete anything, not a single thing from Mindy. He was instructed to take screenshots and email them to his lawyer so they could be safely stored away from his phone, in case his phone was destroyed or damaged. You know, like by Silas throwing it against a wall as hard as he could.

So, Silas dutifully took screenshots of the texts, willfully choosing to not throw up all over his phone. He didn't have any rice to deal with the moisture issue. Then he fired the pictures off to his lawyer with a quick note about whether or not they were relevant. When he was sure they'd sent he promptly deleted all of the evidence from his phone.

Still, he couldn't delete it from his mind. Over and over again he remembered what Mindy had said. He wandered aimlessly through his apartment. Why did she have to text Scott the news? They lived together. Couldn't it have waited until he got home? Why did the text have to accidentally go to him? Scott, Silas, a simple slip of the thumb, and his world crashed.

He opened the fridge, retrieved a beer. It was just one drink. Not like before, when they were first married and they both drank all the time. Not like when she lost the baby and he drank alone all the time. No, she wouldn't get to do that to him again. It was just one drink. Or two. Just a few. It wouldn't get out of hand.

Then somehow, Silas was seven beers in and hardly feeling it when his phone rang. Blythe, of course. It was like she had a sixth sense for damage.

"Hey, you busy?" She sounded preoccupied. Silas glanced at his litter of empty bottles.

"Nope, not busy. What's up?"

"I wondered if you were coming for Thanksgiving."

"I haven't been in Sayen Falls for Thanksgiving since I was thirteen."

"I'm aware, I just wanted to check if you were interested."

"Why?" Silas asked, finishing his current bottle. "What's up for real?"

"Dad is coming."

Silas snorted back a laugh. Maybe it was his dad with the uncanny timing. There's no time for Silas to have a personal crisis. Nick's going to roll into town and inevitably bring drama with him. Well, Sayen Falls wasn't Silas's town on purpose. He could stay here in Michigan, above the fray.

"And you want me to come and do … what?"

"Be there with us. I want to spend Thanksgiving with you because you're my brother."

"Spare me the schmaltz; I don't have the stomach for it right now."

"Okay, I want you to be a buffer. You're the snarky one. You keep it light, break the tension, all that good stuff. I just get emotional and Liam gets wound up."

"You need me to come tell jokes?"

"Basically, yes."

"Well, I just checked and I'll be running out of snark just before the holiday. Sorry."

"Silas, please," Blythe whined, "I really want you there. Gracen will want you there."

"Seriously, you're playing the Gracen card?"

"Is it working?"

"No."

"Well, what are you gonna do if you don't come to Sayen Falls? Go to Mom's? How will that be any better? All Mom does is talk about you and Mindy. And plus you have to deal with Sean's kids. Liam's kids are much better," Blythe reminded him. Their stepbrother Sean had four very unruly children that drove Silas to his wit's end.

"Thanks for that. Maybe I'll stay here and write music."

There was a pause before Blythe scoffed, "Really?"

"Okay, so I don't write anymore."

"You don't even play anymore."

"Well, you don't write anymore either."

"Actually I do, remember?"

"Yeah, I remember you trying to make your high school thought process work for you now. That was when you were ignoring Gracen. More of that high school thought process, I suppose."

"I started a new play. And Gracen has been helping me figure it out. So there," Blythe said childishly. This phone call had taken a weird turn.

"That better be all he's doing. I mean, I know you're dating and all—"

"That's all," Blythe assured him. "He's been a total gentleman. He sorta reminds me of Linus Huxley sometimes. And I did not see that coming."

"Linus, the English gentleman," Silas muttered. Years ago, Linus had been like a big brother to Silas. That was when Blythe and Linus were in college and it looked like they would end up together. But that romance never materialized and she had five years of Ian chaos instead. Still, Silas had always liked Linus. He even did a reading at Silas and Mindy's wedding.

"Do you ever talk to him anymore?" Blythe asked.

"Random email every now and then."

"Maybe you should reach out. You guys were close before he went back to England."

"And met Sophie. And married Sophie. And divorced Sophie."

"I think Sophie divorced him, technically."

"Something we have in common," Silas said, feeling sick again as he replayed Mindy's messages. He imagined her spending Thanksgiving with Scott, oh so happy together.

Maybe it was time to just go home. Not just for Thanksgiving but for life. There was nothing for him in Michigan. No job, no wife, no friends. His mom was here, but she'd be okay without him. She had her other family. There was no real reason to stay, just stubbornness.

Silas said, "What if I came home?"

"That's why I called, I want you to come home."

"No, I mean, home home, not just for Thanksgiving."

"What just happened? Two minutes ago you were adamant you wouldn't come at all. Now you want to move back? What'd I miss?"

"A lot," he surveyed the beer bottles. "But I need more than seven beers to tell you."

"Seven beers? Silas—"

"It's seven, not seventeen, chill out. I'm not even buzzed."

"That's what concerns me."

"We're not all featherweights like you, Miss Three Mixed Drinks and Gracen Has To Walk Me Home."

"Silas, be serious. You want to come home?"

"I might. I don't know yet," his voice cracked, revealing the despair he felt deep inside. He'd lacquered over it with wisecracks and sarcasm for so long that it had taken a significant tectonic plate shift to bring real emotion to the top.

"I've wanted you to come home ever since you left thirteen years ago. If you want, you can come tonight, well, tomorrow since you're seven beers in. Crash on my couch. We can set up an apartment on the river, or make room at Grammy and PapPap's, whatever you want. We want you here."

"I told you I didn't have the stomach for schmaltz."

"I know you want to honor your vows—"

"It's different now," Silas said shortly. "Look, I just need to think. You can tell Gracen, but no one else. I can't be badgered. I'll text you or something."

"Just show up, Si."

"Don't be surprised if I do."

# Chapter 28

The clock on his dash read five-forty-seven a.m. According to Silas's math—which was admittedly fuzzy—he'd roll into Sayen Falls just before six-thirty. He was making good time; the highways were empty at night and there was no construction to slow him down. After calling Scott to settle the matter—definitely the hardest conversation Silas ever had in his life—he threw all of his stuff into clothes baskets and boxes and suitcases and anything else he could find. Most of it was jammed loose into the back of his Ford Explorer. His guitar and concert posters were in the back seat, and his box of vintage records was in the front seat. Nothing else mattered. There was nothing else of value. She'd taken all of it when she moved out. Silas had believed that if he could be generous then she'd be kind, or maybe even want him back. It was clear now that he had just been doped up on fairytales and love songs.

As he left Michigan, southeast bound for Sayen Falls, he had no doubts about leaving. Yet as he approached the Falls, inky night giving way to dawn by slow degrees, the doubts he had about returning loomed large. This wasn't really his home. Hadn't he been saying that for years? So why was he coming now? Just in time for Dad drama. It was stupid. Still, it did seem less stupid than staying in Michigan. It's true that texts and phone calls and social media have no geographical boundaries, but it felt better just breathing totally different air from Mindy. This air was his and his alone. He'd never shared it with her. She'd never wanted to see where he came from. And Sayen Falls was where he came from, even if it wasn't really home.

Six twenty-three; the sun splintered just over the horizon. Silas flipped on his turn signal and exited the highway. Just over the bridge, and then he signaled again to turn into the private lot behind the shops. He couldn't exactly roll into Grammy and PapPap's unannounced. At least Blythe was sort of expecting him. He groaned to himself just thinking of how he'd explain his sudden appearance. Maybe he could laugh it off, chalk it up to impulsive artistic moodiness. He wouldn't actually have to tell them what the last straw had been, what had finally broken his back. That could stay between himself, Mindy, and his lawyer. The divorce would be final soon. Once it was behind him, maybe he could manufacture a version that wasn't humiliating.

A tall slim figure in athletic pants and a lightweight hoodie jogged in his direction. Silas slowed to a stop and rolled down his window. Gracen halted dead in his tracks, at first shocked, then he chuckled and shook his head.

"I don't think she was expecting you overnight delivery."

"I had to get out of Dodge."

"I know the feeling."

"Is Blythe in the shop?"

"No, she's been opening later. The parking garage is closed for repairs so even regular customers aren't coming. At least not in the morning, so she's sleeping in."

"I don't really want to wake her up—"

"My door is unlocked. Crash there. I'll let her know you're here when I finish my run."

"Thanks."

"You're welcome to stay with me as long as you need. I'm probably the least invasive person in Sayen Falls."

"That is probably true. I'm going to talk to Becky about renting out the apartment above the donut shop. It shouldn't be too bad. Jesse lived there before he took off to parts unknown."

"Good plan."

"I had the last five hours to try to think of one."

"I had almost ten, and I can tell you, once I got here, those plans mattered very little."

"I don't plan on falling in love, Romeo. Or is it Henry the Fifth?"

Gracen reddened slightly. "I didn't realize people knew about that."

"This is Sayen Falls, the land where everyone knows everything."

Silas rolled up his window before continuing into the lot where he parked beside the Shelby. Grabbing a backpack with a change of clothes, his toothbrush, and his cell phone charger, he headed up the back stairs and into Gracen's apartment. It was odd turning to the left instead of the right at the top of the stairs. But he wasn't going to wake up Blythe and face her emotional hugs and welcomes with no sleep and an empty stomach. Food first—toast and jelly, good enough—and then sleep. He sank onto the leather couch, pushed his shoes off, and fell into a restless sleep. Exhaustion rarely makes sleep easy, no matter how badly it's wanted or needed. And Silas was exhausted deep down in his soul.

For the next week, he slept on Gracen's couch. He spent most of his time helping in The Yellow Bowl or SIP however he could and fixing up Becky's vacant apartment. Most of his energy was consumed trying to appear nonchalant about his arrival. It helped that all the Elwoods seemed willing to go along with his façade for the time being. Ginnie, true to form, asked the most questions but she was so sincere and earnest about it that Silas could hardly be annoyed.

On move-in day Gracen rounded up his high school staff to help move furniture and boxes into Silas's apartment. They used Blythe's Jeep and Silas's Explorer to gather pieces from all over Sayen Falls. Mae Houser gave him a complete bedroom suite she no longer needed and Sam Buterbaugh donated a set of living room tables to the cause. Becky gave him the couch from the den because no one really used it anymore and he preferred his easy chair. Of course, Miles and Mary Alice instructed Blythe to raid the attic for whatever plates, cups, silverware, and other odds and ends she could find.

Blythe, Lily, and Ella unpacked all the housewares into freshly scrubbed cabinets as the boys lumbered up the stairs with pieces of furniture.

Sawyer backed into the apartment with one end of the couch. It was a narrow space so to get the whole thing in the door he had no choice but to be backed into the wall.

"I'm getting paid overtime for this, right?" Sawyer grunted as he unpinned himself from between the wall and the couch.

"You're not getting paid at all," Gracen said, heaving his end of the couch into the room. "You're just a nice guy."

"Oh, is that it?"

"That's debatable," Ella flirted and Sawyer raised his eyebrows with a wolfish grin.

"Do you mind? Some of us are working here," Finn teased as he lugged a nightstand into the room. Silas and Liam entered a few moments later with a headboard.

"At least you didn't have to help Mindy move," Silas said. "We had an overstuffed couch, a king-sized bed, and two armoires that she took."

"Arm-whats? Armoires? See, here in Sayen Falls, we speak like men," Liam said.

"You speak like an idiot," Blythe said passing by with a stack of collapsed boxes. She handed them to Gracen so he could throw them in the dumpster for recycling.

"Come on, help me with the dresser," Gracen said to Sawyer. "If you ladies are done, there's some lighter things, drawers and the bed frame, stuff like that."

"But it's cold," Ella whined. Lily rolled her eyes as she picked up both their coats and thrust one at Ella.

"I'm the little rich girl, but which one of us is spoiled?"

Gracen laughed; he was proud of Lily's sass. He'd been encouraging her to speak up more. Lately, she came to the riverfront just to talk with Gracen, Blythe, and Finn.

Silas grinned at Lily's comment. "Need some ice for that burn, Ella?"

Ella stuck her tongue out at him. "I can throw your stuff in the river."

"As long as it's not my records, I probably wouldn't miss it."

As Blythe pulled on her coat she said, "I thought we could get some frames for the albums and we could hang them up with your posters."

"Um, that's one option, but I bought them for listening, not decorating."

"People actually do that?" Liam smirked.

"Cool people do," Silas shrugged. "So I guess that's why you don't

175

know about it."

"Ouch, need some ice for that burn?" Ella said. Liam glowered at her. "I mean, Mr. Elwood, would you like the first aid kit?"

"Mr. Elwood, you make these poor kids call you that?" Silas laughed.

"I'm their teacher."

"Not here."

"And technically, I've never had you for a teacher," Lily pointed out.

"But, the million-dollar question is, will you be in his musical this year?" Ella asked. This time it was Lily who glowered at Ella.

"Jury's still out on that one," Gracen answered on her behalf. Lily threw him a grateful look as the group clambered down the stairs.

The musical was something else they'd been discussing lately. Lily just didn't see the point in getting so far out of her comfort zone when no one—meaning, her parents—would be there to see it. Gracen tried to encourage her without pushing too hard. But, someone had to reassure her. She had to know she mattered somewhere.

Outside in the brisk cold, Silas opened his car door and lifted the crate of records. He handed them to Lily.

"Can you handle this?"

"You're trusting me?"

"You can handle it," he grinned. "Put them on the kitchen counter."

"Um, Silas, aren't you missing a record player for those?" Ella asked as she surveyed his pile of, well, junk, in the back of the SUV.

"Don't ask," he muttered. Mindy had taken the record player simply for spite.

"Alright, less talking, more working, come on," Liam said, clapping his hands. He told Ella and Sawyer to bring up the dresser drawers. Liam and Finn took the top of the dining table, Silas and Gracen took the heavy pedestal base. Blythe carried up a chair.

"You know, these riverfront apartments are charming but a total pain in the tush to move into," Blythe said as she made three more trips for chairs.

"What happened to Jesse's furniture?" Liam asked.

"He sold it. He needed the cash before he became a big shot," Blythe explained.

As Liam and Silas worked on getting the table together, Gracen flipped through the record collection. He paused to show Blythe a few of interest.

"You have some really good music here. I mean, really good. How did you ever get some of these?"

"I have good connections. Well, I did. Mindy managed to ruin that too," Silas sighed.

"Well, when you get a record player, let me know. I'd love to hear some of these albums, especially The Beatles. I've heard the remastered digital recordings really aren't the same."

"No, it doesn't compare at all."

"Aww, my boys have a playdate all set up," Blythe laughed, putting an arm around both Silas and Gracen. Silas shrugged her off.

"And this is why I wanted to move into my own space," Silas said. "Gracen's apartment is still too close to you."

"Whatever. You love me," Blythe said as she squeezed him tight.

"Just point her towards Gracen when she starts to get schmoopy," Liam teased as he stood up from the table. It leaned slightly.

"Nice work," she said dryly.

"Just don't put anything that rolls on that side."

"Thanks for the tip," Silas replied.

The group worked a little longer arranging the furniture just right. As the dinner hour approached, Ella and Sawyer had to get home to their families. A text from Ginnie "just asking" when he'd be back was a signal for Liam to leave as well.

"And then there were the misfits," Gracen remarked to Lily after the others left.

"Should that be my audition piece?" she retorted with a grin.

"I'm sure no one has ever used a song from the Rudolph Christmas special before," Blythe remarked. "It would be memorable."

"Anyone else starving? If you're not all sick of it, I can make pizza," Gracen offered.

"Never sick of your pizza," Blythe said kissing him sweetly. Lily made a face at Finn which made Silas chuckle. He pushed them toward the door.

"Alright, get the smoochies out of here," Silas said. "We'll meet you in twenty."

"Come on, Kate," Gracen said as he helped her slip into her coat.

"They're sweet," Lily said when they were gone. "I love it when he calls her 'Kate'."

"You're the only one on the SIP staff who gets it," Finn said.

"That's probably true. But I was raised on Shakespeare."

"Because your father is English?" Silas asked.

"Because my parents are snobs," she explained. "Not that I think anyone who enjoys Shakespeare is a snob. But for them, the arts are only about being accomplished. Or cultural. Or something."

"They're missing the point," Silas said blandly. "They should watch *Dead Poets Society*."

"Anyway, enough about me," Lily said. "What are your plans? What are you thinking?"

"I really wasn't thinking when I came here. I'm in debt up to my eyeballs, losing my job and going through a divorce really wiped me clean," he said heavily, dragging his fingers through his dark hair. His eyes clouded over with worry.

"When is the divorce final?" Finn asked. The first question he'd posed in two weeks.

"Soon, I'll probably have to go up for a court hearing or something."

"If you want me to drive you up there, just say the word," Finn offered.

He reasoned that he could afford the gas more than Silas, and there was no need for Silas to face Mindy alone. He had very few details regarding the divorce, but he rightly assumed that Mindy wouldn't be alone.

"I'll let you know," Silas said gratefully, "but in the meantime, I need a job. There's not much use for a stage manager in Sayen Falls."

"You should work for Gracen," Lily suggested.

"Not my sister?"

"Your sister doesn't need you," she shrugged. "She has Finn to be her right-hand man."

"And Gracen needs a right-hand man?"

"Don't we all?"

Silas raised his eyebrows. He'd hardly noticed Lily on his previous visit. She hid in shadows of the limelight Ella relished. Of course, Blythe had told him about the issues with Brady and Lily because that was big news. It seemed that something had been jarred loose in Lily since then. She wasn't loud or showy, that wasn't her way, but something about her commanded his attention when she spoke.

"And you worry so much about your employer?"

"It's not like that. Ella's the one in love with him, he's so dreamy," Lily blanched. "He's what I think having a brother might be like. Gracen's the only person who's ever stuck their neck out for me. I guess it made an impression."

"I heard about that," Silas said. "So as his sister you're looking out for him?"

"Doesn't Blythe try to look out for you?"

"She does try," Silas agreed.

"You don't let her," Finn pointed out.

"I'm not used to all this Elwood affection. It's been years since I was breathing it in full-time."

"You'll get used to it," Finn said.

"Thanksgiving oughta be fun—my first family Thanksgiving in years and Dad is coming."

"Will there really be that much drama?" Lily asked. "My parents keep an extra tight lid on their issues whenever we're with family, so holidays are actually a bit of respite."

"It's hard to say with Dad. I don't think he intends to cause drama. It's more about, well, it's the wounds that he'll crack open while he's here. And we've all got 'em, every last one of us."

# Chapter 29

The Elwood Thanksgiving was coming together like a Norman Rockwell painting. Despite Mary Alice's difficulty getting around the kitchen she still managed to get out a picture-perfect meal with Ginnie and Blythe as sous chefs. Ginnie whipped up mashed potatoes while Blythe made spiced cranberry sauce entirely from scratch. The turkey glistened as it browned and baked in the oven.

There were thirteen folks to gather around the table. Earlier in the week, Ginnie helped Viola and Teddy make place cards for all the guests. The kids were so excited that Grandpa Dennis and Grandma Linda, *and* Grandpa Nick were all coming. Ginnie was less excited; she knew that her parents and her father-in-law could make the day difficult.

The house wasn't very large so it felt like everyone was sitting on top of each other while they waited. All the people made Silas a little itchy-crawly. With the main floor packed, the only refuge was upstairs in the bedrooms.

"I'm going upstairs for a minute," he mumbled to Gracen. "I can't even hear myself think with that football game on and everyone talking."

"Hey, Silas?" Blythe called from the kitchen.

"No you aren't," Gracen smirked. Silas shot him a look. Blythe came out of the kitchen and found her brother with one foot on the staircase.

"We need more ice. Do you mind running down to the gas station?"

"More ice?" he repeated.

"Yeah, that cold stuff that water turns into when it's put in the freezer?"

"Thanks. Yeah, sure, I'll go get a couple bags," Silas said, relieved to be able to escape for ten minutes.

After Blythe returned to the kitchen, Gracen pleaded, "Take me with you. It's very people-y in here."

"Hey, Gracen?" Blythe called out again.

Silas grinned, "Sorry, sucker. Sounds like the little woman needs you."

"Phrases like 'the little woman' might be why you're divorced," Gracen joked.

"Ha, if only it had been that," Silas snorted. He grabbed his coat off the overloaded hall tree and fished his keys out of his pocket. "I'll be back in ten. Twenty if I decide to sit in the car for a while and ponder my life choices."

"I need you back in five," Gracen told him as he obediently headed into the kitchen.

"Do you mind helping the kids set the table?" Blythe asked him. "Usually we put Finn in charge of that because he's like the Teddy Whisperer, but he's with Reverend Smith and his wife Anna today."

"I'm supposed to be a replacement for Father Finn?" he replied dubiously.

"They're children. Not demons. And yes. They adore you," Blythe retorted. "Besides, this isn't *Downton Abbey* so we're good with a regular place setting, Princeton."

"Forks on the left, right?" he winked.

"Viola will tell you where to find everything," Blythe advised him.

"I would expect nothing less from Vi."

He went back into the living room to collect the kids. As Gracen entered, Becky looked away from the television screen as the referee threw a flag and he sighed.

"These games are getting to be too long. Why do they have to review everything to death? In my day, football was football."

"We know, Pop, in your day, men were men, and dames were dames," Dennis teased his father.

Becky raised an eyebrow, "I have never called a woman a 'dame' in my life, thank you very much."

"Dinner about ready there, Gracen?" Miles asked.

"I think so," Gracen said, clapping his hands together. "I've been instructed to help Viola and Teddy set the table."

"It's a family tradition that the youngest members set the table," Miles explained, "but when they're this little, they need some help."

"We've had some pretty creative place settings over the years," Becky laughed. "Blythe and Ginnie never could get those boys to follow directions and do it right."

"It was more fun to do it wrong and watch them be mad," Liam confessed.

"You better make sure the kiddos get it right," Nick told Gracen, "or Blythe will be mad."

"Not with Gracen," Liam corrected. "She'd *never* be mad at Gracen."

As Gracen rolled his eyes, Viola jumped to her feet and took his hand. Teddy immediately followed, never wanting to be too far behind any adventure or left out of an important job.

With a wry smile, Nick remarked, "That just hasn't been tested yet, son. We're still getting to know Gracen. He might not prove to be any more adept at handling her than the last one."

"Handling me?" Blythe asked. She had come into the dining room with a stack of plates. The dining room and living room bled into each other, almost in an open floor plan. As such, standing in the dining room, she could hear every word spoken in the living room.

"Oh relax, Blythe," Nick scoffed. "I'm just pointing out that we still don't know much about this young man that you're so googly-eyed over."

In his periphery, Gracen saw Blythe wilt. It was a subtle change; her bright eyes cooled, her expressive face stiffened, her graceful shoulders slumped. It was a careless remark, but it hit its mark. And then some.

Liam's tone was caustic as he commented, "Well, that's rich coming from you."

"That's an odd thing to say," Linda smiled, sensing drama.

"Yes, I'd like an explanation," Nick informed his oldest child.

"Dad, seriously?" Liam demanded. "Alright, fine. You had a heart attack in October and a cardiologist wants to put a little box in your chest. That's all. Clearly no big deal."

There was a flash of panic on Nick's face. Then it turned to cool, collected anger. "I'll have to thank Luke for violating HIPAA. So much for privacy laws."

"That's all you have to say?" Liam replied. This was ridiculous.

"Nick, you had a heart attack and didn't tell your kids? Really, man? I know you like your space and all, but that's a little extreme," Dennis shook his head.

At this exact moment, Silas returned with ice. He stepped into the kitchen and immediately heard raised voices in the living room. When he looked at Ginnie, she shrugged sadly. Mary Alice was white as a ghost. Everyone else was in the living room. And that was where Silas directed his footsteps, despite the deep desire to return to his car.

"He didn't tell his parents either," Miles grumbled. "And neither did my grandkids who obviously knew. Right, William? All three of you knew?"

All eyes momentarily rested on Silas as he entered the room, then attention shifted to Liam. He opened his mouth to answer his grandfather, but Silas cut him off.

"Now wait a minute, I'm sorry, PapPap, but you can't make this Liam's fault. He thought, we all thought, it was the right thing to do to save you and Grammy any worry."

"You were part of these discussions?" Nick asked skeptically. "You're around about as much as I am. What difference does it make to you?"

"Dad," Blythe gasped. It was an awful thing to say and an awful thing to hear. She hated what was happening and how paralyzed she felt.

Silas's voice was frigid. "Yes, it's totally the same. A thirteen-year-old moving with his mom and a forty-year-old walking out on his family. Definitely the same."

"Hey, I didn't walk out," Nick protested.

"It was more like running," Silas spat.

"Wait a second, there are things you kids don't know," Becky piped up.

"Nick, you never told them why you left?" Dennis exclaimed, "It's been over a decade!"

"I'm so confused," Blythe mumbled as she rubbed her brow. As she lowered her hand, Gracen took it into his. Viola still stood by his side and Teddy was nearby, looking very overwhelmed.

"Listen, Denny, they're my kids and I don't want to get into it," Nick hissed. "And you don't have a lot of room to judge me. You missed plenty and you were right here."

"So typical. Someone calls you out and you turn it around on them," Linda clucked. "You haven't changed a bit."

Dennis was self-important and Linda was insufferable; how sweet, kind, wonderful Ginnie ever came from their union was a permanent mystery. Listening to the Beckwiths throw in their opinions reminded Blythe why she didn't really miss the huge gathering of the clans. It was better when only a handful of faithful friends came to celebrate together.

Nick threw up his hands, "I don't know what anyone wants from me. I came home to have a nice Thanksgiving with my family and spoil the grandkids a little. But I feel like I'm the piñata at a party."

"What we want is for you to be forthcoming," Liam stated.

"We want you to come home," Blythe said softly.

"Blythe, if you have something to say," her father sighed with annoyance, "speak up."

"She said we want you to come home," Silas informed him bluntly.

"What on earth for?" Nick asked. A mocking grin flickered on his lips.

"To be with family? Or, more practically, so we can help you recover from surgery?" Liam suggested.

"Just give up my life and come back," Nick said flatly.

His mother's tender voice from the kitchen doorway disrupted the building argument.

"You said you would come back, Nicky," Mary Alice reminded him. "It was never supposed to be this long."

He sighed again, but annoyance had given way to something more like resignation. "I thought I'd have to come back but I've done well for myself in Vegas."

"And this surgery business? How's that gonna work out?" Miles asked.

"It's not a big deal," Nick lied.

With careful control of his temper, Liam argued, "I've done my homework, Dad. It is a big deal. The total recovery time is twelve weeks. You can't lift anything for like six weeks. It's insane to hire nurses or go to a rehab place when you could come home and actually be part of the family."

"Just leave everything and come home," Nick said again.

"You left us to go there, why not try it in reverse?" Silas pointed out.

"You kids have a lot of nerve, you know that?" Nick said. "I know I haven't been 'father of the year', but I don't see your blessed saint of a mother here any more than I am. She's the one who ran off to Michigan to marry that man, and she dragged Silas with her. Blythe is just lucky she got to stay here. If it weren't for me, she would've had to go, too."

"What?" Blythe asked. This was a new crumb of information about those tumultuous days.

Her grandparents glanced at each other, and Miles's eyes darkened.

"Nicholas, enough," he snapped. "Don't drag all that up. You just said you didn't want to get into it."

But it was too late. Every human has a saturation point, and Liam had been too strong and too silent for too long.

"You're right. Mom isn't perfect. Okay? Is that what you want me to say?" Liam exploded as a dam of emotions burst. "That it was complete garbage she got remarried like five minutes after the divorce was final? That she spends more time with Doug's kid and grandkids than she does us? That we get the scraps from everyone except Grammy and PapPap? It's been a mess for as long as I can remember. That's why I'm trying so hard to be a good father and brother and whatever else I need to be. I won't add insult to injury. I'm not going to be like you."

"Liam," Mary Alice said gently, "don't say anything you can't take back, sweetheart."

Liam spun on his heel to look at his grandmother. She expected to see coldness in his eyes to match the icy tone of his voice. But he looked like a little boy, like Teddy when all the fun runs out.

"Grammy, I know this is hard for you and for your sake, I'll let it go," Liam sighed. "But I do have one more thing to say. Dad, you are this far away from losing us completely. We can play nice in the sandbox to keep the peace but that will be it. I have to protect my family."

"Mommy," Teddy cried out as Ginnie finally entered the room. She had been carefully waiting for the right moment. Her little boy ran to her, clearly agitated by all the anger spewing from so many people that he adored.

"Dinner is ready," Ginnie said simply. Her voice was calm and kind. She wasn't feigning enthusiasm or dripping with perkiness. She was just Ginnie; it was what the moment needed.

"Really, Ginnie, after all that?" Dennis asked incredulously.

"It's Thanksgiving, Dad," she said, scanning the room to look at everyone. "Mary Alice worked hard to make this day something to remember, for all of us. Blythe and I did too. Even Teddy and Viola worked hard on the place cards for all of us. They used up a whole booklet of stickers, for heaven's sake. So, we're going to be adults here. We're going to sit down at this table where we'll give thanks for what we have and share a meal together," she firmly concluded.

And all of a sudden, Liam was chuckling lightly. He walked over to his wife and gave her a simple kiss. "This is why I need you."

"I know," she replied. And then she looked meaningfully at Gracen who was still holding Blythe's hand, with Viola at his hip. "It's good to be needed."

# Chapter 30

The remainder of the meal was uneventful. The conversation was light, mostly directed by Ginnie. Without question, she was the MVP of the day. And she appeared to do it all so effortlessly.

Blythe knew that Ginnie was actually working hard to steady the ship. They were lifelong friends and sisters-in-law so she knew well enough that Ginnie really wanted to tell her parents off or put Nick in his place. But, she sure made things look so smooth and easy. Blythe envied her. It was taking all her willpower to put bites of food in her mouth and make simple conversation. A bubble of tears hovered at the bottom of her throat for the remainder of the day. She was sure as soon as she got away from this ridiculous hoard of people the bubble would burst.

Dennis and Linda left first. Then Silas took his leave; he'd had his fill of family to last for several days, maybe weeks. Next, Ginnie and Liam bundled up the kids and strapped them into the van to head for home. Gracen felt that he and Blythe should leave as well, but he was waiting for her to initiate their departure. The trouble was that Blythe was becoming more and more catatonic as the day went on.

She could feel herself slipping away and she lectured herself harshly. All of this was to be expected of her father. It was just an unkind remark about her; it was just an unfeeling joke about Gracen. It was just his harsh tone. It was just his denial he needed them. It was just the deflection to their mother. It was just the refusal to come home. It was just the usual. And maybe that was the problem. More of the same and it was mind-numbing, so Blythe had finally just gone numb.

At last, Gracen stopped waiting and simply announced they were leaving. Let the remaining parties—Miles, Mary Alice, Nick, and Becky—conclude what they wanted. There was a round of goodbyes, handshakes, and hugs. Blythe merely went through the motions. Saying goodbye to Nick was wretched; she felt nothing except deep, deep down she wanted desperately for him to recant it all and say he'd come back. Of course, he did not.

Silently she and Gracen walked out to the car. After he started the engine, he allowed himself a moment to study her. She was so lost inside herself. Without a word, he backed out of the driveway then started for home. He knew that the silence filling his '67 Shelby was not about him. The woman he knew and adored was hurting, and not for the first time, at the words and actions of her father.

When they arrived at the plaza, he exited first then came around to open her door. Mechanically, she slipped out. Her thoughts had taken her deeper and farther away.

"Do you want to talk about it?" he asked gently.

"No."

"Alright."

"Alright?"

"Alright."

Experience taught Gracen that silence was better than trite sayings and admonitions to not cry. He simply held Blythe and waited for her to show him what to do next. As she slipped her arms around him to hold on tight, he made sure he held on even tighter. Because experience also taught him that when the world is falling apart, even if it has a thousand times before, all you really want is someone to help hold onto the pieces.

Refusing to succumb to the cries at the base of her throat, Blythe just clutched Gracen as tight as she could and waited for the tornado inside her to settle. She knew it would. It always did. Every time a little bit faster than the time before, and having him near helped keep her grounded. She wasn't going to get swept up inside the cyclone this time.

"I don't know why it still bothers me."

"Because he's still your father and you deserve better."

"We won't see him again for months. Everyone leaves me for the easier things. I know I'm difficult but I just want to be worth staying for."

"Hey, hey," Gracen whispered, cupping Blythe's face in his hand and turning her to meet his eyes. "You're not difficult."

"Yes, I am. I keep telling you, I'm a mess. My family is a mess."

"Am I supposed to be relieved I'm not the only one that comes from chaos? I'm not. It breaks my heart to see you this way."

"I just want to feel like I matter. And I know that's stupid because there are people who care, I know that. But I still feel so insignificant. Like if I slipped away the world would just keep spinning on its axis and no one would notice."

"The world might keep spinning on its axis but mine would come to a crashing halt," Gracen told her. "How is it that you've only been in my little corner of the world for a short time and yet you make up so much of it?"

Stroking his cheek with her hand, Blythe smiled at him sadly. "It hasn't been long enough for you to get tired of me."

As badly as Gracen wanted to tell her that wouldn't happen, how could he know for sure? He had no idea how much time was left on the meter. Maybe he would get tired of her. Maybe she would need too much from him. Or maybe would stop wanting him. There was so much Blythe still didn't know about him. Most relationships aren't built to last. Was there a real reason to believe theirs would be different?

"I hope that never happens," he said at last. He took her hand and kissed her fingertips.

"Me too," she whispered as tears slipped from her eyes.

The kids knew that something had gone wrong tonight. Daddy was mad and Mommy was sad, but not because of each other. There had been so much yelling. Then, Aunt Blythe had been quiet and weird. It was all very strange, but Viola had learned to expect this kind of thing from the grown-ups when Grandpa Nick came around.

Teddy asked if he could sleep with Viola, and she said it was okay with her. Liam volunteered to do bedtime. He very much needed some quiet time with the loves of his life. Ginnie eavesdropped from the hall while he pulled the quilt up snug around the kids to tuck them safely into Viola's bed. Teddy popped his bottle out of his mouth to ask for a song. Ginnie knew exactly which song he wanted. It was the special song Liam had sung to him since he was born.

When Teddy was in the NICU they couldn't hold him very often and it was agony for them both, especially when Teddy would cry. Liam had started singing to him through the glass around his small bassinet, and Paul Simon's "St. Judy's Comet" soon became a favorite.

Liam looked at his kids, so trusting of his love, so adoring of his person, and his throat choked with emotion. There was absolutely nothing in the world that would induce him to hurt his children the way he'd been hurt. Swallowing hard, he took their hands into his and began to sing Teddy's favorite song.

Tears slipped down Ginnie's cheeks as Liam's strong tenor voice cut through the darkness and into the hallway. Her heart was heavy with sorrow for her husband. Most of the time Liam dismissed the issues with his parents and they caused him little pain. But since the children had been born, the wounds cut deeper. Particularly after they almost lost Teddy. His mother, Carrie, made slightly more of an effort than Nick, but it still wasn't much. Ginnie often felt bad that her parents lived close and treated the kids to special weekend outings when they weren't busy. They wanted to do more but still worked full-time so they were limited. Still, it was the desire that mattered. Liam understood that Nick and Carrie maintained lives separate from each other and away from Sayen Falls. He didn't understand why they didn't desire more, even if they couldn't achieve it.

Long after the children slipped into peaceful sleep, assuming the faces of angels before his very eyes, Liam remained on the bed just watching them. When Ginnie had been pregnant with Viola people told him there was nothing like parenthood. It was a love like no other kind of love. Liam had doubted that could be true. Then, when Viola was placed into his arms for the first time it felt as if he was being baptized into a new dimension of love. Life was richer with Viola. Every experience meant more and he wanted to shout his love for his daughter from the rooftops. She gave his life new depth, new meaning, new purpose.

Then, when Ginnie was pregnant with Teddy everyone told him that his heart would expand so he'd have enough love for both. Liam worried that wouldn't be the case. He feared he would favor Viola because she was the first-born, or he'd favor Teddy because he was a son. But when Teddy was delivered by emergency c-section, green with meconium poisoning and the room remained soundless without his cry, Liam felt his chest explode. Fear, grief, and love held him in their clutches as the room spun around him. Day by day he sat by Teddy's bassinet, singing whatever he could think of to bring his son peace and so he would know that Daddy was there. It seemed impossible that the rambunctious little boy now affectionately nicknamed Teddy the Terror was that same fragile newborn he had prayed over for so many days and nights.

In the present moment, when at last Liam crawled into bed beside his wife, he slipped his arms around her to pull her tight. Burying his head in her hair, he breathed in deep and felt peace spread through him.

"I know I don't always love you the way you need me to," he murmured, "but you do know that I love you right?"

"It's never easy for two to become one," Ginnie said, rolling to face her husband.

"Obviously my parents never figured it out."

"We are not your parents. You are not your father."

"I'm not so sure sometimes," Liam exhaled. Memories of his father yelling at him the way Liam yelled at Teddy for just being a kid, then darker recollections of drunken phone calls to Blythe and to Ginnie from 'the lost years'. Nick had never been a drinker; his cruelty came without intoxication. There were moments when he feared he was a carbon copy of his father. Scar the people he loved with words that couldn't be taken back, and then cut and run when the siren call of another life lured him away.

"You are not Nick. You have a few things in common, I'll give you that. But we all turn out more like our parents than we want to. That's why I quit my job, you know. I didn't want to put my students ahead of our own children like my parents put their work ahead of me."

"At least your parents made up for it in other ways."

"By smothering me, yeah, it was great," Ginnie said, rolling her eyes. "You know, your parents aren't wholly bad. That's your problem, you and your siblings. You see the world like a fairy tale, good guys and bad guys. We're all just people, even Nick and Carrie. Your parents did some really great things with you guys before the divorce. And even after the divorce, there have been good times. It just doesn't look like the storybook that's in your head."

"I don't want our kids to ever lie awake and have a conversation like this one," Liam said firmly. "No matter what, I'm in this for the long haul. You're stuck with me for life, no do-overs, no mulligans," he promised, lacing their fingers together and kissing her in the dark.

"For better or for worse, like Miles and Mary Alice, and Pearl and Becky," Ginnie nodded.

"Til death do us part," Liam whispered, nestling his head on the pillow by his wife. Her slender fingers stroked his hair with tenderness until he fell asleep.

* * *

"Nicholas, I don't understand why you always do this," Miles said with a weary sigh. "Every time you come home, you sabotage whatever chance you have to make things right."

"They weren't supposed to know about my heart attack," Nick mumbled.

"How could you keep that from us?" Mary Alice asked.

The dishes had all been cleaned, the leftovers tucked into the fridge, and the kitchen had returned to normal. They were sitting at the round kitchen table, talking hard and honest with their boy as they had done so many times before.

"I didn't want any of you to worry, first of all," Nick shrugged. "And I don't know. It's like when I'm there, it's easier to keep the kids at a distance."

"Nicholas, they want more from you and they deserve it. They always have," Miles said.

"I know, I know. I'd like to be the father they always should've had, but I don't know how. I never did, and now? They're adults."

"That doesn't mean a thing," Mary Alice said gently. "It's not too late. Very clearly, they want to have another go at being a family with you here."

"Mom, the fact is, sometimes I think about coming back to Sayen Falls. But I don't know if there's room for all of us here," Nick confessed. "Especially now that Silas is back. He came here to start over, and obviously, I'm not a big source of help for him."

"Son, we've been praying for you to come home ever since you left," Miles told him.

"We can help you with the kids," Mary Alice added.

"You've done more than your fair share already, Mom."

"A mother's work is never done."

"I guess Carrie and I missed those parenting classes. We signed up for Lamaze instead."

"It's a load of hooey," Miles scoffed. "Breathing and huffing."

"You said that then," Nick laughed. "Carrie was so mad."

"She brought my grandbabies into the world with that hooey," Mary Alice chided her husband, "and she did a good job raising them."

"Until she left," Nick said darkly. "I drove her away."

"She made her choices, and you made yours," Mary Alice said. "The only reason to look back is so you do better moving forward."

Nick sighed, "I look back on it a lot, but it doesn't seem to push me forward at all."

"You know what we think," Miles said. "And the kids have said their piece. It's up to you, Nicholas. If you want to come home, then come home. If you want to make it work, then make it work. And if you want to stay out there, there's nothing the rest of us can do."

# Chapter 31

The fortunate aspect of drama on Thanksgiving was that Black Friday followed immediately, and Blythe could focus on The Yellow Bowl. Every shop in the plaza had sales of one kind or another to lure customers, so the work was steady. Not like a festival, but enough to be a distraction.

Then, on Saturday night Nick left for Las Vegas. To their surprise and his credit, he sought out each of his children before he departed. Liam was at home with his family, so Nick got to spend a good hour with his grandkids. He found Silas working at SIP, but Gracen made Silas take a lunch break to chat with his dad. Of course, Blythe was at The Yellow Bowl, where Nick ordered a mug of chai and bought a book for his flight. There was an air of sincerity about Nick that hadn't been there before. Blythe was grateful for that, and they all appreciated his efforts. But no more was spoken about his health, and there was no indication that Nick would be reaching out for their help.

On Monday morning, Gracen knew that Blythe was running errands before they decorated the shop with Finn and Silas. As such, he expected The Yellow Bowl to be dark and quiet, so it came as quite a surprise to hear the distinctive sounds of banjos and fiddles seeping through the floor and their shared wall. Knee deep in curiosity, he got up from his couch where he'd been reading and headed down the stairs. He found The Yellow Bowl closed but lit up. Finn was sitting at a table with a teapot and a laptop, and his phone was plugged into the sound system. Gracen gave a good rap on the door to get his attention. The sound startled Finn. His head snapped up, then he smiled sheepishly.

"Sorry about the music," he said as he unlocked the door for Gracen.

"I don't mind. I was just a little confused," Gracen replied. As he spoke, the song ended and in the quiet, he heard the bells on the backdoor jingle. In a few moments, the next song started and then Silas appeared. He was there to start prepping for Christmas.

"I listen to Irish folk music when I'm dealing with writer's block," Finn explained, "and that's also why I'm here and not my apartment or the church. There's a little more inspiration just lingering in the air here."

"Writer's block? Must be going around," Silas commented. "I still can't write anything. Blythe said she's stalled out too."

"It's the season," Finn shrugged.

"Shouldn't Christmas drip with inspiration?" Gracen asked. "Particularly for sermons?"

"One would think, but you try coming up with something that's not been said before," Finn said flatly. "At least I don't have to do Christmas Eve this year. Talk about pressure."

"You hit it out of the park last year," Silas told him.

190

"Yeah, I did so well that your sister ran out crying."

"Okay, it wasn't quite that dramatic. And besides, that had nothing to do with you. It was Dad and Ian and all that garbage. This year should be better for her with Princeton here."

"She's the only one who calls me that," Gracen informed him. Then he asked, "She ran out crying last year?"

"Christmas is usually a time when she's flooded with memories," Finn explained, "and not all of them are good and even the good ones are bittersweet. It sorta came to a breaking point last year, but she really seemed to turn a corner after that."

"And then you rolled in," Silas added. "So now you're all caught up."

"Thanks for the backstory," Gracen bantered.

Finn sighed, "Well, Blythe isn't the reason I have writer's block anyway. Eddie asked me to preach the first week of Advent, which of course is this week, and I'm at a loss."

"Hence the banjos and fiddles and whatever else that is," Gracen said.

"It's a concertina," Finn informed him, "and it's my youngest brother playing it. It's like a tiny accordion. You've seen them, I'm sure."

"Your brother is a musician?" Gracen said with surprise.

"Both of my brothers are. This is their band," Finn told him. "All of us were taught how to play at least one instrument. My mom's parents are your stereotypical good Irish country folk and very musical."

"So then, *you* play?" Gracen questioned.

"Very little. Drums mostly. But I can do a little banjo or guitar if absolutely necessary."

"You really are a jack of all trades, master of none type, aren't you?"

"I think 'renaissance man' sounds better," Finn grinned. "Hey, that reminds me, it was a good thing I was here this morning. A package came for you and they left it with me."

"They left it with you again?" Gracen asked, recalling the movie posters.

"I might've suggested that I take it. I was very intrigued," Finn shrugged. He disappeared into Blythe's office for a minute and came out dragging an enormous box.

"Aunt Grace strikes again," Gracen whispered as he glanced at the shipping label. He stood the package on end and it came up past his waist.

"It's not going to open itself," Silas prompted.

Gracen gave him a look as he tore the box open. He dug through a mess of packing peanuts before feeling the top of a guitar case. Closing his eyes and shaking his head, he gripped the case to pull it out of the box. Bits of styrofoam littered the ground as they fell away from the case.

"She finally figured out how to ship it. And her timing is impeccable," he noted, given their current topic of conversation.

"You play the guitar?" Finn asked dumbly. "So I'm not the only one with hidden talents."

"I'm a nominal player at best. Aunt Grace and Uncle Harry wanted me to be musical. Ten years of piano and half as much guitar."

"Should we be on standby for the piano to arrive? We'll need more help getting it up the stairs," Silas joked.

"Dare I ask what kind of guitar that is?" Finn asked. "After seeing the Shelby, and those vintage posters, my money is on a Gibson."

Gracen clicked open the case, and gingerly removed the guitar. "It's an acoustic Martin, mahogany wood."

Silas's eyes bulged as he drank in the sight of the beautiful guitar. He'd sold his good Gibson to pay his lawyer. His remaining guitar was cheap, with a hollow, tinny sound. The Martin before his eyes was like an oasis in the desert. "Are you serious? A Martin?"

Gracen strummed the strings and winced. He held the guitar out to Silas, "Needs tuning."

"You … you want me to tune your guitar?"

"I want you to keep it for me," Gracen decided. "It's unlikely that I'll play it much, and someone should. It's too beautiful of an instrument to sit silently when it could be played."

"But … this is a Martin. And you just want me to take it?"

"Think of it like boarding a horse. I couldn't keep a horse here, that'd be ridiculous. I would stable it somewhere. I want you to stable my guitar."

"You don't have a horse, do you?" Finn asked. "I'm not signing for any horses."

"No, no horse," Gracen grinned. "Besides, I left this guitar behind in Summerstead, clearly not a prized possession."

Silas still looked spooked, but he couldn't tear his eyes away from the rich wood and shiny frets. There was a slight chance he was going to start drooling.

"Liam drove the Shelby," Finn smirked, and promptly Silas took hold of the Martin.

"I can't figure you out, Hall. I don't know if you really don't care or if you're just acting too cool for school or if this is your way of ingratiating yourself to us."

"Yes. All of the above," Gracen replied.

The fact was, the guitar had been bought with college graduation money from Roy. He was supposed to invest the money, but Gracen had deliberately bought the most expensive guitar he could find to spite him. It had never been about music or craftsmanship. Now, the guitar reminded him of his grandfather and of his own stubbornness. But for Silas, it was a thing of beauty. As soon as he saw Silas's face, Gracen knew he should get it into his hands. It might help cure his writer's block, just as the music of his people was helping Finn find the inspiration for his sermon.

"Seriously, take it for a while," Gracen said earnestly. "It won't do me any more good here than it was doing in Summerstead. But you need a better instrument to mess around with than that beginners' special."

"Thank you," Silas said humbly.

Just then, the next song on Finn's playlist began with a guitarist doing some intricate picking and plucking of the strings. Then, a mandolin and a banjo joined in.

"That was my brother Carrick on the guitar, and Aiden on the banjo," he commented. "This is one of my favorite pieces. Aiden wrote it. He said he was inspired by his dog."

"His dog?" Gracen laughed.

"Inspiration is a tricky thing," Silas replied. "Must be one heck of a dog though."

"Well, you definitely won't get any writing done with us distracting you," Gracen said, remembering why Finn had this music blasting in the first place. "I'll help Silas get boxes out and let you work until Blythe gets here."

"Actually, I had a thought just before you both turned up and I wanted to run it past someone before I bothered hammering out a whole outline," Finn said.

"I know almost nothing about sermons and church," Gracen confessed. "We were a Christmas and Easter only family."

"That's alright. I don't need an expert on exegesis and expository teaching," Finn replied. "The theme for the first week of Advent is hope."

Gracen snorted back a laugh, "I don't know much about that either."

"Yeah, coming to the two of us for feedback on hope is like going to a deaf man for feedback on a song," Silas pointed out.

"I don't care about your qualifications, guys. I just need to hear it out loud," Finn said with exasperation. "The first candle symbolizes the prophets and the hope of the Messiah they foretold. So, I was thinking about Elizabeth and Zechariah. You know, how they'd given up the hope of having a child. Zechariah was so shocked that he didn't really believe the angel and then he lost his ability to speak until the baby was born. And that made me think about how much we lose when we don't hold onto our hope. When our hope is anemic we become so cynical and unbelieving that we start doubting the very words of God. We could end up with faith that misses miracles."

"Anemic hope," Gracen pondered, "I like that phrase."

"It's a good name for an emo band," Silas agreed. He added, "I think using Elizabeth and Zechariah in the first week of Advent makes sense. I mean, their kid was kind of a big deal too."

"Who was their kid?" Gracen asked, working hard to recall the smattering of sermons he'd sat through. "Oh, wait a sec, the Baptist guy, right?"

"John the Baptist," Finn grinned. "He was 'the voice in the wilderness'; the one who prepared the way for Jesus to begin his ministry," he elaborated, then he snapped his fingers. "And if John had been born years before when Elizabeth and Zechariah first wanted a kid, he wouldn't have been a peer of Jesus. I mean, he would've missed his calling. God's timing was perfect. It's not that he didn't hear their prayers, it's that he had a better plan."

"I think if you take all this and iron it out smooth, you've got yourself a sermon," Silas nodded. "It sounds good to me."

"I agree," Gracen shrugged. "I might even come and hear the rest of it. I want to see where you go with this anemic hope idea."

"No pressure there," Finn remarked as he tapped some notes into his computer.

"I promise not to run out crying," Gracen joked.

"Hey, I did not *run* out *crying*," Blythe said as she marched down the hall. The celtgrass music had completely muffled the sound of the bells on the door when she entered the building, so she took them by surprise.

"I'm just repeating what he said," Gracen said, pointing at Finn like a little kid.

"I defended you," Silas was quick to mention.

"They're quoting me out of context," Finn said defensively.

She laughed at his expense, "It's okay. Last year was a rough one."

"And this year?" Finn asked tentatively.

"My dad tanked Thanksgiving; he's not getting Christmas too. I think I've done rather well this year at making different mental choices and living here in the present moment," Blythe said proudly. "I refuse to go down in December."

It was a strong statement. And it was clear that she wasn't quite up to it yet. There was residual weariness in her eyes from the disappointment with Nick. After all, only three days had passed.

Finn snapped his laptop shut and stood to unplug his phone. Before he did, though, he gave Blythe a hug. "I'm proud of you, woman."

"Thank you, Finn," she smiled as she squeezed him back.

Their moment reminded Gracen how new he still was to Sayen Falls. As much as Blythe cared for him, their shared history was so short. The length and depth of what she shared with Finn was sometimes intimidating. At least, he wasn't Jesse. There was a lifetime of relationship there to compete with.

"Any chance your brothers' band has a Christmas album?" she asked as Finn picked up his phone. "I'm kinda partial to the fiddles and banjos."

"They put out a single last year, but that's it," Finn said.

"Well, leave it on anyway. We have the rest of the month to listen to Bing Crosby and Mannheim Steamroller," she shrugged.

Then she clapped her hands and started firing off the directions. Clearly, the woman had come with a plan to get Christmas on display in a hurry. Before long, Silas was complaining about the ridiculous amount of Christmas décor his sister had amassed and she was telling him to stuff it.

"I think I pulled something," Silas said rubbing his neck.

Blythe slapped the back of his neck, "There you go, all fixed."

"This is why I actually work for him now," he pointed at Gracen. "He's not abusive."

"Aw, poor baby," Blythe said. She thrust an armful of garland at him, "Go hang this."

In spite of his sister's bossiness, Silas soon found himself fairly enjoying the work. He had some fresh ideas for how to hang and display the lights and garland. His theater background gave him a bag of tricks to work with. Like his sister, it'd been a while since creative juices had room to flow. The Yellow Bowl and Christmas decorations seemed like unlikely inspiration and yet Silas was having fun. The shop took on a rustic nostalgic feel as garland bedecked every bookcase and trimmed every door and window frame. He hung the lights three times before they looked just right in the window. He'd almost forgotten what a perfectionist he could be.

Ordinarily, Blythe looked forward to getting lost in private memories as she took beloved decorations from the worn boxes to display proudly on the shop's pale yellow shelves. However, right now she didn't feel much like getting lost in memories, so it helped that Gracen was doing the digging. She was standing on the counter, and they chatted back and forth as he handed her things and she gave him back others. It was nice that she wasn't incessantly climbing up and down, up and down like she usually did. Gracen cut her workload in half, and, just by being there, he cut her mind's workload in half as well.

They were nearly finished when Silas took a good look at the shelves and noticed what Blythe was setting on display: their mother's Santa Clauses, the ones their father had given her year after year. Each one was unique, some round and rosy, others stern or austere; most wore red but the collection was spotted with Saint Nicks in other types of garb. Carrie had loved her Santas. Nick had loved buying them for her. And the children had loved getting them out of the boxes and helping their mom find places for them all. Then, Carrie and Nick divorced and the Santa Clauses disappeared.

"Those Santas are still around? I thought they were yard sale fodder years ago."

Standing high on the counter Blythe turned abruptly, and Gracen instinctively reached out his hands to steady her.

"So did I. Grammy saved them. She saved a lot of things no one else wanted. You know how sentimental she is. I found them in the attic. I

195

couldn't believe it when I found them," Blythe said. She had knelt alone in the dim attic for almost an hour, taking out each Santa, remembering and grieving. "I couldn't bear to leave them there once I knew they still existed, so I brought them here."

"They look good here, they belong here."

"I never told Mom, I figured it didn't matter. It's not like she's going to see the shop."

"I think she'd like to know," Silas replied. The shop had remained neutral territory through all the ugly. It was a refuge for all of them, the grandchildren, Carrie, and Nick.

Silas pulled a wrapped parcel from the box and carefully removed the tissue paper. It was a Victorian Saint Nick; tall and thin, he had a long wiry beard to match his rather pointed hat, and his colors were muted shades of red and cream. And it was snapped in half.

"It was broken when I found it," Blythe said, looking down at her brother.

"It could be glued. Didn't you pick this one out for Mom?"

"I did. But I didn't see the point in fixing it," she answered. In fact, Blythe had figured it was quite fitting that the one she'd chosen all those years ago was broken. Pasting it back together wouldn't fix much.

"Do you mind if I have it then? I always liked this one. He's different from the others."

"Go ahead." She looked away from Silas and the broken Saint Nick to Gracen who had been taking this all in very attentively. "These were our mother's, Dad gave most of them to her."

"I figured they had meaning, but I didn't want to pry."

Gracen handed her a Santa teapot which she set on top of a milk-glass cake stand in the center of the top shelf. Of course, a set of Santa mugs followed, displayed beneath the cake stand. The final piece was a vintage set of three Santas in various gymnastic positions.

"Recognize these?" Blythe asked Silas as she arranged them just right.

"Those were Pearl's."

"Becky said I should have them here with the other Santas, I always loved them."

"I think Pearl would like that."

She turned on the counter and gestured to her work, "What do you think?"

"It's very festive," Silas said approvingly, "but not too ... red."

"It suits you," Gracen remarked. "This is you, I think."

"I'm a collection of Santa Clauses?"

"Each one has a story. You see meaning in things." He considered carefully, "You find hope in all sorts of places, even a box of forgotten Santa Clauses."

"I think keeping my hope alive has been one of the most important parts of my journey," Blythe replied. "And I nearly lost it a time or two."

Taking his hand again she slipped down from the counter, and their eyes lingered. Gracen wondered if he'd ever get to the end of all her stories. And she had yet to really get to the beginning of his, this woman who loved stories and hope and saw them in everything.

# Chapter 32

"I'm just relieved we didn't have a repeat of last year," Liam declared as he and his family bustled out of the cold and into The Yellow Bowl. "I don't care if his eyes are closed or his hair is sticking up or whatever else could be happening in that photo. At least, the kid saw Santa and didn't lose his ever-loving mind."

"So I take it 'pictures with Santa' was a success this year?" Blythe asked. Last year's attempt was a notable disaster. Teddy hadn't tolerated waiting in line well and then decided Santa was the most terrifying person on the planet when it finally was his turn.

"Teddy did nicely. I think he was still a little s-c-a-r-e-d," Ginnie spelled out so the word wouldn't trigger him.

"I know what that spells," Viola said proudly.

"I'm sure you do, darling, but I don't want Teddy to hear that word," Ginnie explained.

"Because then he'll be sc–," Viola started to ask.

"Nope! Don't say it!"

"But it's over now."

"Viola, please, just go look at books and let Mommy have a minute," Ginnie sighed. Viola shrugged in that patronizing way little kids have, then trotted off to the kids' section to pick out some new-to-her books. Sinking onto one of the bar stools, Ginnie confessed, "I love her to pieces. But sometimes she's too smart for her own good. Or my own good, anyway."

"You're amazing, Gin," Blythe reassured her as she poured a cup of coffee. "You're really such a good mother. Are you driving yourself crazy again this year?"

"Not as bad. Liam convinced me the wrapping paper doesn't need to be quite so methodical," she replied. She took a tentative sip of the coffee then made an approving face.

"Yeah, Finn made it before he left. He's booked solid in activities at the church again this year," Blythe explained. "But I think he loves it."

"Where Finn?" Teddy demanded when he heard the name of one of his favorite people.

"He's at the church. He's working there right now instead of with me."

"Where Sen?" Teddy asked instead. It had taken his people a full week to figure out that 'Sen' was meant to be Gracen in Teddy's two-year-old broken English.

"He's next door working hard," Blythe replied, careful to avoid using the word 'pizza'.

"Pia work?" Teddy asked anyway, knowing that Gracen and pizza went hand-in-hand.

"Yes, pizza work," Blythe smiled. "How about a donut, Teddy Bear? I have some cinnamon sugar ones that look really good."

"Okay! Yeah!"

She plated the donut and set it before her beloved nephew after he climbed up to sit at the counter. As she looked away she found a glowering stare from her big brother.

"What? He was good this year, right? Do you want him to obsess about p-i-z-z-a?" she demanded.

"It just so happens I'm about to go order some for our dinner," Liam retorted.

"Well, you should've spoken up sooner, goonie bird," Blythe teased.

"That's a name I haven't heard in at least a decade, probably more."

"Do you still believe there are goonie birds in the Beckwiths' attic?" she laughed.

"I'm sure *you* do. You probably still have a nightlight."

"So what if I do? It happens to be a nightlight with a silhouette of George Washington on his horse. Jesse got it for me at Mount Vernon a few years ago," she fired back smugly.

"You two are ridiculous," Ginnie said rolling her eyes. "Is this what I have to look forward to with Viola and Teddy?"

"It's better than Alex and Jesse trying to beat each other's brains out," Blythe shrugged.

"Those two idiots," Liam grumbled. "I like them both pretty well on their own, but together is a different story."

A muffled buzzing sound started from somewhere in the pile of coats and hats and outerwear the Elwoods had shed when they came into the shop. Liam was closest to the table containing their mountainous mess so he began digging through pockets.

"It's your phone," he said. It stopped buzzing just as he found it, but he handed it to his wife anyway. "You never have your ringtone on."

"I'd rather miss a phone call every now and then than have my ringer wake up a napping child," Ginnie retorted. She swiped the screen open and discovered that Jesse was the missed call. "Do you care if I call him back? I'll make it quick."

Blythe waved her hand dismissively, "Go ahead, it's not like we're crowded in here."

In fact, the Elwoods were the only people in the shop. This December was a little slower than previous years. It was a strangely rainy month with temperatures hovering around freezing, but not quite committing. No one in their right mind enjoys driving in the dreaded 'wintry mix' and even fewer people enjoy schlepping purchases on sloppy sidewalks going to and from stores with poor parking.

"Hey Jess, sorry, my phone was buried under some coats. We just saw Santa … Yeah, it went pretty well this year. We got there early so the line wasn't long … I'll definitely send you the pictures when we get them. They're emailing me the images … I know it's totally beneath you, but I always feel like I don't get good pictures of the kids unless you take them … Well, I'll hold you to that," Ginnie said. She cupped her hand over the phone to tell Liam that Jesse had just offered to take family portraits when he came home next.

"He's been saying that since Teddy was born," Liam said to Blythe. "I'm still waiting."

"So where are you?" Ginnie continued. "Oh, you're in France again this year? … Is that near Paris? … Stop laughing, I've never been to France."

"He forgets some of us haven't filled one passport, let alone multiples," Blythe mumbled.

"Yeah, I'm at The Yellow Bowl," Ginnie said, her tone changing dramatically. She looked at Blythe as she said, "No, Blythe is in her office."

Immediately, Liam and Blythe shared a look. Liam took a step closer to Ginnie to try to overhear exactly what Jesse was saying.

"Jesse, what are you talking about? … C'mon, are you serious? You're kidding me. You didn't … You're serious … No, I don't want to know."

"This doesn't sound good," Liam said to his sister. Her eyes narrowed.

"Jesse Thomas, stop talking … *No*, I'm not listening to you. I'm not going to be party to whatever it is you're trying to do … She's happy. They're happy … *Jesse*, listen to me. It's not just about Blythe … No, it's not. He's my friend in my own right. I've worked alongside him for six months now. Even Liam likes him … No, Liam doesn't want to know either. We're not going to be your allies," Ginnie said flatly, glaring at her husband.

"I didn't do anything," he said, holding his hands up.

"Okay, listen, I'm going to let you go," Ginnie sighed harshly. There was a pause as Jesse talked. "I love you, Jesse, but you're better than this. I'll talk to you in a few days."

"Gracen?" Blythe asked simply. Her voice was cold with irritation. She wasn't close enough to make out any words, but she heard the urgency in his voice, and the frustration with Ginnie when she wouldn't hear him out.

"Yes," Ginnie said, exhaling heavily again. "Jesse claims he found out something important that we need to know. I told him that we do not."

"He was digging around back in May when he came for our birthday. I told him to lay off it then," Blythe muttered. "Glad to see he's listened."

"He's never liked the idea of you with anyone else. It's probably driving him insane that you could be falling in love with a guy we all actually like this time," Ginnie scoffed.

"Did he say what it was about?" Blythe asked as she chewed on her left thumbnail.

"I didn't let him tell me anything," Ginnie told her. She frowned, "Do *you* want to know?"

"I just … I don't know. I don't want Jesse to snoop around and then try to turn my friends and family against Gracen. That's so wrong on so many levels."

"Well, I would hope you don't want that," Liam commented.

"But if Jesse did find out something big and bad and scary, shouldn't someone know?" Blythe asked with some genuine concern.

"Do you think there is something big and bad and scary?" Liam questioned. "Because if you have a feeling there is, then someone needs to listen to Jesse."

"Now, hold on," Ginnie argued. "I know Gracen can be elusive, but I figured the two of you have been talking and getting to know each other better. Right?"

"Yeah, but not 'getting to know each other better,'" Liam said with heavy air quotes.

Blythe rolled her eyes, "You can relax and lose the air quotes." She turned to Ginnie, "Sometimes I feel like I know him. We talk all the time. He talks a lot about Aunt Grace and Uncle Harry. He's still grieving his death pretty deeply. Uncle Harry was the closest thing to a dad he's ever had. I know all about his brother and sisters. They're not close, but he worries about them—especially Michelle. She's a mess. He told me a little about his mom and her anxiety. Of course, we've talked about Roy, the evil grandfather. Gracen didn't have a lot of friends; mostly he left behind business associates. And, well, there are no real exes in his background to talk about. I know he's not exactly Mr. Innocent."

"It sounds like you know quite a lot about him," Ginnie reassured her. "I think if Gracen has something to tell you, he'll open up when he's ready."

"That's just it. I know there's something more about why he's here or who he was or something. I can't place my finger on it."

"Some guys aren't riddled with mystery. Some guys just don't like to talk about themselves," Liam offered in an effort to be fair. "Gracen could be either."

"Blythe, in your gut, do you trust Gracen?" Ginnie asked pointedly.

"I do," she answered instantly. "I told Jesse that in May. My friendship with Gracen was about learning how to trust again. And, I don't know, it's like our relationship is putting that trust in action. But I don't want to be blind and stupid, I did that once."

"No one wants that," Liam said firmly. "Maybe I'll call Alex and vet him a little. After all, he was the one who put Gracen in our midst."

"You know, that's probably the other reason Jesse has his britches in a twist," Ginnie said frankly. "Gracen was Alex's friend before he was anything to any of us. That fact alone is enough to get Jesse in a snit. Throw

Blythe into the mix …"

"But there's never been anything between Jesse and me," Blythe insisted. His behavior was making that illusion harder and harder to preserve.

"Forget Jesse for now. He's been making mountains out of molehills since we were kids," Ginnie advised. "And enjoy your holidays. Gracen has been here since April. Whatever big bad boogeyman secret Jesse thinks he discovered can wait. I have no reason to distrust Gracen just because Jesse says so."

"What do you think?" Blythe asked Liam. "No offense to Ginnie, but I did the Pollyanna routine before. It didn't end well."

"I think Ginnie is right, in that, Gracen hasn't done anything to deserve suspicion. But only you can decide if you're comfortable with letting everything lie," Liam said honestly. "The power is always yours, Blythe. We can give you advice, one way or the other, but it's up to you to figure out what to do. But, I don't think it's fair to compare him to Ian. He doesn't deserve that."

Gracen most definitely didn't deserve that, not based on his Sayen Falls behavior anyway. And Blythe knew exactly how dramatic her oldest friend could be. She also knew how stupid she could be. The fear was that only one of them could be in the wrong on Gracen.

* * *

"You'll have to thank your brothers for me," Blythe told Finn. "I love this set of Christmas music they put together."

"They were overjoyed that a fan had a request," Finn replied.

"Well, you can also tell them I'm totally fangirling then," she giggled.

"They have social media, you know. I don't need to be the go-between for this particular dialogue," he groaned. As proud as he was of Aiden and Carrick for pursuing their music, it was weird to have one of his best friends fangirling over them.

"I'll make myself President of the American chapter of their fan club."

"I'm just glad to hear you a little more like yourself. You've been weird the last couple of days," Finn remarked.

They were alone in The Yellow Bowl. Christmas was now just four days away, and four days had passed since Jesse's call. In that time, Blythe had chewed off all her fingernails, as she tried to decide if it was foolish to ignore Jesse or foolish to hear him out.

"I'm really angry with Jesse," she confessed. "He knows how hard December already is for me. Memories and all that nonsense. He should've kept his yap shut until January."

"You're worried about what he found out."

"Of course I am. Ian managed to hide a whole other relationship from me for months. Clearly, I am not the type to pick up on danger."

"The old you maybe, but you learned from that."

"One would think."

"Blythe, come on. Is there anything about Gracen that indicates that he's unfaithful?"

"I don't think that's the big fat secret. No, this is about his past."

"Then maybe that's why he hasn't told you about it," Finn reminded her. "After all, you're the only one who knows my backstory—other than Reverend Smith. And I only told Eddie because he's my boss. Sometimes the past needs to stay there."

"You really think that?"

"I think you and Gracen have only been dating two months. The man has only been here nine months total. He pulled into town completely closed off, angry, and grieving. If anyone is expecting total transparency, that person is going to be disappointed and rightly so."

"But what if it's a big deal? What if it's a deal breaker? What if I'm wasting my time and his because I don't know?" Blythe asked. "What if he breaks my heart?"

"Those are valid points and I'm with you in the trenches. My curiosity is as piqued as anyone else, but I won't ask Jesse. He went about this all wrong."

"I know he did. But that's Jesse. He goes about everything all wrong."

Finn eyed Blythe closely as he spoke. "The other side of this coin is your own backstory."

"Gracen knows all about Ian."

"I don't mean Ian. I mean the thing you've not told anyone, not even me. You bloody well know we've all guessed at it, but my best guess is that the truth is actually messier."

"Yeah, I know. I've thought a lot about that. I don't think Jesse has though."

"Maybe he has and he's factored all that in."

"I just want a good Christmas. Just one. And Jesse has no right to ruin a Christmas that would otherwise be really good."

"Then don't let him," Finn recommended. "Keep your Christmas. And see what happens next."

"That is what Ginnie and Liam said too."

"Aye, there it is. Good sense all around," Finn smiled. "I will pray about this for you. I'll pray that the opportunity comes at just the right time for you both to show your full hands."

"Can you also pray that we survive it? I don't want to lose him," she admitted. "I didn't think I'd fall in love again after Ian. I'm quite sure I won't have the stamina if I lose Gracen too. Not if this all falls apart because of some past mistake, of his or mine."

# Chapter 33

In the days leading up to Christmas, Blythe made a firm decision that Jesse wasn't going to erode the trust she felt Gracen deserved, nor cast shadows on her Christmas. After all, wasn't it Jesse just last year who had told her she needed to come out of the shadows of the past? Particularly at Christmas? So whatever shadows lingered in Gracen's past could stay there. She knew enough and the rest could wait. Besides, she had her own secrets she wasn't quite ready to reveal either. Only Ebenezer Scrooge should have to deal with ghosts in December.

The Yellow Bowl was closed the day before Christmas. It was unlikely she'd have any business, and she still had presents to wrap before the Christmas Eve service at First Church. She was downstairs in her office rummaging around for more tape when Gracen knocked on the front door.

"I really should just give you a key," she smiled as she unlocked the front door for him. He gave her a kiss for a greeting, and Blythe felt pretty happy with the way things were.

"I thought I'd make you lunch," he offered. "I know you're busy today."

"I need to wrap your gifts first," she instructed. "They've been hiding at Finn's apartment, but he put them upstairs yesterday."

"Well, that's intriguing," he grinned, kissing her again. "Give me a hint."

"No, you're like Viola. If I give you a hint you'll figure it out and ruin everything."

"Ruin *everything*?"

"Yes, *everything*," she laughed. Her arms slipped around his waist and she hugged him as she giggled. He kissed the top of her head as if it were very natural. And it was.

A knock on the door prompted Blythe to whirl around and she was quite surprised to see a package delivery person holding a small brown box.

"Packages on Christmas Eve?" she remarked to Gracen. "You let him in; I'm going to fix him a cup of tea real quick."

He flipped the lock and opened the door for the carrier. "I hope you don't have many more stops to make."

"Just a few," the carrier replied with a jolly smile. "It's not so bad. I get paid overtime to play Santa Claus."

"Well, here Santa, I hope you like English Breakfast tea," Blythe said as she handed him a hot takeout cup. She gestured to the sugar bowl.

"That's very kind of you. Thank you," he said. He scanned the package with an electronic device and read the name, "So Gracen Hall?"

"Special delivery from Summerstead Isle?" Blythe grinned as Gracen held out his hands.

"Indeed. Aunt Grace," Gracen confirmed, eying the label. He slipped his hand in his pocket to retrieve a specially marked business card. Giving it to the carrier he said, "Come in sometime and get a free lunch on me, okay?"

"I'm just doing my job," the carrier shrugged as he accepted the card, "but I appreciate the kindness."

"I appreciate this," Gracen said, indicating the package. As the carrier left, he relocked the door but never stopped looking at the package.

"You know what it is, don't you, Princeton?"

"I sure do, Kate."

"I love it when you call me 'Kate'," she told him, tucking her arm into his. "So what is it?'

"A book. A very special book," he said. He put the package into her hands so he wouldn't have to unlink their arms, and fished his knife out of his pocket. Carefully, slicing open the tape on the box he tilted it to remove a small parcel covered in bright Christmas wrapping. He repeated softly, "A very special book."

His slender fingers peeled back the wrapping to reveal a careworn hardback copy of *A Christmas Carol*. Unbidden tears stung his eyes as he flipped open the cover to read the inscription. There were two—one inscribed to Harry and another inscribed to Gracen.

"This was Uncle Harry's," Gracen explained. "Aunt Grace gave it to him the first Christmas they were married. It was his favorite book."

"I love that she wanted you to have it."

"We had a tradition. From the time I was little, Uncle Harry read me this book every Christmas," he said fondly, then his voice cracked. "Last year, he was really sick with radiation and chemo. I came every evening after work to read a few pages until we finished it."

"Gracen," Blythe breathed, wrapping her arms tight around him again.

"He died six weeks after Christmas," he added, swallowing those tears. "I think the reason I didn't get this gift sooner was that Aunt Grace wanted to read it one more time first. I hope she's doing okay without him."

"It's very sweet and thoughtful that she sent it to you. Having his book will be like reading with him again. I always feel so connected to someone I love when I read one of their books, knowing that our fingers turned the same pages, our eyes read the same words, we laughed at the same jokes, and cried at the same sad parts."

"Sometimes I wonder if one reason I love you so much is that I know he would've loved you," Gracen said without thinking. When he saw her eyes grow twice their size, he realized what he had accidentally said. In their three months together, Gracen had avoided taking her to bed and telling her he loved her. Neither had been easy, much to his surprise. He hoped the look in his own eyes now wasn't panic.

"Gracen," she said gently, "how should I interpret what you just said?"

He was relieved she was asking instead of slathering accolades of her own love all over him. Still, he knew he could only spare a few seconds to think of a reply before his awkward silence would be hurtful to her. He was sure he loved her. So he said, "'I love thee, Kate'."

"*Henry the Fifth*?" she grinned slowly. "At a time like this?"

"'Dost thou like me, Kate'," he continued quoting. She rolled her eyes and he knew what that meant. It meant he was making her a little weak in the knees.

"Stop that and give me a real answer, Gracen Henry."

For a moment, he laughed and it shoved his renewed grief out of the way. In his laughter, he set the book on a nearby table to pull Blythe close so he could kiss her.

"'There's witchcraft in your lips, Kate'," he whispered, quoting one more time.

"Stop doing that. You know what it does to me. It's Shakespeare and your ridiculous voice and your eyeballs. It's too much, I don't like it."

"What's wrong with my voice and my eyeballs?"

"Nothing. That's what's wrong with them," she retorted. Her eyes danced with his as they gazed at each other. She touched his cheek, "I do love you. I don't know if you want to hear that or not, but I've known it for a while."

He took hold of both her hands and lifted them to his lips. Meeting her eyes, he answered straightly, "I love you too, Blythe. I told you in September I was afraid I was falling for you. There's no doubt for me now. I just have no idea how to express that normally."

"Normal is stupid. Shakespeare is better, Princeton," she declared. She gave him a quick, playful kiss, then redirected their conversation, "You promised me lunch."

"You said you had to wrap my gifts first."

"Give me fifteen minutes. No, twenty. I still need to find tape," she remembered. "Oh, and I was thinking we should exchange gifts tonight. Tomorrow will be crazy. The morning starts at seven at Grammy and PapPap's. There are so many gifts, too many gifts. And a lot of people. Not as bad as Thanksgiving though. Ginnie's parents won't be there. Or my dad, obviously."

"Yeah, Silas gave me the run down. It sounds more laid-back than Thanksgiving."

"It's all about who's there and who isn't."

"Well, I'm good to do our gifts tonight. After church?"

"Yeah, let's come back to my place and watch *It's a Wonderful Life*, too. We haven't done that one yet."

"So, lunch in twenty, gifts and movie tonight. Sounds like a plan, Kate."

"And please, no more Shakespeare. It just isn't fair."

"Whatever you say, Kate," he grinned.

After lunch, Gracen attempted to call Aunt Grace to wish her a Merry Christmas and to thank her for the book, but she didn't answer. He left a voicemail expressing his thanks and glad tidings, but it really wasn't the same. He decided to try again tomorrow on Christmas Day if she didn't call him back.

The Christmas Eve service started at seven, so he jumped in the shower around six to give himself plenty of time. Just as he finished rinsing the soap off his body, he heard his phone ringing. Figuring it was Aunt Grace, he hopped out of the shower, wrapped a towel around his waist, and scrambled to answer his phone. However, when he looked at the screen he did not see Aunt Grace's picture; instead, his mother's face was smiling nervously at him. She always looked nervous in pictures. Chrissy looked nervous period.

He was not prepared for a Christmas Eve phone call from his mother. He'd been in Sayen Falls for nine months with no word from her. He thought about ignoring the call. No one would be the wiser. Besides, he was legitimately busy. But as he looked at the thumbnail photo of his mom lighting up on the touchscreen, he just couldn't. Love answers the phone when it hurts. Love listens anyway.

"Hi, Mom."

"Gracen," she breathed. "For a minute, I thought I'd missed you. I mean, I thought you weren't going to answer. I mean, I thought you didn't hear the phone ringing."

"Mom, it's alright, I knew what you meant."

"Right, of course, you did," Chrissy laughed uneasily. "So, how are you? Aunt Grace told me you're doing okay. You're okay?"

"I'm doing pretty well actually. Business is good."

"I hope you're not working too hard. I mean, that there's more than just work in your life. You're so young, Gracen."

"I don't just work. I know that's probably surprising," he said with an awkward chuckle.

"You were so focused on your work here."

"It was all I had."

"Yeah, I know," Chrissy said softly. "So, tell me about it. What do you do when you're not making pizza?"

"Well, there's a girl. She owns the place next door."

"Aunt Grace mentioned that too. That's really great. What's her name?"

"Blythe Elwood. I'm getting ready right now to meet her for the Christmas Eve service at church."

"You're going to church? I didn't think you went anymore. I should be getting ready too. Daddy will kill me if I'm not ready when he wants to go."

207

"You're never ready when Roy, I mean, when Granddad, wants to go," he grinned. "But, yes, I'm going this year. I went to church a couple weeks ago too."

"You went to Ohio and found religion and a girl," Chrissy giggled.

"Something like that. My friend Finn is an intern at the church, he gave the sermon."

"You have friends. I'm so relieved, Gracen, I've worried about you."

He bristled. It was so easy to say that she had worried about him, but how had she shown it? She hadn't called. She hadn't reached out. When he was there, she hadn't defended him to Roy. She hadn't done anything to take his part in his entire life.

Gracen hung his head. A trigger in his brain counted the toes on his bare feet, but he wasn't conscious of it. "You don't need to worry about me. I'm sure there's enough on the Isle to think about."

"I am worried about your sister."

"Which one?"

"Well, both of them, but Josselyn. She seems so unhappy with her work."

"Is she still working for Wallace Corp?"

"Yes, she has part of your old job. Or something. I don't really understand it. Jerry tried to explain it all to me when you left, but you know how I get," she said, sounding nervous again. Yes, Gracen knew exactly how his mother could get. She was essentially a bundle of nerves gingerly wrapped in skin. It seemed to him she had no bones to make her strong, no guts to give her stamina.

There was a knock at his door. Gracen glanced at the clock on his nightstand. It was almost time to leave for church and he still wasn't dressed.

"I'm sorry, Mom, I have to go. I am glad you called though."

"Well, just one thing. Jerry and I are going to send you a check for Christmas. It's right here actually, I'm looking at it right now on my dresser," she said with a little titter of laughter. "I just haven't gotten around to actually mailing it."

"It's okay, Mom, don't worry about it. I don't need anything."

"You sound so good, Gracen."

"I am good. I'm doing fine," he assured her. The words almost stuck in his throat.

"Good, good. Okay then, I'll let you go," she said softly. "Have a Merry Christmas, son."

"You too."

"I love you, Gracen."

"Love you too, Mom."

Gracen tapped the screen with his thumb and his mom's picture faded away. He stared at the screen for a moment longer. Blythe knocked on the door again. He combed his fingers through his hair as he threw the phone down on the bed.

"Just a minute," he shouted, quickly pulling on a pair of pants. Rushing with a shirt in hand, he opened the door. Blythe's eyes bulged as he slipped his arms into the sleeves and began buttoning it up. She'd never seen him without a shirt on, and it was not a bad sight.

As soon as he saw her, he kissed her. His mind cleared for a moment. Then, he caught himself counting the length of their kiss, one one-thousand, two one-thousand, three one-thousand. It was an anxiety trick, counting. Abruptly he stopped kissing her.

"Sorry, I'm running behind now. My mom called me."

"Your mom called?" Blythe asked with equal parts surprise and confusion. She followed him through the apartment. She'd only ever been as far as the living room or the kitchen. Maybe she had used the bathroom once. They spent most of their time at her place. In his bedroom, Blythe sat gingerly on the bed as if it might burst into flames.

Gracen fumbled in his sock drawer for clean dress socks. He found a pair of black ones and sat on the bed next to her to put them on. "Yeah, I'm not sure why."

"It is Christmas."

"Yes, it is. Apparently, she and my stepdad are sending me a check."

"That's nice."

"Is it?"

"Isn't it? I'd love some money. I'd buy myself an old-fashioned typewriter. Or one of those cat clocks, you know, with the moving eyes."

He had to laugh, "You would."

Gracen felt like his mother was just throwing money at him again. Sure, Chrissy meant well, but where was the love? Still sitting, he straightened up to button his shirt. As he finished each button, he counted. Stop. Counting. He couldn't remember the last time he'd counted things to cope. It was an old familiar reflex brought on by an old familiar stressor.

"I should've told her to send me my favorite flavor of salt water taffy. Or even a mixed box from my favorite shop. In either case, I bet she doesn't know."

"American Flag taffy from Waite's Candy Shop," Blythe recited. He looked at her curiously. "It came up when we discussed which shop has the best taffy and which one has the best fudge. The Fudge Pantry has the best fudge. Rocky Road, by the way."

"Why do you remember these things?"

"Because I love you and I think you're interesting. And probably because I want someone to remember the minutiae about me too."

"All good reasons, I suppose," he kissed her gently then rested his forehead on hers, and for a minute, all was calm. He stood and went to his closet to pick a tie off the hook. She pushed herself up off the bed, and went to tie Gracen's tie for him. "We better hurry. The church fills up fast on Christmas Eve."

* * *

When the flicker of the candles hurt Blythe's eyes she wanted to cry. The candles had always been her favorite, even last year in the emotional melee. But this hurt. It definitely hurt.

She lowered her candle as she squeezed her eyes tight. Her brain had little men inside of it and they were pounding with pickaxes to get out.

"Are you okay?" Gracen whispered. He thought of what Finn had said about Blythe running out last year crying.

"Headache," she mumbled. "Correction: migraine."

"Not again," he groaned quietly. She'd been fighting headaches all through December. Only one other had gotten license to turn into a migraine; she had ignored it instead of cutting it off at the pass with cold water, ibuprofen, and quiet.

When the service ended, most of the Elwoods lingered to chat with friends and give out hugs and Christmas cards. But Gracen made Blythe's apologies for her before ushering her out the door and into his car.

"Have you hit the nauseous stage?" he asked as he cranked the heater.

"I think maybe yes. I can't tell. My eyes are really angry right now."

The drive from First Church to the riverfront plaza was very short, but he took it slowly. When he parked, he insisted on opening her door for her and helping her up the stairs. Blythe was grateful because any doubt about the nausea had been erased.

"What do you need?" he asked as he turned on the light above the sink in her kitchen. He wanted to keep the lights dim so her retinas would stop trying to murder her.

"Um, first, I'm going to get changed so I can breathe," she said. "This dress is great and all, but it's not doing my respiratory system any favors."

"You do look beautiful. Did I tell you that?" he asked, stealing a moment to kiss her. "Absolutely stunning, as always."

"Thank you. You're about to see me absolutely frumpy in pajamas. Don't be too shocked at the transformation."

While she went about changing out of her ivy green dress and into something actually comfortable, he busied himself in the kitchen. He wet a washcloth and stuck it in the freezer so it would be icy cold. Then he poured two glasses of ice water. Next, he went into the living room. He grabbed a quilt from an oversized basket and fluffed a throw pillow.

"You look like such a fussbudget," she giggled. "Even better, you look like my grandfather getting the couch ready for my grandmother."

"I will never be offended by any comparison to Miles Elwood," Gracen replied. "And I'm getting it ready for you to lie down. No arguments."

"Who's arguing?" she said, sinking down onto the sofa. Gracen retrieved the washcloth from the freezer and brought along the ice water. Gingerly, he laid the cloth on her forehead. The frosty cold immediately helped. She sighed in relief, "Thank you."

"What else do you need?"

"Nothing right now," she replied. Then her eyes popped open, "Gifts!"

"But your migraine?"

"No, we have to. I've waited so long to give you your presents."

"Okay, give me a minute to get yours from my apartment. I'll be right back. Don't move."

"I don't plan on it."

She closed her eyes again as he walked away. She heard the door open and shut. The cold washcloth had already cut the pain almost in half. Medicine. When they'd gotten home, she'd been so focused on her dress that she'd forgotten to take any ibuprofen. She stood up and walked into the kitchen, just as Gracen returned with her gifts.

"What part of 'don't move' wasn't clear?" he grinned.

"I needed some ibuprofen," she explained. "Besides, my legs still work. Stop hovering."

"I'm not hovering. I just don't want you to be miserable. I wouldn't think that migraine-induced vomiting on Christmas Eve is really on your bucket list."

"That's valid. I'm just not used to *you* treating me like a broken thing."

"You're not broken just because your brain is trying to hold you hostage," he said as she returned to the sofa. Delicately tossing her head back, she swallowed three ibuprofen effortlessly. She slapped the cold cloth back on her head.

"Okay, your gifts are those giant ones leaning on the wall by the tree," she said, pointing to the live Christmas tree they had decorated last week.

"Why didn't you get me the big one?" he smirked facetiously. The packages were of identical shape and size, tall enough to reach his waist, and wide enough to be awkward to carry. "I have no idea what this is."

"That's because I didn't give you any hints, Princeton."

With no further ado, Gracen started tearing off the wrapping paper. His fingers brushed big round light bulbs and then he discovered they were attached to a bright brass frame. It was a vintage poster frame, like the ones at an old-time movie theater.

"For your Alfred Hitchcock posters," she explained smiling.

Gracen was completely impressed, which was hard to accomplish. "This is amazing. I love it."

"The other one is exactly the same. I was so excited when I found them

211

at Buterbaugh's."

"He really has everything in that antique shop, doesn't he?"

"If it's old, he's got it."

"Well, I love this. Do the lights work?"

"They do now. Becky and PapPap helped me tinker around with the wiring."

"Becky helped you?"

"That surprises you?"

"Only because it's for me. I'm sort of the thing standing between you and Jesse."

"There's like a zillion things standing between Jesse and me. You're just the tallest one. Becky likes you. And, he really likes to tinker with things with my grandfather out in the shop. It's their pastime."

"I'll have to thank them both tomorrow," Gracen nodded. He leaned the frame carefully against the wall, then crossed over to Blythe. As he kissed her forehead gently, he said, "Thank you. This is really thoughtful."

"I'm so glad you like them."

"Your head is really cold," he laughed softly.

"It feels better actually. The nausea has subsided."

"Good," he pronounced. "And now for your gifts. They're much smaller in comparison."

He had set them on her easy chair when he came back in, so Gracen retrieved them now as he explained, "You'll get another one tomorrow with everyone else. I'm afraid I didn't get very personal with your family. I ordered taffy and caramel corn from Summerstead."

"Are you serious?" she exclaimed. She sat up and the cold cloth came off her head.

"Yes, I even got tiny buckets of caramel corn for Vi and Teddy," Gracen grinned. "If everyone is half as excited as you are, I'll feel like I did okay."

"They will *love* it," she insisted. She turned her attention to the two presents in her lap. She picked up the smaller one to unwrap and soon found that she was holding a leather-bound planner. The front read 'Once More Unto the Breach' and on the title page, it stated it was an organizer for writers. Beneath the title, Gracen had written an inscription.

*Hail to Thee Blithe Spirit, My Kate,*
*You see the world glittering with possibility. You see potential even in me. The rest of us need you to write so we can draw on the hope you see.*
*With love,*
*Gracen*

"Oh, Gracen, I love it! I promise I'll use it," she gushed. "No one's ever gotten me a gift like this before. It's so meaningful and thoughtful."

"I know you're really more of a pen-and-paper type so I thought it'd be useful to map out your plot points and jot down any ideas you have."

"I tried using an app but I felt like it was taking me forever to just set up my goals and whatever. This is perfect," she told him. Then, she tore into the other gift, anxious to see what it would be. It was in a box of its own and the image on the box confused her. "It's a typewriter? How'd they fit it in this skinny box?"

"You're adorable," he grinned. He opened the box and slid out a keyboard which would attach to any computer with a USB cord, but it looked and felt like typewriter keys. "I saw it online and couldn't resist getting it for you. You have such a retro vintage vibe, and I thought it might help transition you from paper to digital."

"This. Is. Amazing!" she squealed. "Oh my head, too much. Calm down. But seriously, I couldn't love this more."

He grinned at her, rather pleased and proud of himself. Exchanging Christmas gifts was another first in his book. Until now, the only women he'd bought gifts for had been his mother, Aunt Grace, and his sisters. He usually got them all a variation of the same theme. Not a lot of sentiment or personality. But with Blythe, he just knew she had to have these things and he wanted to be the one to give them to her.

"I knew you'd like them," he said, "but I am glad to see I was right."

"Gracen, I'm really happy with us," she said, turning rather serious. "You don't know everything about me but I feel like you *know* me. And I feel like I get to know you in a way no one else does."

"You do. You know talking wasn't really my thing," he said with a sheepish look. Inwardly, the shame was nagging at him. He was ashamed not only for his past actions but also for hiding it all from her. On the other hand, telling her was a level of transparency he'd never broached before. He was not ready for that now. This day had seen enough firsts—first professions of love, first exchanging of Christmas gifts.

These are things teenagers do, he thought to himself. But when he was young, managing panic attacks, working a steady job, and keeping his grades up had taken up all his energy. This was the first time in his life he'd had enough of himself to share.

"Do you still want to watch *It's A Wonderful Life?*" she asked, derailing his train of thought.

"You should sleep off the rest of your migraine."

"I'm turning it on whether or not you stay," she informed him. "I always watch a movie on Christmas Eve. It's a tradition."

Tradition. Uncle Harry. *A Christmas Carol.*

"Have you ever read *A Christmas Carol?*" he asked suddenly.

"No actually, I haven't. I've always meant to," she replied, looking a little confused.

"Then, let's start it tonight. I'll read to you until you fall asleep," Gracen suggested. "It's my only tradition and I want to keep it."

"I would love that, Gracen. That sounds perfect."

Presently, he left to bring the book from his apartment. When he returned, Blythe was nestled into the couch, waiting expectantly. He sat down on the end of the couch where her feet could rest across his legs. Before he cracked open the book, he studied her face, particularly her eyes. Seafoam. That's what color they were. Seafoam green. She gave him a curious smile, and he leaned over to return it with a kiss.

"Alright, chapter one," he began. His deep voice was warm and soothing as he read page after page. About three chapters in, Blythe began to doze. At the end of the chapter, she was sound asleep and looking as pristine as a Christmas angel.

"I love you," his voice was nearly inaudible. Gracen lingered for almost thirty minutes, watching the steady rhythm of her breathing and getting lost in his own thoughts.

This was a strange Christmas Eve; a last-minute delivery, an unexpected phone call, the slip of his lips which had made 'I love you' accessible. Aunt Grace and Mom and Blythe. These were the women in his life, and the only thing they really had in common was love. And tea. They all loved a good cup of hot tea.

This made him smile before he carefully slipped Blythe's legs off his lap and onto the couch so he could take his leave. He paused to kiss her forehead again, hoping the migraine would be completely gone by morning. The day ahead would be loud and full.

Outside in the space between their apartments, Gracen made up his mind that he needed to run. His running shoes were just inside the door, so he quickly exchanged them with his dress shoes. Running in his dress pants and a double-breasted peacoat would be a little awkward, but this was not about form. It was always about function.

He started jogging uptown towards The Deighton Inn, relieved that the city workers had salted and the plaza was mostly dry. It would be a quick run. There was no need for a marathon. Just a few paces to order his thoughts. Things are going well, there's no need to start reciting monologues in iambic pentameter just to think straight.

However, his brain began chanting Aunt Grace, Mom, and Blythe. Shakespeare, Uncle Harry, and Blythe. It was becoming a mosh pit of thoughts and memory. This run was possibly doing more harm than good as his brain obsessively recited Aunt Grace, Mom, and Blythe. Shakespeare, Uncle Harry, and Blythe. At least it wasn't counting.

In the distance, church bells began ringing. It was midnight, the moment when Christmas Eve becomes Christmas Day and all the magic and mystery descends on earth. Somewhere a dog barked. Aunt Grace used to say that the animals talked at midnight on Christmas Eve.

"So much for magic, Aunt Grace."

Then, all of a sudden, his brain stopped the recitation like someone screeching the needle off a record player. In its place, a torrent of scrambled thoughts came loose.

The magic is love. Love is vulnerable and vulnerability. 'Stiffen the sinews, summon up the blood.' You told her you love her, now tell her the truth. She says she loves you. Tell her your story. She sees the world with glittering possibility. That is magic. And she sees the magic in you. Love is magic.

"Well, that's ridiculous," he muttered. He turned his body back towards his apartment and focused his brain on the Bard. He took the cue from the quote which had just surfaced and recited the 'Once more unto the breach' monologue until he reached his doorstep.

* * *

Just after midnight Blythe startled awake as her dreams cracked away from her conscious. She heard the last chords of the Christmas bells ringing above the church. Some things never change. As her mind cleared she realized she was in the living room. She stood up to move to her bedroom, but something drew her to the glass doors. Blythe took the detour to look out into the starry night, hoping it had maybe clouded over and was unloading buckets of snow for a freshly white Christmas. Instead, she saw Gracen pacing with his hands on his hips, and breathing deeply. Clearly, he had been running. Suddenly he looked up so she jerked back from the window, holding her breath and praying he hadn't seen her. It felt too much like spying, which was perilously close to prying. He had his secrets. Blythe had accepted that, at least for the time being.

As she stepped away from the door, Blythe wondered though if she was wrong. If maybe it was time to push. Pushing wasn't the same as nagging. And she'd already proved that she wasn't clingy and demanding, right? If this relationship was going to continue, then she needed more facts.

She glanced at the couch. The man had essentially just read her a Charles Dickens bedtime story. This relationship was making her really happy. It wasn't fair for Jesse to try to poke holes in it.

She padded to her bedroom, pulled her covers back, and pushed aside her cares. Out of habit she picked up her phone to check for texts and scan social media one last time. As her news feed began to fill with Christmas wishes, a text message from Jesse arrived. *I'm sure you're angry with me, but I'm trying to look out for you. Don't hate me, you know I only do this because I care. Merry Christmas, babe.*

All at once Blythe was fuming. She felt like smoke was about to start pouring from both ears. She just wanted one Christmas Eve without drama, one Christmas without a lot of broody internal processing, and Jesse couldn't let her have it. If he really cared, he'd back off and let her make her own mistakes. Like he had with Ian. There it was again. The ugly past that she couldn't escape even when she'd put it behind her. Until they were all working with the same set of facts, no one could know if Jesse was in the right or if he was just causing trouble.

And so, in the darkness of this quiet Christmas Eve, Blythe wondered what she didn't know, and how much longer she could act like it didn't bother her.

# Chapter 34

Two days after Christmas Gracen finally got Aunt Grace on the phone. He hoped a good chat with her would settle his nerves and help him see what to do. For the last three days, whenever he thought about his mom he started counting. After he spent time with Blythe, Shakespeare looped. His brain would not slow down. As much as he wanted to, he couldn't override the sequence and get past this.

"I really appreciated your gift," he told Aunt Grace right away. "I started reading it with Blythe on Christmas Eve. She's never read *A Christmas Carol*."

"I found it in Harry's study and I just knew you should have it. I read it before I mailed it to you. I couldn't help myself."

"I had a feeling. Was your Christmas okay?" he asked tentatively.

"It was lonely without Harry and it was strange to not have you," Aunt Grace confessed. "But I spent the day with family. We made the most of it. JJ sure has changed since you left."

"How do you mean?"

"Well, he's trying so hard to be thoughtful. I guess he still has his temper. Josselyn told me that he argued with Roy just before the holidays. But I don't see any sign of that in him. He comes over a few times a week."

"He does?" Gracen was incredulous. None of his siblings would've stopped to give Aunt Grace the time of day before he left.

"He sure does. Josselyn comes often too. I suppose they don't want to neglect an old woman in need," Aunt Grace said and Gracen could hear her smile. "They take the packages I send you to the post office."

"I wondered how in the world you were achieving that," Gracen remarked. "So the twins are your co-conspirators. I bet Roy loves that."

Aunt Gracen let out a little sigh, "Roy isn't himself either. JJ says he obsesses about you. He won't talk about you with me at all. But his health hasn't been too good. In my opinion, he's not taking care of himself."

Roy was obsessing about him? What did that mean? JJ was probably just spouting off. They'd always been rivals. This conversation was not doing much to still the wheels spinning in Gracen's mind. In fact, it had ignited a few more into motion.

Count five things you can see. No. Don't start counting. Gracen thought of his mother.

"Mom called me on Christmas Eve," Gracen said. He wanted to steer the conversation away from Roy.

"She told me all about it. She was so happy. Gracen, I hope you believe me, but your mother has been so anxious about how things were left."

"I believe you."

It wasn't hard to believe his mom was riddled with anxiety, about him or anything else. In fact, the affliction seemed to be spreading.

"She wanted to know more about Blythe. I hope it's okay that I told her the bits and pieces that I know."

"It's okay. I tell Blythe about all of you so it only seems fair, I suppose."

"Did you have a nice Christmas with her?"

"I did," he replied, launching into a recap of the highlights of Christmas Eve and Christmas Day. Hearing it himself, he realized what a nice, normal holiday experience it had been. And yet his anxiety was still making him count things.

"So, you had a good Christmas with your girl and her family. I'm so happy. Uncle Harry always said it would take someone really special to get you to sit up and take notice, let alone settle down and behave. I'd like to meet this girl and shake her hand."

He smiled to himself. But the nagging thoughts would not just shut up and go away. With a heavy sigh, he asked Aunt Grace, "Do you think I should tell her why I'm here? The whole story?"

There was a beat of silence. "You mean you haven't told her?"

"When I first got here she asked some questions and I was evasive. I didn't want to get into it. Now she's stopped asking and I … I don't know."

"Well, in my wise old opinion, it's never too late for the truth. If she cares for you even half as much as you so clearly care for her, then she'll hear you out. It might even do you some good to get it all out of your system. Nothing good comes from bottling up pain."

"There's a good chance I'll lose her if I'm entirely forthcoming."

"Can you really love her if you keep her in the dark? Can she really love you? I know it's scary and it's messy, but if you don't want to be alone, you have to face it sometime with someone."

"This whole thing came out of left field," he stammered. "You know that. You know I always banked on being alone."

"Then why do you sound so worried about losing her?" Aunt Grace asked gently. "Gracen, my boy, you not only owe it to her but to yourself as well. And the truth has a way of catching up to you. You know that already. Don't wait too long."

* * *

Gracen had a strong suspicion that Aunt Grace was probably right. After all, when had Aunt Grace been wrong? Still, there was the trouble of figuring out how to launch that conversation. Where to begin? How much to say? He'd never had to tell his story before. The population on Summerstead Isle just knew it, they'd watched it unfold in living color. And there was the other issue of finding words to explain the behavior. A lot of words were needed, and quoting Shakespeare was not going to help him this time. Until he had it well sorted, he wanted to keep his mouth shut.

The variable Gracen couldn't factor in was Jesse Beckwith. The people around him had kept Jesse's communications under wraps, so he didn't know that the clock was ticking.

That is, until Alex Beckwith called on New Year's Eve day, hours before Gracen was supposed to be with Blythe.

"I just found out something and I don't think you're going to like it."

"What is it?" Gracen asked with heavy skepticism.

"My brother went to Summerstead Isle. He had a long chat with Vanessa Bentley. I don't know for sure, but I think she told him everything."

"Your brother. Your brother … Jesse?" Gracen said almost dumbly as the meaning sank in. His color drained. He considered exactly what Vanessa would have to say—none of it would be good. In fact, it would be pretty awful. Gracen imagined how Jesse would spin the story to make it even worse. Suddenly, the past he'd so carefully tucked in neat sentences and evasive replies was a snowball gathering volume and velocity as it rolled downhill. "What is he doing investigating my private life?! Is Vanessa aware she broke her agreement by talking?"

"Vanessa? I have no idea what her goal or thought process is. But I'll give you three guesses what Jesse's end game is."

"Blythe," Gracen sighed. Cold beads of sweat formed on his neck.

"I guess he's been digging around for something on you ever since you rolled into town," Alex explained. "I heard that when you two met it was like Julius Caesar and Marc Antony. I'm not a giant nerd, so I'm not sure what that means, but I gather it's not good."

"They were both in love with Cleopatra," Gracen said through gritted teeth. Caesar and Antony. Ridiculous.

"Look, all I know about Caesar is that he gets stabbed in the back."

"Okay, so how do I make sure Jesse is Caesar in this scenario then?"

"You can't. He has the upper hand. When Jesse finally gets to spin his story, it's over. I know Jesse and I know my people. They will listen to the golden boy. Then they will judge you and you'll be toast."

"He hasn't tried yet. Maybe he won't."

"Gracen, he called Ginnie a couple weeks ago. He told her he was in France when he was really driving from Summerstead to New York City. He tried to tell her then, to get an ally, but she wouldn't hear him out."

"How did you find out about this?" Gracen demanded.

"Liam called me."

"What did you tell him?"

"I said that everyone has stories, but you're not a criminal. Which is more or less true."

"It's only true because of Roy."

"Those things were blown out of proportion."

"Says the lawyer. If this all took place a couple weeks ago, why are you calling me now?"

"I just found out. Liam said something about wanting to make sure Blythe had a good Christmas. He's pretty angry with Jesse."

"That makes two of us," Gracen grunted. He couldn't believe this was happening. Aunt Grace had just warned him to tell her before it was too late. He wondered if she knew about Jesse. Had Jesse talked to his family, too? "I can't believe he actually went to Summerstead."

"Can I completely level with you? I know Blythe is a great girl and all, but maybe this is for the best anyway. She's a distraction. You're an entrepreneur. It's in your blood. And you're really good at making businesses grow. If you stay focused, you could open another location across town on campus. You could open a new business entirely; you're not limited to food service. Frankly, your goal should be getting to where you're not throwing the pizza dough, and you're just making money. But Blythe seems to be holding you back."

"So just cut my losses and focus on work?" he said.

"Wasn't that the plan when you left?"

"Alex—"

"Listen, Gracen, I grew up in Sayen Falls. They're nice people, but they can be judgmental. The details of your story don't sound good in any light, let alone, how colorfully my brother will put it. I'm telling you, your calling in life is business. Forget the girl and get your head back in the game. When the bottom line is good, you won't even miss her."

Gracen knew Alex was wrong. Maybe not about the Elwoods, but about how much he would miss Blythe. She'd be right there, still next door, but closed off to him.

"I really thought you knew better than to get involved with the girl next door," Alex sighed. "If I'd had any idea you'd really go for her, I wouldn't have put you on the riverfront. Or in Sayen Falls at all, for that matter."

"I owe her an explanation. I can't just end it like it's no big deal."

"I have a feeling you'll be explaining plenty once Jesse makes his presentation. He's probably working on the visual aids right now."

"That's encouraging. Thank you," Gracen said with heavy sarcasm.

"Like I said, I know my brother and I know my people. And I know you. It's all oil and water," Alex said simply. "In the cold light of day, it just won't mix."

"I will deal with this, Alex. Thanks for the warning," Gracen said dryly before he tapped his phone and ended the call.

His brain was sounding every bell, whistle, and alarm it could find. It was also simultaneously launching stray lines of Shakespeare and trying to count the bricks in the wall. He felt his breathing becoming erratic. He knew what was coming.

"Get your shoes," he told himself. He had to coach himself through the moment. His shoes were by the door, so he put them on. "Go outside. You need to run. You need to breathe."

Obediently, he did what he told himself to do. It was a cold day, and he was only wearing a Henley shirt and jeans. He shivered once in the cold, but his brain didn't seem to want to register senses very well. His brain was interested in counting what he could see or hear or smell, but it refused to compute any sensory input properly.

Out of habit, his feet turned to the left towards The Chatterbox. It was about a half hour until sunset now, so the sky was turning gray and pink. The electric street lamps turned on to illuminate the plaza. Gracen knew it well now, every cobblestone, and every missing paver. He knew what was in every window and what used to be in every empty space.

His mind returned to his first run in Sayen Falls. He'd known only grief and resentment then. That was the grit he used to set up his new life. The Elwoods' collective kindness had tempered that grit and with their help, he'd been able to construct a pretty good life. And now some jokester he barely knew was trying to dismantle it with missives from his past.

He wondered who else Jesse called. Why not call Blythe herself? Maybe he had and she wouldn't listen. Or maybe she listened and didn't believe Jesse. It was all in the past anyway. Obviously, that wasn't who he was anymore. He barely recognized himself these days. Maybe that was the illusion. It was quite possible this new and improved Gracen was just a passing fad.

Reaching the pylons he stopped to catch his breath. He had shared just enough to keep her from asking more. It was the story of his life in facts and figures. But the minutiae of a life rarely matters; it's the sum of the parts, what it all means, how it all plays out that makes a difference. Sometimes the sum total makes a person stronger, but sometimes the combined facts just leave a person crippled. Gracen felt as crippled and helpless as Tiny Tim. It was painfully clear that no matter how far he ran from Summerstead Isle and his grandfather, he'd never get away.

After all, it wasn't just Jesse and the threat he posed. Gracen had been dancing with his demons ever since his mom called. He could keep a lid on the anxiety until Summerstead came knocking. It felt like waves crashing onto the shore. When the ocean rolls back out, it always takes a little sand with it. His family eroded his good senses with every phone call; it was probably good they didn't call more.

When he circled back to his apartment, he saw the light on in Blythe's side. Daylight was fading fast now, darkness was almost upon him. The light from her apartment spilled out onto the balcony and the pavement below just as it had the night he'd arrived. She had been a passing curiosity then, this girl with life in her voice and her soul in her eyes.

"You have to tell her before he does," he commanded himself. He thought of the first time he'd kissed Blythe. On the night of Becky's party, no one had counted his drinks. He'd had two tumblers of scotch neat and one beer. Alcohol wasn't a regular vice for Gracen, but the appeal of liquid courage tempted him. Instead of going upstairs to prepare for his evening with Blythe, he got into his car and drove to the closest liquor store. He came home with a bottle of scotch.

# Chapter 35

Blythe was already talking freely to Gracen when she opened the door to her apartment, "I'm so glad we decided to stay in tonight."

Then she looked at his face. Immediately, she knew something was wrong. The smile slid from her lips, her brow furrowed, and her voice dropped. "Gracen, what's wrong?"

"Your old friend Jesse," he replied, marching into her living room. He was wound tighter than a spring by now. His deep voice was biting.

"What do you mean?" Her heart clenched as she thought about the phone call Ginnie had received. She wondered what Jesse had done now. Couldn't he just leave well enough alone?

"He's quite the investigator, it seems. He even went to Summerstead."

"I had no idea he went to Summerstead!" she exclaimed. All of a sudden she was on the defensive like she had to explain herself or Jesse's pathological behavior. She was sick of feeling like Jesse was a problem that needed to be explained away, but that is exactly what he was.

Her words were an accidental confession of her knowledge. And it was the last straw for Gracen. He stood behind her easy chair and gripped the back of it so tightly his knuckles turned white.

"But you knew I was his little research project?" Gracen seethed.

"No, not exactly. I told him back in May to lay off. When he came for our birthday," Blythe tried to explain, "I told him I wanted to get to know you my way and to leave it all alone. I know he tried to talk to Ginnie but she told him she didn't want any part of it."

"You knew he called Ginnie and didn't tell me? You didn't think that was something I should know?" he demanded, throwing his hands up.

"What was I supposed to say? 'Hey Gracen, Jesse wants us to break up because he thinks you're the Big Bad Wolf.' That really would've gone over well?" Blythe retorted. She put her hands on her hips and stared at him from her spot in the dining area.

"A heads up would've been nice. Liam called Alex, and then today Alex called me. He wanted to warn me before Jesse tells all my secrets and your people turn up their noses at me."

"Turn up our noses. You really think we're that type?"

"You religious sort tend to monopolize the corner on passing judgment."

"That's completely unfair and unfounded," she said hotly. "We've been nothing but good to you despite the fact that we don't know anything about you. I went ahead and fell in love with you. Do you think I'm so fickle?"

"I think you'll see that you fell in love with a falsehood," he told her with his voice cold and dark. "You fell in love with what you wanted to see in me and not what's really there."

"Well, how in the world do I know what's really there if you never tell me? I thought I was getting to know the real you but now you're freaking out like you've been living some kind of double life and the jig is up."

Blythe had no idea where her words were coming from. It was unlike her to hold her own. But everything about this was surreal. She'd never seen Gracen so unhinged. Sighing dramatically, she stepped further into the room, closer to where he was standing, and that's when she noticed that he smelled of alcohol. "Have you been drinking?"

"Scotch. Just a little liquid courage to face the firing squad."

"Seriously—you're that afraid of me? Am I such a prude that I can't hear your stories?"

"I have no idea what I'm doing here," he stepped out from behind the chair as he spoke. "All I know is I've managed to manipulate you so far and keep you from asking for more details."

"Manipulate me. You think I've been satiated with what you give me? Gracen, please. Everything you tell me just makes me want to know you more. That's how it works when you love someone. I just don't ask because I don't want you to retreat into your shell, or start running laps."

"Yes, I'm aware. You think you know everything because you've been in love before," Gracen spat. "Being in a toxic relationship that left you emotionally charred has really made you an expert on how healthy relationships work."

Immediately he regretted it. Gracen took a step toward her but as he did Blythe lifted her hand and slapped him full across the face. The stinging slap left a red handprint on his cheeks. The sound reverberated in the tension between them. For a split second, Blythe was more shocked than Gracen. And then she came to life.

"How dare you," she fumed. "You told me to slap you if you ever treated me like I was broken, or if you ever acted like an idiot. Right now you're doing both."

"Blythe—"

"I took a huge risk trusting you, and that's probably my own fault. But the fact is you're too big a coward to just talk about who you really are and what you really want from life. You can spout poetry and promises all you want, but it isn't real. You're not real."

"I haven't made you any promises," he sputtered. On some level, Gracen knew that was a stupid thing to say at that moment but his brain was on hyperdrive and too busy to think.

"That's a technicality. It's a loophole. Alex probably helped you find it. You guys are all alike. You, Alex, and Jesse. You're a bunch of cowards. Jesse didn't even call me himself because he knew I'd be furious. You must be hiding something pretty big. Did you leave behind a litter of illegitimate kids? Do you broker kidneys on the black market? Hitman?"

"That's it, start cracking jokes. You're just like Silas. You want to embrace all this beauty and truth in the world, but when the truth is ugly, you hide behind sarcasm."

"I haven't heard anything yet, so I'm not hiding anywhere. I'm waiting."

"You're waiting to hear about how my grandfather railroaded me out of Summerstead Isle with threats to unbury my dirty little secrets?" Gracen said vomiting up the truth. "How I got arrested for having sex on the beach when I was twenty-two? How I had sexual harassment charges brought against me just last year because I apparently slept with too many girls at Wallace Corp? I don't even remember it, Blythe. I don't even remember it."

In all his imaginings, he had not pictured this conversation unfolding like this. But he was lit now and spewing like a geyser.

The words hit her like a slap in the face. Her voice was surly, "Good grief, I didn't know you were a womanizer. I thought you were just allergic to commitment."

"I'm not a womanizer," Gracen argued. His eyes flashed.

"What do you call it?" she countered.

"It's not about women! It's just about sex!"

"What?! Gracen, that doesn't even make sense," she cried. None of this made sense. Her ideas of him were getting jumbled, and she still felt on the defensive.

"That's because you can't understand it. You're so *good*," he said as though it were an insult. "Sex for me is about clearing my head. I get wound up. I go for a run. I count things. I quote Shakespeare. And when all the tricks stop working, I need something more cathartic."

"So you find some witless girl to spend the night with."

"I used to. That's not me anymore. But thanks to Jesse, I don't get any do-overs."

"No, we're not blaming Jesse for this. And Jesse doesn't get to decide what happens in this relationship."

"Well, it's thanks to him that we're standing here yelling at each other about it."

"Hey, we could've talked about this over donuts and tea on the balcony anytime you wanted to. You waited until you got caught and then you came at me like a bat out of hell."

"Oh, right, yeah. You would've been completely swept off your feet if I told you all about my sexual exploits and my anxiety. Yeah, you would've loved that. It's what everyone wants to hear."

"Of course I don't want to hear it. You don't want to say it. It's gross," Blythe pointed out. "But you're the one who chose to get loaded on scotch tonight. Clearly, you are a grab bag of issues, and yet you were so worried about me having cocktails at Becky's party."

"I did the right thing that night," he insisted. He stalked away from her and stared out the balcony window for a second. Then, he turned to face her again, "And I'm doing the right thing now. It's time for you to see me just as I am—a workaholic with an anxiety disorder and a penchant for meaningless sex."

"Then how do you explain us? That's not the Gracen I know."

"Only one of them can be real, and you tend to believe illusions. Don't hit me, but you did that with Ian. I may not be much better in the end."

"You really think I'm this sheltered little ding-dong who doesn't know anything," she mused, still very angry.

"Blythe, I know you. You're sweet as sugar and believe in fairy tales."

"Thank you for giving me the depth of a puddle, Princeton."

"You know what I mean."

There was a pause before Blythe spoke again. Her voice was spiked with resignation and regret. "Yes, I do. It means the pedestal is going to come crashing down and I'm probably going to break my neck."

"What are you talking about?"

"For your information, I know exactly what it's like to use sex to feel better for all of five minutes. I know exactly what it's like to try to figure out just how deep you can bury a secret," she said, rubbing her forehead hard. "Why not? Let's just have it all out. I've been sleeping with Jesse, whenever he's home and I feel like it, since we were seventeen. There. Do you still think I'm so 'good' and sweet as sugar?"

The quietness sizzled with tension as Gracen absorbed her confession. Of course, no one had believed there was 'nothing' between Blythe and Jesse, but Gracen had never suspected quite this much.

His voice bellowed, "That's twelve years! You've been sleeping with Jesse for twelve years and no one knows? I don't know if I should congratulate you, ask for advice, or throw up."

"Are you serious right now? You have the pukes because I slept with Jesse after everything you just told me?"

"You've been insistent that there's nothing between you and Jesse. I might be a womanizer, but I didn't blatantly lie about it!"

"It's not a total lie," Blythe stammered. "We've never officially been a couple. And when I was with Ian, we didn't even so much as hold hands or hug inappropriately. Jesse didn't even try anything!"

"Oh, well, three cheers for Jesse. Clearly, he's the gentleman here and I'm just a pig," Gracen grumbled as he ran his fingers through his hair.

"I didn't say that! I don't think that!"

"Did you sleep together when he came for your birthday?" he barked.

"No. I was mad at him for wanting to investigate you."

"You shouldn't have let that stop you, apparently. It didn't stop him from investigating."

"I didn't want to sleep with Jesse! It's been more than a year actually.

About the same time that I stopped getting involved with Ian."

"Wait a minute—there was overlap? You just said there wasn't!"

"When I was officially with Ian, there wasn't. But those two years afterward …" Blythe shrugged her shoulders helplessly. Her voice dropped, "It was messy. I told you I'm a mess. I'm no different than you when you boil it down. We're really quite a pair."

Stripped of their mutual progress and left only with the desperate foolishness of their past, neither Blythe nor Gracen had much appeal. The anger was gone. There was nothing left to hide, so there was less to fear, and there was less to yell about. It was all out there now, just stinking and waiting to be dealt with.

"I told you the fall off the pedestal was going to hurt. Guess I'm not the only one who felt it," Blythe said at last.

"I don't know how I'm supposed to react to any of this," Gracen sighed. "I've never wanted to break someone's neck before. That's JJ's style. Rage and yell and hit people. I'd love a few minutes with Jesse right now. He put all of this in motion and it turns out there's a lot more to it than I ever imagined. The idea of him in your bed," he gestured to her room. "Ian and Jesse. I know it's hypocrisy of the grossest kind, but I want to kill them both for messing with you."

Blythe sank onto her couch, and looked up at him. "The question is: can you live with it? Can you stay with me? And can I stay with you? The past is ugly, but maybe we shouldn't confuse who we used to be with who we are now."

"How do we figure that out?" Gracen asked, sitting on the easy chair across from her.

"We stay here and talk like rational people until we know," she replied. "Or we flip a coin."

"The coin toss might be faster," he sighed, "but fate has never been my friend. Let's talk."

227

Across the plaza, Silas sat alone in his darkened apartment. There was a light on above the kitchen sink where a plate and a glass half full of water remained after his dinner. His television was off. The countdown and New Year's bashes held little appeal for him. Gracen's guitar leaned against his couch. It was an amazing instrument, but it wasn't his. He couldn't bring himself to really play it. Not that he was really playing much of anything these days. It was like he knew how to play the music, but the music didn't speak to him anymore.

Silas set the priceless Martin on a guitar stand in the corner of the room. When he sold his Gibson, he had saved the stand to remind him that better days were surely coming. With the Martin safely stowed, he retrieved his shabby cheap guitar from the coat closet. He'd lost so much over the last couple years—his job, his stuff, his wife, his dignity. Slowly, he strummed the guitar. It sounded about as empty as he felt. He returned it to the closet.

With a glance at his phone, he saw that it was a quarter 'til midnight. He powered off his phone, stood up, and padded to his bedroom. His bedroom faced out to the plaza and he could see a light on at Blythe's place.

The young lovers, he thought grimly to himself.

Then, Silas took off his wedding ring and put it in his top dresser drawer. New year, new life. It was time to accept it was over. The papers were signed and it was just a matter of days now for it to all be official.

Shutting the drawer, Silas turned and flopped onto his bed. He wondered if the music would ever come back to him, or if he'd lost it too in the divorce.

* * *

Elsewhere in Sayen Falls, Lily was spending her New Year's Eve holed up in her bedroom alone. Sawyer and Ella were at a party with Sawyer's parents, so there went her two friends and the entirety of her social life. She popped some popcorn and settled into comfy clothes to watch the New Year's TV special alone in her room.

Then just before midnight, the fighting began. Her parents were supposed to be out at some posh New Year's Eve party, but a door slam signaled their return. There was a lot of yelling, most of it coming from her mother, Karen. At some point, Julian smashed a vase. Lily wondered if this one would be it, the perfect storm that would sink them. She almost hoped it would be. At least they could move on with their lives. As it was they were stuck, the three of them, in a squall that allowed for little rest and even less joy.

The people on TV started counting down. Lily counted down with them. Her father bellowed expletives Lily rarely heard. The Morgans were too polished and demure for coarse language. And then it came. The final wave that sank the ship.

"It's over, Julian! I can't do this anymore!" Karen screamed. Lily leaned forward in her bed, listening intently.

"I hope you mean it this time," Julian growled.

"Oh, I mean it. I'll sign the papers. I'm done. You win."

Papers. Apparently Julian had been pushing for this. Lily shut her eyes tight as they started to sting. One of her father's specialties as a lawyer was divorce. He was surrounded day in and day out by crumbling marriages. That line of work would either push him to protect his marriage with fierce loyalty or to lose all faith in the institution. A tear slipped down Lily's cheek. Her dad had lost all hope in his marriage, in his family.

"Who's telling Lily?" Karen asked hotly. Their voices weren't as pitched now but sound carried in their austere home.

"I doubt it will be any great surprise," Julian grumbled. "She'll be fine."

"We have to do this carefully."

Lily sat straight up in her bed, clutching her pillow to her chest. She strained to hear her mother's voice.

"I don't want the neighbors going wild with gossip."

"We can't lose any clients either."

Sinking back into her bed, tears obscured Lily's view of the perfect lace canopy above her. The people on TV blathered about resolutions and hopes for the New Year. But they were far away, somewhere in TV land. Lily was here on a sinking ship with little more than a pillow and a shred of hope to cling to, and all her parents could do was think about their reputations. She hugged her soft down pillow close to her chest as tears slipped down her cheeks in a soundless cry. At least she had that shred of hope to keep her from drowning.

\* \* \*

Across the Atlantic in a luxe hotel room in the heart of London, Jesse took two aspirin for his hangover and sank back into bed. It was only seven-thirty in the morning there and he had no idea why he was even awake. Nor did he have any idea what the girl's name was beside him. He hoped he hadn't called her Blythe. He was making that mistake more and more often, particularly since Blythe had gotten romantically entangled with Gracen.

The thought of Gracen Hall turned Jesse's stomach. When Ginnie wouldn't listen, he decided to bide his time until after the holidays. With any luck, he could get stateside again and have a face-to-face conversation with Blythe about Gracen.

Of course, the truly troubling part of all this was why it bothered Jesse so much. All he could think of anymore was going back to Sayen Falls and Blythe. He'd started dreaming about high school again. All these years later, he couldn't forgive himself for being so stupid, for walking away when he'd had his chance.

The girl stirred, stretching a lithe arm across his chest. Jesse swallowed hard. This wasn't the life he really wanted.

He remembered what woke him up. In his dream, he was with her. They had made love and Blythe turned to tell Jesse that she loved him. He wanted to tell her that he loved her too, that he had always loved her. But Jesse woke up before he could. As usual.

* * *

"He's asleep," Ginnie sighed as she crawled under the covers back into her warm bed. She and Liam had been taking turns rocking Teddy back to sleep all night. Their clock projected the time onto the ceiling in huge numbers to accommodate her fuzzy eyesight: three forty-two.

"Remember when holidays were fun?" Liam mumbled as Ginnie slipped under his arm.

"Very vaguely."

"Viola was never this hard."

"God bless Viola."

"I'll get up with him the next time," Liam promised, kissing her frizzy hair. Ginnie didn't answer; she'd drifted into much-needed sleep. He held his wife close and breathed in the lingering scent of her vanilla perfume.

Their entire evening had been a derailment. Liam had wanted to get a sitter and take Ginnie out for dinner. Lily even offered to watch the kids for free again, but Christmas cost more than they'd planned. There was no money left for a New Year's Eve dinner date, not even if they did it on the cheap. Ginnie was far too money conscious to let Liam spoil her. He knew that in the long run that was for the best but every now and then he wished they could be irresponsible. What's a little more debt? They were in over their heads anyway.

So they had stayed at home with the kids. Ginnie wanted to make the best of it. She found some New Year's themed crafts and prepared a special meal. But Viola didn't want to try the food. That girl was so picky. It reminded Liam of his sister who was a special kind of stubborn when it came to new foods. Then Teddy tore up everyone's crafts when they were half-finished, just because it brought him great joy to do so. Viola cried and when Liam raised his voice, Teddy screamed and Ginnie ended up scooping him up for snuggles. Which in turn set Viola sulking. It wasn't fair that Teddy caused all the trouble but got all of the attention. Liam wanted to tear his hair out. Their home felt like a three-ring circus most of the time.

Which reminded him of the dog. During the craft debacle Bandit stretched up to reach the table and cleaned everyone's plates, including Viola's full helping of her untouched dinner. Then when all the crying and screaming began Bandit got nervous and threw up all the food. The dog that normally had an iron stomach. At least Ginnie had let Liam clean it up. She usually took it upon herself to do it because it didn't seem that Liam could or would do it correctly.

They missed the ball drop because Teddy refused to sleep. Then, promptly at five after twelve, the boy fell sound asleep. Liam had offered to rewind the DVR so they could watch the ball drop but it wasn't the same five minutes late. Ginnie poured them each a glass of wine and they snuggled on the couch to make fun of the performers. Teddy woke up. And Teddy kept waking up. What a night.

Most days Liam wouldn't have given up fatherhood for all the riches in the world. His kids were the most precious thing to him, save his wife. But every now and then he missed having Ginnie all to himself. He missed being the master of his time. He missed thinking complete thoughts. And he missed having money.

Outside snow was beginning to fall. Frost was etched across their windows. He needed to weatherstrip the windows. He'd have to look at the budget again too. They couldn't afford to keep the heat this high. Then again, he couldn't afford to have his wife and kids shivering all day either. He would never hear the end of it.

In her sleep, Ginnie exhaled. She sounded like a kitten, just like Teddy when he actually slept. Someday that child will sleep, Liam assured himself as his eyes drifted shut. Twenty minutes later Teddy cried out for Mommy.

"Today is not that day," Liam groaned as he rolled out of bed.

* * *

Mary Alice reached for Miles but he wasn't there. Her wrinkles creased as she squinted at the clock. It was nearly six but Miles hadn't gotten out of bed this early since he retired. Well, since the paper mill closed and he was given a retirement package instead of a severance like the younger men. But he hadn't been sleeping well these last few nights. It didn't seem to matter if he slept in the bed next to his wife, or out on the easy chair while she slept on the couch. Sleep was evading him.

Her bones and joints creaked and crackled as she shifted to the edge of the bed and straightened. Her left side was still slower to respond than her right, a side effect of that stroke that had clipped Blythe's wings. Mary Alice wanted to make it up to her granddaughter somehow but she hadn't figured out how. Heaven knows she prayed about it every day.

Miles stood in the living room, staring out at the blue dawn stretching across Sayen Falls. Sunlight shyly sparkled on the fresh-fallen snow. Mary Alice wrapped her arms around her husband's waist and nuzzled her chin on his shoulder as she had done countless times in their lifetime together.

"You're worrying about Nick and the kids."

"I want to know they'll be okay."

"They will be. I just feel it in my bones."

"I thought that was rheumatism."

"It's arthritis."

"It's love, Mary Alice. You have love in your bones."

# Chapter 37

Where do we go from here? It was a short question, but not a simple one. Andrew Lloyd Webber had gotten an entire heart-wrenching ballad out of it. That paled in comparison to the hours of conversation that took Blythe and Gracen through the night and into the morning.

He explained all the dirty details of his past, and she told him how things had even started with Jesse in the first place. It was a raw, simple honesty neither of them had really tried before. This level of vulnerability was like undressing their secrets and baring their souls.

"Is there anything more I need to know? About what you're feeling?" Blythe asked as she blinked fiercely at the dawn. "Or, heaven help me if you're deliberately keeping anything else from me. I can promise you, you know all my secrets and demons now. There might be the odd fact here and there, but nothing big."

"There is one more thing," Gracen admitted. "I should've told you the truth when you asked about my family months ago, but I've lived with this lie my entire life. I saw no reason at that time to start living in the truth."

"About your family? Why would you lie about your family?"

"Because a lie is all I've ever known. I was spoon-fed the lie until I was eleven and then I was expected to live it," Gracen sighed wearily. "Robert Hall isn't my father. I don't know who my father is."

"Did your mother have an affair?" Blythe questioned. Her brain felt so fuzzy and this was a very strange lie to process.

"No. I was conceived three months after Robert's death. I was born a year almost to the day after he died. Anyone with a brain on Summerstead Isle could figure out that I wasn't his kid. I have no idea really how I was conceived. When Robert died my mother was devastated. Her anxiety spun out of control. That's all I know."

"That's it? That's all? That's like nothing," Blythe said with a frown.

He shrugged, "I've been informed that I was supposed to be aborted several times but Mom kept missing the appointments. Finally, it got to a point when she couldn't legally do it, and then eventually I was born. But I've been a liability to the Wallace family ever since."

"But this is the twenty-first century. It's not exactly unheard of for kids to be born to unwed parents."

"Not on Summerstead. Small town, old money, lots of gossip. I grew up wondering why people always looked at me funny and why the PTA moms whispered. I figured it out when I read Robert's obituary. I asked Aunt Grace, and she explained they thought it was for the best if I didn't know the truth until I was old enough to handle it. I can understand that, actually. Would you tell Viola if Liam wasn't her father? Now, at the tender age of nearly six? I wouldn't."

"But to treat you like that? It's insane. It's not your fault. It's your mother's."

"I don't blame Mom," Gracen shook his head. She wasn't much of a mother but she was his. And having inherited—or imprinted—her anxiety disorder, he understood. He knew how hard it was to think clearly and make good choices when overwhelmed by crushing thoughts and feelings. His mother lived in a haze of medications because without them she could not cope. "She's had a rough life. Her mother died when she was a teenager. Roy was a controlling father. Mom has been on anti-anxiety meds for the last forty years. I'm not going to say that Roy uses it to control or manipulate her, but I will say it is a side effect."

"Gracen, this explains so much to me about you," Blythe breathed as she took his hand into hers. They were sitting together on her couch and had been for the last several hours. "No wonder you're so closed off and you don't talk about yourself."

"Well, that's it, more or less. Now you know everything."

"I will never know everything about you."

"Because this is it? The end of our run?" Gracen asked, peering at her through tired eyes.

"No. Because you're so much more than all of this," Blythe explained, "and I don't want to lose us without a good reason."

"The fact that I'm an emotional cripple isn't a good one?" he said attempting to joke.

"Hey, I have abandonment issues and you only associate love with manipulation. That's either a Molotov cocktail or matching baggage."

"And you think it's matching baggage."

"It could be matching baggage with a bomb inside of it for all I know. There are no guarantees. That's why it takes trust."

"It's like you're fighting for us. And I don't know why you think I'm worth it. It makes me wonder if you're clinging to romantic illusions. I don't want that for you."

"I'm fighting for us because you are worth it, Princeton. I might slap you again."

"I can feel the love," Gracen replied wryly.

"I'm tired, we've been at this all night," she smiled, "but seriously, we both can sit here and say that no one has fought for me, stayed for me, worked for me. You know my story and now I know yours, and I'm staying. What are you going to do?"

She posed the question again, bouncing the ball squarely in his court. Morning light splintered into her living room. Blythe looked exhausted, of course, she hadn't slept, she hadn't eaten. Neither had he. Gracen knew he couldn't end their relationship without regretting it. There was no just cause, only fear that he would hurt her and lose her in the long run.

However, this wasn't the long run, not yet. This was now. She was here now and so was he. And maybe that's all he needed, for now.

Gracen cupped her sleepy face in his hands and kissed her lips softly. She sighed ever so slightly at his touch.

"I'm staying," he whispered, and she melted into his arms. Overcome with exhaustion Blythe felt that she could fall asleep in that instant, in his embrace. "Baggage and all, I still love you, Kate."

She stroked his cheekbone in that familiar way, and smiled. "I hope you never stop calling me Kate."

They kissed again, then as he studied her face, he pushed the hair out of her eyes. "You should go to bed."

"It's morning."

"Your bedroom doesn't have any windows."

"That's not exactly the point."

"Well, take it from someone who has often had their days and nights mixed up, it helps."

He stood and extended his hands to lift her up from the couch. Placing his hand on the small of her back in the way that sent shivers down her spine, Gracen walked with Blythe to the door

"So, not the New Year's Eve I pictured, but this was … important," Blythe said.

"I'm sorry, I'll make it up to you."

"Next holiday, no scotch."

"No scotch," Gracen nodded.

He paused at the door, and Blythe suddenly lunged to give him a fierce kiss. This had been a very long, very draining New Year's Eve. Yet when all was said and done and the sun dawned on the first of January, Blythe felt that it had been for the best. It wasn't smooth sailing but they had weathered a storm. Storms roll into every life, every relationship, theirs could be no different.

When at last Gracen returned to his apartment, he collapsed onto his couch. He remembered his first sleep in Sayen Falls on that very couch. He'd arrived here with a whole lot of pain and very little hope. Now for the first time, Gracen had more hope than he had hurt. He wasn't sure how long it would last or what exactly to do with it to make it last. With Blythe's sweet kisses lingering on his lips, Gracen smiled. For this moment, it was enough to have hope. He'd worry about what to do with it when he awoke.

# Chapter 38

"So, I wanted to let you know that I talked to Jesse," Blythe said to Ginnie. It was the first day back to school after winter break. Ginnie treated the kids to a trip to The Yellow Bowl once she picked up Viola from school. The littles enjoyed some hot cocoa and powdered sugar donuts while they looked at picture books. Ginnie enjoyed a chat with Blythe as she sipped an espresso. She really needed the pick-me-up.

"How did that go?" Ginnie asked.

"I told him to let it go. Gracen told me everything. We had it all out on New Year's Eve."

"And is it as bad as Jesse says?"

"It is, in a way. But like I said to Jesse, Gracen wasn't hiding anything from me, not really. He came here hoping to start a new life and leave the past behind him. And that's precisely what he did."

"I can understand that," Ginnie nodded. "I think we all have things we'd rather leave behind us if we can. Even Liam wanted his return to Sayen Falls to be a fresh start when he came back. He didn't want the darkness from 'the lost years' to define him forever."

"Exactly. I know that Jesse understands that. He just doesn't want Gracen to have that luxury. Well, anyway, I think Jesse will let it lie, and it was the strangest New Year's Eve ever, but Gracen promised me that Valentine's Day would make up for it."

"I hope it does," Ginnie sighed. "I doubt we'll do anything for Valentine's Day. Liam will probably be at musical rehearsal."

"Oh, right, that's starting soon," Blythe sighed, knowing what a strain the musical sometimes put on their marriage.

"He's in a meeting right now lobbying for *Les Mis*."

"So he decided that's the show he wants?" Blythe grinned. "I can only imagine how well it's going with Debbie and Russ."

"Probably not well at all."

\* \* \*

Blythe and Ginnie's assumptions were correct. The minute Liam suggested *Les Misérables*, Debbie became smug and dismissive.

"It's too much, Liam, even the youth version."

Although she loved *Les Mis*, she felt it was too ambitious for this group of kids. She had it in her mind to do something classic like *Guys and Dolls*.

"There's no choreography, what do you want me to do? Block fight scenes?" Russ pointed out. This was a man who had danced on Broadway with Angela Lansbury. His talent as a choreographer was not to be squandered on shows without big dance numbers. He was pushing for *Forty-Second Street*.

"Ken, please," Liam said, turning to the stage manager, "*Les Mis* has some great sets, it's not just background pieces. I mean, the barricade is iconic."

"We don't pick a show based on the set pieces," Debbie said sharply. "It's either *Guys and Dolls* or *Forty-Second Street*. Personally, I think we have a better cast for *Guys and Dolls*."

With a sigh, Liam rubbed his chin. He hadn't shaved in a couple of days and his carefully maintained stubble was becoming an itchy beard. It was a wonder Ginnie hadn't complained about it yet. He needed to stay focused. Debbie was a steamroller, which is why the program had almost collapsed in the first place. No one wanted to work with her. Three years ago Liam had stepped in to be the hero and had been bullied into shows he hated.

"Let me make this clear," he said with sudden authority. Their eyes turned toward him; Debbie was smirking. "We do a show that matters, or I'm out. I quit. I'm done."

He needed the stipend to survive the winter's heating bills. This was a bluff he desperately hoped they wouldn't call.

"A show that matters," Debbie repeated, with a patronizing grin.

"*Les Mis* matters," he said simply. Her eyes narrowed, she regarded him closely. There was emotion brewing inside him. That was highly unusual for Liam Elwood.

"What exactly has prompted this all-or-nothing demand?"

"I'd prefer to keep that to myself," Liam replied.

Debbie drummed her fingers on her desk. "There must be a reason."

Liam scowled, he should've known that Debbie wouldn't back down.

"To be frank, I'm tired of abandoning my family to help you out with shows that don't mean anything to anyone. My kids are only going to be little once. I missed Teddy's first steps during *Brigadoon*."

"We all make sacrifices."

"Right. But you get to call the shots," he countered. He noticed Russ covering a smile as he shared a look with Ken. "It's easier to make sacrifices when you're doing what you want to do; when you're doing something you believe in."

Debbie leaned back in her desk chair, her brow furrowed. "I've been doing this a long time. I gave up a lot of time with my family to put on these shows. I think they all have mattered. But. You're right. If you're going to give up time, it should be something you care about," Debbie conceded, "and I know what *Les Misérables* means to you, to all of you."

Liam cracked a smile. "It was the first Broadway show we ever saw."

"I've heard Blythe tell that story a dozen times," Debbie said with uncharacteristic fondness. Generally, there was little love lost between those two. "She used 'On My Own' when she auditioned her senior year. So many girls attempt that song, but Blythe was one of the few that nailed it.

And of course, you used 'Master of the House' for your *Music Man* audition."

"It worked," Liam grinned. "And this show will work."

Typically, Ken didn't say much at these meetings. He'd learned quickly that Debbie's bossiness ruled the roost. But today he had something to say. "I think Liam is right. *Les Mis* will resonate with the kids. They don't listen to Rodgers and Hammerstein, they listen to *Once, Next to Normal, Rent, Wicked*—shows that make statements and stand for something."

"So the math teacher and the stage manager have gotten poetic on me and decided we need to do something deep and meaningful," Debbie said. "How interesting."

"Hey, even math teachers and stage managers have souls. You artistic types think you own the market on depth," Liam argued.

"Alright, fine, I can tell when I've been beaten."

"You can? Since when? I've never seen it before. This should be documented for the yearbook," Russ teased. In twenty-six years working together, he'd never seen Debbie Reitzel not get her way, at least not without a lot of yelling. Liam hadn't raised his voice a single time.

"I can't believe I'm agreeing to this. If there's backlash from the parents, you're explaining it, Mr. Elwood," Debbie sighed, "but I'll secure the rights and get it posted. *Les Misérables* is the Sayen Falls spring musical, heaven help us."

* * *

When the show was announced the music department began buzzing with excitement. Straightaway, Ella and Sawyer began preparing audition pieces for the romantic leads, Cosette and Marius. Ella desperately wanted Lily to audition but she was stubbornly refusing. Day after day, Ella pleaded, but Lily only became more adamant.

After five days of listening to the harassment and refusal, Gracen asked Lily why. They were in his office rolling silverware while Silas and Sawyer manned the front. It was a quiet night on the riverfront, with almost no customers.

"I just don't see the point," Lily shrugged.

"Because your parents won't come?" Gracen asked. She nodded. He said, "Can I give you some advice?"

"You know you can, but I can't promise to take it."

"What else is new?" Gracen winked. "Alright, here it is: You're not a kid, Lily. You've just turned eighteen; you're about to graduate high school and go off into the world. You need to make decisions for yourself, what makes *you* happy. You can't live for your parents."

That was a solid point. She looked away. "Well, I doubt I'd get a part."

"So now you're switching tactics," Gracen had to laugh. "There are a thousand reasons to *not* do something. All it takes is one good one though."

Lily eyed Gracen skeptically. "One good reason? That actually seems like a really poor way to make a decision."

"Okay, we're not talking about getting married. It's a musical. A musical. You get that right? Singing, dancing? Alright, very little dancing in this show, but still."

"Will you and Blythe come?" she asked, turning a bit shy.

"That's even a question? We're committed for several reasons already, but yes, we'd come to see you. Blythe and I will sit in the front row and throw roses."

"That seems like overdoing it," Lily teased. She scooped up the stack of rolled silverware and tossed them into the clean dish bin. "Gracen, I don't even know what song I could use to audition. The others have like a 'go-to' song. Ella uses 'I Could've Danced All Night', and Sawyer uses 'If I Loved You.' I don't really have a song that's mine."

"That could be a good thing. You're not auditioning as Lily Morgan. You have to be a character. Your song should reflect that."

"You say that with experience."

"I helped Uncle Harry a lot at his theater. Just because I couldn't get on a stage without going into cardiac arrest, doesn't mean I don't understand how it works."

"It also apparently doesn't preclude you from pressuring other people into it."

"Do you have an anxiety disorder?"

"I could," she grinned. "If that would get me out of this."

The front door chimed and there were voices murmuring in the dining room. Gracen assumed—hoped—customers. A few moments later Silas appeared in the office door with Blythe.

"Hey, I have like seven copies of *The Great Gatsby*, any chance you're a Fitzgerald fan?" Blythe began, looking down at the book in her hand. When she glanced up and saw Lily she smacked her brother with said book. "Why didn't you tell me she was here?"

"You didn't ask?" Silas offered.

"I wouldn't have just barged in," Blythe said. She knew Gracen was concerned about Lily with her parents' divorce progressing. It was strange to think of divorce as progress.

"You're still beautiful, even when you barge," Gracen flirted. Silas blanched and Gracen looked at Lily. "Sorry, are we being nauseating?"

"No, it's cute when it's you guys."

"I'm a little nauseated," Silas said raising his hand.

"In that case," Gracen said, pulling Blythe into his lap with a loud kiss.

"Seriously, my sister."

"I had no idea you were such a puritan," Lily said to Silas playfully.

239

"Oh, and now I get to hear it from this one," Silas rolled his eyes.

"This is actually perfect timing," Gracen said. "I have Lily just about convinced to audition for the musical."

"Really?" Blythe gasped. "Liam called a little bit ago. They haven't found a Fantine. I think you should audition for her. You could totally do it."

"Fantine?" Lily's eyes grew wide. "She's really important."

"There are only four female roles to speak of, dear, they're all important," Blythe replied.

"Fantine, I don't know," Lily said. Gracen could see she was back-pedaling. He shot Blythe a look. But it was Silas who spoke next.

"I think you can do it. I think you can connect with the character."

"Because I'm a depressed single-mother turned prostitute?"

"You don't have to literally be the character, for crying out loud. This isn't method acting," Silas retorted. "You have to get the emotions of the character. I think you get that."

"Because of my parents," Lily said rather matter-of-factly.

"That's part of it, sure. Use that drama in your favor. But Fantine isn't hopelessness. She is hope," Silas explained. "She's trust. She trusted the guy who got her pregnant, she trusted the innkeepers to take care of her child, she trusted her employer to be fair, she trusted the police to listen to her story. Over and over again, she trusted. And then we get 'I Dreamed a Dream' when she realizes that all of that trust brought her to ruin. That's gut-wrenching. If you can nail that, you steal the show."

"And you actually think I can do this?" Lily was incredulous.

He shrugged. "Hemingway said that writing is easy, you just open up a vein and bleed. Singing, acting, it's similar. You open up a vein and bleed all over the stage."

"That sounds terrifying."

"Hemingway was the one who said it was easy, but he was kinda nuts," Silas said. "It makes you vulnerable, putting that kind of emotion out there for the world to judge. But it's the only way to be authentic."

"I forgot that you liked Hemingway," Blythe said. It'd been a long time since Blythe heard her brother talk like this about music and performance. Maybe he'd finally been out of the Mindy atmosphere long enough to get his bearings straight.

Silas smirked. "He's the only one that I can understand. You can keep your Shakespeare; I'll take Papa Hemingway and his cats with thumbs."

"Lily, I think this whole thing could be really good for you," Gracen said earnestly. "You can prove to yourself that you can do something that scares you, and be good at it."

"And it might be cathartic," Blythe said. "Believe me, this is one of the more healthy ways to deal with feelings. I think that's why Silas and Liam and I all became such theater geeks."

240

"I know it's why I did," Silas admitted. "I got obsessed with music, and then theater by association after our parents split up. It was something I could get lost in. I could express whatever I was feeling. I didn't have words for it most of the time, but I always had music."

"That's actually a very beautiful sentiment," Lily said.

"Every now and then I come up with something that isn't sarcastic," Silas grinned.

Lily chewed on her bottom lip. Lately, she'd felt like a mess of emotions loosely held together with twine fraying at the ends. This audition would either send her over the edge or set her free. There was only one way to find out.

"Okay, let's figure it out. What do you think works?" Lily asked. Time to take the leap.

"Hold up, before we jump into show tunes and American Songbook, let's move this conversation," Blythe said. "We need a piano. There's one in the banquet center. I have keys and we have Piano Man here."

"I take it you mean me?" Silas said.

"Yes you," she said shoving her brother out the door. "Come on, you two, get your coats. I'm sure Sawyer and Finn can keep our places from burning down for a half hour."

Minutes later Blythe had them gathered around the grand piano in the banquet center in the plaza just down from her shop. She had access to the building since they often supplied tea and coffee for the events there. It was chilly inside so they kept their coats on and their hands in their pockets, except Silas. Silas was playing scales, loosening the music in his muscles, as the others chatted about the audition.

"I was in the musical my freshman year, and I used 'My Favorite Things'," Lily told them.

"Okay, well that's out," Blythe groaned. "Liam hates that song."

"If I recall, it makes him want to stick a rusty ice pick in his ear," Silas said as he played another scale. Over and over again his fingers graced the keys, limbering up the music that used to fill his brain. Suddenly he thundered the theme from *Phantom of the Opera* on the grand piano and music filled the entire space.

"I've never understood how you can just do that," Blythe shook her head.

"I didn't know I still could. It's been a while since I've been able to really play. I sold my keyboard to pay the bills. But that's a sad story for another day," Silas said. He did another scale, then burst into something fast and jazzy, very ragtime. "Yup, still got it."

"I guess sometimes we don't know what we're capable of until we're already doing it," Blythe remarked.

"That should be on a keychain," Silas quipped.

"Remind me to find him a keyboard," Blythe said to Gracen. "Or did you leave one of those in Summerstead?"

"What do you want to hear?" he asked and Blythe shot him a look.

"Okay, before he starts calling her 'Kate'," Silas said, "let's get back to the task at hand. Miss Morgan needs a song that will win her Fantine."

"Something sad, but strong … poignant," Blythe said thoughtfully. "How about that one from *Cats*? 'Memory'?"

"Can't do it," Silas said, making a face. "These hands don't play 'Memory'."

"The song is a little cliché," Gracen said. "What about something from *Phantom*, like 'Wishing You Were Somehow Here Again'?"

"That could work," Blythe said thoughtfully.

As Blythe and Gracen bantered titles, Silas's fingers scattered up and down the keys, trying out pieces of songs, his selections more from muscle memory than conscious choice. He drifted away from musicals and into his old set pieces. Because Coldplay had been heavily featured in his sets back when he played, he found himself tapping out the chords to "Fix You". He stopped short. The sudden silence grabbed the attention of the others.

"Lily, ignore them. Forget everything we said. What do you love? Just pick a song."

She closed her eyes and an answer came. "There's a song we did my sophomore year in choir that I really liked. But I don't know if it's a good idea to use it."

"What's the song?" Silas asked.

"'Love Changes Everything'."

"I know that song. It's from *Aspects of Love*," Silas replied. He thought hard for a minute, his right hand plunked out a piece of the melody. "I think I can find the sheet music online. Just a second."

"It's a beautiful song," Blythe said to Gracen. "It's about how love changes you forever, no matter how it works out. You're never the same."

"Then it should be perfect," Gracen said. He hoped they weren't bullying Lily into vomiting up emotions she wasn't ready to deal with.

"Okay, here we go, finally got it," Silas said, squinting at the tiny screen, "I hope."

He directed her to stand in front of the piano, her heart thumping out of her chest. He began planning a brief intro, then nodded to give her the cue to start. Lily's voice trembled through the first verse but settled considerably by the chorus. Silas gave another nod so that she'd continue through the second verse and by the time she hit the chorus a second time she had found a sweet spot. He kept playing and she followed his lead through the end of the song. Lily hadn't taken her eyes off Silas for a single note; she turned now to look at Gracen.

"That was amazing. I'm so proud of you."

"It was just a first try," Lily said feeling self-conscious.

"So imagine how good it will be when you know it cold," Silas said. He stopped playing and the keys made a jarring sound. "Is there anyone that can help you practice tomorrow?"

"I can play myself if I have the music, eight years of piano lessons."

"Huh, I got you beat," Gracen snorted. "Ten."

Blythe rubbed her forehead. "You really did leave a keyboard in Summerstead, didn't you?"

"I'm supposed to inherit Aunt Grace and Uncle Harry's piano someday. It's a Steinway."

"This clown," Silas said dismissively. He turned his attention back to Lily. "I just don't want you to get used to me and then miss your cue. Someone here always missed their cue."

"Shut it," Blythe sassed. "I still got Dolly even with my missed cues."

"Yeah, we know, we know," Silas said. "I can come to play for you if you want."

"It's really okay, but I appreciate it. I appreciate all of your help. I just hope I can do it tomorrow," Lily said nervously.

"Well, we know you can," Gracen said firmly. "You have so much potential."

"Enough of this schmaltz, I'm about to choke on all the feels," Silas said as he resumed tinkering on the piano. "We have to chop this down to sixteen measures and then sing it about forty-two times."

"Forty-two?" Lily repeated; her smile was coy.

"Well, we don't want to overdo it."

* * *

The Martin had joined Silas's cheap guitar in the coat closet. He didn't like it sitting in the open, just staring at him. He couldn't feel the music. And without feeling, there was no point in doing it.

With trepidation, he pulled open the closet door. It creaked, it needed oil and use. He picked up the guitar case, the hard fiberglass case familiar to his skin, and took it to his room. Carefully he set the case on the bed and opened it to reveal Gracen's guitar. He was almost afraid of it. It didn't matter how meticulously the instrument was made if the music inside of him was gone.

Silas slid the strap around his neck then began to fiddle with the knobs to get the tuning just right. His mind drifted, back to Lily, her song and her uncertainty. The girl really had no idea how good she was.

And it occurred to him that maybe he was living vicariously through her. If Lily moved past her personal fear and her pain to find her voice, then maybe he could move past his own devastation and find his voice again too. There were a lot of ifs and maybes in that sentence. Silas figured the forecast didn't look promising.

He picked out the melody line to "Love Changes Everything", humming and lost in thought. Mindlessly his fingers drifted to different frets and chords, and he found himself back at Coldplay's "Fix You". He had played it in almost every set in college. Mindy didn't really like the Coldplay pieces, but in those days Silas played what he loved, and she overlooked it. "Fix You" meant a lot to him, he knew that song longer than Mindy; he learned it in high school after Grammy had her stroke, and Blythe took over the shop. A loss and a sacrifice, and he had been miles and hours away unable to help either one of them.

He let himself play the song once, and then another time with singing. Tears pricked his eyes but he kept on playing. He had to push through this pain, this blockage in his heart. He had to find the music again. Silas played and played, songs he had learned, songs he had written, songs he had started and never finished. His fingers cracked without calluses to protect them; the physical pain eased the torment inside.

"Because it's just once more, once more," he sang, "until I get it right. Once more, once more, won't give up the fight, once more, once more, until we get it done, once more, once more, you're the only one."

Silas stopped. He hummed the melody again. It was new. It was brand new. It was a tune the world had never heard before. It was music.

He scrambled for paper. All he could find was a receipt. He needed a pen. Where was a pen? He rummaged in the guitar case. Two nickels, a stick of old gum, another crumpled receipt—a pen!

Strumming the chords, he hummed along, then jotted down the words. He tucked the pen behind his ear. Closing his eyes, he let his fingers move without thinking and his lips sing with just feeling.

His eyes popped open. The music had come back. A vein had opened in his soul, the vein with notes and melodies, with words and feelings. Now all Silas had to do was let it flow.

* * *

A week later, Liam was ready to post the cast list on the choir room door after school. There had been several heated arguments over the cast. Only two parts had been cast without a single debate, Jean Valjean and Fantine.

He taped up the list then ducked out the side door to avoid the impending mob of students. As he climbed into his car, he dialed his sister. It rang four times, then he heard her cheerful voicemail message.

"I thought you should be the first to know what we decided. No surprise, Sawyer will be Marius, the romantic lead, and Ella will be his Cosette. They'll play perfectly together. The big news is Lily. She was the only one we even considered for Fantine. Her audition blew us away, even Debbie. You and Gracen should be proud."

# Chapter 39

The rest of January proved to be a meteorological disaster. Temperatures plummeted and snow began falling. The city workers spread salt in vain as it was too cold to do any good at all. There was no choice but to repeatedly cancel school. The first few days it was funny. Then it hit double-digit cancellations and it wasn't amusing anymore.

Ginnie was bearing the brunt of it. Teddy was swinging from the rafters with all his boisterous energy cooped inside their small house. Viola desperately missed seeing her friends and being at school, so she was sulking and moody. But Liam was the worst. His students were behind with their schoolwork, and his cast was losing precious time with the show.

When the pipes burst in the old section of the high school, effectively canceling all activities at the school regardless of weather, Liam snapped.

"This is great, this is just really great," he seethed. He slammed down his phone and stalked into the living room to vent to Ginnie. He glared over the tops of his children's heads, wishing with all his might that he could use big ugly grown-up words. Teddy was trying to climb up Ginnie's legs like a jungle gym, and Viola was crying over the broken VCR.

One look at her fuming husband and Ginnie knew she had to end this mess with the kids immediately. She peeled Teddy off her and set him down firmly on the couch.

"I told you not to put anything in there," she said pointing at the VCR. Of course, if they could afford to upgrade their kids' movies to DVD it wouldn't matter, but that was a comment to keep to herself right now. "You need to tell Viola you're sorry."

Teddy scowled, his hands balled into fists.

"Theodore," Ginnie said quietly. Staying calm was taking the very last shards of her sanity; she could feel her hands starting to shake.

"No."

"Theodore William Elwood, tell your sister you're sorry."

"NO!"

There was a nearly audible snap as Ginnie's last nerve gave way. She snatched Teddy's favorite toy, a clunky yellow tractor she was forever tripping over.

"Then I'm taking the backhoe away."

"Nooooo," Teddy howled and big crocodile tears puddled in his eyes.

"You know the rules," Ginnie was shouting now, "and I've had enough. I told you not to put things in the VCR; you did anyway! The dog's been hiding most of the day because you slap him every time he shows his face. And I'm done. I've given you enough chances!"

"Mine backhoe," he sobbed as he watched Ginnie put the backhoe in the hall closet—toy jail. Viola watched silently, feeling sorry for herself, sorry for Teddy, and even sorrier for their mother. They had done this. They had broken Mommy.

"Gin—" Liam began, his voice was stern.

"Don't you dare," she hissed. The air crackled with tension. Viola knew what was coming. It was a fight. Instantly, she forgave Teddy for the VCR and held her arms out to him. Teddy snuggled close to his sister, wiping his snotty nose with the back of his hand.

"You didn't even warn him," Liam said. Clearly, the man had no sense.

"I've been warning him all day!"

"That's not what I meant."

"If you can do it better, then, by all means, go ahead. You're home enough these days."

"There's no winning with you! If I'm at work, then I'm not here enough. When school is closed, and I'm home, it's still not good enough."

"That's because when you're here you don't help."

"What do you want me to do?"

"Not sulk and pout and throw fits like the children, for starters!"

"Excuse me?"

He was bellowing, she was screaming. The children looked from one to the other and back again like a tennis game. Bandit peeked his head out from Viola's bedroom. As irritated as he was with Teddy's abuse, his instinct to be here for the children was stronger. Quietly, Bandit crept down the hallway into the living room and curled up at their feet.

"All I'm saying is that you're not helping. We have to walk on eggshells around here because every little thing sets you off," Ginnie stated.

"Do you want to go back to work?" Liam sneered. "I'll stay at home with the kids, is that what you want?"

This was Liam's most used line in every argument. No matter the catalyst they ended up in this same exchange. Ginnie's eyes narrowed, her voice lowered.

"I'd be home from work too," she snapped. Truth be told, there were days when Ginnie missed her history classroom and walking away from kids at the end of the workday. "But I really can't do this. I can't have this same stupid argument again."

She glanced at the kids. Bandit's tail thumped against the floor when she looked at them. Her heart broke. She loved Viola and Teddy, and even that dopey dog, more than anything in the world. It immediately grieved her to see them scared, and it chastened her to know that she and Liam had caused it.

As she knelt on the floor next to them a tear slipped down her cheek, and she whispered, "I'm sorry."

"I'm sorry I cried about the VCR," Viola told her mother.

"I sowwy, I-lah," Teddy said to his sister. Bandit scrambled to his feet, licking tears off faces and trying to do his part.

Liam watched at a distance. He felt bad, but he couldn't bring himself to join this tender scene. No one had ever apologized to him, and that was okay. That's life. Life isn't fair, life hurts, life doesn't apologize and make things right.

* * *

Across town, snow drifted and gathered in the riverfront plaza. Finn donned his hat and coat to shovel outside of The Yellow Bowl. Again. They'd kept busy, as busy as they could, but the dropping temperatures and rising snowfalls meant a significant decrease in business. At least today there was some life in the store; Ella, Sawyer, and Lily had come for tea and sympathy when they learned that the burst pipes canceled their rehearsals indefinitely. They were sick of their own houses and each other's houses and the houses of anyone else they knew.

"This is ridiculous, if this keeps up we won't be able to do the show," Ella lamented.

"At least we know our lines," Sawyer pointed out with typical optimism. He took a sip of his coffee, scowled and added more sugar.

"We can't just stand at microphones and sing. We have to learn the blocking, there are a couple dance numbers, all of you bozo boys have to figure out how to die correctly," Ella said.

"Hey, I don't die, I almost die, get it right."

"They actually did stand at microphones and sing for the Tenth Anniversary Concert of *Les Mis*," Blythe said, taking the remaining chair at the table where they were sitting.

"I don't see that working for us," Lily sighed. "I bet Mr. Elwood is getting stressed."

"Liam? Liam lives in a constant state of stress these days," Blythe said.

Ella groaned, "We just need someplace where we can learn our marks and get the staging right. It wouldn't be too hard to adjust to the school stage for tech week and dress rehearsals."

Silas chuckled as he shelved some books. With nothing to do next door, he was helping Blythe and enjoying the distraught conversation very much. The teenage melodrama was so much more amusing than his full-blown adult drama.

"Listen to you, like you know what you're talking about."

"It could work!" Ella insisted.

"I know it could, that's how a lot of shows do it," Silas replied as he flipped a chair backward and sat down. "I used to be a stage manager. I majored in theater, you know."

"How would I know that?" Ella asked. She glanced at Lily, then back at Silas. "I'd think that you'd want to see this show come together. You went to all that trouble to help Lily."

Immediately Lily reddened and she fumbled under the table to kick Ella. Of course, she missed and nailed Sawyer right in the shin. Still, Ella's provocative comment about Silas set wheels turning for Blythe.

"Hey! What about the banquet center? That'd be big enough, I think it's as long as the stage is wide," Blythe said. "And there's a piano."

"Give me a minute to process that," Sawyer said, "I didn't quite get it. Long? Wide?"

"Wouldn't we have to rent it?" Lily asked.

"I don't know, let me call Kyle. It hasn't been used in weeks and he's paying to heat it for no reason, someone might as well be using it," Blythe said as she headed towards her office. She hoped she could sweet-talk him into it. It would give her something to do.

"So you were a stage manager?" Ella asked Silas.

"Yeah, until the place got shut down for mismanagement of funds. It was a mess. I lost my job, that's all I know for sure," Silas sighed.

"What kind of venue was it? Concerts, plays, musicals?" Ella prodded.

"All of the above, but mostly concerts. It was a good venue for up-and-coming acts. I love seeing bands before they really become big."

"Were you ever in a band?" Lily wondered.

"In college, but I'm more of a solo act kind of guy apparently," Silas said, and the implication wasn't lost on Lily. She knew his story. They were living alternate versions of a similar reality. Divorce meant solitude for all the players involved.

"Kyle saves the day! The banquet center is all yours," Blythe announced as she returned. "Ella, call the cast, or text or whatever it is you kids do to communicate with each other."

"It's too cold for the carrier pigeons," Sawyer said dryly. "Too wet for smoke signals."

"I'm calling Liam," Blythe said, with her phone up to her ear. "Hey, I got you a rehearsal space … The banquet center … Yes, I'm serious. Call Debbie and get down here."

* * *

Liam legitimately had no idea what to do. He stared at Ginnie with the children, he gaped at his phone. He needed this rehearsal time very badly. He was also sure that if he left, Ginnie would lose every last one of her marbles.

"What is it? Who is that?" Ginnie asked, trying unsuccessfully to read his expression.

"It's Blythe. She said that we can use the banquet center to rehearse."

"So why are you looking at me like that?"

"I don't know what you want me to do."

248

She closed her eyes and took a deep breath, "I want you to go rehearse."

"Ginnie, we just—"

She squeezed the kids' hands before she stood up. Her tone was gentle, "Seriously, get out of this house. You're going insane here and the show needs you."

"You won't be mad?"

"No. I got all the mad out of my system five minutes ago."

Liam frowned, "Are you sure? I can take one of the kids at least, I'm sure Blythe can keep an eye on them."

Ginnie looked back at her children. They were exhausted, sick of the house, sick of each other. Still, they couldn't crash Liam's rehearsal. He needed to focus.

"I think I'll take them to your grandparents. Or maybe Gramps. Someone might want this three-ring circus."

Liam still looked unsure but he turned back to his phone and dialed Debbie. Once it was settled with her, he called his grandmother to see if it was okay for Ginnie and the kids to come. Mary Alice was thrilled. They could use some energy and life in the house.

With the announcement that they were going to Grammy and PapPap's, whoops and hollers and barks rang through the house. As she moved past Liam to get herself ready, Liam took Ginnie's hand.

"I'm sorry," he said quietly.

"Me too," she replied, and knowing how hard it was for him to say those words, she added, "Thank you."

* * *

An hour later a pack of teenagers in yoga pants and gym shorts moved chairs out of the way as Silas and Sawyer moved the baby grand piano into place. Liam, Debbie, and Russ talked amongst themselves to determine which area would be the so-called stage. As they finished, Debbie took her place at the piano, and Liam thanked Silas for his help.

"It's no problem. I'll go get coffee for you and Debbie and Russ," Silas offered.

"Why are you being so helpful? Are you really that bored?" Liam asked.

"Yes, I'm really that bored. Humor me."

"Okay, kids, sit down, get a grip, and listen up!" Liam shouted. A few minutes later forty-three kids were seated in relatively rapt attention. "We're behind; we all know that, so this is a great opportunity to make some headway. It's time to focus and buckle down. Opening night is in six weeks and we have a lot to learn. We'll take it from the top, get set!"

Kids scrambled out of the way as a group of guys took the area that Liam designated as center stage. Debbie pounded out the opening chords on the piano and the show started to take shape, even in a banquet center.

As Jean Valjean and Javert began singing their first argument Liam's phone rang loudly, his generic old-fashioned telephone ring. He motioned that they should keep going as he walked to the back of the room, close to where Blythe was observing. It was a short call but long enough to put Liam in a terrible mood again. He shoved his phone in his pocket with a ferocious scowl. He paced over to Blythe, muttering under his breath.

"We're doomed. Doomed and cursed, that's all."

"What is it now?"

"Ken, the stage manager, fell on the ice this morning, broke his leg and fractured his arm in two places," Liam explained hotly. "He'll be gone for the rest of the school year. We can't do a show without a stage manager, especially this show. It's impossible."

"That's like adding insult to injury. Or maybe injury to insult, in this case," Blythe said sympathetically.

"I really don't know what we're gonna do. Ken had a few pieces started, but the barricade hasn't even been sketched, as far as I know. You can't do *Les Mis* without a barricade."

"Not well."

Liam glared at his sister; she shrugged, undaunted.

"I guess I need to tell Debbie," Liam sighed. "That oughta be fun."

"I'm sure it's why he called you instead," she patted him on the back. "Good luck."

Grimacing, Liam prepared for Debbie to really give it to him. She was famous for her outbursts. Maybe he should tell Russ first so he'd have an ally or someone to hide behind. That seemed like a better plan; Liam rerouted his steps to interrupt the choreography Russ was directing with Ella and Sawyer in the far corner.

When Silas and Gracen arrived with the coffee, a lightbulb went off in Blythe's brain. She was having quite a day of bright ideas.

"Hey," she said, grabbing Silas's arm. Coffee sloshed out of the tiny hole.

"Watch it," he said.

"So the stage manager just broke his leg and his arm."

"That sounds painful."

"Silas, you're a stage manager. You just said that."

"I ... I, I mean, I did, I was, but I can't just step in and be the stage manager," Silas stuttered. The prospect of working that closely with Liam was not appealing. They hadn't played that well together as kids, and hardly knew each other as adults.

She stared at him. Gracen smirked as he came around behind her to slip his hands through the triangle holes she made with her hands on her hips.

"Buddy, whatever it is, give in now. This is never good. This is her warrior pose."

"Not with you hanging on me," she tried to shrug him off. Gracen laughed, Blythe glowered.

"Blythe, they can't just hire someone like that," Silas said, snapping his fingers. "There's a process, there are credentials I don't have. These are kids, and in this day and age, they don't just hire the director's brother because they're in a pinch."

"You used to be more determined."

"I used to be a lot of things," he said. "So did you."

Gracen felt her shoulders tense, then slump. That dig had hit its mark. Then, Gracen's attention was dragged from Blythe to the bang Debbie made as she slammed her hand down on the top of the piano. Instantly all movement stopped. Lily stared with wide eyes from where she stood at the makeshift center stage.

"What was he doing out on the ice? He's not in the Ice Capades!"

"He slipped, Debbie. I really think some compassion is in order," Russ pointed out. He wasn't afraid of Debbie.

"I'll have compassion when my show isn't in danger."

"We'll have to just keep working," Liam said with clearly feigned optimism. "At least we have a rehearsal space."

"Brilliant. We have a drafty banquet hall, a few tables, and fifty chairs, what more do we need?" Debbie snarled. "We'll never be ready in time. This show is too much, the kids don't know what they're doing, and now we're down a stage manager."

"This isn't the time," Russ raised his voice. "The kids are doing the best that they can."

"Russel, I don't need you telling me about my cast."

"They're my cast too, Deborah."

"Mom and Dad are fighting again," Sawyer whispered to Ella, who smothered a smile.

"Enough, enough, this is ridiculous," Liam said as he waved his hands between them. "Enough. We'll make it work. I'll make it work. I'll do the work if I have to."

Blythe turned to Silas with a long look. He sighed. He walked slowly toward the powwow at the baby grand. Lily watched him, those doe eyes still large and scared. Silas smiled at her and she relaxed ever so slightly as she returned the smile.

"What are the rules for volunteers?" he asked. "I have experience and I'm available."

"No, I won't let you do this for free, it's too big a job," Liam said firmly.

"Well, I'm not going to let you do this without me. Have you ever built a set before?" Silas asked. "Have any of the three of you built a set? Designed a set? Worked out a lighting plan, mic cues?"

Russ threw his hands up in the air, "If you ask me, you're hired."

"We can't just hire the nearest Elwood because he's available," Debbie barked. "What next? Blythe for costumes?"

Blythe broke away from Gracen to throw her two cents in. Liam braced himself for more shouting. Blythe and Debbie blended about as well as oil and water.

"He's very good," Blythe said. "We both know that I'm a total theater snob. If his work was terrible I'd be the first to tell him."

"That is true. You did tell me my blocking for *Brigadoon* was a mess," Liam nodded.

"Well, it was," Blythe shrugged. "Silas went to school for this, and he has experience."

"That's great, Blythe, but we don't have the authority to hire him," Debbie argued.

"I volunteered," Silas pointed out, trying to remember why.

"Enough," Liam repeated loudly. He took his phone from his pocket, "I'm taking care of this. Silas, you need a job, we need a stage manager, and we all need this musical to succeed."

"I wish you luck, Mr. Elwood," Debbie said deprecatingly. "If you can get the board to approve a contingency contract, I'll be quite impressed."

"Then be prepared to be impressed," he retorted as he sauntered away for his phone call. Silas looked at his sister; she was smirking.

"What makes the two of you so smug?" Silas asked.

"Do you know who the president of the school board is?" Blythe asked.

"Santa Claus?"

"Hattie Farriss," Blythe grinned. The Farrisses and Elwoods were old riverfront friends. After all, Kyle had just given them this rehearsal space. And Hattie would want the musical to have a fighting chance.

"Let's just hope Hattie can convince the board. It isn't her choice alone," Debbie sighed.

As he returned with a wide grin, Liam shook his brother's hand. "It's temporary for now but Hattie is working on it. The contingency contract will be approved at the board meeting next week. And we're having that meeting, come hell or high water."

"Or ice and leaky pipes," Blythe said. Liam rolled his eyes but gave his sister a quick hug of gratitude for her quick thinking.

"Okay, kids, take it from 'At the End of the Day'. And don't stop for anything."

# Chapter 40

Ginnie tiptoed down the stairs and back into Mary Alice's living room. Teddy was napping upstairs in the blue room to the left, and Viola was reading a stack of old picture books in the pink room to the right. Quiet time, the best time of day.

Especially on a day like this. The VCR incident and blowout with Liam had just been the final straw. For starters, Ginnie had awakened after Teddy crawled into bed with her for a snuggle and her shirt was soon dampened with the telltale warmth of urine. Then she'd stepped out of bed onto a cooling pile of dog vomit. Bandit had decided to retch up some carrot sticks from two days ago. Ginnie still couldn't figure out how it was only carrot sticks when he'd eaten about forty-seven other foods since then.

With as much grace and patience as she could muster first thing in the morning, Ginnie had cleaned the floor and changed the sheets. She'd put Teddy in his big boy underwear for the day, although potty training was iffy at best. It wasn't too long after that Teddy pooped his pants, and smushed it when he sat down to play. Cleaning out his underwear led to scouring the sink, and the toilet while she was at it. While she was cleaning, Teddy had stuck crayons in the VCR—crayons his sister was supposed to have put away. And then followed the meltdown.

Ginnie wasn't proud of her reactions and behaviors. She'd done the work that needed to be done, but it had been with such a begrudging heart and angry spirit. And the fight with Liam was awful. Some days she felt broken before lunchtime, and this was such a day. Truth be told, it was an immense relief to head to Mary Alice's for the afternoon. At least she wouldn't be alone with the kids to say anything else she could regret.

Mercifully, lunch went smoothly and Miles volunteered to teach Teddy checkers afterward. That wasn't successful but it was riotous to watch. Still, Mary Alice sensed that Ginnie's nerves were rather frayed around the edges. When nap time rolled around, she suggested that the kids nap there and they could keep each other company. Ginnie normally didn't like to break routines or consistency, especially with Teddy. But today, routines had to be abandoned for the sake of sanity and quiet time with other adults.

"I'm glad you decided to stay," Mary Alice said. "There's really no sense in bundling them up in this cold weather."

"This weather has been brutal. Liam is worried about the show," Ginnie replied. "I'm glad Blythe got him the banquet center for today anyway."

"That was good thinking," Mary Alice remarked. "But how are you surviving?"

"Oh, I'm fine," Ginnie said pasting on her most assuring smile.

"I remember how draining the little years can be. Those were long days. I had the three little ones, Miles worked second trick for the paper mill. I would've been lost if Pearl hadn't been in the same boat. We'd get her two boys and my three kids and do the best we could."

"I always thought it was easier in your day. More community or something."

Mary Alice frowned as she considered Ginnie's statement. "I think our expectations were different. I knew I'd stay at home with the kids, that was my job, my contribution. And we didn't worry as much about the best way or what all the advice was. We did what we knew. I'm sure some of that has been proven wrong now, but we made it."

"There is a lot of pressure these days, and it feels like there aren't any second chances. They're only little once."

"I know a bit about that," Mary Alice said quietly. "We second-guessed ourselves for a long time after Kate. And again when we lost Bill."

"How did you ever survive losing them?" Ginnie asked softly. Instinctively her hands went to her womb at the notion of losing a child; it seemed an unbearable loss.

"In a way, I think we're still coping. But I leaned on God. And I learned to lean on the people he gave me and to let them lean on me. I had to. I couldn't shoulder my grief alone."

Ginnie typically shied away from asking questions about Kate or Bill's deaths. But this wasn't really about their actual passing; it was about surviving, coping, struggling. Mary Alice was very private in general, but today she was talking. Ginnie didn't want to miss an opportunity to mine for wisdom. She was desperate for some nugget of truth to guide her.

"Is that what solidified your marriage?"

"Our marriage was solid before that. We eloped, you know. No one was on our side. They thought we'd never make it," Mary Alice explained. "And then when Kate left us, there was a moment when I thought maybe the critics would be right. But Miles just reached for me and I reached for him, and we never looked anywhere else, except up to the God we knew had our little girl. There were moments of blame when the grief was really hard and the despair was overwhelming, but we needed each other more than we needed to place blame."

The memories were almost five decades old, but their strength remained potent. On that fateful day, the front office of the mill was in chaos. There'd been a fight in the washroom, then an argument between managers and the receptionist lost the message from Mary Alice that Miles was needed at home. Their daughter fell through the cracks in her hour of need, but it was not the fault of Miles or Mary Alice.

"The fact was it was Kate's time to go home. I still don't know why. And then we did it all over again when Bill wrecked on that God-forsaken motorcycle. People say that you get to the other side of your hardship and you see what it was all for but sometimes that just isn't true. Sometimes you survive and there still aren't answers. You don't bury two of your children and find some neatly wrapped truth at the end of it all." Mary Alice paused. "There isn't an end."

"I can't imagine losing one of my children," Ginnie said quietly. In her most desperate days—like today—she fantasized about getting the car and just driving until she ran out of gas. Although, that would probably just get her to the end of town; even her physical gas tank seemed to perpetually be hovering near empty. Yet to lose a child, to bury one of her babies—it was unthinkable.

"I wouldn't wish it on someone I hated. It's unnatural," Mary Alice said fiercely. For a moment, she closed her eyes, then she continued, "But hardships are part of life. Maybe that was the biggest lesson I learned. No matter how good a person, or how good a Christian I am, it rains on us all. There's no sense in comparing pain; we all walk with it."

"So how did you make it this far? What's the secret to your marriage?"

"When something was broken between us, we fixed it. We didn't just throw it all away."

"But how?" Ginnie pressed. "How did you do it with three little ones and second shifts? And with intense grief and hardship?"

"I told you, dear, we still are," Mary Alice said, patting Ginnie's hand softly. "Just because we're old doesn't mean we've got it all figured out. Miles still boggles my mind. But we press on. We forgive each other as often as we fight. We hold on more times than we let go. We pray together and dig deep and give grace."

"Isn't there a verse like that?" Ginnie asked.

"'I have fought a good fight, I have finished my course, I have kept the faith.' Second Timothy," Mary Alice quoted. "I can tell you, I'm exhausted sometimes but it's worth it. I haven't given up yet."

"To be honest, you're doing some of your best work right now," Ginnie smiled. "I needed to talk today. Not just about me and my petty troubles, but how to do life, marriage, parenting."

"Can I give you a piece of advice? From an old married woman to a young married woman? Talk to your husband. He can't fix what he doesn't know is broken."

"I don't expect Liam to fix anything. He's overworked as it is."

"So are you, dear. It's not easy for two to become one but it is possible. You have to keep talking, pushing through *together*. Sometimes it isn't the big catastrophes that do the most damage; sometimes it's the erosion from the mundane. You grow apart."

"Yeah, I get that."

"Your grandparents faced that. I don't know if you ever knew that, but their marriage was on the rocks after Dennis and Donald both left for college. They had stopped talking and needing each other."

255

"They never said," Ginnie remarked quietly. Her grandparents were Catholic and old-fashioned. As far as she knew divorce was never muttered under their breaths, let alone considered. There was no exit strategy.

"They figured it out, but it took some time. Oddly enough, the donut shop helped. They did it together. That was one reason we all went in at the same time. It gave all of us something to do. It gave us a place to talk and share our lives, and that's what we've always hoped The Yellow Bowl would be for people, a place to talk and share their lives."

"That's what it is for us," Ginnie said. "It's not just where Blythe works or, well, lives. It's a gathering place for all of us. My kids love it there too."

"So maybe you need to sit down for some coffee and reconnect with Liam. Although make sure Finn makes the coffee."

"Poor Blythe," Ginnie giggled.

"But really, sometimes all it takes is a half hour and a cup of coffee to reconnect. Liam is a good man, I couldn't be prouder of him, but I know he gets lost sometimes with his priorities. He's had so much on his shoulders for so long."

"That's why I try to not blame him or get angry. He carries so much."

"But if he's carrying his burdens one way, and you're carrying yours another, then distance comes between you," Mary Alice reminded her.

"So what you're saying is I need to ask my husband out on a date?"

"Valentine's Day is coming up," Mary Alice pointed out.

"We talked about it the other night. There's just no way to do it this year. And that's okay. I don't want to put even more pressure on him."

"Oh, there's that pressure again. In my day we didn't have to buy flowers and chocolate and ride horses bareback at twilight. Your generation has over-complicated everything."

"Ride horses bareback at twilight?" Ginnie laughed.

"It was in a movie we watched yesterday," Mary Alice rolled her eyes. "It was supposed to be romantic."

"I can see how that would be," Ginnie said, "but I don't need all that."

"Of course not, you have your head on right. We were poor as church mice but Miles always bought me a bit of my favorite candy for Valentine's Day," Mary Alice smiled. "If you've agreed that Valentine's Day is just another day, then that's fine. There shouldn't be pressure to do everything to the nines all the time. But can you make it to the end of the musical to stop and catch your breath together? Honestly and truly?"

Ginnie took a deep breath, "I'm struggling, I do every year and it's not getting easier as the kids get older like I thought it would. But I can make it to April. I always do. And then Liam and I will reconnect. We'll find the same page again."

Mary Alice took Ginnie's hand, "Promise me that you will ask him out for that coffee."

"I will," she promised, "and you know what? I'll get him his favorite candy for Valentine's Day. The kids too."

"Get some for yourself while you're at it. You deserve it."

* * *

"So was your day a total loss?" Liam asked as he flopped onto their bed. He stared up at their ceiling fan. It needed to be dusted. This was not something to say out loud.

"It got better at your grandparents."

"They have that effect on people."

"I had a serious talk with Mary Alice today during nap time."

"About what?" Liam rolled over onto his stomach.

"When they lost Kate and Bill, how they survived so much. She gave me some advice."

"That's unusual, she isn't a real big advice giver. So what'd she say?"

"That I need to ask you out on a coffee date," she said simply as she pulled her shirt off over her head, and slipped an enormous oversized shirt on to sleep in.

"That was her big advice?" Liam asked skeptically.

"That was the gist of it, yes."

He shook his head as he wrapped one strong arm around his wife's leg and drew her close. She fell onto the bed next to him.

"There's more to this story."

"Yes."

He undid her ponytail to run his fingers through her hair. "I miss you."

It had been a long time since butterflies had flitted in Ginnie's stomach. She closed her eyes and sighed, "We'll make it, Liam. We always do."

"Why did you ever take me back? After I was so selfish and mean? I know Knox Callahan treated you better."

"Knox was not the right guy for me. And you grew up. You were a college kid sorting out a lot of issues, I knew that then," she shrugged, "and I missed you."

"You're too good for me," he whispered, pressing his lips to hers. They could fight like the dickens but Liam wouldn't give her up for anything. He'd go down with the ship for this woman. Liam just needed to be sure he wasn't the one sinking the ship, flooding it with too many other projects and problems and people. He peered into her eyes, "Are you sure you're okay with skipping Valentine's Day?"

"Yes, I'm sure," Ginnie nodded.

"I just feel like the jerk husband. Gracen is planning this big day trip Valentine's extravaganza for Blythe, and I feel like a bum in comparison."

Ginnie had to laugh as she stroked her husband's neck. "Gracen and Blythe are in that gooey courtship stage. He has to impress her. I already am impressed. You impress me every day when you work extra hours, come home to play with the children and read to them before bed, and then struggle to stay awake long enough to find out how chaotic my day was."

"That's not very romantic."

"Depends on your definition of romance."

"You're being overly gracious and understanding," Liam groaned. "I feel worse."

"Tell you what, buy my favorite candy and you'll sweep me off my feet," Ginnie grinned.

"A dollar's worth of penny candy from Bonsell's Candy Shop?" he smirked. "Mostly gummy candies and a candy lipstick."

"And I wondered if you even knew."

"I haven't bought it yet. I could come home with a dollar's worth of shoestring licorice."

"Yuck."

As Liam kissed his wife again, a small voice cried out in the darkness for his mommy. Teddy couldn't sleep and he was afraid of the dark. Same story, different night. As Ginnie stood to tend to her son, Liam tugged her back.

"Let me," he said. And Ginnie let him. She'd get the next one. And together, they'd find a rhythm and press on. There was no exit strategy.

## Chapter 41

All his life Gracen had believed that being truly known by another person meant discomfort and distance would soon follow. It was a wonder and a joy for him to discover that was not necessarily so. The intimacy he shared with Blythe was unique and rare; the hardest parts had been laid bare and accepted willingly as part and parcel.

Planning Valentine's Day, then, was an enjoyable challenge. Wanting to do something she would never think to do herself, he decided a day trip was in order. It was high time to see someplace other than Sayen Falls. Columbus was only a little more than two hours away, so Gracen picked Liam's brain for the best and worst of the city. Then, it took him a couple of weeks to finalize an agenda that was tailor-made for Blythe's particular personality. The best part was that Blythe knew almost nothing. He wanted it to be a complete surprise that they were even leaving Sayen Falls. She was given two details: their date would take up most of the day, and she should dress comfortably.

"Is the snow they're calling for going to interfere with our plans?" Blythe asked him as she shrugged her winter coat on. Underneath, she was wearing a lilac-colored shirt layered with a gray cardigan. She'd also chosen her favorite skinny jeans and a pair of cute black snow boots.

"It might, but Silas said we can use his Explorer," Gracen replied. "But the snow shouldn't be a bother to us until the end of our day."

"It's supposed to start snowing within the hour," she said with confusion. He only smiled and gestured towards the stairs.

Sure enough, Silas's car was warmed and ready for them. Blythe was rather giddy with nervous excitement as she climbed in and buckled herself for adventure. The self-satisfied grin on Gracen's face only piqued her curiosity more. When he steered them onto the highway, headed south, she laughed as she said,

"Well, I wasn't expecting this. Where are we going?"

"The state's capital."

"Columbus?"

"That's the one I learned in fifth grade."

"What in the world is in Columbus?"

"The governor? *The* Ohio State University? The Olentangy River? Right? Am I saying that right? Olentangy? The names around here are impossible, by the way."

"Gracen, seriously, what are we going to do in Columbus?" Blythe giggled.

"A little bit of this and a little bit of that."

"You're still not telling me anything?"

"Try to enjoy being surprised and seeing a little bit of the world. Just a little though. No passport required."

"Just a little adventure."

"Bite-sized adventure."

"I can handle that," she assured him. She licked her lips and decided she needed her lip balm. The dryness of winter had tortured her skin and lips. As she opened her bag to dig for the lip balm, she remembered the envelope that had come for Gracen. "Here, this came while you were getting gas. You weren't around so I signed for it. It's from Wallace Corp."

Quickly, Gracen glanced at the certified envelope she was holding. "You can shred that. I know exactly what it is and I have no interest in it."

"Do you ever have interest in the things that come for you?"

"That's me being indifferent and cold. This is me being angry. I'll tell you what's in it, or you can open it. I really don't care. It won't make a difference," Gracen shrugged. He took a drink from his stainless steel water bottle. "It's a check from Roy. My second payment."

"Payment? For what?"

"For leaving and keeping my mouth shut. He gave me half a million dollars to get out of Summerstead Isle and start over. That check should be for a quarter."

"Half a million dollars?" Blythe gaped. "And you want to shred a check for a quarter of a million? Just shred it."

"Shred it. I have no interest in his dirty money anymore. I spent most of the first check on the Shelby, just to stick it to him. He hates that kind of 'waste'," he explained. "The rest was spent on furnishing my apartment and setting up the restaurant. I'm living on profits and my savings now."

"I had no idea the Shelby was worth that kind of money."

"I got a good deal on her, but a 1967 Shelby Mustang isn't exactly a car you buy with paper route money."

"But why did he pay you to leave? What do you mean by keeping your mouth shut?"

"When Uncle Harry died—wow, it will be a year next week," Gracen sighed. It didn't feel like a year, he still missed him the same. He started over, "When his will was read and I didn't inherit Louie & Lucy's as promised, I kinda snapped. No, not kinda. I completely snapped. I didn't sleep for two or three days, I don't remember exactly. Between the grief and anger, and a lot of caffeine, I was an insomniac."

"What were you doing for those three days? Do I want to know?"

"There were no girls at all. If anyone even spoke to me, I probably growled at them. I was researching. I wanted to know how Roy had changed the will. I found definitive proof that he manipulated Uncle Harry and fudged legal documents so Wallace Corp would absorb Louie & Lucy's. He only let me inherit the recipe so I would either sell it to him or work for him. Neither happened."

"I still can't believe he paid you that much money to go away."

"I found a lot of Roy's secrets in my digging. I was relentless. And I was ready to go public. You see, on Summerstead Isle a veneer of morality is essential. A couple business owners were caught on tax evasion and the locals crucified them. The stuff I have on Roy is far worse than that—everything from dirty deals to cheating employees. Some of it goes back decades. If I went public, it could destroy him."

"So he paid you to keep quiet?"

"He did. And he threatened to tell all my secrets too. I almost don't care if he does. I'm not there anymore. Besides, I've always been the subject of gossip, my whole origin story and everything. But a couple of those girls have worked hard to be successful on the Isle. A youthful transgression or my senseless behavior shouldn't hurt their business, but it would."

"And so you agreed to leave so he'd stay quiet. But you'd already lost so much. Forcing you away from home seems cruel."

"Summerstead only rarely felt like home. I miss Aunt Grace, I worry about her. But I was glad for an excuse to leave."

"I'm sorry for everything you've lost, but selfishly, I'm happy you landed in Sayen Falls. If you hadn't, I wouldn't be here now, wondering what the heck we're going to do in Columbus when it isn't football season."

"I would never take you to a football game," he laughed. "I know you that well at least."

"It's the only thing I've ever done in Columbus. I came once to a game with Liam and Silas. It was awful. It was cold and I barely understand the sport, and Liam was a jerk then. Other than seeing him graduate from OSU, I've never been back."

"Then, you should leave today with a much better opinion of the city. At least I hope. If not, then I owe you a really great St. Patrick's Day."

But the day was truly perfect. Gracen took them first to the Museum of Art for a special folk art exhibition. They spent some time in the Wonder Room experimenting with textiles and crafting a work of art together. Then, Gracen whisked them away to a private art studio for a glass-blowing lesson. Blythe loved watching the blob of molten glass take shape as she blew air into it and rolled it back and forth. She made a speckled glass ornament in shades of pink, red, and white, while Gracen worked on a paperweight that was robin's egg blue.

"Will we have to come back to pick them up?" Blythe asked as she slipped her hand into his and ducked behind his shoulder to avoid some cold wind. They were walking up High Street to a vintage store popular with the hipsters.

"No, when I booked the class I made arrangements to have it shipped to us. I promise to not be indifferent when it arrives," he grinned.

"Well, I haven't been this artistic since middle school. That was the last time I took an art class. I had no idea I actually enjoyed it."

"So I've done okay so far?"

Blythe stopped dead in her tracks to give him a kiss, "So far, so good."

The vintage shop was just a few paces ahead and Blythe spotted the goodies spilling out onto the sidewalk. There were two or three wooden sleds, a Radio Flyer wagon filled with old ice skates, and two chubby plastic light-up Santa Clauses marked down on clearance. One front window had mannequins in 1970s suits and dresses posed on mid-century modern chairs and talking on an old rotary phone. The other window held a massive display of phones from across several decades. This display was very fitting, as the shop was named Redial.

"This is like if Sam and Mae combined their shops," Blythe grinned as she stepped inside. The enormous shop was divided into smaller rooms that led from one to another to another.

"Liam told me about this place. It's been here for a while, I guess," Gracen said.

"This does not seem like Liam's scene," she said wryly. They were in a room set up like a 1950s kitchen, lots of chrome and pink.

"He said you'd love it though. I guess this is where he got your graduation gift."

"He got me an architect's table to use for a desk when I graduated high school. It's in my room now. It's a really cool piece."

"Oh, wow, Aunt Grace has this exact same Tom and Jerry punch bowl set," Gracen exclaimed, pointing to a display on a buffet table.

"Did they use it? What exactly is a Tom and Jerry? I've always wondered," Blythe asked.

"They did use it. Every Christmas. It's basically eggnog."

"Gross."

"Have you ever actually had eggnog?" he asked as he picked up a glass to check the price.

"No. It sounds disgusting. Eggnog? What is a nog, anyway? Blech," she made a face.

"I almost want to buy this now so I can make you a Tom and Jerry next Christmas. Not that we'd have to have this punch bowl set."

"Oh, yes, we have to," Blythe said earnestly. "I would love that."

"I'm sure I can have Aunt Grace send me hers," Gracen shrugged, putting the glass down. "It's been a couple of years since she's used it."

"I've just never seen you have an emotional connection to something before," she said, slipping an arm around his waist.

"Is that what that was? I had no idea," he said before planting a quick kiss on her head. "We're going to get something though. You're a collector of things and stories and things with stories. So, we're not leaving empty-handed."

"I never buy things in a place like this," she said in a hushed voice.

"Why not?" he whispered rather loudly.

"No monies, for one, and for two, I get everything for free from people who love me," she giggled. "Everything in my apartment is from someone's attic or something Jesse sent me from some exotic far-off place."

"Well, you're choosing something today so you can always remember our Valentine's Day in this exotic far-off place."

"Columbus," she said flatly, raising an eyebrow.

"It's just a day trip," he shrugged as he took her hand and led her into the next room. It was set up like a living room, and one wall was covered in clocks. The ticking was impressive. The next thing he knew, Blythe was gasping like she'd seen a long lost friend.

"I've always wanted a cuckoo clock!"

"You would," he grinned.

"No, really, I always have. Grammy and PapPap had one when I was a kid. It was in the kitchen. I always wanted to have it, but it broke."

While she was staring at the wooden cuckoo clock, the hour turned and it started to chime. Sure enough, a little bird popped out of his little house to sound the hour six times. The intricate trim along the peak of the house and the bright colors on the face of the clock were in pristine condition. It reminded her so much of the one she used to love.

"Gracen, that bird speaks to me. I love him."

"If you think that bird is speaking to you, Kate, then we have bigger problems."

"I'm serious. This is it. I need this clock," she insisted. "I hope it's not a bazillion dollars."

With a smile, he leaned in close to look for a price. "It's yours, Kate."

He found an employee to take the clock off the wall, and it was carefully packaged up as Gracen paid for it. Blythe was nearly trembling with happiness as he gave her the handled brown paper bag. He held the door open for her as they left Redial.

"Thank you," she breathed. "It's one thing to be given something that no one uses anymore, it's another thing to have someone buy it for you."

"You'll have to tell me what the bird's name is, once you get to know him better," he told her, kissing her. "Now, back to the car. We're headed to the German Village for dinner. I decided to not go upscale so we could be dressed more comfortably. And Liam told me the best place is actually an authentic German Sausage Haus."

"Sausage Haus?" she repeated slowly.

"They have other foods, too."

They also had a live oompah band playing festive music. It was a simple place, no froufrou décor or fussy waiters, but the food was amazing and the atmosphere was warm and welcoming. She and Gracen selected different things from the menu that both agreed sounded delicious so they could share. It was an experience Blythe thoroughly enjoyed.

When dinner was done, Gracen ushered her to one more stop on their tour: a bookstore. An enormous bookstore made of so many rooms they needed a map.

"Is this what you would do with The Yellow Bowl if you could?" Gracen asked as they entered area nine.

"I'd have to take over your half of the building, the empty place next to you, and probably most of Sam's antique shop," she laughed. "But don't think I wouldn't love it."

"I'm sure you would. Why is our building split in two? I don't think it always was."

"It wasn't. A realtor bought the place in the seventies and split it in two so a title office could be right next door. It functioned well for them but it's been a weird set-up for everyone else ever since. I have no idea why PapPap picked that storefront when he set up shop."

"The idea of Miles running a tea room is incongruous to me."

"It was something to keep him busy after retirement. And something he could do with Grammy. She loved it. She had so much fun setting up teas for people. They did a lot of special event type things then, hosting little bridal showers and stuff like that at the shop."

"That makes more sense," Gracen nodded. They had drifted into area thirteen which was chock full of comic books. "I haven't read comics since I was a kid."

"DC or Marvel?"

"Marvel."

"Right answer," she said smugly.

They finished exploring every nook of the sprawling establishment before making a couple of purchases. Together they walked to their borrowed car just as snow began to fall on the city. Blythe looked at the radar on her weather app as Gracen pulled out of his parallel parking spot.

"It's been snowing in Sayen Falls for a while, I think. It's a really colorful blob eating most of the state now."

"Lovely. I'm really glad Silas let us borrow his Explorer then. My Shelby was not made for snow, and your Wagoneer, I can't imagine, handles well."

"It's a dinosaur, I know."

"Why do you have the Wagoneer? I've wondered ever since I arrived."

"It was PapPap's," she smiled. "He'd kept it to haul things, and whatnot. Then the year I graduated high school he got a truck and didn't need it anymore. He was going to take it to a scrap yard, but I asked him if I could have it instead. I was actually crying over the idea of it being scrapped."

"You were crying?"

"I was a teenage girl; when wasn't I crying? But I love that old Jeep. I don't know why. It smells like his garage still, even after I've had it for the last ten years. And PapPap and Becky overhauled it just for me. They wanted it to be as new and as safe as possible. It was so sweet really. It was sort of a graduation present."

"An architect table and a cherry red Jeep Wagoneer. Kate, you are one of a kind, but I wouldn't change a thing."

"I wouldn't change you either, Princeton. Although, I think you've done an awful lot of changing in the last year or so. I'm not sure I would adore the old you quite as much."

"That's very fair and very true. The old me would've missed the real you completely."

## Chapter 42

The closer they traveled to Sayen Falls the more unsettled the weather became. Frigid winds brought a layer of ice to thickly coat and cover everything in its path. The electrical lines sagged under the weight of the heavy sheet of ice. The clouds served as conduits of a seemingly endless amount of snow, quietly covering the slick roads with a blanket of white.

A few minutes after midnight, Gracen finally parked outside their building. "Home again. Did I do okay with our bite-sized adventure?"

"You did real okay," she nodded. "I haven't had a day this busy that didn't involve work or family in ... years. And I loved every minute of it."

An impressive wind gust shook the car. The streetlamps overhead flickered then went out.

"The power is out?" he asked. "Are there generators down here?"

"Not for the whole plaza. The restaurants have them, but that's it. The city has its own power plant so we don't usually lose power, only if there's an accident or something else that brings a pole down."

"Well, let's get inside," Gracen said, casting a wary eye at the electrical lines. He did not like how much ice was hanging on them.

Using their cell phones to light the way, they traipsed up the back stairwell leaving their purchases in Silas's SUV. Just as they reached the top, the lights came back on. The streetlamps cast a dull glow on the gathering snowdrifts and the single light bulb on the landing illuminated their doors.

"Will you be okay?" he asked her.

"It's just some snow."

"But if the power goes out again, I don't want you freezing to death."

"I'll put another quilt on the bed. You're the one more like to freeze to death. You don't have spare anything over there, you Spartan."

"Then, I will call you for an extra blanket," he smiled, hugging her close. Their lips met for a good, long kiss. The lights blinked again but stayed on.

"It's just snow," she said again. Then she unlocked her door and went inside. What a fantastic day it had been. She replayed every part of it slowly as she went about getting ready for bed. No one had ever taken her to the art museum for a date before. She decided they should go up to the one in Cleveland sometime very soon. She loved listening to Gracen explain what he liked or didn't like about a piece of art. He talked about pieces he'd seen at The Met. She wanted to go there with him too.

She lit the candle on her nightstand as part of her nightly ritual to unwind. She crawled into bed and flicked on her TV to stream a show. As the opening credits wrapped up, the electricity wavered again. Before Blythe could even complain, there was an impressive explosion outside as a transformer blew up.

"Good grief, what was that?" she exclaimed as she scrambled out of bed to look out the window. She saw sparks flying from an electric line. Not a minute later, her phone rang. "I'm fine, Gracen."

"That sounded bad. I think we'll be out of power for a while now."

"Yeah, I saw sparks fly from one of the lines. That can't be good."

"We should call the electric company, make sure they know," Gracen said. "And find out how long it'll be."

"I'll call Silas and see if he lost power too. I think the other side of the plaza is on their own circuit but it could all be connected."

"Call me back."

"I'm right next door if you're that worried."

"I don't know, candlelight is very … alluring."

"I'll put on a pantsuit. Now go call the electric company," Blythe insisted and ended the call before Gracen could flirt with her anymore.

With a couple of quick swipes on her touchscreen, Blythe called Silas then checked the time as she moved to look out the bay window. A little after one. It was possible that he was sleeping, but he answered quickly and she could tell that he was still up by the sound of his voice. It wasn't fuzzy at all.

"Do you still have power?"

"It's flickered a few times but keeps coming back," Silas said. He walked to his window to look at the plaza; the adjacent side was completely dark and not a single neon light remained on. "Looks like your side is out."

"Gracen is calling the electric company to see how long it'll be."

"You know they actually hate that, right?"

"At least he'll be nice about it," Blythe shrugged. As she talked she crossed from room to room lighting candles until her apartment was fairly well lit. She returned to the window and waved at Silas now that he could at least see her silhouette.

"If you want to come over here tonight, either one or both of you, just come on over. I still have heat and the temperature is dropping fast."

A knock at her door that Blythe would swear sounded cautious distracted her from Silas.

"Thanks but I think I'll wait it out," she said slowly and then ended her call. She opened the door for Gracen. He was holding a flashlight.

"I know it's stupid, but I have a bad feeling about you being over here alone in this weather. If that's condescending, I apologize."

"You sound like my grandfather. And my brother. He says we can come over to his place if we want to. He has power."

"The electric company said they think it'll only be an hour or so."

"Why are we standing in the doorway?" Blythe asked, realizing Gracen hadn't moved to come into her apartment. "Get in here."

After he stepped inside, she hugged him but his embrace was different. She noticed he was holding something in each hand. She stepped back to look at him; the flashlight was in his right and a book was in his left. He followed her gaze and grinned.

"I figured we could read to pass the time."

"Let me guess. *Henry the Fifth?*"

"The way I see it, it's not just my thing anymore, it's ours. It has been since the undate."

"Which was really a date."

"And why I lost my mind afterward, yes. Anyway, I've read this thing so many times, but I want to share it with you. Reading it is a different experience from watching it."

She gathered up a couple of quilts, and they settled on the couch, snuggling close to share the book and the flashlight. He kissed her cheek as he opened the book. The pages were yellowed and worn, dog-eared and torn, bearing all the hallmarks of a well-loved book.

"So how do we do this? You be King Henry and I'll be everyone else?" Blythe asked.

"Maybe just for the scenes with Henry, I don't know, we'll make it up as we go along. There aren't any rules, it's just us."

And so they spent the next hour and a half reading, rotating parts, stumbling through archaic language, and soaring on magnificent poetry. Gracen delivered a few of King Henry's impressive speeches from memory, which left Blythe fairly awestruck. They skipped a few of the scenes with characters neither of them cared about, and all of the bits containing French since neither spoke it. Around two-thirty, they found themselves at the lone love scene. Blythe assumed the role of Kate and her interpreter lady-in-waiting, and Gracen read for King Henry.

"I think this may be my favorite romantic scene of all time," Blythe said with a breathless giggle when they were halfway through.

"We haven't even gotten to the kissing bit," Gracen laughed.

"I'm not sure I can stand it."

"'There's witchcraft in your lips, Kate,'" he quoted, jumping ahead several lines. Gracen's smooth voice turned Blythe's insides all flittery.

"That's not the line yet," Blythe breathed.

"I really don't care," he replied, kissing her softly. His kiss was so light it tingled. As she melted into his touch the lights sparked back to life and every appliance in the apartment beeped to announce its awakening. The moment was diminished with the electric hum of the twenty-first century and all the romance and candlelight of Shakespeare's poetry faded.

Unknown to Blythe and Gracen, that same twenty-first-century electrical power had surged much too violently through some of the older wiring directly below their apartments. The breakers that controlled the voltage demands of The Yellow Bowl and SIP had tripped, saving both their businesses; the outdated breaker box in the shop next door wasn't so fortunate. That unit hadn't been used as a retail space for years, which made it a convenient storage area for the other shops on the block. Cleaning supplies, paint, even discarded grease from the diner were temporarily housed there.

As sparks spewed forth from an outlet like an unsupervised firework display, the contents of the unit were perfect fuel for a fire. A smattering of sparks landed in a puddle of paint thinner, striking a proverbial match to start a steady blaze. The trail of flames flashed when it reached a crate of aerosol cans. It wasn't long before the drywall covering the brick bones of the room was dissolving into a sheet of hot rage. The fire quickly spread upward and outward, reaching the empty apartment above, then onto the occupied units on either side – Summerstead Isle Pizza and The Yellow Bowl to the right and Buterbaugh's Antiques to the left.

Gracen smelled the smoke first and initially disregarded it. After all, he and Blythe had just blown out about a dozen candles. Then he realized this smoke was different, heavier, stronger, and it wasn't dissipating.

"Blythe, we need to get out, now!"

"What?" she asked, staring at him blankly.

"Grab anything that's important to you – like you can't live without it important!"

"Gracen, what's going on?"

"I think the building is on fire!" he shouted, racing toward the balcony and skidding out into several inches of fresh snow. Immediately, he was met with an impressive blaze that was rapidly coming toward them.

"Gracen!" she called back when she realized that he was serious.

"Call Silas! I'll call the fire department, we don't have much time!" he added, looking back over his shoulder to see Blythe still staring, seemingly paralyzed by what was happening. "Blythe, come on, there isn't any time!"

Leaving her to call Silas, Gracen moved into the bedroom. Anything of real importance to Blythe was in there. With his thumb, he dialed 9-1-1 and told the operator that some shops on the riverfront were on fire. The call ended in seconds, and he grabbed her jewelry box off the dresser as Blythe walked in mechanically. There wasn't a moment to spare for dazed inaction.

"What else? Tell me what else to get?" he demanded.

"I ... I don't know."

She appeared frozen, yet inwardly her mind was racing through an inventory of all she owned. Nearly every item in Blythe's apartment had meaning to her.

Frustration mounted as Gracen ran his fingers through his hair and threw a look around the room. He tossed some photo albums, childhood mementos, and her Bible onto the bed, then tied the quilt up like an enormous hobo sack. Then with the jewelry box in one arm and the makeshift bag in the other he went out on the balcony. He aimed for a snowbank hoping it would be a soft enough cushion that nothing would break and lobbed the jewelry box; the doors popped open, one broke off, and two of the drawers slid out.

Just moments later, Silas came running around the side of the building and into the parking lot.

"You need to get down now!" he yelled. "It's spreading fast, SIP is starting to burn and the books at The Yellow Bowl will burn for hours."

He saw the blanket tucked under Gracen's arm and gestured for him to throw it to him. Gracen pitched it awkwardly and Silas barely caught it.

"Where's Blythe?" Silas called. Panicking, Gracen looked over his shoulder. He had assumed Blythe was right behind him, but she was nowhere to be seen. Shouting frantically for her, Gracen darted to her balcony door. Just before he went in, Blythe emerged from his apartment onto his balcony clutching the banker's box that was the sum of his personal life. He rushed to meet her at the railing that separated their balconies.

"It's all you have," she said simply. Gracen's heart surged as he took the box from her and tossed it down to Silas. Without a word, he put his hands on her hips and effortlessly lifted her over the railing.

"We need to get down the fire escape right now," he instructed her. "You go first."

"I can't do this, I'm afraid of heights."

"I forgot about that," he groaned. He led her to the fire escape and firmly planted her feet on it. Then he cupped her face in his hand and looked her hard in the eye, "You are a strong woman, don't pull the damsel in distress card on me now, got it? You can do this. They're just stairs."

"Come on, Blythe, I'm here, you can do this!" Silas shouted. He was fighting hard to sound calm but his voice betrayed the panic he felt.

Blythe's knuckles turned white as she gripped the railing. The falling snow made the old rust slippery, and the rickety fire escape wavered with every move. The height and the motion made Blythe feel seasick; she just wanted to sit down and close her eyes. Gracen was behind her on every step, urging her on. She kept moving for his sake. Blythe didn't want to be the reason he didn't make it.

"Just drop now, I'll catch you," Silas said as sirens could be heard in the distance. The flames were growing as the fire consumed every book in its path, feeding its ravenous hunger. Blythe couldn't look at the flames; she couldn't look down at Silas. She could only look up at Gracen and the fear etched in his face.

"Jump," he shouted. "Please, Blythe, jump."

Closing her eyes, she let go of the ladder, and the freefall felt endless before she sank into her brother's waiting arms. Silas steadied her carefully, holding her shoulders until he was sure she wasn't going to faint with fear.

Then, as Gracen clambered down the ladder Blythe snapped to life. Seeing the fire engulfing her beloved shop she suddenly realized all that was at stake. This was her home and her livelihood going up in smoke. She was about to lose everything.

She threw herself at the door handle trying desperately to unlock it.

"What are you doing?" Gracen yelled as the roar of sirens drew ever nearer.

"The yellow bowl is in there," she cried.

"It doesn't matter," he insisted.

Her eyes widened and she rushed to the door of SIP. "The paintings!"

She pulled on the handle and it gave way. Gracen had forgotten to lock it when they left for the day. She only got a foot inside before he grabbed her around the waist and dragged her back.

"They don't matter. None of this matters."

"Gracen, it's everything."

"It's nothing."

Inside the building, there was a thunderous crash as the fire weakened the floor joists. Gracen seized her hand and dragged her several yards away from the building.

"You would've been in there!" he shouted. He hadn't meant to shout, but the adrenaline was dictating his reactions.

With tears in her eyes, she grabbed his collar. "It's my life."

He placed her hand on her heart. "This is your life."

At last, the firetrucks pulled into the parking lot behind them. Firefighters jumped from the truck and jogged to attach oversized hoses to hydrants, calling out directions and assessing the fire by the look of the smoke.

"Is anyone inside?" the fire chief asked Silas.

"No, the other apartments are empty."

As Gracen led Blythe into the parking lot, there was another crash, this time from inside Buterbaugh's, and she let out an involuntary scream. It was just too much to take in.

The fire chief spoke into the radio clipped to his shoulder, and Silas heard him say something about shock. He nodded to himself. This was shocking indeed.

"You must be freezing," Silas said as he looked at his sister wearing one of Gracen's old sweatshirts and flannel pajama pants. He shrugged off the coat he was wearing and held it out to her. When she didn't take it, he shook it in insistence.

Before another word was spoken, the upstairs windows shattered from the extreme temperature difference.

"Oh my lord," Blythe whispered, covering her mouth with her hand in horror. Flames had completely overcome most of the block. The firefighters were laboring hard, but the furniture in Buterbaugh's was good fuel for the fire.

Moments later a rescue squad arrived. The EMTs led Blythe, Gracen, and Silas to the ambulance where they could be evaluated. From where they sat on the back of the ambulance Blythe had no choice but to watch as the fire consumed the framework of her life. After they checked her blood pressure, she slipped her hand into Gracen's. He'd have to start over—again.

"Do you folks have somewhere to stay tonight?" one EMT asked. "The fire chief will shut down the area. You can't be here until after the smoke clears."

"It's too late to wake up our grandparents, and it's going to be such a shock," Silas pointed out.

"We'll crash with Finn then," Gracen said, taking his phone out. Silas stopped him.

"I'll call him, you stay here with her."

As Silas walked away to call Finn, Gracen loosened Blythe's hand from his so he could wrap his arm around her.

"It's all gone," she whispered.

"I'm sure we can salvage something."

In all likelihood, Gracen was wrong. Whatever hadn't been damaged by fire or smoke would soon be iced over. The water from the fire hoses would freeze in these insane temperatures.

"How am I going to tell him that it's gone?" Blythe whispered.

"He will only care about you."

"You keep saying that," she shook her head. "That I'm the only thing that matters. You don't understand what The Yellow Bowl is to us."

"You don't understand that you are what makes The Yellow Bowl what it is."

She tore her eyes away from the fire to look at Gracen. "Why aren't you freaking out?"

Gracen considered the question. "Give it time. Tonight I'm only thinking of you."

As Silas finished up with Finn he scooped Blythe's jewelry box out of the snow and added it to the blanket of her things in the back of her Jeep. It was such a small amount of her stuff, her life. When the EMT dismissed them, they climbed into Silas's Explorer. In the back seat, Gracen found the cuckoo clock and the books they'd purchased.

"There's no place for it now," Blythe said softly.

# Chapter 43

Finn paced outside as he waited for them. When Silas parked on the street in front of the brick apartment building Finn dashed to meet them. He shut Blythe's car door for her and wrapped her in a tight hug. She noticed how he smelled the same—he always had an earthy fresh smell like pine trees after a passing shower or something—and significantly, he did not smell of smoke.

"Are you okay?"

"Probably not," she replied hoarsely.

Two more car doors thudded shut as Gracen and Silas climbed out.

"Thanks for letting us stay tonight," Silas sighed. "It's too late to wake up our grandparents."

"We'll have to go over there first thing in the morning. It'll be on the news for sure," Gracen pointed out as they headed into the apartment.

"They don't watch the morning news," Blythe said mechanically. They began climbing the stairs to the upstairs unit. She simply followed Finn wherever he went.

"Well, it's pretty late, so what do you guys need from me?" Finn asked. "I have clothes that may or may not fit any of you. Do you want showers? Do you just want to go to bed?"

She heard him saying words, English words, words she should know but all she could think about was this smoke smell.

"I think a shower would be good," Gracen said. "Get this smoke smell off us."

"I like that campfire smoke smell for about ten minutes and then it's just really obnoxious," Silas said as he sniffed his own shirt.

"That was no campfire," Blythe said quietly. Feeling chastened, Silas opened his mouth to speak but then decided there wasn't really anything to say. Blythe wasn't responding in offense, she was just breathing out the words that managed to come to the surface.

The boys agreed it was the gentlemanly thing to do to let Blythe shower first and get her squared away. Etiquette aside, Gracen was worried about the look in her eyes. Finn gave her some sweats with a drawstring and a baggy sweatshirt to sleep in. As her smoky clothes dropped to the bathroom floor, she hoped that somehow this shower would work some deep magic and do more than just wash away the stink of that smoke.

As hot water flowed from the showerhead and steam filled the room, it seemed to Blythe that the smell may have been washing off her body just to seep into every other available area of her being. There was no escaping it.

Finn's clothes were loose on her, but she could make do for a night. She wasn't really sure what she'd do for clothes. There were maybe a few things at her grandparents' house that had been left there for various reasons.

Hardly a full wardrobe. She'd have to buy clothes tomorrow. Gracen would too. They'd have to buy everything new. Furniture, linens, dishes. Of course, some things can't be replaced by a quick trip to the housewares department. All the books, photographs, knick-knacks that she had collected in almost three decades of life could not be reproduced. Gracen had far less of that. She almost envied him.

In Finn's guest room there was a twin bed and a futon. Finn could've lived more cheaply in a one-room apartment, but he had wanted a guest room so whenever a friend needed a safe place to land he could offer it. Until now, the guest room had only been used by a few teenage boys in the youth group who needed a break from their parents every now and then.

She knew Gracen would insist she take the bed so she sank onto the mattress while he took his turn in the shower.

"I hope it's okay," Finn asked as he brought a tray with a couple of mugs on it and a few shortbread cookies. "I thought maybe some chamomile would be nice."

"You say that funny," she said, pulling herself upright, "'camo-mile'."

"Aha, signs of life, this is a good thing," he smiled as he sat down next to her. Ever so naturally, she leaned her head on his shoulder.

"Tell me it's going to be okay. Maybe I'll believe it if I hear it from you."

"Why should you believe me particularly?"

"Because you were there the last time my life caught on fire."

"That was a metaphor."

"Yes."

"I think that was worse though. This is just bricks and books. We can fix that."

"It's all gone. All of the things that remind me who I am."

"I know who you are. So does Gracen. And that little brother out there who is worried about you and will keep cracking jokes until he thinks you're okay. We can remind you who you are until you've amassed enough clutter to replace us."

A few tears slipped from her eyes and trickled off the end of her nose then splattered onto the bottom of the oversized shirt she was wearing.

"It's okay, you can get snot all over my clothes," Finn teased. She heard the water shut off in the bathroom. Gracen would be joining them in a minute or two after he dried and dressed.

"Finnian, I'm glad we never tried to make us an 'us'. I'd be sad to not have you around anymore after it didn't work."

"I wouldn't want to be the one in his way," Finn said, meaning Gracen. "He's the right one for you."

"He says I haven't lost everything."

"And you haven't."

After Gracen joined them, they talked for a little while about nothing in particular. Gracen and Finn just wanted to help Blythe's brain relax before she tried to sleep. It was a sweet effort, but of little use.

She tossed and turned in the dark for just over an hour before she whispered to see if Gracen was still awake. By this time, his brain had caught up with reality and the adrenaline was giving way to anxiety. He was wide awake.

"What are we going to do?" she asked him as she lay in the dark.

"Rebuild."

"Where will we live?"

"I don't know. You can move back in with your grandparents for a while, I would think," he rolled over on the futon and propped his head up with his hand. "Maybe Finn wouldn't mind having me for a roommate."

"I know I should be grateful that my grandparents will take me in when I have nowhere else to go, but it just brings back memories. I loved living with them, I did, but it still hurt that neither of my parents could be bothered to stay. Or really tried to take me with them."

"You would've been miserable in Michigan."

"I don't think it did Si any favors in the long run."

"Probably not," Gracen agreed. Dim light filled the room as Blythe turned on her phone and opened an app.

"What are you doing?" he asked with concern.

"Checking to see if anyone is talking about the fire yet."

"Blythe."

"Oh my word," she breathed as a video of the fire began playing. When she tapped her screen the audio started. The sound of sirens brought Gracen out of his makeshift futon bed. He watched the footage for a few seconds, then gently took the phone from her hands. She felt his fingertips brush hers, and she grabbed onto his hand. A muffled sob choked her.

"Kate," he sighed, sinking onto the bed next to her and enfolding her in his strong arms. Gracen wanted to say something heartfelt or profound or healing, but all of the words just seemed hollow. Instead, he said nothing at all and just held her a little tighter and a little longer.

"Too bad I didn't grab my copy of *Henry the Fifth*," he said after a while.

There was a timid knock on their door, then Silas's voice followed. "You guys awake?"

"Yes," Blythe answered and Silas cracked open the door.

"Finn and I are up too."

"Why are you two losing sleep?" Gracen asked.

"They're worriers," Blythe answered.

"Finn has *Monty Python and the Quest for the Holy Grail*," Silas said. It was an old favorite.

"Put it in," Blythe nodded as she pulled the comforter off the bed.

In the living room, Blythe settled herself on the couch with her head on

Gracen's shoulder and the blanket pulled all around her for some comfort. Silas curled into the loveseat as best he could and Finn sank into his worn recliner. Monty Python galloped on the screen, but no one laughed much at the jokes. Then as Galahad asked for just a little bit of peril, Gracen noticed Blythe was sound asleep. By the time the movie ended, Gracen had dozed off with his head leaning down on Blythe's.

* * *

The morning light was hazy and gray. Miles shuffled about the kitchen preparing breakfast for Mary Alice and himself. Coffee was filling in the pot, and bread was browning in the toaster. He filled a bowl with cereal for each of them and was about to pour the milk when there was a soft rap at the door. No one ever knocked at the back door, as they had to come into the enclosed porch to do so. And no good news ever came this early in the morning. He looked at Mary Alice with some confusion, then slowly Miles opened the door.

"What in the world are you two doing here so early in the morning?" he asked upon finding Blythe and Gracen on his back porch. She was wearing clothes that weren't hers, and a very grave expression. Immediately concerned, Miles opened the door wider to let them in.

"We have news," Blythe began. Deep down she wanted to do the talking, but the words were now frozen in her throat. She sat at the round table with her grandmother, and looked up at Gracen. He nodded.

"There was a fire on the riverfront last night. I'm pretty sure it took most of our block. It will be on the news this morning, I'm sure."

"A fire?" Miles exclaimed.

"Are you both okay?" Mary Alice gasped.

"We got out alright. We salvaged a few things, and climbed down the fire escape," Gracen said. He sat in the chair next to Blythe.

"You got her down the fire escape?" Mary Alice asked in amazement, knowing just how much Blythe feared heights.

"I reminded her how strong she is," he said as he looked at Blythe.

"How much damage is there?" Miles asked urgently.

"I think it's safe to say almost everything will be lost—between the fire, smoke, and water damage," Gracen surmised.

Mary Alice said woefully, "This is a terrible shame. All of your books, Blythe, oh, that's just awful. Everything you have. I just can't believe it."

"And the paintings of Summerstead Isle," Blythe said quietly.

"I had to convince her that we needed her in one piece more than the paintings," Gracen said as he met Miles's eyes. Miles studied Gracen; the old man was unreadable.

"I appreciate that," Miles said at last.

Blythe confessed as tears pooled in her eyes, "I just keep thinking that

I've lost everything. It's all gone. Everything."

"You haven't lost everything, dear. You have a place to go here, you know that. And we'll get it all sorted," Mary Alice assured her.

"I keep telling her that," Gracen said. He looked at Blythe. "Between your grandparents and me, we're going to make sure you're okay and want for nothing."

"You don't owe me anything," she said in a small voice.

"Owe you? Who said anything about owing? Blythe, I love you. We're in this together, in my opinion. I want to shoulder the weight of this, at least financially. I know I can."

From his vantage point across the small kitchen, Miles studied his granddaughter. He had sensed the heaviness on her the minute he opened the door. That darkness had been on her before: when Nick and Carrie divorced, when Nick and Carrie each left, and when Ian ended their engagement after his affair. It always followed loss.

Now, with the way she was looking at Gracen, the heaviness lifted. Not permanently, but long enough for the real Blythe to smile through. Maybe the darkness wouldn't overtake her this time. Maybe she'd gotten stronger since she'd learned to love again.

"I'm glad to hear you say that, son," Miles told him. "Ian used to say Blythe didn't make enough at The Yellow Bowl to pull her weight. The idea of providing or shouldering anything was foreign to his pea brain. Maybe you're old-fashioned like me, but I like the way you're talking."

"You guys use the strangest words to describe me," Gracen said, finding a grin. "Blythe insists I'm a romantic, you're calling me old-fashioned. No one on Summerstead Isle would agree with these assessments."

"I'm familiar with that too," Miles replied. He shared a smile with Mary Alice. "I changed a lot because of Mary Alice. It's amazing what the love of a good woman can do."

"That's why I agreed to marry you even when everyone thought I was crazy. I knew who you really were. And you haven't let me down," she said fondly. She turned to Gracen, "Did Blythe tell you that we eloped?"

"No, she didn't. I imagine that's quite a story," Gracen replied.

"Tell them how your parents found out," Blythe said. It was her favorite part of the story. For the moment, she nearly forgot the fire.

"The marriage license fell out of my pocket when I came to visit," Miles explained. "Mary Alice had gone back to live with her folks."

"Dad was angry, but he got over it. He saw how good you were to me," Mary Alice said. "And that's what we see in you, Gracen. We already think of you as family."

Miles added, "That's why we're offering you the other room upstairs."

Gracen looked up at him with surprise. "I really appreciate it, but Finn already said I could stay in his guest room."

"Just as long as you both know that whatever you need if we can help you then we will," Mary Alice said firmly.

"Oh, I know that," Blythe said, her voice quivering. "That's why we came here first. I mean, you needed to know, it's your shop. But I also knew you'd take me back."

"Take you back?" Miles shook his head. "This has never stopped being your home. And it's not our shop anymore. It's yours. You've done us proud."

"Miles, would you mind getting my pocketbook? These kids need something to wear, they look like hobos," Mary Alice said. She was keenly aware of her granddaughter's moods and wanted to redirect before her thought cycle got going too quickly.

"We're not taking your money. The bank didn't burn down," Blythe said to her grandmother. It was useless to argue, but she had to put up some kind of fight.

"I don't want to hear it. You're going to need every penny to get The Yellow Bowl and Summerstead Isle Pizza up and running again," Mary Alice insisted.

"Blythe, don't make me worry too much about you," Miles instructed.

"Oh, I'm fine," Blythe said as she accepted some folded-up bills from her grandmother. Everyone in the room knew she was lying. She amended her statement. "I'll be fine."

"I'm sure you will be," Mary Alice said as she shoved a few bills into Gracen's hand. "No arguments from you. Just take it and go get yourself some decent clothes to wear."

"You really don't have to," he said.

"Of course, I don't have to, but I'm a grandmother and I want to spoil my grandkids," Mary Alice said. "Don't deny me this."

"Come back later with the Wagoneer, you're going to need it to move the dresser," Miles said as if they had any idea what he was talking about.

"What dresser?" Blythe asked.

"Whichever one you're not going to use in that bedroom suite upstairs."

"You mean, the one in my room? The one that used to be Kate's?"

When Blythe had moved into the riverfront apartment she'd taken her childhood bedroom suite with her. Her room at their house needed furniture, so Miles had taken Kate's out of storage in the attic. It was a gorgeous walnut set with two dressers and a vanity. Blythe had wanted it ever since she was a little girl. She used to sit in front of the vanity in the attic and pretend she was on TV, talking into the mirrors like cameras.

"Do you still want it?" Miles asked. "Do you mind splitting the set with Gracen?"

The implication was that the set would not be split for long. The idea of sharing bedroom furniture with Blythe in a permanent sense renewed

Gracen's adrenaline rush. He didn't necessarily want to run away, but he was starting to feel like a good run was needed.

"Of course," Blythe said as tears slipped down her cheeks.

"We told you both, anything we have, it's yours," Mary Alice offered. "Do you need a bed? We could give you one of the twin beds from the boys' room."

"Finn has an extra bed, I'm good," Gracen answered. This knee-jerk generosity was not his normal.

"Yes, I slept on it last night," Blythe said, which was, of course, not exactly accurate.

"I'm glad you had a place to go," Mary Alice remarked. "You could've come here though."

"It was late."

"You can always come here," Miles assured her. "You know that."

Blythe nodded as she bit her lip to keep it from trembling. She couldn't speak. If she opened her mouth at all, only sobs would come out. The enormity of it all was sinking in. Miles crossed to her to put his hand on her shoulder, and she began to shake as tears fell in full force. It was awkward for Gracen to wrap his arms around her sitting next to her at a round table, and even more so with her grandparents watching, but Gracen did it nonetheless. As he pulled her closer to him, she sank into his chest.

It was in this moment that he became fully aware of his own skin. This was one of the warning signs of his anxiety. It accompanied the thoughts that had been racing since about three in the morning. His foot began to tap, ever so quietly under the table.

A hand went on his shoulder, then another on his arm. Gracen lifted his head to see Miles above him, Mary Alice reaching across the table. Their eyes were closed, they were praying over him. A memory of Aunt Grace and Uncle Harry came to mind. As he bowed his head, Gracen exhaled. There was a lot of work to do. There were a lot of things to sort out. Thank God he wasn't alone this time.

# Chapter 44

The next morning Blythe's alarm went off at six as it always did. She was in a deep sleep cluttered with fragments of strange dreams. The alarm ripped her out of those dreams which left her in a fog. There was no reason to get up, and she lacked a will to find one so she rolled over onto her side.

When she closed her eyes the dreams came back. She was flying, no falling. Flying always turned into falling in her dreams because she had no control over where she landed. She was falling and Gracen was running to catch her, but he wasn't really going anywhere. It was as if he was on a treadmill and couldn't make any progress. There were others she was shouting to—her father, her mother, her brothers, but they couldn't hear her. She was going to splatter if someone didn't do something.

Her eyes popped open as Blythe willed to be awake instead of returning into that dreadful sleep. She knew what this fly-falling meant in her dreams. It meant that in reality, she felt out of control. It meant that she felt desperate and scared. It meant that she was afraid no one could help her. At least in her dream, Gracen was trying, but of course, her subconscious was aware of his issues and had to work those into her dream. There was no escape from the reality facing her even in her dreams.

The enormity of rebuilding was daunting. She didn't see the possibility in recreating The Yellow Bowl with all of the ideas she'd ever imagined in the long lonely hours she'd spent there. There was just work. And mess. Until it thawed, there was nothing but unknowns. She couldn't even make plans if she wanted to.

Lifting her phone from the dresser which served as a nightstand, she checked the weather forecast. No more snow, but the temperatures were only slowly climbing. It was still only February. They could get another blizzard before spring. After all, last winter had dragged on for ages until at last, spring, April, and The Gala.

The Gala. She wondered if there would even be one this year. How could there be? With half of the riverfront charred to a crisp.

Sliding her phone around, she checked her emails—boring. She checked social media—still plenty of posts, pictures, and videos of the fire. She didn't need the reminder. Pulling up her messages, she texted Gracen.

*Are you up and running?*
A few minutes later he replied: *It's slow going in the snow.*
*You're trying to run in this weather?*
*It's a compulsion.*
*I forgot to tell my alarm to leave me alone. But I was having nightmares anyway.*
*Maybe that's a good sign.*
*How in the world do you figure that?*
*You're alive.*

*That's a pretty low baseline.*

*Gotta start somewhere, Kate. Let's meet for breakfast. You pick the place.*

*There's a greasy spoon diner near campus. Don't run. I'll drive. Pick you up at 7.*

Blythe stared at her phone with a bemused smirk, then worry wiped it off her face. This was actually not a good sign. Gracen should be asleep. Or sitting at Finn's shabby kitchen table eating cereal or something. He should not be running. He only ran in conditions like this when he absolutely had to keep from imploding. He ran when his brain threatened to hijack his entire body with compulsive thoughts.

Quietly as a church mouse, Blythe slipped out of bed to get herself dressed. The only bathroom in the house was downstairs so she had to creep carefully to avoid waking up her grandparents. They didn't usually get up until closer to seven or seven-thirty. At the bottom of the stairs, she strained her ear toward the living room and could hear her grandfather's fluttery snoring. Good. Still asleep.

Safely down the stairs without disturbing anyone, she brushed her teeth and did her makeup. She had used some of the money from Mary Alice to buy new makeup along with a couple of outfits. The foundation and concealer did wonders to cover up the circles under her eyes. She faked a smile to put on the blush and it made her face hurt. Also not a good sign.

When she finished getting her face ready, she snuck into the kitchen to leave a note that she was out for breakfast with Gracen. Then she tip-toed to the hall tree, selected her coat, checked the pocket for keys, and left.

Inside the Wagoneer she caught a whiff of smoke. One of the boys had driven it over to the house last night, but she wasn't sure which one. There had been a lot of talking, and Blythe kept slipping in and out of it.

Her eyes teared up then she steadied herself. "It's just a building. Bricks and mortar. Drive the stupid car."

So she drove the car to Finn's and arrived at ten 'til seven. She was never early for anything in her life. Just as she slid the gear into park, Silas emerged from the apartment. He approached her window.

"Gracen just got out of the shower. He'll be out in a minute."

"You're staying here too?"

"Just for a couple of nights. The city is doing inspections on the other buildings. I'm not sure what they're looking *for*, but they're doing it. Probably an insurance thing."

"You could stay in the other room at Grammy and PapPap's, you know," she said, fully aware that he didn't like staying in that room. He never had.

"I know. I gotta get going. I'm meeting Liam before school starts. I'll see you later. And hang in there. Don't go down the rabbit hole, okay?"

"You know me too well," she replied with a teary smile. Silas frowned but was relieved of the pressure to do something when Gracen appeared.

"Do you want me to drive?" he asked.

"No, it gives my brain something to do."

Gracen slid into the passenger seat and gave her a quick kiss. She sighed reflexively at his touch. As she pulled away from the curb she asked about the Shelby. It was nowhere to be seen.

"Becky said I could park her in his garage," Gracen explained. Becky's house was just around the corner. "There's only on-street parking over here and as laid-back as I can be about her, I don't want to be stupid about it."

"He's probably just overjoyed to have her in his garage. You won't find bigger car guys than Becky and PapPap. They've overhauled so many cars together. Becky insisted on teaching all of us how to change a tire, change the oil, even Ginnie and me. Ginnie was a mess," Blythe said, suddenly laughing at the memory. She shifted into second gear, then third. "But I learned faster than Jesse. I'm not sure I could do it now though, and he's changed tires on the side of the road in Africa."

"They're really good guys, Becky and Miles. I'm grateful for them, especially now," Gracen said. "I'm still getting used to having people around that want to help me out."

They soon arrived at the diner. It hadn't changed a bit since Blythe was a college student. In fact, it hadn't changed in decades. But it was warm inside and smelled of fresh coffee and hot French toast.

Once they were seated at the booth by the window, Blythe said, "I've been comparing your grandfather and mine the last couple days."

"There is no comparison."

"I came to that conclusion. And that saddens me. Everyone should have a PapPap like mine. Or one like Becky. They're different personalities, but amazing grandfathers."

"At least I had Uncle Harry. But I agree with you. That's probably why Miles and Mary Alice mean something to me. Of course, they're the kind of people that mean a lot to everyone."

"This is true. To know them is to love them."

"And respect them. I have the utmost respect for them," Gracen confessed. "And I really like that I can look Miles in the eye and assure him my intentions haven't changed."

"How do you figure?" she asked with a natural smile. That one didn't hurt as much. Her face was loosening.

"When I assured him my intentions were to respect you, to be kind, and to be safe, I thought I could keep a lid on all my feelings. Well, I can't do that but I am managing to keep a lid on some of my impulses. So, my intentions haven't changed. It's rather nice not feeling like he'd kill me if he knew what I was doing to his granddaughter."

She blushed a little as she nodded. "It is nice not having anything to hide. I've spent a lot of time feeling like I've crafted an illusion and if they knew the real me they'd be terribly disappointed with their granddaughter."

"You gave up everything for them and the shop. They'd never be disappointed with you."

"I did that for me."

"You did it for everyone."

"Maybe that's why this loss is so bitter to me," Blythe said heavily. "It's been my home so much longer than the last ten years. It hasn't changed much since I was a kid. I liked it that way, I needed it that way. And now, no matter what happens next, The Yellow Bowl cannot be the same."

"But you didn't lose your memories in the fire. We'll come up with a way to pay tribute to them, to preserve them somehow," he promised.

"The memories are just starting, Gracen," she said softly. "Silas told me this morning not to go down the rabbit hole. He doesn't understand that I can't help it. My mind obsesses. It will eat away at every trail to get at a memory, good or bad. I can try to control it, but so far, I'm not doing so great."

"Just know you're not alone," Gracen said, covering her hand with his. "I'm starting to freak out too. But we'll get it sorted. We'll make it."

# Chapter 45

For the next week, strange dreams of a nightmarish quality continued to litter Blythe's sleep, and her days were pockmarked with vivid memories. Gracen came by the house every day, and she usually had something to show him that she had ferreted out of the attic. Some object that contained a recollection, a story she could tell him, a moment she could have in the flesh for a second time. Aside from these visits, Blythe said very little to anyone as she hid in her thoughts.

Meanwhile, Gracen kept as busy as he could. His laptop was lost in the fire so he bought a new one and was deeply grateful he had backed things up in a storage cloud. Reconfiguring his entire life on a new piece of machinery was still time-consuming. This didn't bother him. He liked having the time eaten up with something he could trick himself into believing was important. His brain needed the activity. It was hard being strong for Blythe, even though he wanted to do it.

Then, when the week had passed, Silas got a worried report from Mary Alice about Blythe, and he shared it with Liam over lunch at school. They agreed to see Gracen the next day after rehearsal to see if he could spur some sense in their sister.

"I'm glad you guys came," Gracen said as Finn ushered Silas and Liam into the apartment. He tapped away on his laptop. "I've been mulling over some ideas for a new shop. Nothing set in stone. The insurance company is still sorting things out. They need to be convinced it wasn't arson."

"Of course it wasn't arson," Silas said shortly.

"It's just how it works. I went through this on the Isle a couple times."

"What does Blythe think of your plans?" Liam asked.

"We haven't talked about them much."

"Why not?"

"She's not ready to talk about the future."

"That's exactly what she needs to do," Liam protested. "She can't stay frozen like this."

"She's grieving," Gracen shrugged. "She needs time."

"It's a building, not a person," Silas countered.

"You should know that The Yellow Bowl was more than that to Blythe. Besides, we're not dealing with what is rational to you guys. She's depressed. The fire was traumatic," Gracen reminded them.

"Which is why she needs to snap out of it," Liam said sharply. Then he back-pedaled, "I don't mean that the way it sounded, it's just, she can't dwell in the past. I don't get the point of it."

"It doesn't really matter what you get or don't get. It's not your life," Gracen replied. "She can't help it. You know that, right? She's not choosing this?"

"She's not choosing to do anything about it either," Silas pointed out. He knew Gracen loved his sister and all that junk, but it was a little annoying hearing him talk like her own brothers were clueless. Silas turned to Finn, "You've seen this before. What do you think?"

"I think it's only been a week and you guys might be expecting a lot from her," Finn answered honestly. "The Yellow Bowl was everything to Blythe."

Silas knew he was right. Safety. Security. Stability. Home. Work. Freedom. Success. The future. The past. All of it had been held in those beloved yellow brick walls. When they caught fire and crumbled, it let loose a host of ghosts from the past. His sister was haunted.

But Silas didn't want to think of his sister sinking into despair again. He countered Finn's statement, "Family is everything to Blythe."

"Family and her friends. And Gracen," Liam added.

"Nope. No, sir, I'm not going to be the replacement for 'everything'. It can't be me. Or you. Or any of us. What if I get hit by a bus? Then she loses everything again," Gracen said, crossing his arms.

"So you're just going to let her be stuck in this loop of reliving the past?" Liam asked.

"For now, I guess so. Basically, my plan is to just be there for her and not look at her like she's broken because she can't stand that. I'm just going to listen when she talks, and be okay with silence when she doesn't."

"I just don't want this to get out of control like it did before. You know, when she got all dark after Ian," Silas said.

"It's only been a *week*," Finn replied. "It took her a couple of months of messy decisions and coming cold turkey off antidepressants to take her to that dark place before. The meds were helping until the other side effects became unbearable. She only snapped because she stopped taking them too quickly."

"So let's cut it off at the pass," Liam said, as if it were a herd of cows coming down a mountain. "Before she even starts talking about meds and everything."

"Blythe will be okay. It may not be your version of okay, or my version of okay, for a little while. But she's alright," Gracen insisted. He had grown up in a home colored by depression and anxiety. He was a veritable expert on the subject.

"I hope you're right," Liam said peevishly. He was about as thrilled with Gracen as Silas.

Finn interjected, "Of the four of us, I'm the one who was there for her the last time. I think talking with her is going to be a lot more helpful than worrying. Or bossing her around."

"I haven't bossed her around," Liam said.

"Yet," Silas added with a smirk.

"Hey, you agree with me," Liam reminded him. "And I just think she needs something to do, a reason to get out of bed in the morning. I'm sorry if that makes me the bossy one."

"She does need a reason to get out of bed in the morning. I agree with that completely," Gracen sighed. "The problem is my plans don't amount to much right now. I'm kinda like a hamster on a wheel. A lot of talk and no real direction."

"So maybe you both need to snap out of it," Liam said.

"You probably should, because the rumor mill says that the city is thinking about evicting whoever is left on the riverfront and moving city hall down there," Silas informed them.

It felt like a bomb drop. The possibility of completely losing the riverfront was too much. Gracen's eyes narrowed, "Excuse me?"

"The mayor's son has been talking about it. He's in the show and our whole cast is wound up over it. They want to raise funds or start a petition or something."

All cylinders fired simultaneously inside Gracen's brain. Too many thoughts at once. Way too much. The overload made his chest tighten, his knee bounced. He could feel the anxiety creep up around his throat, and he began to count things in the room. Eight shoes. Two bottles of water. One can of soda. One wedding ring—Liam's. Ten fingers—his own.

"Okay, then I have to get started on a plan. I have lots of ideas, not just about my shop and The Yellow Bowl but the riverfront in general. It needs an overhaul. It needs a new vision."

"Then I suggest you get started," Silas said.

"And hopefully Blythe finds her reason to get out of bed in the morning," Liam added, "or there's more to lose here than the riverfront."

* * *

Nine days after the fire, Blythe decided it was time to see the riverfront. She felt like she had to face it. Then, after she went once, she couldn't stop, she couldn't stay away. Every day the blinker flipped on, the steering wheel turned, and the Wagoneer slowly crept by the burned-out building. Every day Blythe idled in the parking lot, just staring, just crying, sometimes just wanting to cry but nothing would come. All of the assurances that it could be restored and reopened did little for her grief. It wouldn't be the same. And Blythe had learned to cling to sameness.

That's why she'd held onto Ian for so long. It's why she so often turned to Jesse. It was the same, it was familiar. Out of habit, out of fear, out of stubbornness, Blythe had clawed to keep things the same, and there was precious little. The Yellow Bowl had been the same all her life. Sure, little updates and improvements here and there, a new shade of yellow paint, a new type of tea, a new vendor for napkins—the minutiae mattered very little. The bricks and bookcases and stools and chairs and tables and teacups had been the same year after year. It had been her cocoon. It had been her home.

But now it was a blackened mess. And March surprised them with an early thaw which turned her home into a soggy jumble of ashes, books, and brokenness.

Brokenness was the very opposite of sameness. And Blythe had enough of brokenness already.

With nothing else to do, she kept coming back. Day after day, the blinker flipped on, the steering wheel turned, and the Wagoneer slowly crept by what remained of The Yellow Bowl. She was feeding her depression on the ashes, and she knew it. But what else was there to do?

* * *

Every day he laced on his jogging shoes, his feet hit the pavement, and he breathed out Shakespeare. It was the only thought Gracen would allow. Only monologues that he hadn't created; only words that his brain had memorized. Nothing organic, nothing reactionary, nothing that had anything to do with the here and now. *Henry the Fifth, Macbeth, Hamlet, Richard the Third, Twelfth Night, As You Like It.* This would keep him steady.

Because as soon as he let his mind out of the safety of Shakespearean monologues and into stream of consciousness, the anxiety became all-consuming. Every thought screamed for his attention at once. There was too much to do in too little time and with too little money.

Yes, logically, the insurance checks would be cut—eventually. He'd open a new shop and get going—eventually. The Yellow Bowl would be taken care of—eventually. But in the meantime, there wasn't much to do other than obsess and plan.

A year of grief and a year of growth, a year bookended with loss but with footnotes of love. The juxtaposition left him spinning, so Gracen ran. And he breathed out the Bard. Or else he'd find himself counting every object he could see and naming every noise he heard in an attempt to stay grounded.

It was exhausting.

After watching this for two weeks, Finn gently suggested maybe Gracen should stop trying to sort it all out alone. So when March arrived he went to the Elwoods. If Blythe couldn't help, maybe Miles or Mary Alice could. Maybe someone could help him get over this hump of planning and really moving again. He had to get off this hamster wheel.

* * *

"You want to put a Ferris wheel on the riverfront?" Miles asked as he read through Gracen's plans. That seemed like an ... interesting idea.

"Eventually. It's part of a later phase," Gracen explained. So far Blythe hadn't said a word, she just kept scrolling and scanning the laptop. They were gathered in the living room, and Gracen sat between Blythe and Mary Alice on the sofa.

"I think I get it," Mary Alice said slowly. "You're using what you know from Summerstead and applying it here in Sayen Falls."

"It could work," Miles shrugged.

"It might be just what we need down there. Someone with some big plans for the place. Kyle is a nice man, but I don't think he's ever dreamed quite this big," Mary Alice said.

The words on the screen blurred as tears stung Blythe's eyes. This was not the first time she'd sat in front of a computer screen reviewing big plans for the riverfront. It was, however, the first time those plans had a shot of coming to fruition.

The first time had been with Ian when they'd been in their dream stage. They'd picked out a dream house, they'd talked about their dream wedding, and their dream life together. And they had created some dream plans for the riverfront. Ian had even drawn up blueprints, being an architect and all.

Blueprints. She still had them. They were on the same thumb drive as her play. And that thumb drive was inside her jewelry box.

Without saying a word, Blythe set the laptop on Gracen's lap and went upstairs. Tears started to fall as she opened her jewelry box. Her pearls sat in the drawer, shiny and perfect, untouched by the catastrophe. She picked up the tiny silver drive and steadied her emotions.

Then with her feelings properly seated, she went back down the stairs and thrust the thumb drive at Gracen.

"What is this?"

"Blueprints. That's what you're missing. You need visuals. I have them."

"Ian?" Gracen asked her. He knew that loser was an architect.

"His blueprints, but my dreams," she insisted. She cracked half a smile, "There isn't a Ferris wheel but I kinda like that idea."

A hundred megawatt grin lit up Gracen's face as she snuggled next to him on the couch and rested her head on his shoulder. Gracen inserted the drive and she directed him to the correct folder. His computer required software to open them, software he'd have to pay for.

"Do it," Miles directed. "This is an investment. I'll pay for it."

"No, I can pay for it," Gracen assured him. "This is the kind of thing I should be spending money on, and with any luck at all, it'll pay off."

A couple minutes later, after the website had digested Gracen's debit card information, the laptop displayed Ian's blueprints and Blythe's old dreams. It was fairly user-friendly, so Gracen quickly managed to plug in his modifications. And Blythe had a few recommendations of her own.

Dust was blown off ideas she'd thought of long ago. New life was breathed into her dreams, and a teeny tiny spark of life settled within her. Maybe just enough to get out of the car and do something.

"You need to get these plans to Kyle quickly," Miles said when they finished.

Gracen nodded. "I have a meeting with him in just a couple days."

"You set that up before you came over here?" Blythe asked.

"I had to make something official. I had to get out of my own head."

Blythe bit her lip. "When your meeting is over, let's walk down the plaza together."

"I think that's a good idea," Mary Alice encouraged. "Get some fresh air into these dreams of yours."

But Miles wasn't sure. He too had driven by the riverfront. He knew how ugly it looked in the light of day, and how hard that was for a sentimental kid like his granddaughter. He advised them gravely,

"Just remember, your lives are more than bricks and mortar."

# Chapter 46

Blythe leaned on the brake pedal to creep past the shop at a snail's pace. It was a familiar sight at this point, and yet, still so foreign and surreal. The darkened bricks, the busted out windows, the yellow tape stretched around the building. Not knowing if there was anything salvageable inside was making her crazy. They'd been told that it wasn't safe to go inside. The fire marshal had said that once insurance cleared and work could begin, there'd be a time to see what could be saved. Blythe could only think about how the spring rains would come and ruin whatever was left.

It was the day of Gracen's meeting with Kyle. He was doing something. And that's what everyone wanted Blythe to do. Something.

She scrutinized the building. It was time to take matters into her own hands. It was time to do something.

Shifting into reverse, Blythe backed into a parking spot. Very quietly she emerged from the Jeep, even though she knew all the shops were closed and the place was deserted. Ever so slowly, she approached the building determined to go *inside*. She quickly glanced over each shoulder to be sure she was alone before lifting up the caution tape and ducking underneath. Fumbling in her pocket she pulled out her keys to unlock the back door. The memory of throwing herself at the door flickered in her mind's eye, and she dropped the keys. She cleared her throat, shook the memory off her brain, and calmly picked up the keys. It felt almost stupid to have to unlock the door to a building that looked like a looter could emerge from it any minute. Of course, there'd only be looters of soggy paperbacks and broken teacups coming from the charred Yellow Bowl.

The door groaned loudly as Blythe pushed it open; she threw a look over her shoulder again before tiptoeing inside. The view took her breath away. The buttery yellow walls were black from flames and smoke. She winced as she looked inside her office. The papers on her desk were nothing but ash now. It was possible the files inside the drawers were salvageable, but Blythe didn't want to think about those kinds of things now. Reconstructing the data of her business was a matter altogether separate from piecing together the spirit.

Moving on, Blythe tried to steel herself as she approached the front of the shop. Her efforts were useless. The bookcases were burned and the books inside of them were ashes with spines. It was a strange and chilling sight. She ran her hand down the bar; it still had a layer of water on top. Memories overwhelmed her, fighting for prominence in her brain.

… Being perched up on the counter as her dad tied her shoes after she tripped and skinned her knee outside.

… Swinging her spindly legs on the bar stool as Mary Alice pointed to the words in *Dick and Jane*.

… Playing hide and seek behind the towering bookcases with Jesse, a strawberry donut in her hand, chocolate icing smeared on his face.

… Sitting at the bar after school, not wanting to go home after the divorce. The Yellow Bowl was whole, it wasn't broken like home.

… Crying over geometry and boys and blistered feet because everything, even dancing, was just so hard.

… Opening the shop for the first time all on her own. She was scared to death but she did it. And she did it well. She did it all with a grace that trips over its own feet; beautifully stumbling.

As the memories swam in her eyes, she made her way behind the counter. There was her red gingham apron, in a ball soaked with water and grimy with ashes. She grabbed it as a sob escaped her throat. All of the teacups were smashed, every plate, every dish. They'd all crashed to the floor when the floor joists next door broke and caused such a tremendous shake. Blythe sank to her knees to pick up a few broken pieces. This was Gracen's teacup, in too many pieces to count. Her sob became a scream as she threw what was left of the saucer onto the floor. Her body slumped forward, shaking while tears streamed down her face. After a few minutes, she took a few racking deep breaths, and forcefully wiped her eyes with sooty palms. As the tears were shoved away, she spied a glimpse of yellow ceramic under the broken shelves.

"The yellow bowl," she whispered. With trembling fingers, she lifted the wood out of the way, and there it sat without a single chip. Blythe picked it up in awe. She poured a bit of water out of the bowl, then polished some soot off it.

"Impossible."

This discovery heartened her and emboldened her. She staggered to her feet. Clutching the bowl and her apron she darted down the hall, sidestepped the carnage, and flew outside. Quickly she stowed her treasures in the Jeep, then headed straight for SIP's door.

It was, of course, unlocked as it had been that night. She could hear echoes of the crash from the floor joists breaking, and there they were hanging in pieces through the ceiling. Carefully, Blythe snuck further inside. The floor was littered with the vestiges of Gracen's book collection. His bookcase remained upstairs, laying empty and on its side as if it had vomited out its contents. In the middle of the kitchen, she found half of Gracen's couch dangling through the ceiling. The smell of wet burnt leather filled her nostrils as she cautiously crossed into the dining room.

As the fire had to cross through SIP to reach The Yellow Bowl, the damage inside was even worse. The poster prints of her great-grandmother, grandmother, and herself were completely destroyed. The painting purchased in Summerstead was likewise ruined. There had to be something she could save, just something, one thing.

Blythe looked around frantically, and there she saw one of her grandmother's own paintings of the shore. It was puffy from water damage and the image was clouded over with smoke, but it looked like maybe, just maybe it could be salvaged. Clambering up on a table, she reached to remove the painting from the wall. The table creaked under her weight, and she remembered the time she'd fallen off the chair and Gracen had chided her. Well, if she broke her neck getting her grandmother's painting, he'd just have to understand. With a grunt, Blythe lifted the painting off its nail and it pushed her back with momentum. She hit the floor fairly hard as the painting crashed onto the table. Undeterred, she picked up the painting and started to march it out to her Jeep.

As she inched past the couch obstacle, something brass caught her eye. She stopped dead in her tracks. Leaning the painting against the wall, Blythe maneuvered to the other side of the couch and there she found Cary Grant and Grace Kelly still glamorous and refined. The framed poster of *To Catch a Thief* had fallen through the floor. Aside from a giant crack down the middle and some spidering in the glass, the poster was spotless.

Laying the poster frame on its back and putting the painting on top, Blythe dragged them toward the door. She tramped on a waterlogged book, an anthology of British poets. On impulse she added it to her pile. Then she spied the careworn copy of *A Christmas Carol*. Eagerly she grabbed it and placed it on her makeshift sled. Another idea flew into her brain.

Outside, she popped open the hatch of her Jeep to gingerly add to the treasures inside. Leaving the hatch open, she approached the building again. She took a deep breath, steadying her nerves. She would have to be very careful. Slowly and cautiously, Blythe ascended the stairs then opened her door. She was profoundly grateful her floor joists had stayed intact.

Her eyes flitted around her scorched apartment, tears threatening to fog her view. Memories pounded on the door of her brain. These ones were barking and raving mad.

… Ian was sitting on the couch, promising her the world and she gave him everything without question. She loved him so much.

Her stomach churned as she recalled the touch of his hand, the sly lick of his lips. She shook her head and like some sort of twisted kaleidoscope the memories turned to Jesse.

… Falling into his arms when he finally came home. They talked about Ian and he said all the right things. Jesse was always saying things.

"Not now," she insisted. She'd come upstairs for a specific reason and these memories were not going to derail her now. No. Not now.

She surveyed her apartment again, this time with cold objectivity. It was a mess. Burned up and stinking with smoke and stale water. But her life wasn't that mess. This was just a place full of stuff. Her life was ahead of her, inside of her.

"There," she said out loud as she found the thing worth all this trouble.

Gracen's copy of *Henry the Fifth* lay open on her couch. It looked expectant, like any minute its readers would return and finish the saga. She snatched the book to hug it close to her chest. It was damp and smelled of smoke, but it was there. Somehow it had survived. And it could still be read again someday. It would be read again.

She turned abruptly, the floor groaned under her weight. This was, without question, the most foolish thing she'd ever done. Yet in a strange and macabre way, it felt like living. It felt like she was doing something in the midst of her emptiness. It felt like she was taking something back. And Blythe was not one to take.

That was the moment she realized that Gracen—and everyone else— was going to chew her out as soon as she showed them all the things she'd saved. Still, it was too late now. She was invested. And Blythe was proud of herself. She had done something.

Without another look, she bolted out the door and down the stairs.

* *.*

City hall was buzzing with energy; phones ringing, people coming and going, voices floating out of offices. Gracen's leg bounced with similar energy as he sat in a chair outside of Kyle's office. His folder of plans lay on the chair next to him, lifeless and yet holding his livelihood. With great effort, Gracen reminded himself to breathe and he exhaled a bit of *Hamlet*. At least Kyle was a known entity and a nice one at that. It was the rest of the schmucks in this building that would threaten his plans.

Kyle's door clicked as it opened. A familiar but very unexpected voice wafted out before his person came into view.

"I have to say, this was a big surprise, but I hope it works out," Kyle said. He clapped a hand on the back of none other than Jesse Beckwith. Gracen had to tell his eyeballs to get back into his head where they belonged.

"I'm hopeful. The riverfront has been through big changes before, and I want in on this. It'll be good, I'm sure of it," Jesse said with his characteristic optimistic charm. As he turned, Jesse saw Gracen rise to his feet, and he extended a hand, "Hey, Gracen."

"Blythe didn't say you were coming back to town."

"She didn't know," he grinned. "No one knows. I wanted to touch base with Kyle first."

"That's …" Gracen trailed off as a myriad of words trickled through his brain. None of them seemed wise to let out of his mouth. He settled on, "Nice."

"Well, I'll let you get started," Jesse said, zipping his coat. "Little colder here than Peru."

293

Something about Paddington Bear flickered in Gracen's memory, but he dismissed it. Picking up his folder, he followed Kyle's gesture into his office.

"That's quite a surprise, isn't it?" Kyle said as he settled into his desk chair. Slightly unnerved, Gracen took the seat across from him and laid the folder on the desk.

"What did he want?"

"He wants to open a studio on the riverfront, among other things," Kyle explained. "It turns out that while we've all been assuming that he's been living the high life, Jesse has actually been living on peanuts and saving most of what he's made."

That had to be a staggering amount, Gracen realized. Jesse was a pretty well-known photographer in the right circles. He was constantly in demand, and most of his expenses were paid to get him where people wanted him.

"Anyway," Kyle continued, "Jesse wants to invest in the riverfront."

This made Gracen bristle, and he hated himself a little bit for that reaction. He redirected his focus. "Are there plans for the riverfront yet?"

Kyle exhaled loudly, "That's the million dollar question, and believe me, everyone wants to know. Right now, I just want to keep my job."

"The city is blaming you?"

"Not exactly blaming. They're looking for a scapegoat since the fire started in an empty building with bad wiring. If the riverfront is going to stay as is, everything needs to be inspected and updated. But they don't want to sink money into a property that isn't exactly thriving."

"It's not your fault that so many of the buildings are empty. The plaza hasn't been taken care of," Gracen said. "The city needs to invest money if they want it to make money."

"I've been telling them that for the last decade," Kyle said. He nodded at Gracen's folder. "Which is why you're here. Whatcha got?"

"I think I can help you out. I don't want either of us to lose our jobs," Gracen grinned. Time to focus, flick on the charm, turn up the confidence, and stow the anxiety for later.

"That's a good start," Kyle chuckled warmly.

"I think if I can apply some of my boardwalk sense with some of my business sense, and use Blythe's vision for the riverfront, we can all work together to bring the place back to life and get things booming again."

"Booming?"

"Yes, booming. Go big or go home, Kyle." Gracen flipped open the folder and lifted out the pages of architectural renderings. He cleared his throat, "These should be presented on a grander scale, but I'm not an architect."

"No, you are not an architect," Kyle said as he scanned the images. He was impressed. "In fact, how did you do this?"

"Full disclosure, these aren't exactly my plans. This is Blythe's vision."

A smile stretched across Kyle's face, then he chuckled, "And she just happened to be engaged to an architect once upon a time."

"Yes, yes she was. And she happened to save the plans they dreamed up on a thumb drive in her jewelry box, that I just so happened to chuck off her balcony the night of the fire."

"How fortuitous."

"Finn called it providential."

"I don't care if little fairies made it happen," Kyle grinned. "These are good plans. It ties it all together. The old buildings, the crazy eighties experimental architecture. Is this the entire riverfront?"

"Yes. And that's our proposal. What's the sense in fixing five buildings? The entire plaza needs a facelift. And, let's be real, some of it needs a total overhaul."

"Ah, but that's the stumbling block," Kyle said, dropping the plans on his desk with a sigh. "City council is obsessed with the money, and well, I shouldn't say this, but people around here have been wanting to relocate city hall."

"I heard that rumor."

"Businesses like The Chatterbox and The Deighton Inn can stay, they're the bookends and they're doing pretty well, so there's no reason to tamper with them. But pretty much everything else in the middle gets gutted, and all the city offices get moved down there. They're even talking about moving the police station down there."

"Good grief," Gracen muttered. He slicked his hand through his hair.

"But I like this, Gracen. I like these plans. What kind of financials do you have to go with this? That's your expertise, isn't it?"

This stoked Gracen's fire a bit, and he brightened as he pulled another sheet from his folder. "Yes, that's my wheelhouse. I broke down what the cost should be. I talked to the other businesses affected by the fire and got rough estimates of what the insurance payouts will be."

"And I have the numbers for what the city will get from our insurance plan," Kyle said.

"Good, good, excellent," Gracen nodded. "I deliberately left that number out of my plans so I'd have to deal with the big scary numbers."

"That is a sizable number," Kyle said, glancing at the bottom line.

"But it's achievable, with a couple investors and some fundraisers."

"I don't know if the community cares enough for that, frankly."

"We have to make them care, and believe me, I'm your boy for that," Gracen said with his megawatt smile. He handed Kyle another page.

"What's this?"

"My credentials," Gracen said as Kyle scanned the page. "I worked for my grandfather for over a decade and he moved me around quite a bit, honing my skills and using my talents. To diversify Wallace Corp, and keep up public appearances, he had me head up some historical preservation projects. I did all the financials, drummed up all the investors, and planned some pretty successful fundraisers."

"Couple that with your accounting, you really are the boy for the job," Kyle said. He tapped his nameplate, "Should I put this in a box?"

Gracen laughed, "I don't want *your* job. I just want a shot to keep my business."

"Level with me, you could easily move to campus or anywhere else in town and probably do better than you were."

"You're right. This is about the riverfront."

Kyle lifted the blueprints, "This is about her."

"Okay, so it's about her," Gracen shrugged. "Is that a problem?"

"Nope, that's what I wanted you to say. In my experience, love is a pretty big motivator. And judging by your plans and your history, you're not the type to fail anyway."

"Not unless I'm set up for it," Gracen muttered.

"Hey, I want to see the riverfront come back to life as much as anyone," Kyle assured him. "Can I keep these?"

"Yes, those are yours to keep."

Kyle said, tapped his thumb on his teeth, "You know, Nick Elwood is a contractor."

"He's also in Vegas and doesn't show any signs of coming home."

"True," Kyle sighed. He remembered the old days when they'd had cookouts with the Elwoods, and sometimes a Beckwith or two, and all their kids would play together. "At any rate, I like what you have here. I think I can float this."

"I can attend any meetings you need. Whatever you need from me. Not like I'm doing much else these days anyway."

"Perfect," Kyle said. He reached to shake Gracen's hand. "I'll do everything I can to get this ball rolling and I'll keep in touch."

"Sounds good," Gracen grinned as he stood up to leave. He had expected Kyle to be encouraging and was relieved to have been right. However, right now there was a loose cannon rolling around Sayen Falls that had him a little worried. As Gracen burst through the doors of city hall and climbed into the Shelby to meet Blythe at the plaza, he hoped that Jesse hadn't gotten to the riverfront before him.

# Chapter 47

"What are you doing?" Jesse barked as he saw Blythe exiting the stairwell with a book in her hands. She stumbled at the sound of his voice and cursed a little when she dropped the book.

"What are you doing here?" she shouted. Her nerves were jumpy from being in the forbidden building to begin with, let alone being caught—especially by Jesse Beckwith who was supposed to be on another continent.

"Were you inside? Were you *upstairs?*"

"Why aren't you in Peru?" Blythe demanded. She reached the yellow tape and Jesse lifted it for her. She stomped past him to her Jeep.

"I can't believe you would be reckless enough to go inside of a building very clearly covered with caution tape. For a book none less. What book could be that important?" Jesse grunted. Loudly and deliberately, she slammed the hatch.

"*Henry the Fifth.*"

"Of course, I should've known, bloody Shakespeare."

"I'm still trying to figure out why you're in this hemisphere."

"I'm here because of this!" he declared, waving his hand toward the hollowed-out building. "You know, the fire, the loss, the destruction."

"You always manage to turn up when there's been loss and destruction, don't you?"

"What does that mean?"

Admittedly, she wasn't sure what it meant but it sure felt good saying it.

"It means you can never just turn up on a Tuesday."

"Okay, what does *that* mean?"

"It means what it means, Jesse. Good lord."

"I'm here because I'm worried about you."

"And there it is," she said with a dry laugh. "Jesse the Hero has come home, all is well."

"I'm not saying that."

"Why don't you just get in line, Jess? Everyone is worried about me. That's nothing new. That's nothing particularly special. What exactly do you think you can fix by being here?"

"I'm here for good," he snapped.

His words echoed strangely in her ears. "What do you mean?"

"I quit. That's why I'm in this hemisphere. I gave all my gigs to friends and I'm done."

"You're done being a photographer?" She said with immense confusion.

"Not exactly, I'm opening a studio here. But I'm home for good now."

"*Why?*"

"Seriously, why? Because this is my home."

"Just like that," Blythe snapped her fingers. "If I'd known that all we had to do was burn down five buildings, my goodness, we would've done it years ago."

"What does that mean?"

"I don't know!" Blythe cried. It seemed as though nothing either of them was saying was making very much sense. Never before had she been so angry at the mere sight of Jesse. But she was. She was furious that he was here. She didn't want him here. She didn't need him here.

"Blythe, this isn't all about you. When I saw the video of the riverfront burning down it just hit me. I need to be here. I'm tired of living out of a suitcase. I'm tired of feeling like I rush home just to miss everything."

"And you're worried about me."

"Forget I said it."

"I won't be able to. You'll stare at me like everyone else does."

"And how is that?"

"Like I'm going to explode."

"Not explode. You always implode. You self-destruct."

"Is that why everyone acts like I'm helpless? Like … like … I'm some wounded bird," Blythe stammered, her mind racing for words. "I'm a wounded bird who can't fly."

"Well, you kind of are," Jesse shrugged. It seemed like a fair comparison to him.

Fire flashed in Blythe's eyes. "Excuse me?"

"I've known you your entire life, and whenever life comes along and kicks the crap out of you, you curl into a ball. I'm not saying there's anything wrong with that, but yeah, that's why we all look at you like you're helpless."

"Do I look helpless now?" Blythe said. She stretched her arms open and gestured toward her filthy clothes.

"You look like a woman who doesn't care if she lives or dies."

"I have something to live for, thank you very much."

"Good, I'm glad," Jesse said. Then, because she'd made him angry, he added flippantly, "I wasn't sure since Ginnie said Gracen had to drag you away from the building. Seems like strange behavior for someone happily in love."

The smack of her hand meeting his cheek echoed through the quiet riverfront. Her hand stung, but it was nothing compared to the mark she left on his face. Jesse gaped at her as he rubbed his smarting stubbled cheek. For a moment, it was unclear which one of them was more surprised by her actions. Blythe scrambled to find her voice.

"I don't need a hero. And if I did, it wouldn't be you."

And without giving him a split second to reply, she jumped into her Jeep and sped out of the parking lot. Within seconds, the Shelby pulled in, and Gracen found Jesse alone in the parking lot with a very red cheek.

Through the window, he asked, "What'd you do?"

"She was in the building when I got here, and I freaked out."

"She was in the building," Gracen repeated as his eyes widened.

"She had a copy of *Henry the Fifth*," Jesse said coolly.

"Did … did she hit you?" Gracen asked with a nod to Jesse's cheek.

"I might've questioned her behavior the night of the fire. And her happiness."

"That's helpful. And here I was worried that it would be weird having you around," Gracen sneered before he stepped on the gas and peeled out of the riverfront to find her.

The trouble was Gracen really didn't know where to look. First, he turned toward her grandparents' house, but not surprisingly, her Jeep was not in their driveway. He considered the options: the valley, the theater in the high school, maybe even her childhood home. She had told him once that she used to drive down that little side street and cry. As he paused at the stop sign, Gracen exhaled loudly. He figured he'd try them in order geographically, and then just wait for her back at Finn's. There wasn't much else he could do.

He fired off a text to Finn to make sure she wasn't there. An almost immediate answer back confirmed that she was not. Of course, she wasn't answering her phone. It went straight to voicemail, over and over again, straight to voicemail.

Gracen wasn't overly worried that she was going to drive off a cliff or into a telephone pole. The fact that she had slapped Jesse was a good sign. She had some life in her. She had some fight in her. But still, he didn't like the idea of her out there brooding and alone.

He drove past the house she'd grown up in, and there was no sign of her. The next stop was the high school before he'd get on Sayen Trail to take it all the way into the valley. It would be the hardest to find her down there. There were so many parks. At least, it was unlikely she'd be tromping through a muddy trail.

As he stopped at a light, his phone rang and he scrambled to answer it without looking.

"Where are you?" he asked, assuming it'd be her. He assumed wrong.

"I'm in my office," Roy said wryly. "Where are you?"

"Roy—Granddad," Gracen stammered. All of the blood drained from his face, sounds became tinny in his ears.

"I expected to hear from you after I read about the fire."

"Why … why would I call you?"

"Well, because you have nothing."

A car honked behind Gracen, and he stepped a little too hard on the gas. He needed to pull over to have this conversation.

"Give me a minute; I can't talk right this second."

"I'll hold the line," Roy said, not trusting his grandson to call him back.

Gracen threw his phone down on the passenger seat and took the necessary turns to the high school parking lot. There was the Wagoneer. He'd found her. First, he had to deal with Roy.

"Okay, I can talk now. What exactly do you want?"

"I wanted to see how you're doing?"

"I'm fine. Are we done now?"

"I'm not the enemy here. I want to help you," his voice was slimy with false kindness.

"I'm sure you do."

"I do. And I want to congratulate you."

"Congratulate me?"

"On the girl. I hear you're in love with her. She's a pretty little thing, too, this, um, let me see, Blythe Elwood. Yes, she's very pretty. Not your usual type though. Not blonde."

"How do you know about Blythe?"

"I've read everything I can about this place you're living in. Sayen Falls, it's a nice enough place. The riverfront needs some work though. Well, now it really does."

Gracen worried he would retch if he didn't get off the phone quickly. It was too much. His grandfather knew too much. He felt so violated.

"What do you really want?"

"Alright, I'll get down to brass tacks, if you want me to be frank."

"I just want you to get whatever it is out of your system so I can carry on with my life."

"Fair enough," Roy snidely chuckled. "The fact is, I really have no idea what you're thinking. You're involved with this sweet young lady, and yet have nothing to offer her. You lost that sad little pizza place in the fire."

"This is very inspiring," Gracen muttered as his brain began to take off. It'd been racing for days, and now there was no hope of catching up with it.

"I just want to make you a couple offers. First of all, cash the check I sent you before. Or if that one burned, I'll send another. In fact, I'll send more. But then I'd like to be considered an investor. I can send the usual paperwork; you're familiar with the percentages."

"I would say so," Gracen said. He had created the documentation Roy was currently using for his investment projects.

"Or, if that's not to your liking, just come back to the Isle. We'll tear up our agreement, I'll give you a good place in the company, and we'll get you set up with a house here and everything. Your girl likes Summerstead Isle, doesn't she?"

In the haze, Gracen wondered how Roy knew that Blythe had been to Summerstead Isle. The thought drifted just out of his reach. His brain was stirring too quickly for him to keep up.

"Absolutely not. Her life, our life is here."

"You have no life," Roy said with a laugh. "Your life just burned down."

"We're rebuilding."

"You can't do this without me. You gave it a good go, and you might've had a chance without the fire, but you can't start over with the insurance money. We both know that."

When Wallace Corp had dealt with a property fire, Gracen had chased down every dime he could find from the insurance company but, Roy was right, it had to be supplemented. And it wouldn't be enough this time. However, that was exactly what Gracen had planned for.

"I'm taking care of it. And I'll be just fine without your money."

"I won't offer again."

"Good."

"I mean it, Gracen. You turn me down, no more chances," Roy seethed.

"Let me make this perfectly clear: I don't want your money, I don't need your help."

"You'll regret this, boy."

"Maybe," Gracen said with finality. He tapped his phone to end the call and threw his phone down on the seat. His hands were shaking with anger, with anxiety. His body pulsated as he leaped out of the Shelby. He wanted to peel off his own skin and let his nerves splash all over the ground.

"Count to ten, then go find her," he instructed himself.

With this command, Gracen's brain summoned all his memories of Blythe. It was like a traffic jam in there, but at least his mind knew what it was there to do. Get the girl, and talk it out. He didn't have any magical things to say to her to make it all better. Still, Gracen knew he wanted to see her, he needed to see her, and he needed to talk to her. And maybe they'd both walk out of the building just as broken and bruised as they went in, but they'd be together. And that was something. It had to be something.

* * *

"Knock, knock," Jesse called as he opened the front door of Becky's house. He hoped the welcome here would be better than it had been on the river. The fact was, Jesse had nowhere else to go. In his haste, he'd offended most of his clients. His colleagues thought he was having a nervous breakdown. Maybe he was.

When Becky saw him, Jesse knew that here he had sanctuary. His grandfather did his best to scramble to his feet, and Jesse closed the distance between them so they could hug.

"Why don't you ever tell anyone when you're coming home?"

"I used to think the shock value was fun. I'm not so sure anymore."

"Why? Who else have you seen?"

"Blythe and Gracen."

"I wouldn't expect them to be happy to see you. After that stunt you pulled at Christmas."

"It wasn't a stunt. I was genuinely concerned."

"If you came home for her, you're too late," Becky sighed. "This one seems real."

"I didn't come home for her. Not exactly. Not exclusively anyway," Jesse struggled to explain. "Gramps, I'm tired. Living in airports and hotels, I feel like a nomad. Do you have any idea how hard it is to file taxes without a permanent address?"

"I've never understood wanting to be a wanderer. You or your dad."

"I don't want to be like Dad," Jesse said harshly. "It hit me all at once when I saw The Yellow Bowl going up in flames. I wanted to be home. But it looks like I'm the outsider now."

"Nonsense, boy. Now get your bags and get settled. We'll have to get you a real car," Becky said as he looked out the window at the rental.

As Jesse headed out to his rental car to retrieve his duffle bag, Ginnie's minivan pulled into the driveway. She had just picked Viola up from school and was headed over for a helpful visit. That's what Viola called them— they would visit with Gramps and do some laundry and housekeeping. Ginnie no sooner parked than the van door came open and Viola burst out of it. She threw herself around Jesse's legs.

"Jesse!! This is the best day ever!" she cried. "Teddy, look who it is!"

"Ee-ee!!" Teddy shouted. "Mommy, it Ee-ee!"

"I'm still Ee-ee, huh?" Jesse grinned as he picked Viola up and hugged her tight. Ginnie unstrapped Teddy from his car seat and released the Kraken. Just as Jesse set Viola down, the little cannon shot from the van into Jesse's arms. "Hi there, Teddy Bear."

"This is surprising," Ginnie said to her cousin. "Why aren't you in Peru?"

"I quit. Like I told Gramps, I couldn't do it anymore."

"Your timing is a little messy."

"I already saw Blythe. It didn't go well."

"Jess, she's drowning in trauma right now and she's not sure she can trust you. Of course, it didn't go well."

"I'm not here to cause trouble. Good grief, Gramps thought that too. I'm here because I thought Sayen Falls was my home."

Ginnie put her hand on his arm, "Hey, it is your home. If that's what you want. I sorta thought you'd pick London or New York to call home when you were tired of roaming. But you know I'm always happy when you're in Sayen Falls."

Teddy happily slapped Jesse's face then gave him a big kiss on his cheek. Jesse smiled, "I guess this guy is happy to see me too."

"I'm happy to see you too!" Viola said as she took hold of his hand.

"Me too!" Teddy exclaimed.

Jesse snuggled his face against Teddy's cheek. His stubble scratched and Teddy giggled as he shoved him away. It was better than a slap. Still, he wondered if there really was room left for him in Sayen Falls, or if he'd just torched his career for nothing.

* * *

Blythe was sitting in the back of the auditorium staring at the rehearsal. It was hell week: the last week of rehearsals before opening night. Those kids were singing their faces off, but the only voices she heard were the ones in her head. They were singing, laughing, dancing. They were her and Jesse when they'd been teenagers on that stage.

"What are you doing?"

This time the voice was soft, it was gentle. It was Gracen's.

"Remembering."

"That's usually dangerous for you."

"It's emotional suicide."

"Can I talk you off the ledge?"

"Too late. I took the plunge."

"And yet, you live."

Gracen ascended the balcony stairs as he spoke, and he sank into the chair next to her. Taking her left hand in his, he kissed her Claddagh ring.

"I exist. I survive. I am a wounded bird," she said grimly.

"Who said that?"

"I said that. And Jesse said I like it that way," she muttered. The callous words of her oldest friend had dragged her away from the breakthrough she'd had about life and mess in her apartment.

"I saw him. You left quite a mark."

"You told me once to slap any guy that made me feel inadequate or something to that effect. I didn't really think though. It was probably the adrenaline from being inside."

"Yes, about that," Gracen said sternly. "What were you thinking?"

"I'm tired of being in limbo. I know it was stupid, but I needed to see the damage. I needed to see what could be saved. There isn't much. Your apartment is basically caved in on the shop. But I found the yellow bowl on my side. And one of your posters. And one of the paintings."

"One of my posters?"

"It fell through the floor. So did *A Christmas Carol*. I don't know why it isn't burned up."

"Jesse said something about *Henry the Fifth*," Gracen said. "It couldn't have fallen through the floor. It was in your apartment."

"I went upstairs for it," she said casually, hoping that if she was nonchalant he wouldn't lecture her.

303

Gracen didn't lecture. He was incredulous. "You risked life and limb for that?"

"I guess so. I was just ... doing things. There wasn't much of a thought process. Jesse seems to think it means I don't care if I live or die. Or that I don't love you very much if I don't care about living. That's when I slapped him."

"You love me more than anyone ever has. I don't need Jesse to validate that," Gracen assured her.

"I'm tired of him just swooping in and trying to save me."

"Kate, you don't need saving."

"You say I don't need saving. But I feel like I'm drowning. I feel like I should just be able to get over it and see it for what it is."

"You lost a lot. It's not just a little fire, a little loss."

"It all connects for me," she sighed.

"I know it does."

"With the shop gone, I'm reminded of everything, everyone, else that's gone. But I don't want all that loss to define me."

"I know that too."

She asked him and her voice was earnest, urgent, "Why can't I just get over it? Everyone else is over it."

"Everyone else is not over it," Gracen said firmly. "It just manifests differently. If they think you should get over it, it's because they can't get over it either and it's easy to pick on the most emotional one of the tribe."

"Emotional. Is that another word for weak?"

"No, emotions aren't weakness." Blythe cocked an eyebrow, and Gracen smiled, "I know, shocking coming from me."

"Very surprising, indeed. You were allergic to emotions when we met."

"You were my antidote."

"So I've been some good to someone."

"Don't talk like that."

"I'm just worn out. It's too much. The emotions are too heavy for me to bear. I think that's why I sink like this. It's just too big of a burden."

"That makes perfect sense to me," he said, pulling her hand to his heart. "You feel big, you love big, you live big."

"My life is rather small if it can be burned down like that."

Inside her apartment, she'd had a burst of clarity about life and meaning. But it had slipped away again. Blythe craved steadiness.

For a few minutes, they were quiet. He held her hand, running his thumb along her fingers, and just resting in the silence with her. His mind started to slow its pace, and eventually, it ceased its frantic search for the right turn of phrase to fix her. If she didn't need saving by Jesse, then she didn't need fixing by Gracen.

"You know something, Kate," he said at last, "There's not a thing I can say that will make the world right again. This is a big loss. I have every right to run ten miles a day, pace the floor at night, and fill up pages with ideas that I just need out of my brain. You have every right to slip through the slideshows of memories and moments in your mind, to feel them, to mourn them, and to dream about them. But neither of us can go into the dark place, okay?"

Her voice shook as she whispered just one word, "Okay."

She rested her head on his shoulder and stared forward at the stage as tears slipped down her cheeks. The voices were gone. The kids on stage were singing "One Day More".

"It's just gonna take time, but I've got nowhere else to be," Gracen said. "Do you?"

"Nope."

"Good," he said, reaching his arm around her to pull her closer. As he glanced over at her, she reached up to his face. Their lips met in a much-needed kiss.

"I love you," she breathed.

"Thank God for that."

# Chapter 48

"I just want to know which one of them said 'Macbeth' in my theater," Silas groaned as he flopped into a chair at the kitchen table. Miles and Mary Alice were in the living room watching a game show; Blythe and Gracen were working on the riverfront plans in the kitchen. "Seriously, they're not kidding when they call it hell week."

"It looked pretty good when we were there the other day," Blythe tried to encourage him.

"No offense, but you had tears in your eyes. And you were in the last row."

"Okay, well, that's rude but true."

"Our mics are shorting out, set pieces are toppling over. A piece of the barricade broke today when we turned it around after the battle. Oh, and a light burst which showered the cast in glass. Thank God no one was hurt," Silas elaborated. "I was there until two in the morning, changing every light, testing every mic, and checking each and every set piece. That's why I'm not at the school now. I told Liam I needed a minute. I'll be there at four-thirty to get ready for opening night."

"No wonder you look like a zombie," Blythe said. "Do you want me to make you something?"

"A stiff drink? Oh, wait, definitely no booze in this house."

"Plus it's one in the afternoon," Blythe pointed out.

"I'll just make myself a black coffee."

"You sit. I'll make you a dirty chai."

"How? You don't have any of your equipment here."

"I'm magic," she smiled as she set to work fiddling around with coffee and tea and liquids and steamers and other doodads and whatnots. As she poured the frothy drink into a coffee mug, she said, "You know what they say, bad dress rehearsal, good opening night." Silas stared at her flatly. She handed him the mug, "Geez Louise, you're cranky."

"I'm exhausted. And I'm nervous about tonight. We all are. It's probably good I won't see Liam today, we'd reverberate off each other."

"It's a high school musical. It's okay if it's not flawless," Gracen said.

"In reality, yes. But Liam staked a lot on this. If the show is a flop there's going to be a lot of 'I told you so'."

"Well, that's just childish," Blythe replied.

"It's the theater," Silas grunted, taking a sip of the chai. It was rich and smooth, not at all bitter like the black coffee planned on. He took another drink. This was better. And still highly caffeinated with the shot of espresso.

"You know people in Sayen Falls support the arts program. There'll be a full house, and it's always easier to play to a full house than empty seats," Blythe assured her brother.

"I hope so. We did sell a lot of presale tickets, mostly parents and grandparents, but it gets the kids excited," Silas nodded.

"Any chance the Morgans are among those?" Gracen asked, his voice thin and expectations low.

Silas sighed heavily. "No. I heard Lily tell Ella that they're not coming."

"Neither of them?" Blythe asked.

"Not together, not separately, not at all. They're both staying in the house for appearances until Lily graduates. Then they're selling the house and officially divorcing," Silas informed them. He'd been able to follow the drama in tidy installments at rehearsals. He added with a scoff, "They're thinking of her about as much as our parents thought of us."

"Well, that tells me everything I need to know in as few words as possible," Blythe said sardonically.

"It was a rather economical way of putting things actually," Gracen sighed. He glanced at the microwave clock. "I have a meeting with Kyle in a little bit."

"How are things going with the riverfront?" Silas asked cautiously.

"Being proactive with plans has helped. And that petition Ella and Lily took up with the students really impressed the mayor. I'm meeting with Kyle to discuss turning The Gala into a fundraiser."

"You'll have to let the girls know it was helpful. They really hustled," Silas smiled.

"I plan on sending them both roses for opening night," Gracen replied.

"They will love that. Becky always sent me roses," Blythe said fondly. "He got them at Little Lambs and Ivy. It's the one on Sayen Trail, right next to the law offices."

\* \* \*

Gracen left his meeting with Kyle feeling cautiously optimistic about the future of the riverfront. City council still needed to meet and vote on a final decision, but there had been heavy pushback from the citizens once the rumor got out that the riverfront plaza would not be restored. This, more than anything, gave him a boost of confidence that their vision was achievable.

The drive from city hall to the florist on Sayen Trail was short and easy at that time of day. Little Lambs and Ivy was a quaint little florist just bursting with blooms, quite befitting its adorable name. No wonder Blythe recommended it. Gracen had a friendly chat with the flower designer who helped him select pink roses for Lily and yellow roses for Ella. On a whim, he also ordered an arrangement of wildflowers for Mary Alice's kitchen table. He knew Blythe would enjoy them too.

When he left the florist, he paused outside considering whether or not he should march into the neighboring law offices of Morgan and Morgan.

He wanted to give at least one of the Morgans a piece of his mind. But what would he really do? Barge in without an appointment and accost someone he'd never met to tell them to be a better parent to their teenage daughter. That sounded ridiculous.

He shook his head and got into his Shelby to go back to Finn's. There was another car leaving ahead of him, a black Jag that purred as it pulled out of the lot. Gracen noticed that he needed to refuel so he headed towards the gas station just down the street. The Jag also pulled into the gas station. As he climbed out of his car, he heard a voice from the other side of the pump.

"That's quite a car you have there. You certainly don't see one of those every day."

It was a deep male voice with a British accent. No way. Couldn't be. Gracen peered around the gas pump with a friendly smile. The man he saw had Lily's eyes.

"Thanks, man. I've enjoyed having her."

"Enjoyed? Are you thinking about selling?"

Until that moment, the idea had never crossed Gracen's mind. But it did make sense. He needed money. He didn't need an expensive collectors' car.

"Possibly. I hate to let her go, but I have to think a little more practical these days than when I bought her," he took a deep breath. Time to get real. He extended his hand, "Gracen Hall."

"Hall. I know that name," the man said slowly. "Julian Morgan."

"I wondered if you were Julian Morgan. Your daughter works for me at Summerstead Isle Pizza. Or did, anyway, until it burned down three weeks ago."

"That's it. Gracen Hall. Right, Lily talks about you. I'm sorry we haven't been into your establishment. My wife and I don't eat pizza very often. She's a bit of a food snob."

"Well, hopefully, we get the shops on the river up and running again here very soon, and you can come let your daughter serve you a slice," Gracen smiled, then he added, "You must be very proud of Lily and all the work she's done on the musical."

Julian nodded vaguely. "It's kept her very busy."

"Are you coming to the show tonight?"

"I have a meeting with a client," Julian answered, unsure why he owed this guy an explanation.

"Your wife? Is she coming?"

"I really have no idea what Mrs. Morgan intends to do with her time," he said with an icy tone.

"I think you should come," Gracen said. "Hear me out, just for a minute. I realize you don't know me from Adam but I know Lily. It would mean the world to her if you were there. It would be everything to her. All the work would be worth it."

"You presume to tell me about my daughter?" Julian said brusquely. "Gracen Hall, you're also the one who dealt with Brady Carmichael."

"Yes, that was me. Lily's really come into her own since that mess. I'm proud of her," Gracen said carefully. "And, frankly, sir, you should be too."

A cloud crossed in front of the sun, immediately cooling the spot where they were standing. This was the most unlikely conversation Julian Morgan had participated in for a long time. He shifted uncomfortably.

"I'm not used to people, strangers particularly, telling me what to do."

"Do you want me to draw up a contract? Would you be more comfortable with some paperwork detailing the specifics?" Gracen suggested. "Your client can get divorced another day; this is Lily's opening night. She almost didn't audition because she was sure her parents wouldn't care enough to come."

Gracen knew he was pushing it so he told himself to cool it. Lay off.

"It's not that I don't want to go," Julian said defensively. "Work comes first in our household."

"Then maybe that's the problem. Maybe that's why your daughter dated Brady Carmichael in the first place. And maybe that's why you and your wife are on the brink of your own divorce," Gracen said simply. So much for holding back.

"Look, I came here for a tank of petrol, not a lecture on my family life," Julian retorted.

"I know. I apologize for my rudeness, but not for speaking up. Lily thinks the world of you, or would if you came," Gracen sighed. Tank of petrol. Tank of gas. The car. The Shelby. "Hey, I'll make you a deal. You come to the show tonight and I'll sell you my Shelby at a good price."

Julian's jaw went slack, then he laughed. "You can't be serious. You'd sell your car to me just to get me to a high school production?"

"Not just to get you to the high school musical. For you to understand how important this is to Lily. How important Lily is to all of us. She's going to have a cheering section there tonight. You should be part of that. If you can only see in numbers and contracts, then let's make a deal," Gracen shrugged. "And I could use the money."

"It's an interesting offer," Julian admitted. "But I really need to get going. I have a meeting in Felicity Springs in twenty minutes. It was good meeting you, not so great talking with you, and rather entertaining thinking about your offer for the car. Goodbye."

And just like that, Julian went into the gas station to pay cash for his gas. Gracen assumed that was simply to get away from him, so he swiped his card and filled his tank. At least he had tried. As he climbed back into the Shelby and turned the key, he considered again the option of selling her. The longer he thought about it, the more it made sense. He just needed to find a serious buyer.

# Chapter 49

The curtain was going up in fifteen minutes. Ginnie picked crumbs out of her mini-hairbrush before she ran it through her hair. She checked her lipstick in the rearview mirror, still unconvinced this bright red worked, but she was committed now. She had just enough time to run in and find Liam before he called places for the kids. Stowing the brush and her keys in her oversized purse she slammed the door and flitted as fast as she could into the school.

Liam was backstage in the hallway between the dressing rooms helping his lead get the mic wired through his costume. Lily and Ella were giggling about flowers that had arrived for them, from Gracen of course, and proudly showing them off to the other cast members. Ordinarily, he would've snickered at their giddiness but there was no time for that now. The curtain was going up in less than fifteen minutes and right now the star of the show did not have a working microphone. He talked to Silas through the headset he was wearing to ask him to try it again. And again. Finally, the microphone came through loud and clear on the headsets which meant it would work in the monitors as well. Crisis averted.

"Okay, guys, break a leg, don't screw up," he said and headed for the stairs to the hall.

"Thanks, Coach, you always know just what to say," Ella scoffed.

"I don't do inspirational speeches."

"Sure you do. Remember when we did *Brigadoon* and you told us that if we dropped Mike out of the tree you'd kill us all? That was very inspirational," Sawyer joked, as he shuffled cards. A good number of the main actors had half of the first act to kill playing spades.

"Oh, or remember when we did *Meet Me in St. Louis* and you told us that if anyone got in front of the trolley while the stage crew was pulling it that you'd taser us? I found that highly motivational," Ella added.

Liam looked at them flatly as he shook his head, covering a smile with his hand. "Okay, you want some inspiration then? Don't get hit by the barricade or I'll make you run laps tomorrow before the show."

"You wouldn't dare," Lily gasped. Russ was notorious for making the kids run laps around the auditorium if they were unruly during a rehearsal. Builds up stamina, he'd say, as he cackled at their agony.

"We're artists, not athletes," Ella said haughtily.

"Then don't get plowed over by a giant revolving set piece," Liam grinned. "But seriously, you guys have got this. I've never been more proud of my cast. No matter what happens tonight, if there are mistakes, and there will be, you'll get through it because you're tremendous."

"That's more like it," Ella beamed.

"There you are!" Ginnie cried as she cracked open the door to the dressing room hallway. "I've been looking everywhere. I think Debbie is about to have a conniption fit because she can't find you and you're not responding to the headset."

Liam glanced down at the controls he wore on his belt loop. He had flipped the headset off after talking to Silas.

"She'll get over it," he shrugged. He told the kids to break a leg one more time as he jogged up the stairs to his lovely wife. He pressed his lips to hers, breathing in her familiar scent of vanilla and peaches, and exhaled slowly.

"Watch the lipstick," she admonished him, then she squeezed his hand tight. "You ready? They're waiting for you."

"I didn't think you could make it tonight," he said as they walked over to the set of double doors where he would make his official entrance in front of the crowd.

"My parents agreed to take the kids at the last minute. They know how important opening night is and how much I wanted to be here."

"Wow, I'll actually owe them for something."

"Hey, they gave you me. But I'm just happy I can be here with you. This is your night."

"It's the kids' night."

Giving him a look, Ginnie planted a fat kiss on his bristly cheek, then she tried to rub away the lip print with her thumb. A stagehand opened the door and Liam stepped into the spotlight, holding Ginnie's hand. He gave a short wave to the audience as they made their way to their seats. Liam and Ginnie always sat in the third row on the aisle. She was more nervous and excited for her husband this year than ever. Liam needed a good break.

In the balcony, in her usual seat, Blythe reached across the armrest to slip her hand into Gracen's. As the house lights went down and the overture started, he smiled wide at her and squeezed her hand three times. He'd learned the code from watching Miles and Mary Alice.

"I love you too," she whispered. She was wildly nervous for her brothers and for the kids. It'd been a good long while since she'd had so many people she loved in a show. It made her miss it. Her days on stage were long over. But writing could be her outlet now. And, she realized, there was more time for it since the fire wiped out her usual obligations.

As the curtain opened and the show began in earnest Blythe started to relax. She eased back in her chair but didn't loosen her hold on Gracen's hand. The kids were doing a wonderful job. She was very impressed with how gritty the boys managed to play the chain gang and was particularly spellbound with the vocal talents of the leads, Jean Valjean and Javert. Liam had lucked out with a strong talent pool.

Then, shortly after the first song, a tall, dark figure snuck into the auditorium. He immediately ducked his head in an attempt not to distract the audience members in the balcony. Blythe straightened in her chair then leaned forward. She caught a glimpse of his profile as he scanned the rows for an empty chair.

"That's Julian Morgan," she hissed. Gracen grinned to himself; he truly hadn't expected to see him there. He nodded to the empty chair next to Blythe.

"Julian," she whispered as she released Gracen's hand. She stood halfway up and stretched across the balcony railing to tap him on the shoulder.

"Blythe?" he asked in surprise. He used to be somewhat of a regular at The Yellow Bowl before his business started thriving. She beckoned him to sit with them, and when Julian saw Gracen he gave a half wave. Gracen nodded with a friendly smile.

"Lily hasn't been on yet," Blythe said in hushed tones. "She'll make her entrance soon."

It surprised Julian how nervous he was to see his daughter's performance. He hoped, for her sake, that she'd be wonderful. He had spent the afternoon in distracted thought, wanting to get work done but being continually drawn to thoughts of Lily. She was such a shy girl, so unsure and quiet. It seemed so incongruous that she'd be on stage in a lead role of a very emotionally charged show. How had his little Lily grown up so much and he missed it all? She had gotten lost in the abyss of paperwork and the sea of meetings. Julian wasn't demonstrative or affectionate by nature and his estrangement from Karen only made him worse. None of it was Lily's fault, but he could see how she bore the brunt of it.

When she appeared on stage Julian twisted his program so intensely it had a permanent curl. Then, as she sang out her first solo notes, crisp and clear and brimming over with poignant feeling, his heart about burst with pride. He had never felt such joy. No case or client had ever given him this high. As the story progressed and it was time for Lily's solo piece, "I Dreamed a Dream", her father sat on the edge of his seat with tears in his eyes. Pride mingled with regret as his heart connected with her through the music floating from her voice. He'd had no idea she had all this talent and feeling inside her unassuming frame. He really didn't know her at all. He wondered if it was too late.

At intermission, he thanked Gracen. "You took a risk calling me out."

"I did and I didn't actually think it made a difference," Gracen admitted.

"Well, it did and I'm grateful. And in all seriousness, if you're interested in selling the Shelby, I'm interested in buying. That has nothing to do with me being here, other than it drove your point home."

"Selling the Shelby?" Blythe asked with considerable surprise.

"I don't think he meant it. He was just trying to get me here," Julian explained.

"No, that was a serious offer. Well, not the part about coming to the show. But I am ready to sell her. I bought her in anger to prove a point. I'd like to sell her to prove a different one," Gracen said honestly.

"Gracen, you can't sell the Shelby," Blythe protested. "It's your only car. You can't just walk all over Sayen Falls."

"I thought about it all afternoon and talked it over with Finn. He said we can share his car or something."

"Finn. You talked to Finn but not me?"

"Blythe, I'm doing this for you. For us. We need money more than we need an old car."

"But I love your car," she argued. "It feels like part of you."

"It's part of the old me, trust me. I was angry and bitter when I bought it. I picked it because Uncle Harry always wanted one, and I wanted to show Roy that I didn't need his money to make it on my own."

"And what point are you trying to make now?" she demanded.

"That I know when a car is just a car, and when the better investment is in people."

She opened her mouth to argue, but stopped. "I think Uncle Harry would be very proud of you for that."

"I know Aunt Grace will be when I tell her," Gracen grinned. He turned to Julian. "Let's meet tomorrow to talk about a good deal for us both."

"That works for me," Julian answered. A funny smile spread across his face. "Karen is really the one who likes Mustangs."

"Julian, maybe there's more than one relationship that can be saved," Blythe suggested. "You should have Karen come with you to tomorrow night's show. And go from there."

The lights flashed twice to signal that the second act would be starting soon. Gracen took Blythe's hand.

"First, we have to finish tonight."

* * *

When the show neared its emotional finale a pin drop could be heard in the auditorium. Pure silence filled the room as the lights came up for the death of Valjean. Lily appeared as Fantine's spirit to welcome Valjean into heaven, extending a hand to the faithful servant. In his seat, Julian leaned forward to hang on every note.

As the scene unfolded, Sawyer and Ella as Marius and Cosette rushed on stage in wedding clothes. Faint sniffles could be heard as Cosette pleaded with her adoptive father to not die but instead join in her happiness. Ella played the scene with flawless emotion as she sank onto the stage, her white dress billowing around her. Sawyer knelt behind her, clasping her hands with his. In the balcony, Gracen reached to still Blythe's wringing hands. She glanced at him, relieved at his touch. Salty tears left streaks on her cheeks, but she didn't mind. This ending got her every time.

Suddenly, the auditorium filled with sound as the cast lined the aisles, seeming to appear from nowhere. They had practiced their silent unseen entrance a hundred times but no one knew it would work until there was a captive audience. Liam's gamble had paid off; the audience was so invested in the death of Valjean on the stage that they didn't notice the appearance of thirty students in the darkened auditorium.

As they bellowed the last refrain of the show, chills ran down Liam's spine and tears streamed down Ginnie's face. Silas cut the lights and the auditorium went completely black for the cast to make their well-rehearsed exit before the bows on stage. In the darkness, Ginnie leaned to kiss her husband. She felt a tear on his cheek. It had worked and he was so proud.

First Ella and Sawyer appeared on stage for their bows, Sawyer striding in from the left and Ella skipping from the right. She flashed a flirtatious smile at him before jumping into his arms. The audience cheered as Sawyer backed towards stage right with Ella in his arms so that Lily could come forward for her bow. Every chair emptied as people clambered to their feet to give a thunderous round of applause for shy, quiet Lily. She looked genuinely surprised and thoroughly overjoyed with the reception the audience gave her.

After the curtain call was over, the cast filtered into the hallway to mingle. Nothing prepared Lily for the feeling she had as her father pushed through the crowd to swoop her into his arms. Julian hadn't hugged Lily like that since she was a little girl, and she felt small and safe and happy in her dad's strong arms.

"You came," she breathed as she met his bright blue eyes. He nodded, unfamiliar with being overrun by his feelings. Lily hugged him tight, "I'm so glad you came."

Over her dad's shoulder, she caught a glimpse of Gracen and she heard Ella's girlish squeal as she hugged him. Blythe opened her arms to Sawyer for a hug. Julian hung back as Lily bashfully approached Blythe and Gracen. Gracen slipped one arm around her shoulder and squeezed her close.

"You were just as amazing as I knew you'd be."

"Thank you," she smiled. "The roses were really thoughtful."

"Every actress deserves flowers in her dressing room on opening night," Gracen grinned.

"Be careful, Gracen, you're setting the bar awfully high for the poor guy that falls in love with this one someday," Silas said as he joined them.

"I feel sorry for that guy," Gracen said, shaking Silas's hand. "He's got us to deal with."

Lily flushed slightly and cast a glance back at her father who was watching her with curious fondness. He liked seeing her interact with her friends. She seemed so vibrant, not like the ghost of a girl that hid away in her room at home. He motioned for her to come over, and shocked her when he suggested she invite some of her castmates over to watch a movie and unwind after the show. Lily had never had friends over before. It didn't seem like her home was a place she could invite people. She had no idea what had come over her father but she loved it. She hoped it would last, feared that it wouldn't, but figured she'd ride the wave as long as it crested.

# Chapter 50

Gracen walked up the drive to Becky's garage for the Shelby. This would be the last time. He was meeting Julian that evening to complete the transaction. It was unseasonably warm and the snow had entirely melted now. It was good weather to go for a couple of joy rides, which was on the agenda before the big sale.

He punched in the code on the garage keypad and at the same time, Becky came out of the house to join him. He called out to Gracen, "I still can't believe you're really selling her."

"It's time to say good-bye, Becky," Gracen grinned.

Just then, Jesse pulled in the driveway, home from grocery shopping. The drive was wide enough that Jesse could pull over to the left and Gracen still had plenty of room to back out on the right. To say that they had been avoiding each other for the last two weeks would be putting it lightly.

"I still can't believe you're really selling her," Jesse said, a perfect echo of his gramps.

Gracen shook his head, "It's just a car, guys."

"If you really think that, then you never deserved her," Becky said.

"Nah, I think Gracen is right at the end of the day," Jesse said. "He has other priorities right now. If Julian backs out, I'll buy her for Gramps."

"What does an old man like me need with a car like this?" Becky chuckled.

"What does a snob like Julian need with it?" Jesse replied.

"Actually, he intends to give it to Karen for an anniversary gift," Gracen told them.

"I thought they were getting divorced," Becky said with surprise.

"It seems that Julian wants to move towards reconciliation."

"And nothing says I'm sorry like a fully restored 1967 midnight blue Shelby Mustang," Jesse said wryly.

"I would think it would be a good start," Gracen shrugged. "Provided he backs it up with some action and feelings or something."

"Speaking of apologies and actions and feelings," Jesse cleared his throat awkwardly, "I want to try to clear the air."

Gracen raised his eyebrows, "Clear the air?"

"I know I just came crashing into town with no explanation. I think I finally realized how hurtful that's been for Blythe," Jesse admitted. "But I want you to know that I didn't come back to interfere with you two. She said some things to me after New Year's that made me realize I was in the wrong. So, seriously, I'm just here because it's home."

Gracen didn't mean to, and in fact, he didn't know he was doing it, but he shook his head slowly. This was not only unexpected but a little surreal.

"Well, I appreciate that, Jesse."

"I want to help however I can with the riverfront project. I think Kyle already told you I intend to be an investor, and I also want to open up a studio."

"I told Jesse that in the meantime he can use my office downstairs," Becky interjected. "I don't do much writing anymore."

"Excuse me, writing?" Gracen asked.

"Gramps is a bit of a creative writer," Jesse grinned. "Short stories, mostly. I like to think I got my creative expression from him."

"Who'da thunk it, right?" Becky said to Gracen. "But I just scribble things down now, I don't need an office anymore. Haven't needed it since Pearl passed, come to think of it. So Jesse can use it for whatever he needs until the riverfront is open again."

"You're really prepared to do senior photos and pet photography?" Gracen asked Jesse with heavy skepticism. "After the career you've had?"

"I draw the line at pet photography but I think ordinary people should have their memories captured just like the rich and famous, or for that matter, the mountains and oceans that couldn't care less if I take their picture," Jesse answered.

"I think you'll do well here," Becky said.

"I thought about offering a photo booth at The Gala. We can charge twenty bucks to have their picture taken and I'll email them the digital files," Jesse said trying to sound excited. "It's kitschy but people like it."

"That pained you a little bit," Gracen snickered.

"It did a little. But I'll adjust, especially if it helps the riverfront. That's why I'm here. I came here to get my own self in order, and to do what I can to get the riverfront in order."

"Then I guess the riverfront is our common ground. We both want it rebuilt and better than it was before," Gracen conceded.

Jesse stuck his hand out to Gracen. There was a moment's pause then Gracen extended his hand and they shook.

"I feel like I should take a picture of this for that Tweetergram," Becky remarked.

"Oh, Gramps, give it up," Jesse said as he shook his head. "And get in the car before the man sells it. Enjoy your joy ride."

\* \* \*

"Did Becky do okay saying goodbye to your car?" Miles smirked as he eased himself into the hotrod. This was a car made for a young man.

"He did alright when all was said and done," Gracen replied. "We talked about his creative writing. I won't lie; it blew my mind a little."

"Yeah, old Becky has a way with words," Miles snorted. "He talks enough so it's never surprised me he could make words stay on paper too."

"So where are we headed?" Gracen asked Miles.

He thought for a moment then told him to head out of town towards the Valley, using Sweet Street. They chatted politely about nothing in particular until they reached the edge of the city. Then, Miles gave a few more detailed directions leading them to a row of houses on what was arguably the last street in Sayen Falls before the countryside.

"Okay, what's special about this house?" Gracen asked as he parked where Miles instructed. He knew there must be a reason they had come to this exact spot.

"This was our first house, Mary Alice and me. Do you know how I paid for the furniture?"

"Not a clue."

"I sold my car. It was a sky blue 1953 Pontiac, but we needed a table to eat on and a bed to sleep in more than I needed to be motorized."

"How did you get to work?"

"Becky picked me up. It was handy working together. I spent the next year fixing up car engines for people and then we had enough to pay cash for a car, a '55 Buick Roadmaster. Cherry red."

"So you get it. You understand why I'm doing this," Gracen nodded. "You can talk all you want about love being enough to build a dream on but the cold hard fact is that money makes the world go round."

"That's the truth. Mary Alice and I pinched a lot of pennies in our day."

"And you made a lot of sacrifices, I'm sure."

"Sure did. That's part of what you sign up for when you get married."

"Everyone is making a big deal out of it because it's such a rare car. But I don't care. I really don't," Gracen said emphatically. "By selling the Shelby, I have enough to take care of myself and Blythe until the insurance checks come and the shops are not only rebuilt but making a profit."

"The others don't get it. William is a realist; romance baffles him. Silas defaults to sarcasm, it's just his way. And Jesse Beckwith, that boy has always been inside out and upside down. It's not all his fault, but it's true all the same," Miles summarized succinctly. "And none of those yay-hoos know that I did the same thing for Mary Alice. That woman took my breath away and all my common sense with it. When you feel that way about someone then cars don't matter."

"The future together is all that matters," Gracen nodded.

Miles smiled, more to himself than for Gracen's benefit, as he said, "I always wanted this for Blythe, someone who would see her the way I see her grandmother. And I know, without a doubt, that you do."

"I just want to be worthy of the way she loves me. I need to be worthy of this second chance. Take the opportunity, explode all the possibilities out of it. I guess that's why I'm so invested in the project. It's one giant second chance for the riverfront."

"You sound like her, talking about possibilities and all."

"I've learned a new vocabulary here in Sayen Falls. Not just from Blythe, but from all of you," Gracen swallowed, surprised by his emotions. "I owe you and Mary Alice a lot too. I don't know how I'll ever repay you for believing in the screwed up guy that rolled into town a year ago."

"You don't owe us anything, son," Miles assured him. "You're family. We told you that. And family doesn't owe. Family gives."

"Not my family."

"I know, we've talked that saga out before. But as far as we're concerned, you're one of us now," Miles reiterated. He fished a set of car keys from his pocket. "That's why we want to give you one of our cars. Mary Alice doesn't drive anymore and it's not good for it to just sit in our garage. I know it's an old man's car and nothing like this Shelby, but it will get you from Point A to Point B faster than your feet. Even jogging."

Astonished, Gracen began to protest, "Miles, I can't take your car."

"We're not asking you to take. We're giving it to you. You can't refuse a gift." Miles thrust the keys into Gracen's hand.

He stared at the keys as he absorbed Miles's words. Gracen shook his head, "I just hope I don't let you down."

"Just take care of the car. And, more importantly, take care of my granddaughter. Even if the two of you decide to part ways, just go about it with kindness and decency," Miles told him simply. "And keep making decisions that would do your Uncle Harry proud. I think he and I would be of the same mind."

"I think Uncle Harry and you would agree on a lot of things. Especially Blythe. I can't imagine parting ways," Gracen said slowly. "She's the best thing I never knew I needed."

"A good woman is like that," Miles nodded. "Well, we better head for home before the lady folk set to worrying."

"Dinner will be ready soon," Gracen pointed at the clock. "Blythe said they were working on ham pot pie while they stuffed envelopes for The Gala."

"Well, get to getting then. I'm not much for missing meals."

# Chapter 51

When Miles and Gracen arrived back at the Elwood homestead, they found Mary Alice at the kitchen table surrounded by envelopes and invitations, and Blythe sitting on the staircase with a very strange look on her face. She was on the phone. Gracen lingered in the doorway between the kitchen and the dining room where he could watch her. Once she saw him, her eyes never left his face. She looked very similar to the night Luke called about her dad's heart attack.

"So that was my dad," she said as she ended the call.

"Your dad. What did he have to say?"

"He's coming home."

Shell-shocked. That was the look. It was how she looked after the fire too.

"He's coming home?" Gracen repeated as a question.

"In a few weeks, well, probably right after The Gala. Since he'll have to move in here, he wanted to talk to me first and make sure I'm okay with that," Blythe explained. Her voice sounded mechanical. The wheels in her head were still turning the information over and around.

"And how do you feel about that?"

"I … I'm not sure yet. I think I should be happy. But mostly I feel confused. I really didn't see this coming."

"Hey, you kids, get in here for dinner," Mary Alice called from the kitchen. Blythe and Gracen shared a long look riddled with thoughts unspoken before she got up from the stairs and obediently came into the kitchen.

"Your Gram just told me about Nicholas coming home," Miles said as he set the table. Evidently, Mary Alice had overheard Blythe's half of the conversation and filled in the missing pieces.

"Did you two have a nice talk?" Mary Alice asked with classic optimism.

"He asked if it was okay and I told him of course. I want him to come home. I've always wanted him to come home," Blythe's brow furrowed, perplexed. "This is good, right? It feels like it can't be good because this is March and something always goes wrong in March."

"Oh, enough of that hooey," Miles scowled.

Mary Alice interjected, "Blythe Katharine, I will allow you to have all the feelings you want on the matter, but we're not going to chalk anything up to that superstition."

"What superstition is that?" Gracen questioned.

"I always get bad news in March. My parents split up in March, Grammy had her stroke in March, I found out about Ian in March. It's always March. And it sounds like good news with Dad but this could be a disaster," Blythe sputtered.

"And what did you find out last March?" Mary Alice asked her with a coy smile.

"Last March," Blythe had to think. "That was when Alex called about Gracen."

"Not exactly bad news in the long run," Mary Alice said almost smugly.

It was a strange feeling for Gracen to be considered 'news' and not bad news at that. He felt this was a good time to kiss Blythe on the cheek to assure her he was good news after all.

"Okay, so not every March is riddled with pandemonium," Blythe conceded. "It just feels surreal. After all these years? And after the way he left at Thanksgiving, I really didn't think he was ever coming back. I think I was finally accepting that."

"Then, open your heart to him one more time," Mary Alice suggested.

"For Nicholas to realize that he needs somebody, anybody, let alone you kids and his old parents, is a minor miracle," Miles said. "If you ask me, this is an answer to our prayers."

"He told me that he's coming home because of the surgery, but also because he wants to help with the riverfront. He says it's the right time to come home," Blythe told them.

"That sounds like Jesse," Gracen mumbled.

"Jesse? When did you talk to Jesse?" Blythe demanded.

"Today at Becky's. We buried the hatchet, I guess. Or he called it clearing the air. Either way, he swears he's not here to break us up."

"Darn right he's not," Blythe declared. "If we break up, it's not going to be because of Jesse Thomas Beckwith, that's for sure."

"He genuinely wants to help get the shops on the river going again. I think he has the kind of scope and vision we need," Gracen admitted.

"Nicky would be a great asset too," Mary Alice pointed out. "The project will need a capable contractor to head things up."

"Dad won't be able to lift anything for six weeks and nothing heavy for twelve. He can't exactly jump into construction," Blythe reminded them.

"No, but he can hire and supervise," Miles said. "But all of this is putting the cart before the horse. First things first, you kids need to have that gala fundraiser and see what the future realistically holds. And then, Nicholas comes home and has his surgery. All the details will be sorted after that."

"What a very weird day," Blythe murmured. "Gracen is selling his car, my dad is coming home, Jesse wants to be useful."

"I found out Becky writes short stories," Gracen added. "I'm still reeling."

"I should let Becky read my play," Blythe said absentmindedly. "He always had good insight with my work before."

"Oh, and your grandfather gave me a car," Gracen told her

nonchalantly. Her eyes bulged. "I wondered if you knew. I'm assuming by the look on your face that you didn't."

"No, that was something only Mary Alice and I had discussed," Miles informed him.

"You gave him a car?" Blythe asked Miles. "But you don't just give people cars. You're a car guy. You love cars."

"We'll consider it my contribution to the riverfront project," Miles winked. "I have a feeling Gracen will be in high demand getting The Gala turned into a fundraiser."

"That's just the start," Gracen nodded. "I'll have to keep hitting people up to be investors or donors. Organizing other events. And then, you know, overseeing the actual reconstruction of my own shop. And Blythe's, as much as she wants my help."

"You kids will be very busy," Mary Alice said. "Which is why we should eat now while the food is hot."

* * *

Blythe's last ride in the Shelby was to the Morgans' lavish house. Gracen let her drive it while he followed behind in the car Miles had given him. The drive was bittersweet. She rather loved the car, but this transaction made her feel loved in a way she was unaccustomed to. A tear escaped her eye and slid down her nose just as she turned into the drive.

"Julian has assured me we can come for visits," Gracen said after they parked and he saw her face. He kissed the tip of her nose and wiped another tear from her cheek with his thumb.

"I'm not just crying because you're selling the car. Well, I am. But, it's just, it means a lot to me. I know you're doing this for me. No one does this kind of thing for me," Blythe explained as she stared hard at the car.

Gracen's lips grazed her cheek just for a moment before he leaned inside the car to retrieve something. He handed Blythe the silver cross necklace.

"Aunt Grace gave this to me the day I left Summerstead. She told me to think of her every time I saw it and I would know she was thinking of me and praying for me."

"You want me to have it?"

"Yes, because you'll wear it, and whenever I see it, I'll think of Aunt Grace. And I'll keep trying to do things that she'd like."

"It's been a really weird year for you, hasn't it?" Blythe remarked as she put the necklace on. "Today is just another weird day in a long string of weird days."

"It's been a crossroads. Maybe Robert Frost is right. Maybe taking the road less traveled does make all the difference."

"You and your poets," Blythe smiled. She kissed Gracen, then slipped

322

her hand into his and gave him the keys to the Shelby. Together they walked into Julian's house. An hour or so later, they left together.

Being together now felt very natural. In fact, it had stopped surprising Gracen how easy and normal it was to love someone. He undeniably was living a new life in Sayen Falls. A new life required a new future. His dreams weren't all about business and success anymore. Not that kind of success anyway.

Oddly enough, when he stopped and really thought about it, what Gracen wanted was success of the white picket fence variety. He wanted what Liam and Ginnie shared, what Miles and Mary Alice had built their life on, what kept Uncle Harry and Aunt Grace united even after death.

He went for a jog that night. Gracen ran the blocks from Finn's apartment to the riverfront in fifteen minutes flat. The caution tape still hung on the building, draped across the windows.

"I can't believe she went in there," he murmured, shaking his head and combing his fingers through his hair.

But she had. And she'd rescued *Henry the Fifth*. They would take little from their old lives into their new lives, but what they could hold onto was thanks to Blythe.

"'A good heart, Kate, is the sun and moon'," he whispered. He looked away from the darkened buildings and turned toward home. With every step, he breathed out King Henry's courtship of Katharine.

Halfway back to the apartment, his phone rang. Aunt Grace.

"I'm glad you called," he said when he answered. He slowed his pace to a walk.

"I was just sitting here watching an old Cary Grant movie on the television and I got to thinking that I should call you up."

"Is it one of my favorites?"

"No, it's one of my favorites. *The Philadelphia Story*."

"That's a classic, definitely one of my favorites."

"You have better taste than I thought."

"Well, Blythe loves that movie."

"That explains everything."

"And actually, that's why I'm glad you called. I wondered if you could send me something."

# Chapter 52

In the remainder of March, the only flurries were of activity. This pattern continued into April as Gracen and Blythe, and whoever they could find, prepared all the details for the Spring Gala. Their biggest triumph was in convincing Silas to be the entertainment.

With a little help from Blythe, he assembled a band. Finn agreed to be his drummer, Ella volunteered to play guitar, and Lily said she'd play the keys if it would help. It seemed a most ragtag band to Silas. When Ella dubbed them 'Silas and the Understudies' he didn't gain much more confidence. The first week of rehearsal was dicey. They were simultaneously too rusty and too inexperienced. Still, he chose a set list and carried on as planned.

As the weeks turned into days before The Gala, Silas became tentatively confident that it would go well. His pick-up band was beginning to gel. Their efforts sounded like real music, even the pieces he'd written himself. It was actually possible they could help The Gala be a smashing success.

* * *

On the day of The Gala, a thousand tiny details came unraveled that kept Kyle, Gracen, and Silas insanely busy. Gracen was starting to feel like a proverbial chicken with his proverbial head chopped off. Finally, at four-thirty, he insisted that enough was enough and no one would know that the tablecloths should've been yellow instead of powder blue, or any of the other compromised details. He got dressed at Silas's apartment so he wouldn't have to waste any time driving back to Finn's. As grateful as he was to have a place to live, he was very anxious to get back to the riverfront where all the action took place.

Gracen quickly changed into a heather gray pant and vest combination with a sky blue shirt. His tie was pink, blue, and green plaid. The entire outfit had come from Mae Houser who had insisted on just giving it to him. She had also given Blythe a new-to-her pink dress, which Gracen had not actually seen in person yet.

When Gracen appeared outside The Yellow Bowl at a quarter 'til five, he found Finn ready and waiting for the others. Finn had asked the members of the Elwood and Beckwith tribe to gather outside The Yellow Bowl at five.

"Last year I was the one wearing the pink tie to match Blythe," Finn chuckled. This year Finn wore a navy blue shirt with an emerald green tie. All the members of the band were going to wear navy in one capacity or another.

As they talked, Miles and Mary Alice arrived, then Becky with Jesse. They parked in the parking deck and crossed the plaza.

"It's so strange seeing the place like this, especially on Gala night," Becky remarked. Fence pieces barricaded the damaged block from the ticketholders. The Gala was contained strictly to the Sayen Trail block.

"At least you have a beautiful evening for this," Mary Alice said to Gracen. He leaned to kiss her cheek.

"I couldn't have custom ordered a better one."

"Where's Blythe?" Jesse asked carefully. "She didn't come with you?"

"She wanted to drive herself," Miles shrugged.

"Dramatic entrance probably," Silas said, straightening his navy blue tie as he joined them. At the same time, Ginnie and Liam came up the stone steps from behind the building. Her parents had volunteered to babysit, truly a surprise blessing.

"Should we wait for her?" Finn asked, checking his watch. It was now after five.

"You tell me, this is your big moment," Gracen answered him.

"It sorta loses some meaning without her," Ginnie said as she craned to look for Blythe. She and Liam were in on the big surprise with Finn.

"Well, he who hesitates is lost," Becky said simply. "On with the show."

"Alright then," Finn said. "Well, I wanted you all to come here because I have something to show you. I wanted to contribute in some meaningful way to this project. So Ginnie and I talked and came up with something we hope you'll really love—"

A door slammed in the back lot and moments later Blythe rushed into view with only one shoe on. She was shouting something about being sorry and being late and knowing this would happen. But she looked amazing. The dress fit as though it had been made for her. Her hair was up in a French twist, a few hairs left down to frame her face. At her throat was the strand of pearls from Miles. Gracen couldn't take his eyes off her—just as he couldn't the very first time he'd seen her. He met her at the top of the stairs, where she steadied herself on his arm and slipped on the other shoe.

"I'm sorry," she said breathlessly. Gracen had to kiss her before linking her hand with his as they joined the group.

"I'm just glad you didn't miss it," Finn grinned. "This is for you and Gracen really."

Without any more ado, he pulled a rope which caused a massive canvas drop cloth to fall away from the side of the building and reveal an enormous, colorful mural.

"'Once more unto the breach'," Blythe whispered as she read.

"That's my tattoo," Gracen laughed. "Literally."

The design was exactly the same, the colors, the font, just much larger and on brick instead of forearm.

"Ginnie, Liam, and I spent the last few evenings working on this," Finn explained, more than pleased with their reaction.

"It was all Ginnie and Finn. I just handed them paintbrushes and rollers," Liam insisted.

"I forgot how artistic you are," Blythe said to Ginnie, as she hugged her. "You used to sketch all the time when we were kids."

"This was easy, just a projector and paint," Ginnie said. "I only had to color in the lines. Liam did help, no matter what he says."

"This is really beautiful, Finn," Mary Alice said.

"I thought the riverfront could use a permanent reminder. Life will always shove you back, but you keep rallying."

"That'll be a hashtag by morning," Jesse said, snapping a picture of the mural. "It'll go well with this image."

"Is that all you think about?" Silas asked.

"My brain is basically hardwired for graphics and images," Jesse answered. "I'd kinda like to take the lead with social media. Gracen has enough on his plate."

"Have at it," Gracen said with a nod.

"Jesse's right. Social media will love this," Liam said as he put an arm around his wife.

Ginnie added, "It's the rallying cry of the riverfront."

"It's Shakespeare," Gracen said humorously.

"A year ago none of you ding-dongs had ever heard this quote," Blythe laughed. There was a pause as her laugh bounced off the brick around them. It had been two months since the fire, and she had been walking steadily through the darkness to come back into the bright light of hopeful living again. It was clear now she had truly arrived, despite the mess ahead.

Gracen pulled her into a kiss. The others made their leave and headed down the plaza towards the amphitheater. He took a deep breath to steady himself. Then Gracen began to talk to Blythe. His low voice shook and betrayed his nervousness.

"Before I came here and met you I thought I could live my life apart. I'd be able to shake off my grief and the way I grew up and just force life to bend to my will. Then, I met you, more or less in this exact spot about a year ago today. I knew that night that you were much more than what I came here for. Now the idea of being without you, that's a future I don't want. I don't want to live a life apart, not apart from the world and not apart from you."

"I'm not going anywhere. I love you," Blythe promised. Her voice was husky as every nerve ending in her body was vibrating with electricity.

Gracen cupped her face in his hands. His eyes drank her in. As he pulled Blythe close, her hand rested on his chest. She felt his heart beating wildly.

"Loving you has been a new experience. And yet loving you is the most natural thing I've ever done," he breathed. He slipped one trembling hand into his pocket and removed a tiny box. "I know people will think I'm crazy, but I've never been so sure of anything in all my life. I'm more sure of you than I am of oxygen and gravity and the North Star."

Opening the box, Gracen dropped to one knee. He clasped her left hand in his, his hands trembling. Inside the box glistened Aunt Grace's rose gold emerald ring, the one Uncle Harry had bought for their tenth anniversary. It was an art deco piece, stunning craftsmanship from an era of optimism and opulence. He heard Blythe gasp, her right hand flew to her mouth.

"Will you marry me? Be my wife?" he asked her unsteadily.

All the words Blythe had ever learned stood still in her mouth in complete surprise. Even in her wildest dreams, she hadn't expected Gracen to propose. Certainly not like this, on bended knee outside of the ruined Yellow Bowl just before the Spring Gala. Blythe's hand shivered in shock and joy; tears sprang to her eyes.

"Blythe," he whispered with urgency. She could see his eyes swimming with love and emotion that she knew he was so unaccustomed to feeling.

"Oh, Gracen," she finally exhaled. "Yes, of course, I'll marry you."

As he clambered up to stand on both feet, she slid the Claddagh off her finger, so he could slip the stunning engagement ring on instead. It fit perfectly, just like she fit in his embrace, as though she'd been sculpted from his own rib. She turned the Claddagh around so that the point of the heart would face in towards her, symbolizing that she had found her true love, and put it on her right hand.

It was then that she became aware of the whoops and hollers and whistles and clapping. She whipped around to see her friends and family standing strategically around the plaza where it seemed they had disappeared but could, in fact, see the whole thing.

"They knew?" she demanded of Gracen.

"Of course they knew. I'm not dumb enough to ask you to marry me without checking with home guard first," he laughed.

Liam and Silas took turns slapping Gracen on the back in congratulations. With a steady gaze, Miles shook his hand. "Giving you my blessing was easy. But letting her go is going to be hard."

Blythe gave his cheek a peck. "PapPap, you're not letting me go. Don't you know? We fools on the riverfront have to stick together."

Wrapping her arm around his, Gracen escorted her down the plaza just as he'd done that fateful night they met. If he'd only known then that the distractingly beautiful woman on his arm would be the love of his life, he could've saved himself a lot of hassle.

* * *

The first song in the set was one Blythe had not heard Silas and the Understudies practice. It had been a secret selection to celebrate the engagement. Since she'd said yes, they launched the evening with a cover of the American Authors' song "Best Day of my Life". It turned out to be an excellent kick-starter for the crowd. Some of the ticketholders sat in the amphitheater, enjoying the music on a warm spring evening, but most of the guests filled the dance floor. Seeing how much fun and enjoyment they were having fueled Silas and his pick-up band. The relationship between performer and audience is both cyclical and essential, and on this night it was perfection.

From her spot on the keys, Lily could see her parents dancing. Her mother was giggling girlishly at Julian's ridiculous moves. It was extremely rare for Julian to let his guard down so drastically and make an utter fool of himself.

Nearby, Gracen led Blythe onto the dance floor. They talked to each other, rehearsing the details of the night they had met, lost in their love bubble. When the band finished the bridge of the song, Silas announced,

"Ladies and Gentleman, I want you all to be the first to know that my big sister got engaged tonight. Give it up for Blythe and Gracen!"

"I didn't know he was going to do that," Gracen murmured as he leaned in to kiss her.

A cheer went up from the crowd as Blythe blushed. She heard her brother chuckle before he sang the chorus again to finish the song. As an appreciative crowd clapped, he seamlessly led the band into the next selection.

"I need a minute," Blythe told Gracen. "I feel like everyone is staring now."

"That's because they are."

As they exited the dance floor, he retrieved two flutes of champagne. He took a sip and nodded approvingly. "I made sure they got something better than last year's."

"As long as the bubbles tickle my nose, I'm happy."

"Of course," he chuckled.

Blythe tasted hers and wrinkled her nose with glee, "Bubbles!"

He kissed the tip of her nose, which was sickeningly cute.

"Congratulations! We're so happy for you. You kids are the sweethearts of Sayen Falls, you know," Hattie Farriss gushed as she and Kyle approached. The ladies shared a dainty hug as the men shook hands.

"I'd call this event a success, Gracen," Kyle pronounced.

"It's the first of several events we'll need to have."

"I'll follow your lead," Kyle said. "Just don't take my job."

"I have no intentions," Gracen laughed.

On stage, the band began another song; this one Silas had written. Blythe and Gracen remained at the outskirts of the dance floor. Her eyes drifted down the plaza toward her beloved shop.

"Listen to what he's saying," Gracen whispered into her ear.

She turned her attention to the stage where Silas was singing. His eyes were closed as he crooned.

*"So you hold on to me and I'll hold on to you,*
*With a little bit of love and a whole lot of glue,*
*We'll hold it all together,*
*Just me and you,*
*You hold on to me, and I'll hold on to you."*

A smile spread across her face as Blythe relaxed. She glanced down at the ring sparkling on her finger. She was going to marry Gracen.

"Come on, Kate, let's go dance," Gracen urged. "That's us he's singing about."

"Did he tell you that?"

"It doesn't matter if he wrote it for us or not, it's us. We're going to hold it all together ... together," he said, kissing her. "And this night is for celebrating. Not for looking at what we've lost. The riverfront survived."

And then it hit Blythe. The riverfront had survived and she had too. So had Gracen and Silas and Liam and Ginnie with Viola and Teddy the Terror. And her grandparents had circled the sun another year. As Blythe looked around she realized, they all had pulled through another year. There was a lot of work ahead, but this moment was theirs to celebrate.

For as long as the music played, their troubles were kept at bay. There'd be another time to worry, another time to plan. This was the time for celebrating and, evidently, for dancing.

So, Blythe put her hand in Gracen's and they danced.

# ABOUT THE AUTHOR

Rebecca J. Berry is a graduate of Bowling Green State University with a BA in literature. Currently, she's living outside of Columbus, Ohio with her hard-working husband, two adorable children, and one rather loud dog.

Her debut series set in an ordinary Ohio town, Sayen Falls, features the beautiful triumphs and dark sorrows of everyday characters like you and me. As a busy homemaker with big dreams, she knows that heavy doses of inspiration, a tribe of good friends, and a hot cup of tea can change everything. Follow Rebecca on social media under the name Plotting Possibility to get inspiration for your own big dreams. Check out www.amazon.com/author/rebeccaberry for more info and to order other books in the Sayen Falls series.

(And yes, that's her on the front cover!)

Made in the USA
Columbia, SC
29 November 2018